"ALL I WANT IS FOR YOU TO BECOME MY WIFE.

Let me take care of you. You're all alone with nowhere to go." Joshua's eyes pleaded with her.

The entry in Rachel's diary swirled through her mind. *Joshua was not found.* Joshua had died, unmarried. She'd never been here. Nor did she belong. Her world existed 120 years in the future. His ended in less than two. Fate had never meant them to be together. "I wish I could."

He stared at Sarah for a moment, then stormed down the aisle toward the door.

YESTERYEAR'S LOVE

Janet Quinn

JOVE BOOKS, NEW YORK

TIME PASSAGES is a registered trademark of Penguin Putnam Inc.

YESTERYEAR'S LOVE

A Jove Book / published by arrangement with
the author

PRINTING HISTORY
Jove edition / June 1999

The Penguin Putnam Inc. World Wide Web site address is
http://www.penguinputnam.com

ISBN: 0-515-12535-0

A JOVE BOOK®
Jove Books are published by The Berkley Publishing Group,
a division of Penguin Putnam Inc.,
375 Hudson Street, New York, New York 10014.
JOVE and the "J" design
are trademarks belonging to Penguin Putnam Inc.

PRINTED IN THE UNITED STATES OF AMERICA

10 9 8 7 6 5 4 3 2 1

To my sons, Tom, Michael, and Robby.
Thank you for all your love, confidence, and support.

To my sister, Kathy.
Thank you for being my biggest fan.

To my critique group, Debra and Delilah.
Thank you for all your help and encouragement.

Chapter 1

SARAH MARTIN BRUSHED at the front of her blue silk blouse with a paper napkin as she choked. "Now look what you've made me do." She hiccupped, a giggle getting caught in the cough.

"Me?" LeeAnne batted her thick eyelashes at Sarah.

"Yes, you." Sarah threw the wadded-up napkin at her friend. The tight red dress made LeeAnne's pale skin glow and her blond hair shine. Blue eyes smiled mischievously from behind the fluttering lashes.

"You're the one who made the comment about Elvis's pants being too tight and being able to see—"

"Stop." Sarah burst into another fit of giggles and looked away from LeeAnne. She stared up at the ceiling at the shiny silver orb shooting out rays of light across the dance floor and tried to push from her mind the image of the slightly overweight Elvis impersonator jiggling his way across the dance floor. She mopped at the tears of laughter streaming down her face with the damp cocktail napkin stolen from beneath LeeAnne's drink. "I'm going to the ladies' room to fix my makeup and see if I can get this drink out of my blouse."

LeeAnne chuckled. "No use. The grenadine's going to stain."

"It's your fault." Sarah wrinkled her nose and slid down from the bar stool, holding onto the table until her heels clattered against the floor. Straightening her skirt, she stomped off toward the rest room. She held her head up, eyes forward, pretending to ignore the gauntlet of men she traversed, but inspecting every face she passed. She caught smiles out of the corner of her eye, but she couldn't tell if they smiled or smirked at the stain across her left breast.

Returning to the table, she hoisted herself up onto the stool, using the rung as a step. She glanced around for her friend and caught a glimpse of LeeAnne's red dress behind a lumbering form gyrating his arms. *Serves her right, getting stuck with godzilla.* Sarah laughed and reached for her drink. After taking a sip, she propped her chin in her hands and leaned against the bar.

The decision to come tonight had been a good one. After hiding out at LeeAnne's for a week, she needed some diversion. The flashing red and purple strobe lights made the people on the dance floor seem to jerk from spot to spot, rather like an old silent movie. A mass of humanity moved in front of her in time to the music. Off to the left the Elvis impersonator wiggled his hips and she quickly looked away, stifling another giggle. The man in front of her, dressed in tight pants and an even tighter shirt, twirled and spun and threw his arms out in strange gestures. His anorexic-looking dance partner wore a bored expression above an extremely short and tight orange dress. Her body swayed softly, but never really moved.

"Sit up straight."

Sarah jumped, nearly spilling her drink again. She turned and looked at LeeAnne, who slid back onto her bar stool. "Is your dance finished?"

"My feet have been trod on enough. Now get your chin out of your hands and sit nicely. No one will come over and ask you to dance if you slouch."

"I don't care. I'm having fun watching these wackos."
She didn't want to be noticed by anyone. She preferred to
stay on the outside, observing.

"That's not the point. We're here to find you a boyfriend."

"You're here to find me a boyfriend. I'm quite happy on
my own. Besides, as many hours as I work, who has time to
start a relationship."

LeeAnne eyed Sarah closely. "Don't worry. You won't
meet any more loonies like Jack."

A shudder ran through Sarah. She looked over her shoulder and scanned the faces around her. She adjusted the scarf
wound around her neck and rubbed her left arm softly
through the silk. Wincing at the pain of even that slight
touch, she shook her head. "I certainly hope not! He nearly
killed me!"

LeeAnne reached over and patted Sarah's hand. "Don't
worry, the scarf hides the bruises he left around your neck. I
don't know how you can still function. If some nutcase had
stalked me, broken into my house, and tried to choke me to
death, I'd still be locked in a rubber room screaming my
lungs out."

Sarah's stomach twitched. "Without your support, I *would*
be."

LeeAnne wrapped her arm around Sarah's shoulders and
hugged her.

"Ouch," said Sarah.

LeeAnne jumped back. "I'm sorry. I forgot he bruised
your arms when he attacked you."

Sarah shuddered and glanced over her shoulder again.

LeeAnne leaned close to be heard over the music. "Did I
tell you I really like your hair short? You've finally stopped
hiding behind all that hair you had falling in your face all the
time."

"I'm getting used to it." A coldness settled in her bones as
she remembered the steel edge of Jack's knife against the back
of her neck. Death had touched her that night. "He didn't leave
me much choice after he took a hunk out of the back. It truly is
short."

"It's cool and easy to take care of." LeeAnne fluttered her eyelids. "And it makes your huge gray eyes stand out."

"Like an owl's?" Sarah smiled.

LeeAnne smacked Sarah's hand. "No, you brat, so people can see how beautiful they are. I'm just thankful he only cut your hair."

"Me too." Sarah sighed. Even after a week she still hadn't mustered up the courage to go back to work. Only with a huge amount of pleading on LeeAnne's part had she been persuaded to leave her sanctuary tonight. She had to get on with life. She couldn't spend the rest of her life hiding. The bruises were starting to fade, but the memories haunted her day and night. "I can't stay with you forever. I'm going back home tomorrow." She hated being afraid, but more importantly she hated putting her friend in danger.

"Of course you can stay with me forever." LeeAnne sipped her drink.

"No. He might hurt you as well if you get in his way." The hatred that gleamed in Jack's eyes haunted her dreams. She shook her head to clear the vision, trying to focus on the dancers in front of her. She didn't want to remember his eyes focused on her.

"He doesn't know where I live," LeeAnne reminded Sarah. "Besides, he's probably found someone else and you won't see him again. Psycho stalkers are that way."

"And how would you know? If only the police would keep him locked up." Sarah shivered. "You weren't there. He said he'd see me dead before he'd let another man touch me." The look in his eyes had backed up his words. "And I don't even have a man in my life."

"Hell, the man's slipped a gear. You never even dated him." LeeAnne ran her finger around the edge of her glass, staring down into its contents. "See anyone out there you want to dance with?"

Sarah laughed a nervous hiccupping laugh and took a sip of her drink. "Stop changing the subject. I can't concentrate on my business at your place."

"So, take a vacation. You deserve it."

"Pete's having fits. He can't do everything on his own."

She thought of her gray-haired partner chewing on the end of his index finger. He'd been patient the last few days while she'd hid out at LeeAnne's. But two new big accounts needed computer systems installed and employees trained to use them, and their other accounts required attention as well.

"Stay a few more days. Jack'll get bored and wander off to pursue some other woman."

"Excuse me."

Sarah tipped her head backward to look up at the sound of a male voice. A tall, muscular man with red hair and pale green eyes smiled down at her. "Yes?"

"Would you care to join me in a waltz?"

"Of course she would." LeeAnne smiled broadly.

"I can answer for myself." Sarah swiveled around on the bar stool. Her gaze traveled over the man from his green flannel shirt and tight blue jeans down to the top of his boots. Glancing back at his face, she flashed him a smile. Red hair curled slightly at his ears. His eyes seemed to swallow her up. "Yes. That would be very nice," she stammered.

She stiffened as he placed his hand at her waist to swirl her around the dance floor. His hand warmed a spot on her back. He smiled down at her. A body jostled into her and someone mumbled a "sorry" under his breath. A jumble of perfumes and colognes assailed her. He caught her free hand with his and tightened his grip at her waist, pulling her into him. He smelled of citrus, and the soft fibers of his shirt caressed her face. She couldn't breathe. The room seemed to shrink in on her. A sudden urge to pull away and rush off the floor raced through her. He stood too close. Stepping back half a step, she took a deep breath and tried to calm her racing heart. She would not allow Jack to make her afraid of every man she met. "I'm Sarah." Her voice came as barely more than a whisper."

"Josh." He jerked her to one side. "Sorry. This place is so crowded."

Sarah glanced over Josh's arm and saw the Elvis impersonator gyrating next to them. Giggles bubbled up from within her. Tension flowed out of her body and she relaxed into his embrace.

"What's so funny?" A grin that made his teeth flash and his eyes sparkle spread across his face.

"Nothing—nothing that I can say right now, anyway." She buried her face against his shirt and let the rhythm of the music flow over her. LeeAnne had been correct. She needed to get out more.

After the dance, Sarah took Josh and led him off the dance floor. "Come and meet my strange friend who dragged me here."

"Only if you'll tell me what you keep giggling about."

Sarah glanced over her shoulder. Not seeing Elvis anywhere, she said, "Did you see . . . ?" She launched into the story as they maneuvered their way through the crowd.

Josh was laughing loudly by the time Sarah found LeeAnne. Jumping up onto the bar stool, she introduced Josh to LeeAnne and reached for her drink.

"The waitress stole it while I wasn't looking." LeeAnne held her hands up and let them flop back at the wrists.

"I'll get you another one. What were you having?" Josh leaned against the high table in front of Sarah so his chest brushed against her arm.

A shiver ran through her. "That's not necessary."

LeeAnne kicked her. "A Vodka Collins. Two of them." She fluttered her eyelashes at him.

"You know," Josh said, "this place is terribly crowded. I heard about another place about a mile from here that isn't quite so popular and a person can breathe. If you lovely ladies would be of a mind, I'd be glad to buy you a drink down there. We might be able to talk without screaming."

Sarah tensed and shook her head.

LeeAnne smiled at Josh. "We feel safer here in a crowd." She reached over and patted Sarah's hand.

"I meant we'd take separate vehicles and meet there. I'd never presume to ask two ladies I'd just met to ride with me." Josh's cheeks turned pink.

"You go on." Sarah leaned away from him so he no longer touched her. "We're fine here."

"The other place is safer, Cath." His eyes pleaded with her.

"My name's Sarah. Here is perfectly safe." She gripped the edge of the table.

"We couldn't go anywhere safer." LeeAnne's smile started to fade. "I know several of the bartenders and patrons."

"It was just a thought. Two Vodka Collins. Right?" Josh smiled and moved off across the room to purchase drinks.

"He's cute." LeeAnne watched him walk away.

"And very pushy. Maybe we should leave before he gets back." Sarah studied him from the back. His jeans clung to his firm buttocks and defined his long, muscular legs to the top of brown leather cowboy boots. "You don't suppose he's a psycho too?"

"Sarah! Give me a break." LeeAnne smacked Sarah on the arm. "Not all men are psychos."

"Ouch!"

"Lighten up. He seems nice. And you can't blame a guy for trying to hit on you. You are a beautiful woman. The least you can do is be nice to him. You don't have to go home and crawl in bed with him." LeeAnne gave her a smug smile. "Now aren't you glad I made you come?"

"Yes, I'm glad, but it's only been one dance and a drink. Doesn't mean I'll ever see him again."

"You'll see him again. He's got that 'I want to take her to bed' look." She held her hands, fingers intertwined, beneath her chin and smiled sweetly while she playfully batted her eyes at Sarah.

"You're incorrigible." Sarah laughed.

"I know. I work at it." LeeAnne dropped her hands into her lap. "You two would make a great couple, even if he can't remember your name."

"We'd look strange. I barely come to his armpit."

"But his being tall could be very convenient. He could lift you up on the bar stool so you don't have to jump. It would keep his muscles in shape for other things."

Sarah smiled as he disappeared into the crowd. "You're terrible." Maybe it would be nice to have a man around once in a while. But first she had to make sure Jack disappeared from her life.

"You need a man to permanently liven up your boring existence." LeeAnne's eyes twinkled.

"I didn't say I wanted to run off and marry the guy. And life has been anything but boring lately."

"Yeah, but he's a good not-boring. And, is he a looker."

"Good grief, LeeAnne. I just met the man. Give me a break." She searched the crowd to see if Josh was returning. She gasped and her hand went to her neck. Her heart caught on a beat.

"What's wrong?"

"Jack's here." Sarah watched his dark shoulder-length hair bounce softly as he strode through the crowd. His brow wrinkled as his dark eyes darted from side to side. The veins in his neck popped out. For a second, she couldn't move. The room started to spin wildly and she could feel the cold steel edge of Jack's knife against her neck.

She had to escape.

Sliding from the stool, she edged toward the rest room.

A hand grabbed her arm roughly and spun her around. "What are you doing here?" Jack's eyes burned into her.

She backed away, but he increased the pressure on her arm and dragged her to him. "None of your business," she snapped, trying to sound more sure of herself than she felt. His fingers added new bruises to her arm. Ice filled her veins. A tremble raced through her. Searching the crowd, she sought help. "You're hurting me," she cried, yanking and twisting to pull away.

"I told you I wouldn't let you be with anyone else. We're getting out of here." He turned and jerked her after him. She stumbled.

"Jack, let go. I'm not going with you. I told you there's nothing between us. I hardly even know you." She pulled back.

"You're mine until I say different and I don't say different." His eyes flashed fire as he looked back at her.

"Let her go, Jack. I'll call the cops." LeeAnne suddenly stood in front of Jack, her hands on her hips. She tipped her head up to glare at him.

"Get out of the way, bitch." Jack shoved her into a passing man who kept her upright.

"Chill out, fella. Leave the women alone." The man supported LeeAnne by the elbows.

"Butt out. It's none of your business," Jack snarled. He dragged Sarah toward the door as the man backed away, letting LeeAnne fall into the gathering crowd.

Sarah leaned back, trying to dig her high heels into the floor to slow him down. Finding sudden traction, she pulled away from Jack and lurched backward. He yanked her back up, nearly dislocating her arm from her body. She grabbed him to steady herself. His muscles rippled against his shirt's sleeve. Fear coursed through her. "Help me. Someone help me." She tried to scream but it came out as only a faint whisper. Her lungs screamed for air. The mass of people parted like the Red Sea as he dragged her along.

LeeAnne caught up with them. "Someone call nine-one-one. He's going to kill her." Her shrieking voice drifted across the room, melting into the raucous voices and laughter that surrounded them.

Jack stopped suddenly and Sarah slammed into his back. Shaking herself, she looked around him to see Josh standing in front of him, three drinks in his hands. Sarah prayed he would come to her aid and free her from this nightmare.

"Let her go. She doesn't want to leave with you." Josh's voice was even, his stance rigid.

"Get the hell out of my way. It's none of your damn business." Jack shoved Josh. The drinks crashed to the ground, soaking the bottom of Josh's pant legs.

"Let the lady go." Josh rocked forward on the balls of his feet.

Jack pulled a knife out of his jacket and held it to Sarah's throat. "Back away."

"He's got a knife!" someone screamed.

"It's all right. Calm down." Josh held his hands in front of him, palms out. "Let the lady go."

Jack shoved Sarah in front of him, twisting her arm behind her. "Walk." He brandished the knife toward Josh.

"Help me," Sarah mouthed. She prayed someone would take the knife from Jack before he used it on her. She didn't want to die. Her entire body shook. Her legs could hardly hold her. This nightmare kept recurring, like an old late-night television movie. She still couldn't believe this was happening to her. Lunatics didn't stalk people in real life, did they?

Jack pushed her forward, keeping her between him and Josh. As he shoved her through the door she saw Jack's red pickup truck parked against the curb.

"'Bout time . . ." a male voice sounded next to Sarah. She turned her head to plead for help from the valet parking attendant. His jaw dropped open. He stared at them with eyes wide. "Hey, mister. Let the lady go."

Jack turned and flashed the knife at the attendant. The man held his hands in front of him as if to ward off a blow. Sweat beaded on his sunburned forehead. "It's okay, man. Don't want to get involved in no domestic squabbles." The short man stepped backward.

Sarah tried to force air into her lungs. If she screamed, maybe someone would do something. She couldn't see Josh anymore. The crowd had swallowed him up along with any hope of rescue. She was alone. She had to calm down. Her survival depended on getting out of this by herself.

Jack slammed her against the cab of the truck. The door handle cut into her back. The knife clattered against the roof. "Whore. What were you doing with that guy?"

"What guy?" She held her voice steady. *Think,* she told herself. *Think and look for a chance for escape.*

"Liar." Jack's fingers tightened around her throat.

Black spots formed before her eyes. The air in her lungs burned as she tried desperately to get a breath. Sarah clawed frantically at Jack's hands. Kicking him, she slammed the pointed toe of her high heel into his shin. For a blessed second, Jack loosened his grip around her bruised throat.

"Bitch. I'll teach you." Jack's hands closed tightly over her throat once again.

Her body sagged as she futilely struggled for her next breath. Something knocked against her, pushing her to the ground. Air rushed into her lungs and she gulped it in gratefully.

"Sarah, run," a rough male voice commanded from behind her. Someone lifted and pushed her toward the parking lot. Sirens shrieked in the night air, jarring her back into consciousness. Her eyes cleared and the world came back into sharp focus. LeeAnne sat in the driver's seat of her car, the engine running and the passenger door open. Sarah dove into the car. The door slammed closed as the car sped away from the club.

"You okay?" whispered LeeAnne.

"I think so." Sarah gasped for air. Her throat ached. Her body had gone numb.

"Thank goodness for Josh. If he hadn't hit Jack from the side and pushed you away, I don't know what would have happened." A sob punctuated LeeAnne's statement.

"My God, we can't leave him there to face Jack alone."

"He's safe. The cops arrived as we pulled out."

"LeeAnne, we have to go back and make sure he's okay." His soft green eyes and warm smile formed in her mind. She had to know that he was safe.

"He's fine. I'm not going back and put you in danger."

"But, LeeAnne—"

"No buts. I'm taking you home."

Three days ago Jack had tried to kill her for the second time. The police officer had said if she'd press charges, they'd keep him locked up. She did. He made bail before dawn. She left town before his feet hit freedom.

LeeAnne had been right. She needed a vacation and Pete would just have to survive without her for a few weeks. Maybe by then, everything would have calmed down.

Sarah tugged her pink cotton nightie down as she stretched out on the faded flowered bedspread covering her bed in the cheap motel. A dresser with a broken top drawer stood in the corner. It didn't matter. She would only be here a few hours. Long enough to rest and then move on. Tomorrow she'd find a better place, but at two in the morning in the middle of nowhere, she'd been lucky to get a room at all.

For the moment she felt safe. Jack wouldn't know where to look for her. No one, not even LeeAnne, would have expected her to head northeast from Los Angeles and end up

in Wyoming. But, for a long time she'd wanted to see where
her great-grandmother Rachel had lived. With the trouble at
home, now seemed as logical a time as any to investigate her
roots. In a few weeks, Jack would have forgotten her, she
hoped, and she could return to her normal life. In the meantime, she'd fulfill her fantasy of seeing the town where
Rachel had lived. It was a dream she'd had ever since she'd
found her great-grandmother's diary six years ago, tucked in
a trunk in her grandmother's attic. Sarah, fascinated by the
life her great-grandmother described, wanted to trace her
roots. She had been strong and independent for her time and
Sarah admired her fortitude. After being widowed during the
Civil War, she'd traveled from Boston to Wyoming as a
mail-order bride. There she and Sarah's great-grandfather
raised five children in the wilderness. Rachel's strength and
courage gave Sarah hope that maybe she would find some of
that courage to take home with her so the coldness that
seemed to permeate her would leave.

Tomorrow, Sarah would drive the last hundred miles to
the town where her great-grandmother had lived. She hoped
that the church Rachel had been married in would still be
standing. In three days it would be her great-grandparents'
one hundred and twentieth wedding anniversary. Perhaps
she would stop on the way and pick some wildflowers to put
on the altar in their memory, if the altar still existed.

Lights flashed across the curtains of Sarah's room. She
leapt to her feet and peeped out the window. A sigh rattled
through her as she realized it was a sub compact, not Jack's
red pickup truck.

Exhausted, Sarah snuggled back onto the bed, pulled the
worn brown blanket over her, and leafed through her great-
grandmother's diary.

SEPTEMBER 22, 1870

It has been a glorious day. After everything that happened, I am finally married. Henry is checking the
store and will be upstairs directly. My stomach is all

aflutter. I should be changing to the linen nightdress I had made for tonight, but I want to capture my thoughts before they fly away.

The church smelled as wonderful as a flower garden with bunches of mountain dandelions and columbine. Catherine would have loved the event. The sadness I feel at her death during the stagecoach holdup left a shadow over what should have been a perfect day. Henry says it is not my fault, but if I had not convinced her to go west with me to marry Joshua Campbell, she would still be alive. I guess I should count my blessings. If Henry and Mr. Campbell hadn't ridden up with Mrs. Westall, I might have suffered the same fate. I wished to postpone the wedding, but Henry insisted since the minister will not return to Moose Creek for two months and I have nowhere to live except with him. —

I digress. The whole town turned out for the marriage. After all, a mail-order bride and a stage holdup were more excitement than Moose Creek has ever seen. Mrs. Westall says the last happening to cause such a stir was when the stained-glass window was brought in for the church.

I must admit it is the only bit of civilization in this desolate area, but I will not complain. I chose to come west.

The window is astonishing. It brightens up the church. The figure of Christ seems to reach out his hands to me, beckoning me. Just for a moment, I thought I saw him move. Just the fancifulness of a person who has undergone so much excitement in such a short time. I hear Henry's boots upon the stairs.

Sarah looked up at the single glaring light hanging from the ceiling. Would the church and the wonderful stained-glass window that Rachel described still be in Moose Creek? More to the point, what was left of Moose Creek? She flipped to another page further on.

NOVEMBER 19, 1871

Such a harsh land. It takes so much. My heart is breaking. Today the graveyard claimed a new inhabitant.
Mrs. Westall succumbed to the influenza. I shall sorely
miss her for she has been a good friend and confidant.

Good news comes with bad. We are to have another
babe. I fear to carry this one with the same results as
the last. The poor little boy came too early with the ar-
dors of winter still upon us. This babe is not due until
after the spring thaw. I hope he will be stronger. Tomorrow I go again to pray at the church. Maybe the
Christ in the window will answer my prayers and give
us a strong healthy child.

MARCH 30, 1872

Henry found Joshua's horse wandering loose in town
today after the terrible snowstorm. It is strange the animal would be alone. With no sign of Joshua, we are
very worried. Henry, Cookie, and several other men
will go looking for him tomorrow.

APRIL 3, 1872

It has been four days and we still cannot find Joshua.
We fear the worst. Our friend may be lost in the snow.
We may never know.

Sarah closed the diary and clutched it to her heart. Joshua
had never been found. Others in the Martin family had also
suffered. Strangely, Sarah found comfort in the fact that others before her had also had their trials and tribulations. At
least she didn't have to worry about freezing to death or having babies without the aid of a hospital.

• • •

Sarah climbed out of her blue Camaro in front of the old church in Moose Creek, a town that consisted of a general store, a restaurant, and a few scattered houses. After slinging her Dooney Burke leather backpack across her shoulder, she adjusted the red-and-blue flowered silk scarf she'd tied around her neck to cover Jack's finger marks. The flowers didn't match the ones on her baggy white shorts, but the colors came close.

She picked up her bouquet of flowers and started across the asphalt parking lot toward the small, wood-framed building. The sun peeked over the horizon, giving a soft hue to the surroundings. A riot of pinks covered the walls on each side of the wide wooden steps as wild roses climbed trellises reaching for the eaves. Staring up the steps, a small wooden whitewashed door greeted her. A shiny brass door-knob beckoned to her. Sarah wondered if it looked any different than it had in her grandmother's day, as she imagined her grandmother climbing those stairs, walking toward the waiting arms of her grandfather.

Trancelike, she retraced the steps she knew Grandmother Rachel had taken, imagining her great-grandfather waiting on the other side of the door. Sarah's stomach fluttered in anticipation. Her hand reached out slowly for the doorknob and let the door swing backward. She stepped across the threshold.

A floor-to-ceiling wooden partition blocked her view of the church. It had probably kept the wind and snow from pouring down the center aisle during the winter as the parishioners had sat huddled in their pews. The paint showed faint signs of wear from years of use.

She slowly stepped around the wall, holding her breath. The clacking of her sandals against the highly polished hardwood floor was silenced as her feet stepped onto a rust-colored carpet. Minimal signs of wear showed on the carpet that ran up the center of the tiny church. Sarah bent and touched the edge of one of the pews. The wood felt like satin as she let her hand drift across it from one pew to the next.

She sighed deeply. Her great-grandmother's church. The place where she'd married. Yet the changes that had obvi-

ously occurred in the past few years, making everything
more modern and polished, made it difficult for Sarah to
imagine her great-grandmother standing in this building.

Her gaze floated up to the small stained-glass window behind the altar. The bright morning sun shone through it. It
was glorious, just as her great-grandmother had described in
her diary. That had not changed. Jesus, surrounded by a
beautiful backdrop of color, still ascended to heaven with
his arms outstretched. No wonder her great-grandmother
had been so fascinated with the window. It imbued Sarah
with an incredible sense of awe and peace as she stared at it.

She drifted slowly toward the altar. A simple wooden
podium stood to the left with a white linen drape down the
front. The altar itself wasn't more than four feet long and
years of polish made it shine where the embroidered linen
drape, which hung over the edges, didn't cover it. The sun
glinted off a simple brass cross standing in the center of the
altar.

Sarah let her eyes follow the shaft of sunlight back up
from the cross to the figure of Jesus. The sun streamed in
around his head, giving him a natural halo, and for a moment Sarah thought she saw him look down and beckon to
her with outstretched arms. She took a step forward, still not
sure of what she was seeing. The light blinded her. Her head
spun and she felt like she was floating off the floor. She
grabbed a pew to support herself and rough wood greeted
her hand. She looked down and stood on unpolished wood.
She shook her head. Her desire to see the church Grandmother Rachel had been married in and the sunlight in her
eyes must be distorting her senses.

"My gracious, child, what happened to you?"

Sarah spun to answer the woman, her hands going to cover
the bruises on her arms. Behind her stood a well-endowed
woman wearing a brown dress that hung to the floor. A tiny
edging of lace showed at her neck and the long sleeves had
tiny petal-like decorations at the cuffs. Sarah stopped, her
mouth open. She blinked furiously. If she cleared her sight,
everything would return to normal. She glanced back at the
altar. The linen cloth had disappeared. A rough wooden cross

stood where the brass one had been moments before. The world started to swirl and she tightened her grip on the edge of the pew, the wood digging into her palm.

She forced her eyes to focus on the woman standing in front of her. A large white apron was tied around her middle. The woman's hair was tucked up under a yellow calico bonnet that didn't match the dress. The town must be holding some type of pageant today. The woman had to be sweltering in that outfit. Sarah watched as the woman tucked errant strands of gray hair back under the bonnet.

"Charlie." The woman's voice became a loud shrill call. "Charlie. Run tell Mr. Martin and Mr. Campbell something's amiss. One of the brides is here and hurt. Don't you be peeking in here. And run home and get me my cape. You hurry yourself up now." The woman moved closer to Sarah, clucking under her breath. "Poor child. You been through a terrible ordeal by the looks of it. We'll take you right over to my parlor just as soon as I get something to cover you with. How ever did you come to be in the church?"

Sarah shook her head. If she took a deep breath and shut her eyes, when she opened them, the woman would be gone, the carpet would be back, and everything would be normal again. She held her breath and leaned against the edge of the pew. She waited for the satiny feel of the wood to return to her fingers. Then everything would be fine.

The slamming of the door sounded along with the stomping of boots. She wouldn't look. If she didn't look, it would go away. All of it.

"Joshua Campbell, take yourself right out of here. The poor child's half scared to death and ready to swoon. I don't know which one of the ladies she is, but she's not dressed proper to be greeting either of you fine gentlemen."

The woman's voice swirled around Sarah. Fainting seemed a logical solution. Maybe she *had* fainted. Or maybe Jack had caused brain damage when he'd cut off her oxygen with his hands at her throat. Or, possibly, she'd just plain had a nervous breakdown. Slowly, she peeked out of one half-opened eye.

Peering around the partition in the back stood a large

man. He clutched his hat to the edge of the wall, staring at her. Red tousled hair stood on end. His fury was evident in his sparkling green eyes as his gaze rested on her bruised arms.

Chapter 2

THE WOMAN IN brown planted herself squarely in front of Sarah. "Mr. Campbell, I will ask you to kindly remove yourself until the child has a chance to put on more than underclothes." She whispered to Sarah, "Are these the new fashion in underthings from back East? Most unusual and don't seem right practical."

Sarah blinked at her.

"I'll kill the bastard that did this to my bride." His knuckles protruded, showing white bumps that matched the paint on the edge of the partition.

"Bride?!" Sarah gasped. She looked back at the stained-glass window. Jesus had turned his eyes toward heaven. She plunked down heavily on one of the pews. No padded cushion to soften her descent. A dream. That was all there was to it. She could think of no other explanation as to why Mr. Campbell so much resembled the man who'd saved her at the club the other night. She'd fallen asleep reading her great-grandmother's diary. Any moment she'd wake up in the dreary hotel room and start her trek to find Moose Creek.

"Mr. Campbell, really. Such language. And you don't rightly know whose bride she is. Calm yourself. I'm taking her to my house for a spot of tea and a change of clothes. Then you may talk with her." The woman's voice turned into a soft coo.

"We must talk with her now, Mrs. Westall. We have to find the other woman." Joshua's voice boomed through the church as he glared at Sarah. "Why aren't you waiting at the stage stop?"

Of course, thought Sarah. This woman could be no one but Mrs. Westall, her great-grandmother's best friend in Moose Creek. No dream would be complete without her.

"What's wrong? What are the ladies doing here?" A deep male voice sounded behind Joshua.

Joshua swung his arm and hat sideways to stop the voice. "There's just one inside, Henry, and I don't know for certain which one. I don't even know what's happened."

"Mr. Martin, you stay outside." Mrs. Westall's voice rose sharply.

"Why?" An arm clad in a green shirt pushed against the bare arm of Joshua.

"'Cause the child's not dressed proper." Mrs. Westall's reply came sharply.

"Then Joshua best be hoping he's staring at his bride and not mine."

A deep red flushed Joshua's face so his skin matched his hair. "I was staring at the bruises on her arms."

His eyes locked with Sarah's as she peeked around Mrs. Westall. She could sense the anger emanating from him, tinged with concern. What she didn't know was why. Or for that matter, where or when. She shook her head. She wanted to wake up now.

"Bruises?" Henry pushed past Joshua.

"You can't see a thing. Mrs. Westall's hiding her." Joshua crammed his hat back on his head. "Let's git so she can tend to her. Then maybe she can tell us where the other bride is."

Sarah gasped. Henry Martin. Her great-grandfather. No doubt about that. He had the same black hair she did and the same soft gray eyes. Her father had always said she took after the Martins. But if this was her great-grandfather, where was her great-grandmother? Brides? The diary told nothing about them disappearing. She gasped. "The stage holdup. Where's Rachel?" She tried to stand, but her legs wobbled. She felt as if someone had punched her in the stomach. Henry and Joshua weren't supposed to be standing in the church. They should be riding out to meet the stage with Mrs. Westall. They should be rescuing Rachel.

"Oh, my God, a holdup." Henry's face blanched as he slumped slightly. "It appears your bride is safe, Joshua." He gripped Joshua's arm as he wobbled slightly, obviously concerned about Rachel.

Joshua clasped the smaller man's shoulder. "Don't worry, Henry, we'll find yours. We'll get the men to search around the town while Mrs. Westall takes care of Miss Hodges. Mrs. Stedman can't be far away. If mine is alive, yours must be."

Miss Hodges. Catherine. Great-grandmother's best friend. For the moment it would do. That is, until they found out that the real Catherine was dead. But was she? Could more have changed than the men not rescuing Rachel? Had she saved Catherine and killed Rachel?

They had to find her. Sarah's head started to spin. What would happen to her if Rachel wasn't found? She pushed past Mrs. Westall. "Wait. You have to find Gr . . . Rachel. Henry, Joshua, please."

Sarah shrugged off the heavy woolen cape Mrs. Westall had wrapped her in for the trip across the town of half a dozen buildings. She laid the brown cape across the sturdy four-poster bed and moved to the windows, parting the lace curtains to stare out of the many-paned window. Leaning her head against the cool glass, she sighed. She could see nothing but trees and bushes. She turned as the door behind her opened.

"Here, dear. Some hot water to wash up." Mrs. Westall moved across the small room to set a white ceramic pitcher with tiny pink flowers on it next to a matching basin. She laid a clean white towel down. "The men just dragged your

trunks in for you. They found the coach and horses a couple
of miles from town. The driver was dead, but no sign of Mrs.
Stedman could be found. I'm so sorry. I'll leave you to get
changed, unless you'd like to take a rest. Dinner won't be
served until noon, but I could fix you a little something if
you're hungry."

"No, thank you. I'm fine." Sarah turned her attention to
the two large trunks that took up most of the room between
the bed and one wall. "I'll just take a nap, if you don't
mind."

"Of course not, dear. Those gentlemen should have
waited 'til you'd had time to wash off the dust from the road
and change into proper clothing before they insisted on
questioning you." Mrs. Westall patted her on the shoulder.
"What happened to your lovely hair, dear? Under a proper
bonnet it won't be so noticeable. Thankfully, it'll grow back
soon enough." Mrs. Westall turned to leave the room, tsking
under her breath.

Sarah laughed softly. This definitely had to be a dream.
No other explanation made sense. But everything seemed so
real. It couldn't be 1870. It had to be the stress of the last
few weeks and her fascination with her great-grandmother's
diary. It was the only possible explanation.

Washing her face would make her feel better, Sarah decided. She looked in the small hand mirror that lay on the
dresser to find her hair standing on end. Reaching for her
backpack, she pulled out a hairbrush and some cleansing
cream. Dipping the brush in the water, she combed it
through her tightly permed curls and patted them back into
place. After washing her face, she turned her attention to the
trunks.

She dragged one away from the bed with some effort.
"Damn, these things are heavy," she muttered. Clothes
couldn't weigh that much, could they? She flipped up the
top to find the most beautiful dress she had ever seen. She
ran her fingers lightly across the cream-colored silk. Definitely not very practical for this part of the country. Laying
the dress carefully on the bed, she found dresses made of
wool and other fabrics she couldn't identify. Sarah smiled to

herself. This was more fun than rummaging through her great-grandmother's trunk when she'd found it a few years ago. These clothes were new and smelled slightly of some kind of flower.

At the bottom of the trunk she found two frying pans and a large pot. Cast iron. *No wonder the trunk weighed so much.* Inside the pot, on top of several towels, lay a brown leatherbound book. Sarah picked it up. Staring at the cover, she recognized it. Her great-grandmother's diary. She clutched it to her chest. This trunk belonged to Rachel, not Catherine. Tears welled in her eyes. Her heart raced. This might not be a dream. She must have really stepped back in time somehow and changed history. Rachel wasn't supposed to be lost—she was meant to be standing in the Moose Creek church about to be married. Somewhere out there was her great-grandmother and she simply had to be found.

She had to go after the men. If this was a dream, it wouldn't matter one way or another. She could enjoy the adventure. But, if this was reality, she had to rescue Rachel or her own existence would be in jeopardy.

Going back to her backpack, she yanked out a pair of blue jeans and slipped them on. She wished she had a warmer blouse to wear. Turning to the dresser, Sarah pulled open several drawers and rummaged through the contents. Nightgowns and undergarments. In the bottom drawer she found a man's shirt. Pulling it on over her tank top, she looked around for something to wear on her feet. None of the shoes in the trunk were going to work and her sandals seemed too flimsy.

Sarah glanced at the one remaining piece of furniture in the room, a tall wooden piece with intricate carvings down the front. Flinging open the doors, she found a pair of boots on the bottom. They were a little too big for her, but she found some socks in the dresser to stuff in the toes. She went to the second trunk to see if she could find a coat of some type, not wanting to take Mrs. Westall's cape. Near the bottom lay a blue wool cape. Draping it over her shoulders, it fell below her knees. It would have to do. She hoped no one minded her borrowing the clothes. And she'd have to borrow a horse, also. *Was that a hanging offense?* She shrugged her shoulders. If she didn't find Grandmother Rachel, it wouldn't matter anyway. She wouldn't exist to be hanged.

She scribbled a note for Mrs. Westall on a piece of paper she found in her purse. Hopefully she wouldn't notice it was a cash register receipt from a modern grocery store, but she couldn't allow the poor woman to worry. Fastening her watch on her wrist, she shoved her belongings back in her backpack and crawled out the window.

Sarah gripped the horse's mane as the saddle slipped slightly to the left. Horses tied up in front of the store should have a properly attached saddle. Riding this beast was difficult enough without doing it from an angle.

She knew the men had headed east in search of the spot where the stagecoach robbery had occurred. Since the town only had one street, she had to be traveling in the right direction. Sarah hoped they weren't too far ahead of her. After all, when someone was tracking outlaws on TV, they often had to dismount several times to study the tracks on the ground.

She glanced at her watch. It wasn't quite noon. At least she had many hours of daylight in case she found herself lost in the woods. She glanced to the side of the road at the brush which threatened to retake it. She definitely didn't relish spending the night alone out here. Something rustled in the bushes next to her. All kinds of wild animals lived out here. She glanced quickly to the right and urged the horse on a little faster.

After what seemed like forever, she finally heard voices ahead of her, just beyond where the road bent. Hopefully, Joshua and Martin waited around the curve. The saddle shifted again. She groaned and tried to right herself, accidentally kicking the horse in the ribs. He bolted forward. "Whoa, Nellie," she yelled. They thundered around the curve, the saddle sliding even farther to the side. Sarah clutched the horse's mane. Hitting the ground at this speed would have to hurt immensely. She wondered if she could push herself off without landing under the horse's hooves.

Strong hands grabbed her as she and the saddle slipped completely to the horse's side and she started to fall. She grasped at muscular shoulders. "Thank you," she gasped and looked up into deep green eyes. A red mustache hung only inches from her face. "Joshua. Thank goodness."

He held her tightly, staring down into her face. After several seconds, he finally spoke in a deep, warm voice. "Miss Hodges, what in blazes are you doing?"

"Falling off that stupid beast, but you saved me just in time. I'm grateful, but you can put me down now." She smiled sheepishly up at him. His eyes resembled a green meadow in the mid-afternoon with the sun shining on it. For a moment, she wished she were Catherine.

"What are you doing out here?" His voice became gruff as he continued holding her crushed against his chest with strong arms.

He smelled of the woods. Warmth seeped through her, making her giddy. "Following you."

"Why?"

"To find my gr . . . best friend. Rachel has to be found. I couldn't just sit around and wait." She tried to push herself away from his chest. He had to understand how imperative finding Rachel was.

Henry's voice came from behind her. "She belongs in town. She will only get in our way. Besides, isn't that Jake's horse she's riding?"

"One of us will have to take her back." Joshua shifted her slightly in his arms. She smelled wonderful. He had never encountered such a fragrance before, but he liked it. It smelled nothing like the lavender that most women wore. And she was such a delicate woman. She fit in his arms just as a child would.

"You take her back. She's your bride." Henry turned and walked to retrieve Jake's stallion from where he stood a few feet farther on munching grass.

"I won't go back. Not until Rachel's found." She struggled in Joshua's arms.

"Miss Hodges, you have no alternative but to go back. It isn't safe out here." Joshua looked down at the upturned nose and had an overwhelming urge to kiss it. He looked away at Henry. Later, after they were married, he could find out if she tasted as good as she smelled.

"Put me down. I can't argue like this." Sarah kicked her feet. "I won't be treated like a child. I might be able to help."

Joshua set her on her feet and watched her brush her shirt down so that it covered her bottom. Levi's, the likes of which he'd never seen before, molded her legs to the top of her oversized boots. Tight curly hair framed her face. She made a most unusual sight. Laughter threatened to escape him. No wonder this Miss Hodges was a spinster lady of six and twenty years. No man would have her. She seemed to have no ladylike inclinations nor any delicacies about being seen undressed or in trousers. But, then, in the wilderness, such attitudes might be better. "And how do you intend to help, Miss Hodges? You can't seem to remember anything that's happened." He rubbed the side of his face.

Sarah tipped her head back to stare up at him. "For one thing, when you find my gr . . . Rachel, the two of you will scare her to death. She's already been kidnapped and will think you're doing the same."

"Miss Hodges can't be out at night alone with two men. Think of her reputation," Henry said, intruding on the conversation once again. "Besides, Jake will be wanting his mount back."

"We have more important things to think about," Sarah interjected. "We should be looking for Rachel and Jake'll live without the beast until we get finished with our business." She glared at them. Men. So often they were useless in an emergency. And this could turn into a very dire emergency if they didn't find Rachel and get her married to Henry.

Joshua laughed. "We're damned no matter what we do and I don't think you need to overly worry about her reputation or Jake's. I plan on marrying Miss Hodges as soon as the itinerant preacher comes to town in two days. And I'll make it up to Jake. If we split up and I take her back to town, you may have more than you can handle when you catch up with the bandits. We can't waste any more time by both of us going back. I could try to catch up with you, but it'll be hours."

"Oh, hell." Sarah looked up into Joshua's eyes. "We are all going because I'll be a nervous wreck until I know Rachel's okay. Now, fix that damned saddle on that stupid beast so we can get started." She tapped her foot while she watched Joshua straighten the saddle, tighten the cinch, and shorten the stirrups, then she moved to mount the horse again, taking a deep breath. She definitely didn't want them to figure out she'd never ridden a horse before today. It looked easy in the movies, and this one seemed to go where she pointed it. So far. "I'll only follow you again if you try to take me back, so you damn well better mount up." She gritted her teeth as she held onto the saddle horn.

Joshua shook his head. "What have you gotten me into, Henry Martin?"

"And what does that crack mean?" asked Sarah.

"It was his idea to get mail-order brides." Joshua threw his head back and laughed loudly as he lifted himself on top of his large, gray stallion.

Henry muttered, "Mail-order brides—don't know what you'll get. I just pray Mrs. Stedman isn't cut from the same cloth as Miss Hodges. I may have done both of us a disservice."

Sarah glared fiercely at the two men.

Sarah's stomach growled. She'd had a late breakfast this morning, about 120 years from now, and hours ago. The men seemed in no hurry to stop and eat. She sneaked a peak at her watch. Nearly nine. Didn't the sun ever set in this country? Her legs ached from trying to stay in the saddle and her rear had probably been flattened forever from bouncing. Never would she admit defeat, however. Besides, neither man would take her back after all the miles they'd gone. She'd never figured those damn robbers could have gotten so far so fast dragging two women along.

"I don't think we'll be able to go much farther tonight." Joshua looked back at Sarah.

Thank goodness. She shifted for the millionth time on the

horse, trying to ease the pain in her backside. "Please don't stop on my account," she said through clenched teeth, trying her best to smile at him.

"Don't worry, we're not. The horses need a rest and I could use some food." Joshua reined in his horse and swung his leg over the animal's rump as he lowered himself to the ground. "Henry, you get the fire started. I'll get some water." He reached up and lifted Sarah down.

She leaned against him for a moment while her legs decided they would hold her after all. Heat seared from his chest into her body. Where his hands touched her waist, a charge of electricity shot through her. She pulled away from him.

Following the men had been a really stupid idea. She wanted a shower and a bed. She wanted to wake up from this dream so she could find a cafe where she could get a bagel and cream cheese for breakfast. She wanted to be home even if Jack still stalked her. The great outdoors looked much better on the television than it did up close and personal.

She heaved a big sigh. But if this turned out not to be a dream and they didn't find Rachel soon, nothing would matter. No great-grandmother, no Martin family, no Sarah. A shiver ran up her spine.

"Cold?" Joshua held her by the shoulders.

"A little." His hands were warm even through her shirt.

He pulled her cape from her horse and wrapped it around her. "At least you have *some* of your own clothing on. We'll get a fire started and you'll feel better."

"What do you mean? I only borrowed the shirt." And technically the cape and the shoes, but she didn't think she'd better mention that. She wasn't even sure whose cape she'd borrowed.

He looked down at her legs. "Those pants don't belong to some young boy?"

"No."

"I've never seen anything quite like 'em."

"Stop jawing and get the water. I want coffee." Henry's voice interrupted their discussion.

Sarah pulled the cape around her and went to sit on a rock next to the fire. "What's for dinner?"

"Got some venison. Got some flour. Want to make some biscuits?" Henry fed the fire with twigs.

"Here's your water." Joshua set the coffeepot next to the fire. "You cooking, Henry?"

"Thought Miss Hodges might." Henry grinned.

"I don't do barbecue."

"Huh?" Joshua sat down next to her, holding his hands out toward the flames.

"I've never cooked over an open fire. I'm sure I'd make charcoal." A fire under the stars would be romantic, if she had a hotel room to go back to. She looked up at Joshua. A perfect evening would be sitting and roasting hot dogs and marshmallows, then lying back in his arms and counting the stars. The heavens were filled with them. More than she'd ever seen in the skies over Los Angeles.

"What are you talking about?" Henry dropped coffee grounds into the pot and set it in the fire.

"Never mind." Sarah smiled. "One of you better cook if we're going to eat."

"Cooking is woman's work." Joshua poked at the fire with a stick.

"Says who?" Sarah glared at him.

He laughed softly. "Most people do."

"This woman doesn't cook over an open fire." She folded her arms across her breasts and stared at the two men defiantly.

"We can sit here all night and argue, or we can cook ourselves." Henry took out his knife and sharpened a stick.

"I'll go make sure the stock is secure and get our bedrolls. You cook." Joshua pulled a blade of grass from next to him and stuck it between his teeth before he stood up and strolled away. A woman who couldn't cook. He'd never met one before.

Something about Catherine fascinated him for some reason. Maybe it was her odd manner of dress or her reckless streak. Obviously she'd been in the sun without her hat more than once. Her golden-colored skin attested to that fact. But he liked it just as he liked the smell of her. He'd never been near a woman who smelled like she did. He wanted to fold her into his arms and bury his head in her hair, what there was of it. What had happened to make her cut her hair so short? Had the robbers cut it off? Had she had some strange ailment? He couldn't ask her, not yet, but the desire to know burned in him. Another desire grew beside that—a desire he yearned to do something about.

He kicked at the dust with his boot and strolled back to the campfire.

Sarah bit into the piece of meat Henry offered her. "Thank you." She smiled at him. Venison, biscuits, and coffee. Not a very balanced meal, but hunger consumed her and she didn't care. Anything would taste good right now and, surprisingly enough, it tasted wonderful. She'd have to do with just half a cup of coffee, though. The caffeine would keep her awake all night.

She watched while Joshua poured himself a cup and quickly gulped down most of it. "Nothing like good, strong coffee." He refilled his cup, then sat in front of her, leaning back against the side of the rock. His arm brushed against her leg. He took the meat offered by Henry. "Does it suit you, Miss Hodges?"

"Very much. But please stop calling me miss." She took a sip of coffee, nearly choking. She'd never tasted anything so strong or bitter. Setting the cup down, she tried to shift so Joshua's arm didn't touch her, but to do so would mean falling off the rock. One tumble a day in front of him was sufficient, so she tried shifting her leg away a little. His arm still brushed her leg. A quiver ran through her.

"And what would you have us call you?" Joshua leaned forward to pour himself more coffee.

How he could drink the brew that resembled mud, she simply didn't understand. She'd kill for a soda. "Sa . . . Cathy."

"Cathy?" He looked up at her with his clear green eyes.

"Cathy. Short for Catherine." She'd always wanted a nickname. Sarah didn't shorten into anything intelligible. So, for a short time, she'd borrow someone else's.

Henry threw a stick onto the fire. "Seems a bit informal, Miss Hodges."

"I like Cathy. Is that a problem, Henry?" Sarah asked sharply.

Henry glared at her. "Miss Hodges and Mr. Martin would be more appropriate under the circumstances."

"What circumstances?" Sarah looked from Henry to Joshua.

"We've only just met," said Henry.

"Nonsense. I can't remember the last time I called someone by his surname."

Joshua choked, sputtering coffee into the fire. "You cooked up this idea, Henry. Remember that."

Henry stared at Sarah with narrowed gray eyes. "You're never going to let me forget."

"Not in the near future." Joshua stood up. "Did you think to bring a bedroll, Miss Cathy?" He moved to bank the fire.

"Well . . . no. But I can sleep wrapped up in my cape. It's plenty warm."

"Lay here next to the fire." He pointed to a flat spot covered by grass. "I'll bed down near." He spread out his blanket. "One of us better stand guard in case the thieves backtrack. You want me to go first?" He turned to look at Henry.

"No. Get Miss Hodges settled in. I'll call you in a couple of hours." Henry disappeared into a clump of trees.

"Do you really think the thieves will come back?" Sarah sat where Joshua had pointed, wide-eyed.

"Could be. Don't worry. Do you know how to use a rifle?" Joshua sat next to her.

"No." She shook her head.

"Well, you'd better learn if you're going to live in these parts. Lie down and wrap up in your cloak. It'll keep you warm."

Sarah pulled her head in as she lay down and curled up her legs so she would be completely covered. After a few minutes, she stretched her legs. All of her muscles were cramping from being on the horse, and the ground felt very hard.

Joshua, noticing her discomfort, called out to her. "Get up."

Sarah peeked at him out of the blue material. The fire glinted off his red hair, making it appear to be aflame. "Why?"

"I'll put my other blanket down and then I'll put the cloak over you. You'll be more comfortable that way."

"But what'll you use? You'll freeze."

"Won't be the first time or the last."

Sarah smiled at him. "I've put you out enough. I can't take your blanket."

"Women need to be protected and taken care of. I can't have my future wife getting the grippe because she had to lay on the cold ground."

She snatched her hand away from him. Taken care of, indeed! "Excuse me, but I can manage just fine."

"I'm sure you can." His eyes laughed at her.

She curled back into the cape, her back turned toward him.

"Miss Cathy, you're just being stubborn. Take the blanket."

"I'm fine." Stubborn! He hadn't even begun to see stubborn.

"No, you're not. Besides, I can't have you feeling poorly in the morning. We have a long way to go."

"Hmph."

"Miss Hodges, I insist."

"Don't worry. I won't slow you down." She glared up at him, but the cramps in her legs conspired against her and won the argument for him. She couldn't stay curled up if she ever hoped to move again. "Okay. You win. But only if we share. I won't have you freeze."

After stretching her legs, she stood and watched him make up the bed.

"You can lay down now. Here's my extra shirt you can use as a pillow." He grinned at her.

"Thank you." She took the shirt. "I'm sorry for the inconvenience."

"I doubt that." He lay down next to her and spread her

cape across her. Such a fragile one. He could pick her up and snap her in half like a twig. How she'd managed to escape the stage robbers perplexed him. But then, she was a spunky little thing. They were probably glad to be quit of her.

An owl hooted nearby.

"What was that?" Sarah bolted upright.

"Just an owl out looking for his supper."

A shiver ran through her. "You sure?"

Joshua gently pulled her arm so she would lie back down. "Positive. Go to sleep. We'll be off at first light and you need some rest." Her body trembled next to his. He rolled on his side and pulled her into his arms. "I won't let the wild animals get you."

She snuggled against his chest. One night wouldn't matter. He had promised to marry Catherine Hodges and so until they found the real one she'd be Miss Hodges. If they found her. If she still lived. In Rachel's diary Catherine had died during the stage robbery, but now she'd changed things. How much was yet to be discovered?

Tomorrow they'd find Catherine and Rachel, dead or alive. Then she'd have some heavy-duty explaining to do. All of this smacked of a strange dream. Joshua was a reincarnation of the man she'd met the other night, and being in the church had just set her imagination on a rampage. No other explanation could be possible. "I'm being silly," she said aloud without realizing it.

"Very—but women are allowed."

Her body tensed against his and pulled away. "What?"

He tightened his grip on her. "Go to sleep."

"But . . ." she sputtered.

"We'll argue in the morning. It'll give us something to do while we ride."

She remained stiff for a moment, then relaxed against him. "I'm not used to being outside at night."

Joshua hugged her tightly. Maybe Henry's idea of getting mail-order brides hadn't been such a bad idea after all. If nothing else, this one would make his life interesting. She rolled over so her back curled into his body. He draped his arm around her. Her head nestled beneath his chin. Her hair smelled fresh and was soft against his neck. She fit perfectly against him. His Cathy. No. Cath. That name fit this unusual woman far better.

She was right—the cape was too short to cover his legs. But he wouldn't suffer from the cold. Not with her curled into him. The heat within him would keep out the cold. Sleep would not come tonight. Once she fell asleep, he'd relieve Henry. No sense in both of them staying awake all night.

Chapter 3

THE SUN STRUGGLED to burn off the morning chill as Sarah and the two men continued their ride south. The beauty of the scenery distracted her from the endless distance they traveled. Sarah had never seen so many trees or such thick grass. Wildflowers of every color dotted the green for miles—miles upon miles of nothing but growing things and no signs of civilization. Off to one side a deer peeked out of a clump of bushes. It stared at them with huge brown eyes as they passed, then it darted quickly into the denser undergrowth.

Sarah had been to the mountains around Los Angeles and seen forests of a sort, but nothing to compare with the wonders of this countryside. The green, unlike anything she had ever seen, was deeper and stronger, not the dull brown of southern California's Septembers. Her horse slowed as she watched a beaver repair his dam along a small creek. She laughed softly and breathed in the clean air.

"We don't have time for a rest." Joshua's voice came as crisp as the air.

She jumped and looked over at him. "I was watching the beaver."

"We have to keep going. The tracks look fresher."

"I know, I know," she groaned. Even though she'd dampened her hair before they'd started more than two hours earlier, she knew it stood up on end by now. Her hair, when permed, always frizzed after she'd slept on it. She would give anything to just stand in a hot shower and let the water massage her body. Instead, this morning she had splashed cold water on her face. She felt sticky and she ached from head to toe. And eight A.M. hadn't even arrived yet. This day could prove to be very long indeed.

"Hold up." Henry's voice sounded hushed.

Joshua instantly became alert. "What?"

Henry pointed toward a pillar of smoke in the east.

"It could be a settler's cabin." Joshua took off his hat and ran his fingers through his red hair.

"The tracks are veering in that direction. We'd better take a look. Miss Hodges, stay put," Henry ordered.

"Like hell."

"Miss Hodges, your language is most ill-befitting a lady." Henry straightened in his saddle to glare at her.

"And deserting me out here is none too gentlemanly. I can't even see the cabin." Everything had an unreal quality to it. None of this could be happening. She was riding a horse out in the middle of the wilderness with bad guys lurking who knows where. It reminded her of a television Western, except the reality of it all threatened to overwhelm her.

"We would never abandon you. I merely wish you to be safe," Henry said, looking insulted.

Joshua shook his head and chuckled. "There's no way you'll leave her behind."

Henry gave Joshua a hard look.

They crested the next hill slowly. Nestled amongst a grove of trees sat a dilapidated cabin. A plume of smoke drifted lazily from a stone chimney missing several of the top stones. The front steps had disintegrated into a pile. Off to the right, a single horse stood, tied to a tree.

"A trapper?" Joshua spoke softly.

"Might be," said Henry.

"If we travel around to the south, we can come up behind without being seen." Joshua raised himself slightly in his saddle and surveyed the surrounding area. "I don't see signs of anyone else."

"How many men robbed the stage, Miss Hodges?"

Sarah tried to remember what her great-grandmother had written in her diary. There'd been a stage holdup, but no hostages had been taken. Somehow when she stepped through time, she'd altered something. But had Rachel ever said how many men? A guess would do. No one would ever know. "Three, I think. I really don't remember."

"Damn fool woman."

"It's no wonder. It's caused from being strangled. That scared it right out of your head." Joshua stared at her neck.

Instinctively she put her hand up to cover the bruises. She should have remembered to put her scarf back on instead of leaving it lying on Mrs. Westall's bed.

Henry urged his horse ahead slowly. "No matter. Appears to be just one down there at the moment."

Sarah was glad for the cape she'd borrowed as the tree branches pulled at her. Without it, her arms would have been massively scratched. Time became suspended as they carefully picked their way through the trees and came up near the back of the cabin.

"Now what?" she whispered.

"One of us will have to flush out whoever is in that cabin." Henry slid from his horse.

Sarah looked to Joshua. "Isn't that dangerous for Rachel?"

"It's more dangerous to leave her inside, if she's in there." Joshua joined Henry on the ground. "One of us will have to go to the door, and the other one will cover him." Turning to Sarah, he said, "You stay here on your horse. If something happens, ride out of here as if the hounds of hell were behind you."

"Wonderful thought. And where in hell would I go? I'm completely lost now. I have no idea in the world where Moose Creek is—or any other town, for that matter."

"Head northwest." Henry tied his horse to a tree. "You'll hit the road. It'll take you back to town."

"I don't know north from south. We've made so many turns I'm totally confused. You guys just be careful." Her stomach twisted.

"If there's only one man inside, we won't have a problem." Joshua patted her arm reassuringly. "I'll knock on the door."

Her heart skipped several beats. If Joshua didn't belong to someone else . . . His touch sent heat to the core of her being. "Hurry back."

Henry strode down the small incline toward the ramshackle cabin. "I'll go in first. It's my bride inside."

Joshua followed, the stock of his rifle balanced in his right hand. He stood at the corner of the cabin, his stance wary.

Sarah heard a loud rapping sound.

"Trent, Caleb, that you?" A slurred male voice came from inside the cabin.

"Nope," said Henry.

"Then go away."

"Hey. I was just passing by and saw your smoke. Thought you might have a cup of coffee to share," said Henry.

"Didn't hear you ride in." The volume of the man's voice increased.

"Horse went lame back a few miles. Been leading her. Left her up by the trees to graze."

"You just keep on going. Don't got no coffee. Just whiskey."

Sarah slid from her horse. The man clearly had no intention of coming out. She threw her cape over the saddle and crept through the brush to the back of the cabin. A board had shifted to the side, providing a crack for her to peer through. Sunlight streamed in through a jagged hole where the wood had rotted away, dimly lighting the interior of the cabin. The man stood with his back toward Sarah. A woman huddled on the floor just inches in front of her.

"How 'bout a sip of whiskey?" Henry's voice boomed through the door.

"Keep going," the man snarled back. He lifted his gun.

"Rachel?" Sarah hissed. The woman in front of her moved her head slightly. "Rachel?"

Rachel turned her head. With both hands, Sarah beckoned for her to come.

"Not very neighborly of you. I'm stranded out here," Henry hollered.

"Last warning. I've got my rifle aimed at the door. You skedaddle. Don't want no company." The man lifted his bottle with the other hand and took a long swig. He swayed slightly.

Rachel turned back to look at the man. Slowly, she scooted backward across the floor, her skirt marking a trail in the dust, her gaze riveted on the man's back. Sarah held her breath.

She was close enough to touch and once again Rachel turned to Sarah, her green eyes wide with fear. "Ease out of the hole," Sarah mouthed. "We came to rescue you."

Rachel glanced again at the man and then back again at Sarah. Sarah smiled, trying to appear confident, and beckoned. Rachel turned sideways to squeeze through the small hole and was about halfway through when her skirt snagged on a nail. Her body wedged in the hole. Sarah grabbed Rachel under her arms and tugged, hoping to free her from the treacherous nail. A slight creak sounded. The man wavered and started to turn. Sarah grabbed Rachel under her arms and pulled as hard as she could. They didn't move. Sarah yanked again.

"Hey!" The man's gruff voice accosted Sarah's ears. "What the hell?"

Sarah looked up at the rifle pointed at them. The hole in the barrel seemed to grow and threatened to engulf them. "Oh, hell," she gasped, "we're all going to friggin' die." Sarah planted her feet directly behind Rachel and, holding her tightly, threw her weight backward. They shifted slightly.

"Joshua," Sarah screamed, "he's coming out the back." Her voice mixed with the blasting of a gunshot and the splintering of wood.

Rachel screamed. A tearing sound assaulted Sarah's ears. She fell backward, Rachel landing half on top of her.

Sarah shrieked, "Help!"

Another rifle shot rang in Sarah's ears. She had to get them away from the bullets. She scrambled up and dragged Rachel toward the bushes. The air burned in Sarah's lungs as she plunged them both into the first thicket she saw. She covered Rachel's trembling body with her own as the brambles clawed at her. She had her great-grandmother out and she prayed that they would survive whatever came next.

The world became very quiet, except for Rachel's breathing coming from beneath her. Slowly she let out her breath and listened.

"Cath, where are you?"

She rolled sideways. Joshua. Warmth swept through her. Everything was okay. "Here," she cried.

Hands parted the bushes and reached for her. Crushing her against his chest, he smelled of horses and fear.

"Why did you do such a stupid thing?" His voice brushed against her ear.

"I had to get Rachel out." She snuggled against him. For just a moment more, she could have him. Then she had to turn him over to the real Catherine and find a way home to where she belonged. It was definitely time to end this crazy dream.

"We had things under control."

"It didn't seem that way to me. That man wasn't coming out." She sighed. "Where is he?"

"Dead."

She shuddered.

"You could have been killed. Next time you leave the rescuing to Henry and me." He pushed her back roughly by the shoulders and glared down at her. "You understand."

She yanked away from him. His fingers digging into her arms evoked a vivid memory of Jack's face, contorted with fury. Her whole body went cold. "I understand." She turned her back to him, and took slow, deep breaths.

She couldn't explain her actions to him or the fear his anger created in her, nor how important Rachel's rescue was. He'd never understand why rescuing Rachel was imperative.

And she had saved Rachel.

A sudden chill ran up her spine. Was it Rachel? She'd never answered her when she'd called her name. And two women had been on the stage. Where was the other one?

"Rachel?" Her voice rose on the edge of hysteria.

"Yes."

Sarah shuddered with a sigh. "Better get her out of there. She's probably terrified."

Joshua's hand gently rested for a moment on Sarah's shoulder. "I'm sorry. I didn't mean to be angry with you. But, good heavens, woman, you took half a century off my life."

She turned to look up into his eyes, starting to shake uncontrollably. "I'm scared myself. Now get Rachel, please."

Joshua held her a moment longer before he reluctantly let her go and parted the bushes again to help Rachel to her feet. "Mrs. Stedman, I presume. I'm Joshua Campbell."

"And I'm Henry Martin." His voice right next to Sarah made her jump and clasp her hand to her chest. He had moved up so quietly beside them, she hadn't realized he stood there.

"Oh my." Rachel brushed at her skirt. "Not a very proper meeting."

Sarah looked at the large rip down the side of Rachel's green woolen skirt. "I didn't mean to tear your skirt."

Her great-grandmother cast her a half-smile. "The dress can be repaired." The woman started to wobble. Henry swept her up into his arms.

"All this jawing. Poor thing's been through hell. Oh! Pardon me, ma'am." The color in Henry's face heightened as he held her. "We need to get her to some shelter. Are you all right, ma'am?"

"Yes, Mr. Martin. I believe I'm just fine now. Is that terrible man dead?" She sagged against his chest.

"Yes, ma'am. Most certainly."

"Then we must bury him."

"What?" Sarah looked at the woman in her great-

grandfather's arms. They made a lovely couple. They would
have beautiful children, five living ones to be exact. She
smiled broadly. She had saved her family. She wasn't quite
sure how she'd managed. Rachel had two inches on her and
several pounds, not including the mounds of clothing she
wore. How she'd ever pulled her through the hole in the
wall, she didn't know. But she had.

"We need to get you women back to town." Joshua spoke
with finality.

"Not until the man is buried. You can't leave him out here
for the coyotes or bears." Rachel looked pleadingly up into
Henry's eyes.

"We can't hang around here. The other two men might return," Joshua said softly.

"He has to be buried. It wouldn't be Christian to just leave
him." Hiccupping sobs punctuated Rachel's statement.

"He's scum. He probably would have killed you or . . ."
Joshua let his voice trail off.

"Please," sobbed Rachel.

"If Mrs. Stedman wants the louse buried, we bury him,"
Henry said in a matter-of-fact tone.

"Then we'd best hurry. I have no desire to shoot it out
with those other two bandits. Not with the women here."
Joshua dusted his hat against his leg. "I'll look for something with which to dig a grave. You carry Mrs. Stedman
back to the horses. Cath can take care of her."

"Please put me down here. Will one of you gentlemen be
so kind as to get me my reticule from that shack? My Bible
is in it. I want to read a verse over the grave."

"Why would you want to?" Sarah looked at Rachel
askance. Strands of auburn hair poked out of a bun wound
at her neck. A once-fancy hat sat askew on her head.

Rachel tucked her white linen blouse into the waistband
of her skirt, then tugged her matching green jacket down as
Henry released his hold and set her on her feet. "Everyone
deserves a decent burial."

"Take my rifle, Cath." Joshua held out the weapon.

Sarah put her hands behind her back. "No, thank you. I'll
probably shoot one of us. I'll just scream if I hear anything."

"We'll hear you. You have a scream that could wake a dead man." He smiled at her and brushed his fingers down the side of her cheek.

Warmth flooded over her. Sarah wanted him to wrap his arms around her and hold her tightly again. Her insides still shook. But she needed to concern herself with Catherine Hodges. While the men dug a grave, she would have a few minutes alone with Rachel to find out for sure what had become of the woman.

She watched the men walk around the side of the shack. Settling down on the embankment behind the cabin, she patted the dirt. "Join me. You won't get any dirtier than you already are. That outfit is beyond hope anyway."

"A good washing and a little mending and it will do for household chores, though I had hoped it would last a bit longer. I only have one other walking dress for visiting." Rachel remained standing, tears shining in her eyes.

"How can you be talking about clothes after what you've been through? You should be shrieking hysterically." Sarah folded her arms around her knees, trying to keep control of the hysteria that threatened to overwhelm her. It seemed as though she watched the world move before her in slow motion. Nothing seemed in sync any longer. Nothing appeared real.

"If I think about it, I shall start screaming. If Mr. Campbell thinks your screams would wake the dead, he wouldn't want to hear mine. I've never been so frightened in my life."

"And well you should have been. At least you're safe now," Henry piped in as he returned from fetching Rachel's cloak and her bag.

"Oh, thank you so much. At least my traveling paletot survived undamaged. I'll need it to keep from freezing in these fierce winters."

"Huh?" Sarah looked up at Rachel.

Rachel brushed at the cloak with her hand before folding it neatly. She then sat beside Sarah and reached into her bag, pulling out a small Bible and a pair of gloves. She methodically donned her gloves before opening the Bible.

Sarah could see Rachel shake as she tried to turn the

pages. Reaching over, Sarah placed her hand on top of the book. "It won't matter what you read. A simple prayer will do as well." Sarah hesitated. She knew the moment of explanations was nearly upon her and she still had no idea in the world what to say. Nothing would make any sense. "Where's Catherine?" she whispered.

The tears spilled down Rachel's face and her body started to convulse. "She's dead."

Sarah nodded slowly. Rachel's words came as she expected. A small hope had grown that in changing the past, she had somehow changed Catherine's fate, but it had been only a small hope. "I'm sorry. I know you were best friends."

"I should never have persuaded her to come out here with me." Sobs choked Rachel. "I just couldn't bear leaving her behind. She was so sensitive. Such a shy creature, but so pretty and really such a wonderful person. I knew she'd blossom out here.

"No husbands were available back in Boston after the war with the South. That nice Mr. Campbell offered for her hand. I knew he would come to love her or at least appreciate her. She would have made such a good companion for Mr. Campbell. She just needed a chance."

Sarah took Rachel into her arms, gently rubbing her back. "It wasn't your fault. It's dangerous to travel all this way. I'm sure Catherine understood that."

"But if I hadn't insisted . . ." Rachel rested her head on Sarah's shoulder. The sobs rocked her against Sarah. "They hurt her so. They took . . . liberties. She tried to fight them. I never saw her show such spunk. She clawed one of them terribly across the face. He hit her. Too hard. She crumpled. I tried to help her. They just pushed me away, then tied me up so I couldn't move. They took her away. I knew I was next. But by then they had drunk so much, they could hardly stand. They just passed out."

"It wasn't your fault. She made the final choice to come."

"I don't know."

"Well, I do."

"They wouldn't even let me read a Bible verse over her or

say good-bye. They just laughed at me. Cruel laughter. Then they took her body away."

"Where?"

"I don't know." The sobs became harder.

"Well, at least one of them got what he deserved," Sarah said.

"That's a terrible thing to say."

"They did terrible things." She helped Rachel to her feet and walked around the side of the shack. Joshua and Henry stood not far away in a grove of trees digging a hole. She watched them bending and straightening, dirt flying to the side of them, and contemplated what she was going to do. She simply couldn't explain to Rachel who she really was and who the men thought she was. They would think she was stark raving mad. Hell, she was starting to think she was crazy herself. Yet the question remained: Who could she say she was? Definitely not Sarah Martin. Everyone would certainly question that.

Oh, hell, what was she going to do? It would become apparent all too soon that she wasn't Miss Hodges. Who else could she be? Everybody knew everyone else in these parts.

"Mrs. Stedman, the grave is ready." Henry's voice drifted toward them.

"Coming, Mr. Martin." Rachel walked unsteadily toward the clearing, her Bible clutched in her hand, ready to read a verse over the grave.

Sarah followed slowly, letting distance come between them. Joshua walked back toward her, dusting his hat against his pants.

"You should have brought a hat with you, Cath." His voice was almost like a caress.

"I didn't think about it. In fact, I didn't see a useful one anyway. That hat Rachel's wearing is worthless in protecting her from the sun." He had such warm eyes. Eyes she wanted to watch her always. But . . .

The memory of the entry of her great-grandmother's diary flashed through her mind. *Henry has returned from looking for Joshua. He's found no sign of him.* And they never found Joshua. But that wouldn't happen for a year and a half yet.

It didn't matter. Any moment he would learn his bride-to-be had died and she would be on her own. For some unknown reason she wanted to postpone that moment as long as she could. Long enough to feel his arms around her once more. Just a moment more to enjoy the wondrous part of the dream before it dissolved into reality and she once again stood in modern-day Moose Creek.

He laughed softly. "You're right. It's not really a functional hat for this area. Here." He plunked his hat on her head. "This'll keep the sun off your cute little nose. It seems to have had more than it should have already." He ran his finger down her nose. She was such a little bit of a thing. How she had managed to pull Mrs. Stedman through that wall, he couldn't figure. He'd like to strangle her, though. She could have gotten herself killed. Even if she had just entered his life yesterday, her leaving would leave a hole the size of a dynamite blast.

She was like no woman he'd ever met—mule-headed, rash, with no deference to fashion, and with a habit of cursing in a most unladylike manner. No wonder she'd remained a spinster in Boston. No gentleman would put up with her. But then he'd never had much use for gentlemen.

"Let's get these ladies back to town before we have to deal with the other two rogues." Henry's voice cut into Joshua's thoughts.

"Will it take as long to get back as it did to get here?" asked Sarah.

"No, Cath. We'll cut straight through the woodland. It's much quicker that way. We don't want to be out another night." Joshua untied the bandit's horse. "We'll have to borrow this animal for Mrs. Stedman. We didn't think to bring her a mount. You do ride, don't you, Mrs. Stedman?"

"Why, yes, but only sidesaddle." She smiled weakly at him through the tears in her eyes.

"I'm sorry," said Henry. "We don't have a sidesaddle."

"Then I'll have to make do." She rested her hand on Henry's arm.

Joshua watched Henry lift her onto the horse. Sitting sidesaddle in a western saddle would be awkward for Rachel and would slow them down considerably, but she was a lady. Henry would undoubtedly be happy with her for a wife. Relief filled him that she had turned out to be Henry's intended and not his. Cath might be a bit irregular, but he preferred it that way. He turned and lifted Cath up, after checking the cinch.

He led the way, letting Henry ride next to Mrs. Stedman. She seemed to be crying uncontrollably, which fit the occasion, but she still managed to sit on the horse.

After an agonizing several miles, he called back to Henry, "If we want to get back to town before dark, we're going to have to quicken our pace."

"Mrs. Stedman is having trouble managing the saddle," replied Henry.

Rachel wiped at the tears that streamed down her face. "I don't wish to hold us back."

"Not much we can do." Henry's reply came gently.

"I'm sure as hell not spending another night on the ground freezing my backside." Sarah shifted slightly in her saddle, gripping the horse's mane.

Rachel gasped loudly.

Joshua stifled a laugh. He added forthright to her list of not-so-ladylike qualities.

"Now, Miss Hodges, I realize you're not always quite proper and we are out in the wilderness, but I don't find that reason for a lady to stop acting like one."

Joshua nearly choked on his laughter. Henry, even in the wilderness, remained the perfect gentleman.

"Miss Hodges?"

"Yes, your friend, Miss Hodges," repeated Henry. "The one who insisted upon accompanying us to rescue you. You should be pleased to know she was more concerned about your welfare than her own."

"I don't understand." Rachel started to sway in the saddle. "Catherine is dead. Those men killed her."

Joshua looked at Cath, who had turned white. Hell, they looked like they were both going to swoon. He tried to turn his horse to catch her before she hit the ground. *Catherine is dead* echoed in his mind. That wasn't possible. She rode the horse next to him. He'd held her in his arms last night. Who in the hell was this woman?

"What?" He yanked on his horse's rein. The horse reared. "Whoa," he whispered under his breath.

"Of course she's Miss Hodges," insisted Henry. "We found her in the church. In her underthings. She'd been assaulted by those men, but had escaped."

The blood roared in Joshua's ears. He could barely understand Henry. What was Mrs. Stedman talking about?

"I'm sorry, Mr. Martin, but I don't know this woman. I've never seen her before today," Rachel sobbed. "I assumed she was your little sister. I intended to speak to you about her apparent improper upbringing."

"My sister?"

"Yes. She looks just like you."

"I don't have a sister."

"Who are you?" Joshua stared at Cath, who seemed to shrink in the saddle. "Who in thunder are you?" Damn. He jerked at the horse's reins. He couldn't get his horse turned around among the low-hanging tree branches.

"Name's Sarah." Her voice was barely above a whisper.

Joshua stared at her. His mouth dropped open. He yanked on the reins, jerking his horse around. Something cracked him across the head.

Chapter 4

SARAH GASPED AS Joshua slid from his horse. He landed on his back with a thud and didn't move. A cold chill ran up her spine.

A second shot rang out and bits of bark from a tree sprayed her face.

"Get to cover," Henry ordered in his no-nonsense manner. She saw him drag Rachel from her horse and behind the tree next to Sarah. Joshua lay in the open, his horse standing over him.

The third shot whistled past Sarah's ear before it thunked into the tree behind her.

"Get down," Henry screamed. He covered Rachel with his body and pointed his rifle toward the place where the shots had come. "Can't see a blasted thing," he muttered.

Sarah slid to the ground and ducked behind a tree. Damn, her great-grandmother's diary contained nothing about a shoot-out. They could all get killed. And if her grandparents died right here, where would she be? She had to do some-

thing, and quickly. She sure had jumbled things up when
she'd stepped back in time.

Oh, this was just nonsense. A bad dream. If she was having a dream, then no one could die and everything was fine.
But it seemed that this was a dream from which she couldn't
wake up. And, on the off chance that this wasn't a dream, but
reality, she had better do something and fast. Her stomach
flipped and her mouth went dry. Men were shooting real bullets at them. Oh, geez, when had life become so complicated? She had come to Wyoming to escape insanity, not to
find more of it.

She ducked her head as she heard another shot thunk into
the front side of the tree. She looked over at her great-grandfather. He took aim and fired.

"Can either of you women shoot?" Henry asked as he
surveyed the brush from where the shots were coming.

"I can," said Rachel.

He took one more shot, then handed Rachel the rifle.
"Cover me while I get Joshua's weapon."

"Be careful, Mr. Martin." Rachel took aim with the rifle
and fired into the bushes.

Sarah sat, momentarily frozen. Her grandmother could do
everything. She herself began to feel totally inadequate.

Henry tossed her his pistol. "Aim high so you don't shoot
me in the back." He began a flat-bellied crawl toward
Joshua's prone body. Sarah picked up the pistol and nearly
dropped it. It weighed so much. In the movies they tossed
these things around as if they were nothing. Steadying the
gun, she took aim toward the bushes. Slowly she squeezed
the trigger. Nothing happened.

"Pull back on the hammer," Rachel whispered from the
neighboring tree.

Sarah studied the gun. Holding the barrel steady with one
hand, she pulled on the hammer. It slipped from her fingers
and harmlessly clicked forward against the pistol. Holding
the weapon between her knees, she used both hands to pull
the hammer back until it clicked. At this rate, they'd all be
dead before she got off a shot. She sighted along the top of
the pistol and aimed toward the bushes. Raising the gun

slightly, she fired. She tumbled backward, dropping the weapon into the dirt. Her eardrums reverberated. A pain shot up her right arm.

Another shot whizzed past her head and embedded itself into the tree behind her. Bits of bark sprayed her hand. She peeked around the tree to see her great-grandfather lying across Joshua's body and firing into the bushes. Across from her, her great-grandmother held the rifle steady and cranked off one shot after another.

Okay, she thought. *If Rachel can do it, so can I.* She picked up the pistol and rolled onto her stomach. She planted her elbows in the ground, trying to imagine how she had seen a gun held on the television. She really should start watching more Westerns or police dramas if she was going to run into these types of adventures. Using the palm of her hand, she pulled back the hammer and fired. Surely she would be deaf when this ended. The retort from the gun had to be worse on the ears than rock music cranked up on her stereo.

She repeated the procedure several more times, closing her eyes each time the hammer descended. Her arms throbbed, but she had to do her part to save them. As she aimed the gun once more, she saw the bushes rustle. Two hats bounced above the branches. Henry shot, sending one of the hats spinning into the air. A muttered "damn" wafted toward them on the wind. Hooves could be heard pounding away from them.

"Thank you, God," she whispered softly and plunked her head down on her aching arms. The pistol slipped from her fingers.

"They're gone, for the moment." Henry's voice broke the silence. "But we best be getting back to town before the blackguards decide to return."

Sarah looked up at Henry. He walked toward Rachel. "Are you all right, Mrs. Stedman?"

"Yes, Mr. Martin. I'm fine. Now we need to tend to Mr. Campbell." Rachel stood and brushed off the front of her skirt.

Joshua. Good grief. Sarah realized that amid the terror of

the gunfight she'd forgotten all about him. She jumped up and flew to where he lay, sprawled on the ground, looking for all the world like he was dead. His stallion whinnied and sidestepped toward him. She thrust her hands against the animal's flank, trying to move him away. *Oh my God, he's dead,* she thought. She smacked the horse. "Move, damn it."

She knelt beside Joshua. *Now I've really mucked up the past.* She pushed her fingers against Joshua's neck, praying fervently that she would find a pulse. His heart answered her with a steady beat. Taking a ragged breath, Sarah continued her examination and shifted his head sideways, only to find blood gushing from his temple. For an instant, her heart stopped beating.

"Henry, quick. Some water." She waved her hand toward him while she plopped on the ground and pulled Joshua's head into her lap. "And I need something to wash his head off with."

"Move." Henry stalked toward her with the canteen swinging from his hand. "I'll tend his wound."

Sarah glared at him. "Give me the damn water."

A ripping sound came from beside her. "Mr. Martin, please give this to the young lady."

Sarah looked up to see Rachel offering a piece of her petticoat. "Thank you."

Shooting him one last withering glance, Sarah snatched the material from Henry's hand, poured water over it, and pressed it against Joshua's injury. If he needed stitches or a bullet removed, would there be a doctor around? She knew head wounds bled like gushers. She'd learned that last month when LeeAnne's five-year-old nephew had come to visit. When he'd crashed his bike, they thought he was bleeding to death. In the end, he only needed two stitches.

Lifting the rag, she smoothed Joshua's hair back and examined the cut. A couple of butterfly strips would close it right up. A sigh rattled through her body. She had a pair of nail scissors and some Band-Aids in her bag. Now, if he didn't have a concussion, or worse . . . She pressed the cloth against the gash again to stop the bleeding.

A jumble of words floated through Joshua's mind as

something cold caressed the side of his face. It seemed to lessen the thudding that persisted through his skull. What had happened? He could hear Cath's voice arguing with Henry's. But she wasn't Cath. Oh, hell, who was she?

His eyes fluttered open to find her breasts nearly pressed into his face. Whoever she was, she held him in her lap. Warmth surrounded him and cradled him. He liked her touching him. He closed his eyes and absorbed the sensations of her body pressed against his and moving beneath him and her breasts brushing against his cheek. He had many questions, but for now he just wanted to be near her.

Sarah pulled the damp cloth away. The bleeding seemed to have subsided. "Henry, hand me my bag, please."

"What are you going to do?"

"Fix his head."

"It doesn't look that bad."

"It could open up and start bleeding again. Just hand me the bag."

"I'm more worried about him not waking up than a little scratch on his head."

"I can't do anything about that." She blinked back tears. So many strange things had happened in the last twenty-four hours. She'd nearly caused her great-grandmother to be killed, then Joshua, and then all of them. Joshua had another year and a half to live. She didn't want to be responsible for shortening that time. She wanted to go home. She wanted to be where things made sense.

Her backpack hit the ground next to her with a thump. Unzipping the top, she rummaged through it until she found the box of Band-Aids at the bottom. She unzipped the front pocket and pulled the scissors from the plastic sheath in which she carried them. Hiding her movements behind Joshua, she cut a small strip from the Band-Aid then plastered it across the wound she pinched together.

"Ouch." Joshua jumped. "What are you doing?"

"Appears he's going to live." Henry stomped back to stand next to Rachel. "We have to get moving before those outlaws return."

Sarah pressed her hand against Joshua's temple. "Be still.

I'm fixing your head. It's the least I can do." Sarah finished closing the cut. "Rachel, can I have another piece of your slip to wrap around his head to keep the dirt out?"

Rachel ripped off another strip of cloth and handed it to Sarah. "Can I help?"

"I don't think there's much else we can do. Can you sit up, Joshua?" asked Sarah.

"More to the point, can he ride? I don't cherish being out here all night," said Henry.

"I'll be fine." Joshua forced himself out of Sarah's lap. He wouldn't have minded resting there a while yet. His head pounded. Swaying slightly, he pressed his hand against the bandage.

"Open your mouth." Sarah's fingers brushed against his lips, sending a tingle through him. Something hard and chalky landed on his tongue. The edge of the canteen pressed against his lips. "Swallow."

He swallowed, coughed, and sputtered. "What was that?"

"Something to make your head stop hurting," she whispered.

Henry hunkered down to look Joshua in the eye. "You look a little pale, but you'll live." Glancing toward the sky, he continued, "Best be getting on. Feel up to riding?"

Joshua stood, placing his hand against the tree trunk for balance. "Give me a minute."

"Does anything else hurt?" Sarah clutched her bag to her chest as she watched him.

"Everything." He gave her a puzzled look. "What happened?"

"Someone took a shot at you. Knocked you clean off your horse." Henry glanced nervously around. "I ran them off, but I don't want to be waiting around for them to come back."

"The guys who robbed the stage?" Joshua asked.

"Probably," said Henry.

"Ran them off?" asked Joshua.

"Yep," said Henry. He cradled his rifle in his arms.

"Then we should be safe for a few moments while my head stops spinning." Joshua put his hand to his forehead.

"I'd hate to fall out of the saddle again. Besides, I want a few answers."

Sarah yanked his hat from her head. "Maybe you should put this on. It'll help keep the bandage from slipping."

"No, you keep it 'til we get to town. Now, Cath or Sarah or whatever your name is—start talking."

Sarah put her hand to her throat. The time for the truth had arrived, but what truth could she tell that anyone would find believable eluded her.

"Start with your name," growled Henry. "And make it quick."

Sarah took a deep breath and pulled herself up as tall as she could at five feet one inch. "My name is Sarah."

"Sarah what?" snapped Henry.

Martin, thought Sarah. But that answer would really raise Henry's blood pressure and increase the questioning.

"I want an answer," demanded Henry.

Joshua scowled as he looked at her pale face. "Go easy, Henry. Obviously something terrible happened to her, even if it occurred elsewhere than the stage holdup. The bruises didn't get there by themselves."

"How'd you know about Mrs. Stedman and the stage holdup? What were you doing in the church and in your underwear? Why did you pretend to be Miss Hodges?" Henry fired rapid questions at her.

Sarah looked at Joshua. His green eyes questioned her, but didn't accuse. She glanced at her great-grandparents. Oh, hell, no explanation made sense. She shrugged her shoulders. "I don't know." Which was true. Everything had become so confusing. One moment she'd been in the 1990s, the next in 1870. She started to tremble.

Henry growled, "You don't know! Of course you know. Lying isn't going to improve your situation."

"Henry," Rachel said quietly but firmly, "the poor thing's probably scared half out of her wits." Rachel's voice soothed like salve on an open wound.

Henry stared at Rachel, his mouth hanging open. "Why are you defending her?"

Rachel laid her gloved hand on his arm. "She saved my

life. She offered me comfort. Whoever she is, she has a good heart." A sad smile crossed her face.

Henry patted her hand. "Still, 'tis no excuse for lying."

"I never lied," Sarah snapped. She might not have told the truth, exactly, but she hadn't told any outright lies, either. If she'd had a mind to, she wouldn't know any that made sense. And the truth would land her in a rubber room or the 1870 equivalent, which would probably not be a pleasant experience.

Joshua stared at Sarah's neck. "Who did that to you?"

"Jack." That was the truth. Of course, explaining Jack would be as difficult as everything else.

"I'll kill him for what he did to you."

"You'd have to find him first." And that would take a fancy trick to accomplish.

"I've men to help." Joshua balled his hands into fists. "No man should get away with harming a lady."

"Some lady," Henry muttered.

"Hush, Mr. Martin," Rachel said softly.

"No matter how many men you have, you'll never find him." Sarah shrugged her shoulders.

"I'll find him and settle with him," Joshua growled. "You have my promise on that."

Sarah shook her head. "Not in this lifetime."

"And what does that mean?" Joshua still stared at the bruises on her neck.

Sarah put her hand up to cover them. "He's out of your reach. Way far out."

"Probably did away with him," barked Henry. "Where are you from?"

"Los Angeles." She was three for three on truths.

"Los Angeles isn't so far away I can't find him, if he's still around to find," said Joshua.

"Oh, he's still there," said Sarah.

"How'd you end up here?" Joshua's eyes bore into hers.

"Trying to disappear." And she'd done a real good job of it. Better than she'd ever imagined possible. She clutched her hands into fists at her sides, trying to control the trembling that threatened to make her knees give way. She had to maintain control until she got back to the church. Until she could get home.

"From Jack?" asked Joshua.

"Probably from the law," Henry said. "How do we know she wasn't in with the bunch that robbed the stage?"

"Excuse me!" Sarah exclaimed. "Why would I help to rescue Rachel if I worked with them?" The pompous ass might be her great-grandfather, but she had a definite urge to slug him.

"She doesn't look like a robber to me," said Joshua.

"She doesn't look like anything I'd give a name to," snapped Henry.

"That's about enough, Henry. Accusations aren't helping." Joshua glared at him with cold green eyes. "We'd best move out. You take the lead with Mrs. Stedman. I'll bring up the rear with Cath."

"Her name isn't Cath." Henry shot Joshua a dark look before helping Rachel back on her horse. "Yell if you fall off again."

Sarah turned to pull herself back onto her horse. Why the beasts had to grow so tall, she didn't know. Compact cars were dealt with so much easier.

Warm, strong hands encircled her waist and lifted her into the saddle. "Thank you." She smiled tentatively down at Joshua.

The silence between them bore down on her as they rode. No one spoke a word for what seemed like miles. Sarah tried to concentrate on the beauty of the scenery, but worry about what would happen when they arrived back in town kept pushing everything else from her mind. She had nowhere to go. More to the point, she had no way to take care of herself. She had a thousand dollars in traveler's checks, a hundred dollars in cash, her American Express Gold card and her Gold MasterCard in her bag, and not even one penny dated 1870 that she could spend. She could starve to death, or worse. She could only hope the church window would let her go home.

"Why'd you do it?" Joshua's voice broke into her reverie.

"Do what?"

"Lie."

"I didn't."

"You told us you were Catherine Hodges."

"No, I didn't."

"You certainly did."

"*You* told *me* I was Catherine Hodges. I just didn't correct your assumption."

Joshua slowed his horse down to widen the gap between them and Henry. "What did you throw down my throat?"

"Something to make your head stop hurting. Did it help?"

"Yes."

"I'm really sorry."

"About what? The lying?"

"I didn't lie." She jerked her horse to a stop and glared at him. "I'm sorry you got injured. When I saw you lying there, I thought you were dead."

"Come on," Henry's voice snapped back at them. "We've wasted enough time. Everything else can be settled in town."

"It is settled," Joshua called out. "I'm feeling a little dizzy. Go on ahead. We'll catch up."

"It isn't proper for Mrs. Stedman and me to be out here alone. We'll all rest for a minute." Henry started to pull his horse to a stop.

"Keep on riding. Besides, the preacher's coming in two days. That'll save her reputation. And, after all, she is a widow lady, not a—" He stopped his sentence short, and red crept up his neck to his face.

"Watch how you talk about my intended."

"Stop your grousing, Henry. We're going to rest. We'll be along directly and won't get far behind. Anyway, I don't think Cath will agree to sleep out here another night anyway."

Henry turned in the saddle to scowl at them for a moment, then rode slowly on with Rachel.

"My getting hurt wasn't your fault." He shifted slightly in the saddle to stare at Sarah. Part of him was furious at having been deceived. Part of him wanted to scoop her into his

arms and kiss her to see if she tasted as good as she smelled.
"What do you plan to do when we get back to town?"

"I don't know."

Dampness sparkled on her lashes. Fear echoed in her dark
eyes. *Don't cry,* he pleaded silently. He did have a right to be
angry with her. She'd lied to him. But, if she cried, his anger
would melt faster than last winter's snow. She just looked so
lost and helpless. "You got this far. Where were you planning on going? You must have had some idea as to what you
were doing."

Up until yesterday afternoon, she had. "Sort of. It didn't
quite work out." She blinked furiously.

"What do you plan to do now?"

Sarah shrugged her shoulders. "I don't know."

"The preacher's expecting a double wedding."

"That's a little hard. The robbers killed Catherine."

"It does leave me without a wife."

"I know. I'm sorry about Catherine."

"I am, too. I'm sure she was a wonderful lady."

"You never met her?"

"Nope. She corresponded with me on several occasions.
She seemed the proper lady, but very nervous about the trip
west. But Mrs. Stedman assured Henry she'd make a proper
wife."

"Just like Rachel will for Henry." She smiled at the backs
of her great-grandparents. They definitely seemed suited for
each other. They had dismounted a short distance ahead,
waiting for her and Joshua.

"Except I'm not like Henry." Joshua grinned at her.

"And how are you different?" Sarah turned in the saddle
to look at him. She knew the answer. He wasn't as stuffy as
Henry. But she wanted to know what he thought the difference was.

"Henry is always the proper gentleman. I'm a cowboy."
Joshua paused and his face flushed. "I don't mean I'm not a
gentleman."

Sarah laughed. "You have been a perfect gentleman."

"It's just . . . working a ranch makes a man a little
rougher. I was worried Miss Hodges wouldn't adapt to the

life out here, being a proper Boston lady and all. I had my qualms about this whole idea of Henry's. But Mrs. Stedman wanted to bring her dear friend with her, and the woman had to have a husband. I got elected for the honor.

"From Mrs. Stedman's letters and Miss Hodges's letters, she seemed like a right fine young woman. Well, not so young, but she seemed like she'd make a good wife. Out here, that's about all a body can ask."

"You'd have made a wonderful husband for Catherine."

Joshua smiled as they rode on. He looked at the spunky woman next to him. He was truly sorry about Catherine but he certainly didn't regret meeting Sarah.

"You could do me the honor." Joshua held his breath.

"What?"

"Marry me." Was she about to unleash a torrent of her not-so-ladylike vocabulary at him? He was serious in his proposal. Sarah tugged at his heart in a way no other woman ever had. "You haven't any place to go. A young woman can't be on her own out here."

"And why not?" Sarah's eyes widened and sparks flashed deep within them.

"How are you going to take care of yourself?"

He posed an excellent question. Coldness crept up her spine. She didn't have any skills worth much in 1870 in Moose Creek. The call for computer experts was nil. And after she'd told LeeAnne she could go anywhere and make a living! "That's the dumbest reason I've ever heard of for getting married. I don't even know you. You don't know me."

"I know you're the most unorthodox woman I've ever met. Mrs. Stedman and Henry don't know each other. Lots of people get married without knowing the other person."

"Henry and Rachel are different. And Rachel appears so very capable. They're well suited to each other. They'll be happy and have lots of kids."

"You foretell the future also."

"Yeah, I do. Besides, look at them. They're both so stuffy I'm surprised they can bend."

Joshua's mouth dropped open, then he broke into a loud

gale of laughter. "Henry wouldn't appreciate that comment, but it's the truth. A definite gentleman. Mrs. Stedman is just what he needs."

"And you. Don't you want a lady?"

"Thought I did. That's why I let Henry talk me into this scheme."

"So she's dead and you'll settle for me."

"That wasn't how I meant it." From the moment he'd laid eyes on her, he'd wanted her. He'd never seen a woman more beautiful. Something about her pulled at him—tugged at his heart in a most pleasant way.

"Well, I'm sorry but I won't be a convenient replacement. I have better things to do than be somebody's housekeeper. Besides, I don't cook." She sat, her back rigid, in her saddle.

"I just thought that was outdoors."

"If you can't nuke . . . never mind."

"If I do the cooking, will you marry me?" He'd been cooking for himself for years and was right good at it. He didn't want a housekeeper. Besides, he had Cookie at his ranch, who did most of the cooking anyway. He wanted Sarah with her short curls and feisty temper. She'd bring fires to his lonely days—and nights. The loneliness. That was what had started this derailed scheme anyway. If she left, then nothing but being alone stretched ahead of him. She would fill that void in a way that he knew no other woman would come close to matching.

"No," she said adamantly.

"You aren't already married, are you?" A hand seemed to squeeze his heart while he awaited her answer.

"No."

"What about Jack?" The squeezing tightened.

"An acquaintance, sort of."

"Did your parents approve of him?"

"My parents were killed two years ago in a ca . . . accident."

"I'm sorry."

"So was I." She forced down the pain that engulfed her whenever she thought of her parents.

"No wonder you ended up with a man who would take advantage of you without your father to see after you." Joshua reached over and brushed his fingers against her cheek.

Sarah shivered at his touch. "Jack didn't exactly take advantage of me and my father stopped seeing after me when I turned eighteen and went away to college."

"College? A nice finishing school back East?"

"A what?" She wished she understood what they were talking about all of the time.

"Finishing school. They teach you everything a lady needs to know."

"I must have flunked that part." She pressed her hand to her mouth as she giggled. "No. A regular college where you learn history, math, literature, compu . . . That kind of thing."

"Women don't go to college much. You could be a teacher, but we don't have many young 'uns in the area."

Yeah. And what would she teach them? How to program a computer? How to interface systems? "Probably not."

"Then how did you plan to take care of yourself? You must have some family to see after you."

"I can see after myself." *Well, at least she had until Jack had tried to kill her.* Now instead of being in Los Angeles and happily at work, she sat on a horse next to a man who made her insides quiver every time she looked at him. But he was a man with no future and she was a lost woman from the future.

"A woman can't make a living in Moose Creek. There aren't enough women in the area to support yourself as a seamstress. Most of the women do their own sewing."

"That's probably just as well. I can't sew."

Joshua pulled his foot from the stirrup and stretched his leg. "Then what can you do?"

"Not a hell of a lot worth anything, it appears."

"For a woman who went to college, you have a most improper vocabulary. I wouldn't think your father would approve."

"Hell, I learned it from him and what is so improper about a 'hell' or a 'damn'?"

"Ladies don't use that type of language."

"Ladies don't seem to do much."

"They cook, sew, and take care of their husbands."

"Sounds very boring."

He shook his head and then groaned as pain shot through it. Putting his hand against his forehead, he kicked his horse in the flanks gently. "Best be gittin' on. Another night without shelter doesn't seem like a good idea. I'm sure, like you, Mrs. Stedman will be much happier back in town." He'd be shed of her once they reached the safety of town and she could go to wherever she'd planned on going. It would be better that way. Yet a cold, empty spot sprouted within him at the thought of her leaving. "Are you going to tell me the rest of your name?"

She looked at him for a moment, then rode off ahead.

Mrs. Westall kept Sarah and Rachel overnight. Sarah gathered they were to stay with her until the preacher showed up tomorrow. For some reason, no one mentioned she wasn't Catherine Hodges. They all seemed to be embroiled in a giant conspiracy. She didn't know why. Her great-grandmother had spent most of the night crying and Sarah had gotten almost no sleep because of it. That and the fact that every part of her body ached from sitting on that damned horse. The man she'd borrowed the beast from without asking had been very understanding, and had forgiven her, since she was scheduled to marry Joshua tomorrow.

Catherine had been as tiny as Sarah and since she had no clothes of her own, Rachel insisted she use Catherine's. Rachel still hadn't asked who she was. Actually, Rachel had said very little. She'd just sobbed. Thousands of sobs. So sad for someone who would become happily married tomorrow.

Sarah picked out a pale yellow dress with little flowers all over it to wear that day. The skirt seemed to hang limply as if she didn't have enough slips under it, but the day seemed warm and she was already stifling in the outfit. Who ever heard of high collars and long sleeves when the temperature got above eighty?

And buttons. The dress seemed to have a million buttons

down the front. Her shoes pinched her toes. She wondered if anyone would notice if she put her running shoes on under the dress. The voluminous skirt would hide her feet, so how would they ever know?

She crammed her belongings back into her backpack. The sun had just about crested in the sky and she wanted to be in the church by noon. Taking a deep breath, she exited the bedroom and walked down the hall to the kitchen. She smelled chicken frying and her rumbling stomach made her realize how hungry she felt.

She stood a moment outside the door, then straightening her shoulders, she entered the kitchen.

"I see you're up and about, Miss Hodges. Are you feeling better after a good sleep?" Mrs. Westall, busy cooking, didn't even turn from the stove.

"Yes." Sarah turned to Rachel, who was sitting at the table. "Hello, Rachel. How are you feeling?"

"A bit tired." She sniffed.

If she had the time, she'd take Rachel aside and find out why they were playing this charade, but she needed to get to the church so she could end her adventure. The sun shone brightly and crept higher in the sky. She had to be in front of the window to catch the light.

The time to go home had arrived.

"You can leave your satchel in the room, dear. No one will touch it," said Mrs. Westall. "Would you like some coffee and a biscuit to tide you over? Dinner will be in about half an hour."

"No, thank you. I'm going to take a walk, if no one minds."

"The air will do you good. Come back shortly." Mrs. Westall turned back to the stove. "Mrs. Stedman, it might do you a world of good to go with her."

"I really don't feel up to it. Another time, perhaps." Rachel wiped at her eyes with a lace-trimmed handkerchief.

"Perhaps." Sarah quickly headed out of the kitchen and toward the front door.

Standing in front of the church, she hugged her bag to her chest. This had to work. She couldn't be trapped here. She didn't belong. She'd saved Rachel. Her grandparents were about to be married. Her family was safe.

She couldn't take Catherine's place. She'd read her grandmother's diary. Joshua never married. He'd disappeared in a snowstorm in two winters. She'd fixed all she could.

She wanted to go home now.

It was time to go home.

Joshua leaned against the railing outside Henry's store and watched the slim figure walking across the street from Mrs. Westall's to the church. The yellow skirts swayed as she moved. Her short, curly hair circled her head neatly. Again she was without a hat. He really needed to talk with her about walking around in the sun with her head uncovered.

She had never given him an answer to his proposal. The minister would be here tomorrow and Joshua needed to know if a double wedding was going to take place. He still saw no reason why she couldn't marry him. He'd gotten used to the idea of being married. Why, he'd even fixed his home up for a bride. He supposed he should feel something more in regards to Catherine's death, but she'd only been something in his imagination—someone he knew only slightly from a few letters. He'd never met the woman.

He regretted her death, especially since it had been so violent and brutal. No one should have to suffer that way. And women should be treated with respect. He would find the rest of the men who had done this and make them pay. For Catherine and for Rachel.

But he still wanted a wife. And Sarah fit the bill nicely. He could imagine many cold nights livened up by her presence. He wanted to take her home with him and keep her forever. Growing old with her seemed a delightful prospect.

And she really didn't have any other choice. She had to know that. Marrying him was her only choice. And he'd see to it that she saw reason and did just that on the morrow when the preacher arrived.

He stepped down and followed her to the church. Quietly he stepped inside and peeked around the partition. He didn't want to disturb her if she was praying. She stood in the center of the aisle looking up at the stained-glass window. He glanced up as the sun glinted off the myriad colors. It really was a most beautiful sight. Everyone who passed through admired it and he'd never seen its equal anywhere.

"Please, lower your arms and call to me," she said softly. "I want to go home now."

Joshua stood stalk-still and examined the back of her. He glanced around the edge of the partition to see if anyone else was in the church. He couldn't imagine to whom she was talking. He shifted his gaze to watch her.

She walked slowly down the aisle toward the altar, then stopped. She reached her hands up. "It's only a dream. It's time I woke up. Please, why won't you take me home? I don't want to be here anymore."

He took off his hat and ran his fingers through his hair. The light had to be playing tricks on him. She couldn't be talking to the window. And was the prospect of marrying him really so awful that she wanted to leave?

She crumpled to the ground and buried her face in the mounds of her yellow skirt. "I want to go home," the muffled cry came.

She was such a tiny bit of a thing. Joshua's heart ached and he wanted to scoop her into his arms and comfort her. She might not welcome him, but his legs took him down the aisle anyway. He lifted her and crushed her against his chest. Her hair tickled his neck.

"I want to go home." Her body trembled as she buried her head against his chest.

A dagger pierced his heart. "Then go home." His voice came gruffly.

"You don't understand. I can't."

Chapter 5

"IS IT BECAUSE of Jack?" Joshua held Sarah's trembling body crushed against him.

"No," she mumbled against his chest.

"Then go home, if that will make you happy." A twinge went through Joshua's heart. If he held her long enough, maybe she wouldn't want to leave him. Maybe she'd decide to stay with him, decide to become his wife.

Sarah pushed herself away from him, but not out of the circle of his arms. "If I could, I would." She looked up into his face.

"If it's money, I'll buy you a stagecoach ticket or a train ticket." The light coming through the window created a halo around her head. He stared at her, memorizing her every feature in case she disappeared as suddenly as she had appeared.

"Why? I'm not your responsibility."

Her gray eyes held the same haunted look as an animal caught in a trap. He would do anything to wipe that look away. "Because you need the help. I want to see you happy.

I want you to smile again. I want to argue with you some more."

She gave him a half-smile. "Tickets won't help."

"Then what will?"

"Nothing that you can do." A sigh rattled through her.

"Tell me what you need. I'll do whatever I can." She looked so small. Defeated. The spunk she had shown while they'd ridden the trail had disappeared. It tore his heart in two to see her this way.

"I can't." She shook her head.

"Can't, or won't?"

"Can't. If you could do anything to help, believe me I'd tell you. Neither of us can do anything. It's in God's hands."

"The thought of marrying me isn't so repugnant you want to leave, is it?" The question slipped from his mouth before he realized he'd spoken.

"No, Joshua, you'd make a wonderful husband."

"Then why won't you marry me?"

"Because I don't belong here."

"You can. This place isn't so terrible. Awful cold in the winter, but it's really a nice little town with great people. It would be a real nice place to raise kids. I'm rich enough to give you everything you could ask for."

"You don't have to sell yourself to me." She placed her hand on his shoulder.

He wanted to hold her within his arms forever. If he didn't let go, she couldn't leave him. "Then what can I do to change your mind?"

She stared into his eyes for a long moment. "Nothing. No one can do anything."

Joshua hugged her tightly against his chest.

The next morning, Joshua tugged at Henry's tie. "Hold still. The damn thing's crooked. I don't know what you're so nervous about anyway."

"It's not every day a man gets married." Henry looked at himself in the small mirror mounted on the wall over the bureau. He leaned forward and rubbed his chin.

"You look fine." Joshua smiled. "And remember—you're

the one who came up with this crazy idea for us to get married."

"But I'm the one doing it." Henry rubbed his hands back along the side of his hair, smoothing it down.

"Not because I don't want to." Nothing he had said would sway Sarah. She refused to marry him. And all she would say was that she couldn't and she wanted to go home. Obviously something in Los Angeles was more important than anything he could offer.

Henry turned and strode across the room to the bed and picked up his jacket. "I can't understand why you'd have any desire to marry that woman."

"I find her fascinating."

"That's not how I'd describe her." He bent and smoothed the flowered coverlet on the bed. "Do you think Mrs. Stedman will approve of this room? Do you think it's good enough for her?"

"She came all this way to marry you. I'm sure she will think it's wonderful." Joshua glanced around the room. The four-poster bed took up the majority of the space. Henry had gotten Mrs. Westall to make lace-edged curtains of white material with small pink rose vines entwined on it to match the coverlet. On the bureau sat a white china water pitcher and bowl that were also covered with tiny pink roses. A wardrobe to hold Mrs. Stedman's clothes filled the corner of the room.

"I don't know. She is a lady from Boston." Henry tugged at his bow tie.

"Now you've undone it again. Cath says you'll be very happy." He pulled the tie loose and tied it again.

"Cath? Her name's Sarah." Henry frowned. "Besides, what does she know? She a gypsy fortune-teller?"

"Maybe."

"You know absolutely nothing about her." Henry lifted his chin so Joshua could fix his tie.

"I don't care." He'd take her just the way she was, mysteries and all. He'd have a whole lifetime to get to know her.

Henry moved to look at himself in the mirror again. "But she's so unorthodox. Nothing about her is ladylike."

"A lady would wilt on my ranch."

Henry stared at him for a moment. "You're smitten with her."

"I begged her to marry me."

"And . . ."

"She turned me down."

Henry released a big sigh. "I'm glad. I wouldn't want to see you saddled with the likes of her."

"I'll ask again and again until she finally says yes."

"Are you sure that's what you want?"

"Yes." He had never been more sure of anything in his life. She brought a bright spot into his life; as bright as the pink roses that decorated Henry's bedroom.

"Then I hope she brings you happiness," said Henry half-heartedly.

"She will." Joshua turned toward the door. "I need to speak with the minister."

Sarah watched Rachel brushing her long, brown hair. Sitting on the end of the bed, dressed only in the undergarments she'd borrowed from Catherine's trunks, she wondered what would happen next.

"It would be a good idea to take Mr. Campbell up on his offer." Rachel continued pulling the brush through her hair.

"I don't know him well enough to marry him."

"That doesn't matter. No other choices are suitable under the circumstances."

"What circumstances?"

"You've been alone overnight with him."

"Hardly! Henry was with us the whole time." Sarah smiled. She'd probably better not mention that Joshua wasn't the first man with whom she'd spent the night alone.

Rachel scowled. "It would be more appropriate if you called him Mr. Martin."

Somehow, Sarah had never envisioned her great-grandmother as so stuffy when she'd read her diary. If she ever saw it again, she would have gained a new perspective. She wondered what kind of a reaction she'd get if she called Henry "grandpa." A giggle escaped.

"I don't see that as funny."

"That wasn't."

Rachel turned to stare at Sarah. "You have to do something. You can't stay out here alone. It would be unseemly, not to mention dangerous."

"That's probably a good point. I'm not real big on coyotes." Marrying Joshua wasn't the answer, though. Another choice had to be available. Alternatives in life always existed. She just couldn't see one at the moment; the window in the church wouldn't cooperate and until it did, she appeared to be stuck in Moose Creek.

"Then you shall marry Mr. Campbell?"

"No."

Rachel turned back. "I don't see what the objection is, then. It isn't as if he'd met Catherine. They exchanged but two letters. I arranged it all through Mr. Martin. And Mr. Campbell seems more than willing to take you as a bride."

"That's the same reasoning he used. It seems a pretty poor reason to marry anyone." It seemed rather like jumping from the frying pan into the fire. Besides, Joshua died a bachelor. A shiver ran up her spine. Sometimes she didn't like knowing what the future held.

"As good as some I've heard."

Sarah laughed. "Why haven't you told everyone I'm not Catherine Hodges?"

"Mr. Martin asked me not to. Mr. Campbell wishes it that way and as I don't wish to cause him any embarrassment, I agreed. He was very kind to send for Catherine in the first place." Rachel lay the brush down and picked up a crystal bottle, dabbing perfume behind her ears and between her breasts.

"The whole thing seems strange to me." Obviously neither of her great-grandparents approved of her, but that seemed to be a pretty common thing. The older generation often didn't approve of what the younger generation did. But in this case the whole situation had become highly bizarre, since at the moment she and her great-grandmother were both nearly the same age. Sarah stifled another urge to break into laughter. Rachel might take it upon herself to in-form Joshua she wasn't exactly balanced. And she probably wouldn't be far from the truth.

A sharp rap sounded at the door just as it swung open. "Are you two young ladies ready to get dressed? We don't wish to keep the gentlemen waiting overly long."

"It would be bad manners to be late," said Rachel.

Manners. Her great-grandmother seemed obsessed with manners. Sarah wondered how Rachel had managed to get pregnant six times in her life with all her concern about what was proper. The laughter overtook Sarah.

Mrs. Westall stared at her.

Sarah shook her head. "Nerves." And the fact that the world had tilted off its axis. Her nerves were strung so tight, they resembled a rubber band about to snap.

Mrs. Westall put her hands on her hips. "Suppose you would be nervous. After your wedding night, things will get better. You just have to learn to put up with the needs of men. After a while, you get used to it. But then Mrs. Stedman knows that. It's the price of having a man provide for you."

Sarah broke into a gale of laughter. Pink tinged Rachel's cheeks. She couldn't make up her mind which was funnier—Mrs. Westall's assumption of her innocence or her description of wifely duties.

"I do hope you stop that before the weddings start."

"Wedding," Sarah corrected as she tried to stop her uncontrollable mirth.

"Miss Hodges is quite unstrung after the past few days," Rachel interrupted quickly. "She's had a very difficult time."

"The whole ordeal must have been just dreadful. But it is behind you and you will both be married to two of the finest gentlemen I've ever known. Real gentlemen and good providers. That is so important. Neither of them has a propensity for drinking, gambling, or loose women. If I was twenty years younger I'd have set my cap for one of them myself. Now, Mrs. Stedman, let me help you lace up your corset."

Sarah watched with fascination as Rachel held onto one of the bedposts and Mrs. Westall tugged. Rachel's waist seemed to grow smaller with each tug. Finally Mrs. Westall tied the strings.

"Miss Hodges, your turn." She stepped away from the bed, resting her hands on her ample hips.

Sarah shook her head. "I'll pass."

"Now, Catherine, you must get dressed. You mustn't let Mrs. Westall's chatter make you nervous. Mr. Campbell is a very nice man who'll do you no harm."

"I don't expect him to harm me." The corset, on the other hand, might be another matter. With a sigh of resignation, she moved over to hold onto the bedpost. Mrs. Westall wrapped the stiff-boned garment around her waist and started lacing. *This isn't too bad. Not much worse than a merry widow.* "I don't plan to marry him either."

"Exhale." Mrs. Westall started pulling the laces tighter. "You'll be just fine after you get over your case of nerves. Mr. Campbell is such a fine gentleman."

"Oof." Air rushed out of Sarah's lungs. She tightened her grip on the bedpost so as not to be propelled back on top of Mrs. Westall. She could feel her rib cage bending under the rigidness of the garment. "That's good," she gasped.

"It will need to be a little tighter," said Rachel. "Remember you had the dress fitted so your waist would be as small as possible."

Sarah glared over at Rachel. A tiny grin flitted across her face. Rachel appeared to be getting immense joy from having her squeezed to death.

The strings yanked against Sarah's middle. Her fingers turned white as she gripped the bedpost. She swore she heard her ribs crack. She wouldn't have to worry about marrying Joshua or surviving in this time. Any second now she would suffocate.

"That should do." Mrs. Westall's voice came close to her ears.

Sarah continued to clutch the bedpost. The smooth ridges sculptured into the post had become permanent parts of her palms. If she let go, she knew she would collapse on the floor from lack of oxygen. Her head spun. She tried to take in a deep breath, but her chest didn't move outward to allow her lungs to inflate. No wonder women fainted so often before the invention of civilized underwear.

She took in a tiny breath. It slipped into her lungs and back out without straining against the lacings. *Okay. I can do this if I concentrate. The wedding shouldn't take too long and then I can take this horrid thing off and burn it in the nearest fireplace.* Sarah tried to sigh, except it seemed an impossible action. Whoever had invented these things had definitely had it in for women.

Several small breaths later and she could stand on her own. Lord, was the thing tight! As much as she wanted to burn it, she'd probably have to wear it for months to support her ribs while they healed. And she'd wondered about things women did to themselves to improve their appearances in her time. Liposuction had nothing on the corset.

She stood away from the bed and let Mrs. Westall lower a slip over her head. She tied it at Sarah's waist, then adjusted the back of it, which stuck out several inches. She could have had hips as broad as Manhattan and hidden them under this slip. Mrs. Westall then lowered over her head a dress made of cream-colored satin covered with a matching gauzy material. Sarah waited patiently while Mrs. Westall buttoned, then tied the satin bow at the back. At the moment, standing perfectly still seemed the most opportune thing to do anyway. It took far less air. And to think women actually danced in these things. It definitely took practice to move and breathe while trussed up.

"Doesn't she make a pretty bride?" asked Mrs. Westall. "Now if I could only do something with her hair." She tsked several times. "Such beautiful hair. Too bad it's shorn so short."

"It was an accident." Sarah turned to look at herself in the mirror. The cream satin complemented her tanned skin. A row of tiny pink and lavender roses ran from the waist at the back of the skirt, looped down across her knees and back up, making the dress appear to have a double skirt. The roses decorated the bottom of the skirt with a second row of flowers starting from under the edge of the top skirt and wrapping around the train. Smaller matching flowers edged the neckline, which exposed the top of her breasts. Rachel handed her a heavy gold chain with a cameo dangling from it.

Sarah had to admit the outfit was stunning. Any bride would be overwhelmed to be dressed in it. However, she wasn't a bride, but a bridesmaid. And she knew movement or sitting dwelled among the impossible. She stood stiffly while she watched Mrs. Westall dress Rachel in the satin gown she had found in the trunk the first day.

After Mrs. Westall had patted and pulled and tucked, she stood back and surveyed the two women. "Can't do anything more with Miss Hodges's hair, but you both look magnificent in spite of that."

Sarah reached up and patted the satin flowers fastened in her hair. She no longer recognized the reflection smiling back at her. She'd imagined her wedding day often, but she'd been dressed in a long, white satin dress with a veil covering her face. But, then, it didn't really matter. Today wasn't her wedding day, but her great-grandparents'.

"It's nearly eleven and time to go, ladies." Mrs. Westall held the bedroom door open.

Sarah followed Rachel, unsure the dress skirt would fit through the door. A small giggle escaped. This certainly had twisted into a bizarre situation. She would be her great-grandmother's bridesmaid.

Sarah stood at the back of the church, looking up at the stained-glass window. The afternoon sun glinted through it, giving Jesus the appearance of having a halo. She held her breath and her heart skipped several beats. Maybe the window would take her home now. All of her money was back in her bag at Mrs. Westall's, but she could always call LeeAnne for more. Most of her clothes were still in her car, if her car hadn't been towed. Even in a place as small as present-day Moose Creek, someone was bound to notice an abandoned car and call the authorities.

She started to walk forward when an arm restrained her. She glanced to the side to find Mrs. Westall next to her.

"They're not quite ready for you brides yet. The men are still talking with the minister."

Sarah looked down the aisle to see Henry and Joshua standing on each side of a gray-haired man in a black suit. A white collar encircled his neck. He clutched a leather book in his withered hands. He had to crane his neck upward to look at Joshua. Hopefully Joshua was informing him he would only officiate one wedding today.

Heat stole through her while she watched Joshua, standing hat in hand, talking with the minister. He was the most handsome man she'd ever seen. Red hair curled slightly over the top of his ears, and when he smiled as he did now talking to the minister, her insides ached until she thought she would split in two. She wouldn't mind spending the rest of her life with this man. As big as he was, he was still gentle and sweet. Plus, he didn't seem to mind that she didn't fit in.

But that was the problem.

She didn't fit in. She did not belong in the past. Her best option would be to return to where she belonged before she ruined what little time Joshua had left. Both of them would be happier in the end.

Mrs. Westall handed her a bouquet of flowers. Sarah bent her head to sniff the fragrance. White daisies and yellow asters were mixed with bluebell-shaped flowers. The bunch of flowers didn't have the style of a florist's bouquet but were a quaint hodgepodge of wildflowers tied with a piece of white ribbon.

Sarah clutched the flowers in her hands and watched as the townspeople made their way into the church and sat down. This place had more citizens than she'd realized, and it seemed each and every one of them had turned out for the event. Mothers clutched the hands of their children. Men sat with their hats in their laps looking uncomfortable dressed in their "Sunday go to meeting" clothes. She and Rachel wore the fanciest dresses in the group, but then Rachel was getting married, so it seemed proper.

Sarah looked up at the window again. The halo had disappeared. She should have ignored Mrs. Westall and moved down the aisle while the window still seemed receptive. It might never make the offer again.

The men moved to the side with Henry standing on the inside. The minister moved to the center front of the church and cleared his throat.

Joshua stared down the aisle at Sarah. She was the most beautiful woman he'd ever seen. The pink roses on her dress matched the glow in her cheeks. He wanted to take her into his arms, kiss her, and find out if she tasted as good as he imagined. She was an apparition, a dream conjured up from his imaginings on lonely winter nights. No real woman that beautiful would want a man like him. He sighed. Maybe the reason for turning down his proposal was because he wasn't much to look at. The red hair was a curse he'd lived with all his life. And being a tall gangling man didn't help matters any. No one as beautiful and petite as Sarah wanted to spend her life with a brute of a man like him. Not except out of desperation, and, while she acted like a colt about to bolt, he detected more fear than desperation.

But she had dressed and come to the church. The gown must have been Catherine's wedding dress, though it looked like it had been made especially for Sarah. Rachel must have talked some sense into her. Sarah'd finally seen reason and walked down the aisle to become his wife. He smiled broadly. After all, she had no other choice.

She floated down the aisle toward him, taking her spot on the far side of the minister, clutching the flowers to her breast as if they were a shield against the world. Her eyes kept looking up at the window.

She had been staring at the window yesterday when he had found her in the church. He looked up to see what she found so interesting. He'd seen the window dozens of times. For this part of the country it was unique, but being from the city and having been to college, surely she'd seen bigger, more intricate ones. All he saw was the figure of Jesus ascending toward heaven.

Turning back to look at her, the minister's voice intoned in his ears like the buzz of a mosquito. His concentration

centered on the angel standing next to Rachel. Henry and
Mrs. Stedman would soon be wed. Then it would be his turn
to marry the woman who suited him as well as Mrs. Stedman suited Henry.

Out of the corner of his eye, he caught Henry giving Mrs.
Stedman a chaste kiss on the lips. The ceremony must be
nearly over. He'd best be paying attention or he'd daydream
right through his "I do's."

"No." Sarah's voice jarred him. He looked hard at her
face. Oh, hell, what had he missed?

"N-no?" stuttered the minister. "But . . . I understood—"

"You understood wrong. Joshua and I are not to be married." Sarah spoke softly but firmly.

The minister looked over at Joshua, his eyes questioning.

Joshua looked from the minister to Sarah. Her mouth
steeled into a look of finality. He'd just been kidding himself. She'd dressed up because Mrs. Stedman needed someone to stand up with her and no one had wished it to become
common knowledge about what had happened with her just
showing up out of nowhere. The conspiracy to protect
Sarah's reputation had blown up in his face like wildfire, in-
cinerating his heart. "Miss Hodges has second thoughts." He
had to protect her from what the townsfolk would say. "Her
nerves are most distraught after what has happened."

Sarah looked over at him with sad eyes.

"It could be months before I return to Moose Creek," said
the minister.

"She may be leaving the area." Joshua stared at Sarah
while he talked, willing her to stay, to change her mind, and
to marry him.

The minister shrugged his shoulders. Mrs. Westall
gasped. People stirred in their seats.

Joshua tried to smile as he turned to address the people in
the church. "I know Mrs. Westall and some of the other
ladies prepared food for all of us to enjoy. Shall we adjourn
outside?"

Henry took Rachel's arm and led the way. The townsfolk
murmured as they followed. Mrs. Westall hung back and
walked over to Sarah, who stood alone in front of the altar.

"Miss Hodges, are you all right?" She wrapped her arm around Sarah's shoulders.

"Yes." Sarah looked over at Joshua, who hadn't moved. She wished she could read his mind. His lips smiled, but his eyes didn't. She hadn't wanted to hurt him, but she couldn't marry him just because the minister was available and Joshua's bride had been killed. That would be wrong. Rather ghoulish, in fact. And the biggest mistake either of them could make.

"You can stay with me until the next stage leaves for the East, if you wish," said Mrs. Westall.

"Thank you. That's very kind." Sarah sighed. She couldn't tell Mrs. Westall she wasn't taking the stage east. She couldn't leave Moose Creek until she could find a way back to her own time.

Joshua touched her shoulder. Electricity ran through her and she jumped. "Sorry I startled you."

"I didn't hear you move across the floor."

"Didn't think you were so skittish, except when it comes to coyotes."

Sarah looked up into his eyes. Hurt shown back at her. "I'm sorry."

"For what?"

"This." She waved her arms in a sweeping motion.

"I won't force anyone into marrying me."

"Now, Mr. Campbell, I'm sure she never felt forced into anything." Mrs. Westall patted Joshua on the arm. "All that's happened has been more than her nerves can take. Give her a few days to rest and get used to our town. She'll see things in a different light. She'll see we can be as nice as the people back East and every bit as civilized."

"I'll bring Miss Hodges along, Mrs. Westall. You'd best go and help. Henry will worry things aren't going well," Joshua said.

"You're probably correct. You two come right along and join in the festivities. You should be celebrating the marriage of your friends. Seeing how happy they are, I'm sure the two of you will be calling the minister back in for a repeat." Mrs. Westall smiled.

Sarah watched Mrs. Westall as she moved quickly toward

the door and then turned to look up at Joshua. "I suppose we should join the rest of them. I'm all dressed up, I might as well go to a party."

"You're dressed for a wedding." Joshua stared down at her.

"And I attended a wedding. I stood up for Rachel." She'd been to weddings of friends before, but this one would always have a special place in her memories. She had stood up with her great-grandmother and great-grandfather. She'd seen her family history in the making.

"But it was supposed to be your wedding, also."

"No. Catherine was to be married today, not me. Only the fates never meant it to happen. You are destined never to marry."

"You're telling the future again. And a lonely one for me. I liked your predictions for Henry and Mrs. Stedman better." He gave her a lopsided grin.

"She's Mrs. Martin, now." Sarah glanced back at the window.

Joshua followed her gaze. "Yep. Seems strange Henry's got himself a wife and I'm still out in the cold alone. A double wedding should have taken place today."

"Well, it didn't—it's not going to happen." Sarah's voice took on a shrill tone.

"So you say. And how did you become so wise and all-knowing that you can condemn me to a life alone." His smile faded and the corners of his mouth turned down.

"I just know things." She'd already changed history. If she mucked up anything more, who knew how it would affect the future, her future. She had to get back to her own time before she brought devastation on everyone.

"I don't accept your knowing things. I had my heart set on a wife and I'll have one." He folded his arms across his chest. "And, if what you say is true, and I was never meant to marry Catherine, then why not marry you?"

She stared into his green eyes, eyes as cool as a summer meadow. She shivered. "I can't. History doesn't tell it that way. I don't belong here."

Joshua stared at her for a moment, then his voice boomed

around her. "Then where do you belong? Back in Los Angeles with Jack, who did that?" He pointed at her neck. "From what I've heard of Los Angeles, it isn't all that much. Moose Creek may not be as big, but it's a darn sight prettier."

"It is, but . . ." Sarah took a step back and tried to take in a big calming breath. She pressed her hands against her sides. She wondered if people would notice if she slipped back to Mrs. Westall's house and changed into something she could breathe in. She definitely wouldn't be able to eat, and dancing—well, she could forget about that. She'd pass out in the first five seconds. But then, she didn't know any of the current dances. If she tried any of the dances she knew, she would truly scandalize the local citizenry. A giggle erupted in a rush as though it had been locked inside her.

"I don't see anything funny." Joshua's jaw tightened.

"I'm sorry. You're right. Nothing's funny." She shook her head. "The only thing still holding me together is this damn corset."

He stared at her, expressionless. "Your corset has nothing to do with your mental state."

"It does when it cuts off the oxygen supply to my brain."

"You're far from dim-witted, Cath. Blaming it on your corset is nonsense. Women wear them all the time." His eyebrows pulled together in a look of consternation.

"Not where I come from."

"Los Angeles seems a very unorthodox place." He took a step closer to her. "Stay here with me. The beauty and our ways will become familiar and you'll learn to love it and maybe even me."

"Joshua, I can't. I would if I could, but I can't."

"Why not? Beauty doesn't have the pull Jack does?"

She trembled. "None of this has anything to do with Jack."

"Then why won't you stay?"

"I just can't. You have to believe that." She wanted to explain. She wanted to make him understand why she couldn't stay, why she couldn't leave, and why she couldn't marry him. But she couldn't do that either. She looked up at the window. The sun no longer shone directly through it.

"I don't have much choice, do I?" He crumpled his hat in his hands.

"If I could explain, I would." She could see the pain growing in his eyes and something else. Anger. "You wouldn't understand."

"Try me. I'm not stupid nor mean-spirited. I'll believe whatever you tell me."

Silently she shook her head. She didn't even believe her own story, so how could she make him?

He turned his face away. "I think I understand."

"I wish you did, but I doubt it."

"I understand you can't stand the thought of being married to a big grizzly bear of a man like myself." He stepped away from her.

"Joshua, no. That's not it." She reached her hand out to him.

He brushed it away. "What else could it be if it isn't Jack? Some other man perhaps waiting for you?"

"No other man is waiting for me. Now just isn't the right time or place. We're not meant for each other. You're not meant . . ." She let her hands drop to her sides as her voice trailed off.

"I know. I'm not meant to be married. No one will have me. What would a fancy Eastern lady want with the likes of me? But then, you're not a fancy Eastern lady, are you? You're not a lady at all. No man in his right mind would tie up with the likes of you."

"Excuse me! You have no reason to be rude. I didn't mean it to sound the way it did."

"What's wrong? Your corset affecting your speech now? So addled from the lack of oxygen you can't explain yourself?"

"I can explain myself just fine."

"Then do so." He towered over her and glowered down.

"I can't." She glared back at him. "And I won't stand here and be insulted."

"I'm the one being insulted. I'm not good enough for her ladyship."

"Oh, get a life. You're good enough for any woman."

"Just not you, with all your ladylike qualities." His voice pierced through her as the coldness of Jack's knife blade had.

She raised up on her tiptoes. "I may not be a lady like Rachel, but I have other qualities. Highly valued qualities where I come from." She stamped her foot and nearly lost her balance. "Damn skirt," she muttered as she yanked her foot from the hem and heard the delicate material tear.

"Can't imagine what. You don't cook, sew, or do much at all, really."

"I took care of myself very nicely without doing those things. None of them seemed the least bit necessary. I made a very good living. The computer consulting business was very lucrative."

"Then why did you leave?"

"I told you before—Jack." Her hands went to her throat.

He looked her up and down for a moment. "Can't cook or sew. That doesn't leave much for a woman to do to support herself. In Moose Creek, the proper women will run you out." He paused, twisting the brim of his hat in his hands. "Maybe you should be on the next stage to anywhere."

"Joshua Campbell, I am not a prostitute. How dare you?" She reached up on her tiptoes and slapped him across the face.

He grabbed her hand and looked down at her.

She winced and tried to extricate her wrist from his fingers. "You're hurting me."

He abruptly dropped her arm and stepped back. His arms hung limply at his sides. "I didn't mean to hurt you. I'd never do anything to hurt you, Cath. You have to believe that."

She rubbed her wrist.

"All I want is for you to become my wife. Let me take care of you. You're all alone with nowhere to go." His eyes pleaded with her.

The entry in Rachel's diary swirled through her mind.

Joshua was not found. Joshua had died, unmarried. She'd never been here. Nor did she belong. Her world existed 120 years in the future. His ended in less than two. She couldn't change any of that no matter how hard she wished. Fate had never meant them to be together. "I wish I could."

He stared at her for a moment, then stormed down the aisle toward the door.

"Joshua, wait."

"For more explanations?" He paused for a moment, looking back at her. "I think not." The slamming of the door reverberated around her.

Chapter 6

SARAH STARED AT the partition in the back of the church for several seconds, then turned to look up at the window. The sun had disappeared and it had turned dark, as if Jesus frowned down at her.

"Okay, so I handled that badly. I'm really new at this time-travel stuff. I mean, what do you tell people? 'Hi, I'm Sarah Martin. I'm from the 1990s. How are you?' I've heard that insane asylums during this era were really nasty places. I really wouldn't want to find out for myself or find myself locked in my great-grandparents' attic." She spit at the window. "Why wouldn't you take me home before I got everything so mucked up?" She stood, hands clenched at her sides. "I guess I better find him and apologize. It wouldn't be good to leave things this way. Then, will you let me go home?" She stared up at the window for a long moment, then turned slowly and followed Joshua from the church.

As she stepped outside, she realized large dark clouds clustered across the horizon, blocking the sun. She looked around quickly for Joshua. He stood, his back to her, near a table set up in the street shaking hands with Henry, who sat with Rachel and Mrs. Westall. She lifted her skirts carefully and stepped down into the dirt. He turned as though he felt her presence, and stared at her. Then he strode away.

She tried to move quickly, but her skirts tangled around her feet. She kicked at them, trying to get them out of her way. A sharp pain jabbed her in the side. She paused momentarily and tried to suck in air.

Joshua mounted his horse, jerked the reins to the side, and started on the road out of town at a full gallop. She started to yell to him, but stopped. She didn't need to involve the entire town in their fight. Moving as quickly as she could, she walked over to Rachel and Henry.

"Congratulations." She smiled at them. "Where did Joshua go?"

"Home," snapped Henry. He leaned back on the bench where he sat in front of a long wooden table. "He said he wasn't in the mood for a party."

"Mr. Martin, be nice to the poor girl." Rachel laid her hand on Henry's sleeve.

Absently, he patted her hand.

"Where is home?"

"I don't see where that is any of your concern." Henry glared up at her.

"Oh, give me a break. I'm not in the mood for this. I just want to know where he lives," Sarah growled back at him. Her great-grandfather was truly intolerable at times.

"Why, he lives about ten miles up the road, dear," said Mrs. Westall. "I don't understand why Mr. Campbell left so abruptly. Mr. Martin and he are such close friends, I'm surprised he didn't stay to enjoy the party."

"Miss Hodges put him out of sorts," said Henry gruffly.

"I can't imagine why." Mrs. Westall patted her on the shoulder. "Such a nice young woman who's been through so much. It's not surprising she's so timid."

"Hah." The noise erupted from Henry's throat.

Mrs. Westall stared at Henry as a frown flashed across her face.

Sarah looked up the street. "If you'll excuse me, I'm a bit tired. I'd like to go back to your house."

"You should eat something," said Rachel softly.

"I don't think I could swallow a bite." She was convinced no room for any food existed without letting the blasted corset loose. "Please enjoy yourselves. Don't let Joshua and me spoil the day. This should be a very happy event for you." She moved away from the table. A woman dressed in gray moved up to talk with the Martins and Sarah turned and traveled as fast as she could toward Mrs. Westall's house. She had to get her bag. Then she had to find a way to follow Joshua. A horse wasn't going to do since she couldn't sit one trapped in this dress. She needed a buggy she could "borrow." Lord, but the community was going to get tired of her taking their means of travel. If someone borrowed her car without asking, she'd be furious. But it couldn't be helped. She was determined to set things right with Joshua no matter what it took.

The pounding of the horse's hooves against the ground did nothing to alleviate the anger that had built up in him. Joshua pulled the horse to a slower pace. No sense in killing the animal. His own stupidity amazed him. He'd practically called her a whore. That certainly hadn't been the way to convince her to change her mind and marry him. A little patience would have served him better. But her "I can't explains" bore into him the way a burr trapped under a saddle bore into a horse's hide.

The thought of her standing in the church with the sun streaming in and caressing her in that beautiful gown made him ache. He wanted her. Wanted her more than any woman he'd ever seen. A pretty shaky possibility before he'd opened his mouth, and now after his outburst that task seemed as insurmountable as driving cattle to market in a blizzard. Then he had to compound his stupidity by grabbing her arm and hurting her. She'd run away from one man for just such an action. Someone ought to kick him in the backside.

He slowed the horse to a walk. There was no reason to

hurry home. Nothing but a big empty house awaited him. A house he'd built for his bride. A bride dead at the hands of a stage robber. Maybe Sarah was right. He wasn't meant to be married.

Sarah held the horse's reins in both hands, jiggling them slightly as she followed a narrow wheel-rutted trail. The horse seemed to be taking his own sweet time traveling up the road. She flipped the reins across the animal's back to encourage him to speed up. She didn't want to go too fast, but she did want to find Joshua's place before dark.

Off to the east she could see more and more dark clouds gathering. Just what she needed, a storm while she was trying to maneuver a horse and buggy and dressed in an outfit that wasn't going to like water. "Come on, you stupid beast. I know you can move faster than this." She slapped the horse again. The buggy jolted forward, nearly throwing her off the seat. With all the skirt shoved behind her, she could barely balance on the seat. She wished the bustle would squash so she could sit flat. Placing her feet firmly against the front edge of the buggy, she held herself perched precariously on the edge.

The clouds swirled toward her. The ten-mile drive in a horse and buggy took forever. She'd have been there and back in her Camaro, except it didn't have four-wheel drive. She tried to hold the reins firmly but the rubbing was making the palms of her hands hurt. The lightweight gloves she wore were not made for buggy driving and the material had started to fray.

A jagged light flashed across the sky followed by a deafening roar. Sarah jumped and inadvertently slapped the horse again with the reins. The horse raced down the dirt road.

"Whoa," she screamed, using her body weight to pull back on the reins. The horse ignored her. As the wheel of the buggy hit a rut, she flew up several inches into the air and landed back on the seat with a thump. She tried to draw back the air forced from her body. Pains shot through her chest. Raindrops splattered across her face. "Oh, hell." She grabbed her backpack as she slipped on the seat and shoved it under her skirts. At least having all that material hanging from her waist would serve some purpose. She could keep her valuables dry.

Trying to right herself on the seat she saw a sign off to the side of the road, Crazy C Ranch. The horse galloped past. She put all of her strength into yanking on the reins. "Stop, you dumb animal. Damn it. I wanted to turn back there."

The buggy finally came to a stop.

The horse shook its head, sending out a spray of water. Sarah wiped at her face with her gloved hand to try to remove the rain from her eyes. She took several small breaths to ease the growing pain in her side while she assessed the situation. The rain fell harder with each second. The ground around her, which had seemed hard-packed only moments before, was now transformed into muck. "Oh, hell," she groaned. "What did I ever do to deserve this?"

If she could get the horse to back up, she could turn down the drive. She looked behind her. Then she looked back at the horse. If she pulled on the reins, he'd just stand where he was. If she slapped him on his back, he'd go forward. Stop and go were the only two commands she knew. Reverse wasn't in there anywhere. Life would be so much easier if she had her car. It had reverse. And, at least if she got stuck in the mud, she'd have a roof over her head until someone came to rescue her.

She looked for a wider spot in the road to turn the buggy around. A few feet ahead appeared to be a little wider spot. They really needed to make roads wide enough for two-way traffic. At least then she could pull a U-turn. However, this vehicle had a larger turning radius than her car.

She jiggled the reins softly. The horse snorted and shook its head again. "Move, stupid." She jiggled the reins a second time. The horse started forward with a jerk. She pulled back on the reins. The animal stopped. She gave it a soft slap on the back. "Slowly." She pulled to the right and the buggy veered to the edge of the road.

She took as deep a breath as she could and held it. "We're going to do this. Easy, horse. Real easy."

She shortened the left rein and the horse started to turn.

The buggy wobbled. A small squeak escaped her as the right wheel of the vehicle contacted ground again and she gasped. "Okay. We're almost around." She urged the horse ahead. "Slow, now, horse. Just a little farther and we can head back to the turnoff."

Rain pelted Sarah's face so she could hardly see. Never in her life had she been in such a storm. Lightning cut a jagged edge across the sky. Thunder echoed fiercely around her. The horse bolted forward. The buggy wheels hit the side of the road and sank. The horse strained against the shafts to which he was strapped. The buggy didn't move.

"Oh, God." She put her head forward against the front edge of the vehicle and shook her head. "This isn't happening. Move, horse. You can get us out of this, I know you can."

A small river of water formed down the edge of the road, causing the buggy wheels to sink deeper. The horse strained, but nothing happened.

"Damn it all to hell!" said Sarah. Water trickled down the front of her dress. A puddle had formed in her lap. "Now what? We stay here and drown, or I walk." She saw no way around it. It could be hours before the rain stopped or, for that matter, hours before someone came along to help. From the looks of this road, it could be days.

She looked down at her skirt which seemed to be gaining weight by the second. Large water splotches formed across it. Satin and rain didn't mix. She peeked under the edge of her skirt at the shoes that matched her dress. They weren't even made for walking in the dirt let alone the muck taking over the road. She shrugged her shoulders and climbed down onto the road. Grabbing her backpack, she threw it over her shoulder. If she could get the horse unhooked, she might be able to ride him to Joshua's house.

Joshua. She needed to figure out what she was going to say to him. Help. Definitely, help. Discussing the argument they'd had could wait until he got her out of this outfit that now weighed at least a hundred pounds from all the waterlogging.

She gathered the reins in her hands and eased toward the horse. "Okay, horse. You and I are going to have an understanding. I won't leave you hooked to this damn carriage and you won't abandon me in this terrible storm."

Her wet bonnet slipped sideways on her head. She jerked it off and flung it onto the buggy's seat. The mud pulled at her feet, trying to root her to the ground. She fought her way to the horse's side and looked over the buckles holding the animal to the poles. After some thought, she finally decided which straps would free the horse without unhooking its reins. She yanked and pulled until they came free.

"Okay. Step one complete," she muttered as she watched the buggy poles drop to the ground. She looked up at the horse's back, then down at her skirts. She definitely needed the compact model horse. Somehow she had to find a way up.

"Come on, horse. Such a good horse." She'd heard people talk to their dogs and watched them obey when they told them how good they were. Hopefully the horse would listen to her and obey. She led him back to the edge of the buggy. Holding the reins tightly in her hands, she tried to extricate her foot from the mud to climb aboard the buggy. One shoe stuck in the mud. She shook her head and left it there. The damn things hurt her feet anyway. Standing on the buggy seat, she pulled the animal closer. No way could she swing one leg over and sit. But if she lay across the animal, then maybe, just maybe she could get herself upright. Leaning forward across the horse's neck should leave room for the bustle.

It would work.

It had to work.

Walking through the mud barefoot wasn't a pleasant alternative.

She sucked in as much air as the corset would allow and launched herself over the horse's back. Holding the animal's mane with a death grip, she tried to swing herself around.

A tree not ten feet away cracked in half with an ear-splitting blast as the sky exploded with light. The horse reared and bolted. Sarah screamed as she hit the ground with a squelching sound.

• • •

Joshua leaned back in an armchair with his boot-clad feet
propped up on the polished wooden table before him. He no
longer cared if his boots marred the surface. No one but he
would ever sit in this room. He took a long swig on the bottle of whiskey he clutched in his hand.

He'd taken such care in decorating this house. Mrs. Westall had been his advisor every step of the way. The mantel
clock struck six. He stared at it where it sat on the heavy
stone mantel. He'd imported it from back East along with
half the furnishings in the house. He had made the wooden
pieces himself, but an upholstered couch and chairs had
been beyond his knowledge. Now none of it mattered. No
Eastern bride had joined him to enjoy the comforts imported
just for her.

For himself, he'd be just as happy with the simple
wooden furniture he'd had before. But a fine lady needed
more. An ache filled his heart as he looked at the empty
whatnot in the corner. He had imagined it filled with delicate
items Catherine had brought with her. Cath would have put
interesting items on the shelves. Everything about her
shouted interesting.

He supposed he should call her Sarah, but the name Cath
seemed to fit her better. Sarah was a name for a fine lady—
not the unusual female he'd met two days ago. And, with
one swift motion, the little bitty mite of a thing had turned
his world upside down. And life seemed so bleak without
her around. All last night he had dreamed of bringing her
home with him. And she had looked so beautiful standing in
the church this afternoon.

A jagged flash of lightning lit the room. The windows rattled as the thunder struck. The storm outside fit his mood.
Cath would be safely harbored at Mrs. Westall's house.
Until she left. To go home, wherever that was. It shouldn't
matter so much to him. She was nothing more than a waif
who had stumbled across his path. And now she threatened
to take his heart with her.

He sighed and stretched his legs, knowing his heels dug
into the varnish he had so painstakingly applied to the top of
the table. He should fix himself something to eat. With

Cookie and his cowhands still in town at the party, no one else would need feeding and no cooking would be done. With this storm, they'd hole up in town for a day or two and he'd be on his own. His stomach growled at him. He hadn't eaten all day. But the thought of going into the kitchen and lighting the new stove gnawed at his heart more than the hunger did at his stomach. If the rain would let up, he'd walk across to the bunkhouse and use that stove. He could do without food, but coffee sure would be nice. He tilted the bottle and took another swig.

A strange sound on the front porch caught his attention. His feet landed softly on the rug as he sat up and listened. Probably a wild animal looking for a dry spot. He shook his head and started to lean back. The noise came again. He'd never heard a stranger sound, a sort of squooshing, dragging noise. It might be an injured animal. He guessed he'd better get up and look.

He walked quietly toward the front door across the rag rug Mrs. Westall had made for his new parlor. He didn't want to frighten whatever had sought refuge on the other side. A flash of lightning blinded him as he opened the door. Something hit him against the chest. He grabbed for it. A scream blended into the retort of thunder.

His eyes cleared and he stared down at a rain-sodden, bedraggled Cath. "What on earth?"

"Joshua. Thank goodness. You scared me half to death."

"Why were you hitting me?" He wanted to laugh at the sight she made, but he feared she'd really try to hit him.

"I was knocking on your door to be let in." She wobbled slightly.

She had come after him. She had finally come to her senses and changed her mind. "And what are you doing out here?"

"Who the hell cares. Would you please let me in? I'm half-drowned, cold, muddy, and not in a very good humor."

Joshua stepped back quickly from the door. "Come in and sit by the fireplace where you can get warm."

Sarah took a step in the house and stopped. "I'll track mud all over your floor."

"It'll wash." He looked down the back of her skirt as she trudged by him. Mud caked it from the bustle down and around the hem. The footprints on the floor showed she no longer wore shoes. He suppressed a smile.

She started to sway. He grabbed her up, looking around the parlor for a place to set her down. Water dripped down his arms and soaked into his shirt as he held her against his chest. She had gained a great deal of weight since she had fallen off her horse into his arms days before. The water had to have soaked all the way through her petticoats and to her skin. She'd catch a chill if he didn't get her out of the wet clothes and dried out quickly.

He turned and strode toward the kitchen. Gently he set her down in a chair and watched her collapse against the table. Grabbing wood, he lit the stove and started a pot of coffee. "I'll get you a towel," he said over his shoulder. "But I don't have any dry women's clothing for you to put on." She looked very pale as she lay against the tabletop. He looked down at the bag next to her. It couldn't contain anything dry.

"Doesn't matter." Sarah just leaned against the table, not moving.

"Want me to help you upstairs so you can undress?"

"I can't move."

He knelt down next to her. She seemed to be barely breathing. "You okay?"

She placed both hands against the top of the table and shoved herself to her feet, glaring down at him. "Do I look okay? I'm wet, muddy, and just trudged who knows how far in the worst storm I've ever seen, sinking into mud up to my knees—and you want to know if I'm okay."

He stood slowly. "You shouldn't have gone wandering around the countryside with a storm coming on."

"How the hell was I supposed to know a storm was coming on? I was just trying to catch up with you." She waved her hands at him.

He pushed a wet strand of hair away from her face. "Why?"

"Because of the stupidity that went on in the church." She

crumpled into the chair, swaying and nearly falling to the floor.

"Cath." He grabbed for her. "What's wrong?"

She waved her hand in the air. "Can't breathe," she gasped.

His hand rested on her shoulder as she slumped against the table.

"Stays," she whispered.

He looked at the row of tiny buttons down the back of her dress. He tried to pull one free. His large fingers would not unhook the damn thing. He shrugged his shoulders. The dress was ruined, anyway. Grabbing the neckline, he yanked. Tiny buttons clattered across the floor. Sarah still didn't move. He tried to pull the ties loose on the corset, but they refused to budge. He pulled a knife from his boot top and eased the blade under the ties. With a slicing movement, they popped loose. Sarah's back expanded as air rushed into her lungs.

"Oh, thank you, God. Whoever invented these things must have been trying to rid the world of the female half." She drew in deep breaths. "That feels so wonderful."

"Your gown and . . . corset are ruined." He stared at her back, now covered only by a sheer camisole.

"The dress was beyond help anyway and if I have my way, I will never, ever put on another corset for the rest of my life. Now, what do you have that I can put on so I can get rid of this outfit?" She sat up, holding the front of the dress pressed against her.

He stared into her eyes. With the release of the corset, the color had returned to her face and the sparkle to her eyes. "Nothing proper for a woman to wear."

"Just dry will do. Maybe one of your shirts and a towel to dry off with."

He returned in a moment with both items. "Need any more help getting out of that dress?" His eyes roamed over the slightly browned flesh of her exposed shoulders and back, marked with a distinctive white line. He was intrigued as to how a woman ended up with tanned skin so far down her back. All the women he knew covered themselves from head to toe when they ventured outside. And the smoothness of her skin intrigued him. He wanted to reach over and touch her. Heat surged through his body as he thought about running his fingers over her.

"It should just fall off if I stand up. I can manage that by myself."

"All right." Both disappointed and relieved, Joshua turned and moved into the hall.

"I'm dressed." Sarah's voice floated down the hall toward him. "And I think the coffee's done. I'd love a cup."

He pushed the kitchen door open and stopped. From under his shirt, Sarah's mud-caked, bare legs were exposed from the knees down. As she stretched upward, reaching for a mug in the glass-fronted cabinet, the shirt crept upward and exposed more skin that wasn't covered with mud. His breath caught in his throat. His heart threatened to beat its way out of his chest. He adjusted his pants.

Chapter 7

JOSHUA MOVED QUICKLY across the kitchen floor. "Let me get that for you." His chest brushed across her arm as he reached over her head. Grabbing the cups, he filled them and set them on the table. He sat down opposite Sarah, watching her sip at her coffee. His shirt draped enticingly across her breasts, her nipples silhouetted against the material. The top of the shirt fell open, exposing a vee of flesh. A cameo dangled just above the swell of her breasts.

He set his cup down, unable to look away from the top button of the shirt nestled between her breasts. The room had suddenly become too warm to drink coffee. In fact, a walk in the rain might bring his temperature down to a slow simmer. He shifted in his chair.

Sarah looked up. Holding the cup in both hands, she smiled at him. "This is helping thaw me out. I know I've not given you the most pleasant of days, but can I impose upon you further?"

Thaw out! He'd like to thaw her out. A few kisses down her neck to where that button sat would warm her up quickly enough. He'd never sat across from a half-naked woman. In fact, he'd never seen a half-naked woman, except in bed. If he didn't do something soon, he would lose control and grab her to him.

"Joshua, I know you're still angry with me. I don't know what to say to make that better."

"Huh?" He raised his eyes to meet hers. Her soft gray eyes filled with hurt.

"Are you listening to me?"

"Yes . . . no . . . I guess not." He shook his head to clear out the cobwebs. "What did you say?"

She giggled softly. "I must look like a drowned rat." She pushed the hair out of her face. "I asked if I could impose on you some more."

"You're not imposing." He could sit here forever and stare at her, except that his blood pounded so hard in his ears he was having trouble hearing her.

"Of course I am. I have been imposing on everybody since I arrived."

Joshua stared at her for a moment. She had a point. "What do you want?"

"Something to eat. If it's not too much trouble. I'm starving. Breakfast was a very long time ago and slogging through mud really works up an appetite. Especially when one can't breathe."

"Can't breathe?"

"That stupid dress. Or should I say 'corset.' Rachel took great delight in having it laced as tightly as possible. She seemed to be getting even with me for some reason." She smiled at Joshua.

"You could have eaten at the party." His tone was curt.

"I wasn't much in a mood for a party. Besides, not only couldn't I breathe, I couldn't swallow. I was squashed so tightly, I had no room to put in any food."

Joshua smiled at her. He couldn't stay mad at her. She did resemble some kind of drowned animal. A very desirable drowned animal. "I don't have much. I hadn't planned on fixing supper tonight. Figured we'd eat in town."

"A sandwich, maybe?"

He couldn't let her starve. His own stupidity had caused the scene in the church. Now he had every reason to try to make her comfortable. She had come after him. She'd changed her mind. Otherwise she never would have risked her life trying to get to him. "I can fix something." Moving would get his mind off the front of her shirt.

"Oh, that would be wonderful." She shifted in the chair, watching him move toward the stove.

"Would steak and biscuits be okay?"

She didn't eat red meat often, but anything would do at the moment. Besides, on a cattle ranch, what else did she expect him to fix? "I don't want to put you to any trouble."

He laughed coarsely. "It's a little late for that." He leaned down and pulled a bowl from the bottom of a china closet. The top glass-enclosed shelves were lined with china plates covered with an intricate blue flower pattern.

Joshua walked across the room to a smaller table, set the ceramic bowl down, and reached above the table to a wooden box mounted on the wall. Pulling on one of the knobs, a drawer folded down from the top. He scooped flour into the bowl. He scooped something from the adjoining drawer and then sprinkled in some salt. He uncorked a jar that was sitting on the table, reached in with a spoon, and globbed some kind of fat onto it. Sarah watched, fascinated, while he stirred, then poured in some liquid. After plopping blobs of dough on a pan, he shoved it into the oven and turned back to her.

"I have to go out back to get the steaks." He turned toward the door.

"But you'll get wet. Don't you have anything inside to fix?"

"Meat would spoil in the kitchen. Gets too hot. Anyway, a little rain'll do me good."

Sarah looked around the kitchen after the door closed behind Joshua. She had never seen a more beautiful china closet. The highly polished wood glistened in the slight light. Across the room, white curtains with tiny sprigs of blue flowers and lace trim hung at the wide window that looked out into the storm. The black cast-iron stove emitted a tremendous amount of heat. The room made her feel cozy and safe.

The door suddenly slammed against the wall, making her jump.

"Sorry," said Joshua as he kicked the door shut. "Wind grabbed it right out of my hand." He grabbed a cast-iron skillet from a hook above the stove and tossed in the steaks. Using a towel, he pulled the biscuits from the oven and slid them onto a plate taken from the cabinet.

"That's a beautiful piece of furniture." Sarah watched him closely. He seemed so at home in the kitchen. She'd never managed to be that way. Everything she'd ever tried to cook had turned into cinders. "Where'd you get it?"

"I made it."

She sat up straight. "Really? It must be worth a fortune."

"It's just a cabinet to hold dishes."

"*Just*? Why, I've never seen a more beautiful piece of furniture."

He beamed at her. "You can start with the biscuits. I'll get the butter. I have some preserves Mrs. Westall gave me. Sort of a wedding present."

"Sounds marvelous." She spread the hot biscuit with a thick glob of butter, and then jam. She sighed as she sunk her teeth into it. Butter dripped down between her fingers. She crammed the rest of the biscuit into her mouth and then licked the butter from her fingers. She couldn't remember the last time she'd had real butter. It tasted wonderful. "These are the best biscuits I've ever eaten."

"You must not have much experience with them. I do an adequate job." He placed a plate in front of her with a knife and fork.

She cut into the meat and watched the blood seep out on her plate. Wrinkling her nose, she looked at him. "I like my meat cooked."

"It is cooked."

"I mean without .. not red inside."

"You want me to cook it more?"

"Yeah. A lot more."

"That'll ruin it. Steak shouldn't be overcooked."

"I can't eat it this way." She smiled at him.

Shaking his head, he put the steak back in the pan. "Ruin one of my best pieces of beef," he muttered.

"I'm sorry. I just . . . well, I don't eat red meat much and I can't handle it if it looks raw."

"What are you talking about?"

"Red meat. Beef."

"You don't eat beef?"

"Not much. It isn't healthy."

Joshua's mouth dropped open. He clamped his jaw shut and muttered something under his breath. After taking a deep breath, he asked, "Then what do you eat?"

"Chicken. Turkey. Fish."

"Then I'll take you fishing and you can catch your own dinner."

A shiver ran through her. "Yuck. I couldn't eat anything I caught."

"Cath, you are the strangest woman I've ever met. If you don't catch fish, then where do you get it?"

"The supermarket." She stuffed another biscuit in her mouth.

"The what?"

"Store. God, these are good. And you make it look so easy. Could you teach me?"

"Making biscuits isn't so hard."

"That's what you think."

He laughed at her and brought her steak back. "Your shoe leather is ready."

She wrinkled her nose at him.

After finishing the steak, she pushed the plate back. "Thank you. After what happened earlier, I wouldn't have been surprised if you'd thrown me out in the storm."

"I'd never do that."

"Don't suppose you would. I'm sorry."

"About what?" He leaned back in his chair so that two of the legs came up off the floor.

"About what happened in the church. I didn't mean to embarrass you. You've been so nice." She sighed. Being able to expand her chest as much as she wanted felt more wonderful than she'd thought possible. She'd worn some tight outfits in her life, but today had set a record.

"If you don't want to marry me, then you don't want to marry me." A shadow passed over his face.

"It has nothing to do with wanting."

"Then what does it have to do with?"

She wished she could explain. She wanted to be able to tell someone how disjointed the world had become. She wanted to go home. She wanted her computer and her microwave and a chicken sandwich with sprouts. "You wouldn't understand." She sagged against the table. "Hell, you wouldn't believe me."

"Try me."

She looked at him for a long moment, then shook her head. "I'll wash the dishes. That much I can do."

She moved across to the sink with the dishes in her hand. No faucets, just a spout with a handle. A pump. This couldn't be too difficult. She moved the handle up and down. Nothing. She bent to look at the contraption.

"You have to prime it first."

"Huh?"

"Are you sure you can do this?"

"I said I could wash dishes. I never said anything about getting water."

Joshua laughed loudly. "Also, you have to heat water on the stove."

Sarah watched him, fascinated, while he poured a small amount of water from a pitcher on the sink into the top of the pump and then cranked it up and down. He added more water and pumped the handle again. Water came out in spurts as he worked the handle. He refilled the pitcher, then the pan for the stove. With a few more pumps, he had water in the sink. After depositing the pot on the stove to heat, he picked up a bar of soap and a knife. He shaved off bits and let them fall into the water. Adding the heated water, he swished his hands around until he had soapy water.

He reached for the plates to put them into the water. She pushed him aside. "I said I'll wash. Go sit down."

After she finished the few dishes, Sarah reached for the

pan, nearly dropping it on the floor. Damn. She'd never encountered such a heavy cooking utensil. She glanced over
her shoulder to see him smirking. Done with the pan, she set
it next to the sink and started drying it with a towel.

Joshua reached around her and took it. "Set it on the
stove. It'll dry by itself."

"Can I have another cup of coffee?" After the day she'd
had, the caffeine shouldn't keep her awake. In fact, it might
give her a jolt to get moving again. The meal made her want
to curl up into a ball and go to sleep. She plopped down in
the chair by the table.

He poured the coffee. "Don't you think you should put on
some more clothes? You don't want to catch a chill."

She looked down. "I'm not putting anything else on until
I wash off the mud."

"I could fix you a bath."

A hot bath. That would work wonders on her tired, aching
body. She stared at her feet. "That would be an excellent
idea."

He pumped water and set it on the stove. Then he threw
more wood inside it. "It'll only take a minute."

"Where's the bathtub?" She looked around the room. No
place appeared big enough to hide a tub like in Mrs. Westall's house. "Is there anybody else around here?"

"No. Why?"

"I didn't want anyone peeking in while I'm in the tub."

"The water closet doesn't have any windows."

"The what?"

"Water closet. Where the tub is."

"And where is that?"

Joshua pointed to a door off the kitchen.

"So you hide the tub out of the way."

"No. The tub stays in that room." Joshua sipped at his coffee. "It's close to the kitchen stove. Lugging hot water up the
stairs takes too much effort."

"Okay." No running water. At least he had a tub in a separate room and she didn't have to sit in the middle of the
kitchen in little more than a bucket like she'd had to at Mrs.
Westall's. "Lead the way."

Joshua put more water on to heat before he took her into the bathroom. "I did the best I could." He stood in the doorway while Sarah peeked around him.

One of the most beautiful sights she had seen in days greeted her. A toilet. The tank was mounted at her eye level with a string hanging down, but it was an honest-to-goodness toilet. No more outhouses. Living with Joshua might not be such a bad idea. Just until she could get home. After all, no one else in the territory had indoor plumbing. "This is wonderful."

"You like it? Getting all this shipped in and hooked up was more difficult than I expected. Had a few problems with the plumbing. Never did anything like this before."

"You did this all for Catherine?" The man had obviously wanted to impress his bride-to-be.

"Couldn't have a fine Eastern lady running to the outhouse or using a chamber pot. She'd be used to better."

"She might not be here to appreciate it, but I can assure you I do." More than she could ever express to him. A little piece of home behind a small kitchen door. She might survive yet until she found a way home.

Squeezing by him, she entered the room. A metal rectangular cabinet stood against the wall opposite the toilet. She turned back to him. "Where's the bathtub?"

He pointed to the cabinet.

"Taking a bath in a cabinet might be a bit tricky."

"You have to fold it down."

"Oh." She'd never seen anything so strange. She watched while he opened the tub. Faucets were fastened at the wall end. He shoved a plug into the bottom of the tub and turned on the faucets. Water poured in.

She ran her hand along the top of the cool metal. "Never seen a metal bathtub before." The water looked so inviting.

"The only kind I could get transported out here in one piece. Everyone thought I'd lost my mind when I started building the water closet. Said they'd never heard of anything so ridiculous in all their lives."

"But you did it anyway for your lady. That's one of the sweetest things I ever heard of." She smiled up at him.

"It could be for you." His gaze held hers.

"I'll use it. For the moment. But . . ." She sighed. She saw the hurt in his eyes. "I won't make promises I can't keep."

Joshua turned back toward the kitchen.

"Wait. Where are you going?" She reached for his arm.

He looked over his shoulder at her. "To get the hot water."

"But you have running water."

He smiled. "Yeah, but it's cold enough to turn you into an iceberg."

"No hot water, huh?"

"Nope. Couldn't quite work that one out. Know they have it back East, but just couldn't do it. So I put the water closet next to the kitchen to make it easier to bring in hot water."

"At least I don't have to carry the tub out when I'm through. I had enough of that at Mrs. Westall's. She had a fit when I wanted a bath two days in a row."

"Most people don't hold much with bathing."

"It does get the mud off, though." She glanced down at her feet.

"In this case, a bath is definitely in order." Joshua carried the pot of water into the bathroom and poured it into the stream of water flowing from the faucets.

"How come you have a pump in the kitchen and faucets in the bathroom?"

"Didn't think to have faucets shipped in for the kitchen until too late. It'll be spring before I can fix up the kitchen and get rid of the pump. Still will have to heat water on the stove. Just can't get that contraption that's suppose to heat the water to work right. Finally put it in the barn. Too darn much trouble."

Sarah laughed. "If you'll get me a towel, I'll get cleaned up."

Sarah emptied her backpack onto the bathroom floor and surveyed the damage. Her jeans, which had been crammed on the top of the bag had gotten wet, but everything else seemed to be all right. Her makeup had remained dry because she carried it in plastic bags. Pulling out her cassette player, she shoved in a tape and prayed. As she held the earphones to one ear, she pushed play. Soft music came out. One of her last connections to the future still worked. Hope sprung anew in her life.

She stripped off Joshua's shirt and sank into the water. She could stretch out and let the water cover her up to her neck. In Mrs. Westall's tub all she could do was sit in a few inches of water with her legs cramped up. But in Joshua's tub, she couldn't even reach the far end with her toes.

She closed her eyes and let the water ease all the pains from buggy riding and hiking in the mud. When the water started to cool off, she washed. Then she pulled the plug and watched the water swirl down the drain. It amazed her what a wonderful feeling she got from watching such an ordinary occurrence. She'd thought she'd never see such a thing again.

Joshua was an amazing man. What he must have gone through to fix up such luxurious accommodations for a woman he'd never met! Catherine would have been very happy. This house offered everything a woman could want—at least, a woman of this time. Sarah still wanted her computer and car.

She toweled herself off and put the shirt back on. Shoving everything but her jeans back in her bag, she opened the bathroom door and went into the kitchen. Joshua still sat at the table with his coffee cup in his hand. "Thank you for the use of your tub. I feel so much better."

"Don't you think you should put on some proper clothes?" he growled at her.

"This covers me. Besides, my pants are wet." She draped her jeans over the back of a chair, then filled her cup.

Joshua grunted at her. "Barely."

Sarah looked down at her legs. The shirt went down to about three inches above her knees. She had shorts that showed more than Joshua's shirt did. "What's wrong with the way I'm dressed?"

"It isn't decent."

"I don't understand all this fuss about being covered from head to toe."

"Decent women don't dress like that." He ran his fingers through his hair.

"Well, this one does. Besides, I have no dry clothes of my own to put on." She shrugged her shoulders. She would never fit in here. "Want more coffee?"

He nodded his head at her.

After filling his cup, she sat down. "I left someone's buggy stuck in the mud just past your turnoff."

He looked over at her and shook his head. "That doesn't surprise me. What about the horse?"

"I unhooked him. When I tried to mount him, lightning hit and he dumped me in the mud."

Joshua laughed. "I don't think that will make the buggy's owner feel any better, but it had to be a sight to behold."

She stuck her tongue out at him.

"That isn't very ladylike."

"Neither is sitting in the mud."

"Why'd you come, Cath?" A shadow crossed his face and his eyebrows furrowed together.

"To apologize. I didn't know I was going to get stuck in a storm."

He looked straight at her, his fingers gripping the cup.

His silence made her squirm. "You have a wonderful house. Any woman would be very fortunate to have you for a husband. Not many men would go out of their way as much as you have to make a woman feel comfortable." She smiled at him. Somehow she had to figure a way to offer some explanation that would make him feel better.

He slowly took a sip of his coffee, then set the cup back on the table. He stared into her eyes. "But you won't say why."

"I can't."

"Or won't?"

"I can't. I wish I could. More than you'll ever know."

"But you don't trust me."

"It has nothing to do with trust." Dammit! Jack and his obsessions had gotten her into this mess and she couldn't seem to figure a way out.

"What would a pretty little thing like you want with a

grizzly bear like me? You made that very clear. Said I'd never marry anyone. Not good enough." He shoved the cup aside.

Sarah moved around the table and laid a hand on his arm. She didn't want to hurt him. If it weren't for some bizarre quirk of fate, she would be in the West somewhere having her first vacation in five years while she hid out. She couldn't explain to him why she couldn't marry him. She didn't belong here. She had to go back to her life. Here she was useless and helpless. She'd never been that way in her entire life and it was a very unsettling feeling. "That's just nonsense, Joshua. I've met very few men in my life as considerate as you. I didn't mean you weren't good enough to marry someone. Catherine would have been so happy here."

"But not you." Heat shot through him from where her hand rested. The shirt clung to her breasts as she stood next to him. He wondered if her legs would feel silky soft against his hands. She wore that wonderful fragrance she'd worn on the first day he'd seen her. He wanted to take her into his arms and kiss her full lips.

She looked at him without speaking and shook her head.

Standing up abruptly, he knocked the chair over. "You must be tired. Since there's no way to get you back to Mrs. Westall's until the rain lets up, you'll have to spend the night here even though it's not proper." He stared at her for a moment. "No. It can't be helped. I'll show you the bedroom. Tomorrow I'll return you and the buggy to town."

Sarah looked at him and then slowly nodded her head.

Sarah snuggled under the heavy quilt on the four-poster bed. She wondered if Joshua had made the wardrobe that took up most of one wall in the bedroom. It was as finely crafted as the china cabinet in the kitchen. It stood empty, awaiting Catherine's clothes.

This had to be the master bedroom. It had been decorated with fancy blue drapes while a blue-flowered china pitcher and bowl sat atop the dresser. A fancy kerosene lamp sat on a small table next to the bed. Joshua had put a great deal of effort into every part of this house for Catherine. A small pang of jealousy crept through her. She'd never met a man who'd gone out of his way to please her the way Joshua had to please a bride he'd never even met. Twentieth-century men just weren't gallant anymore. Joshua was one of a kind.

She wished he were hers.

She leaned over and blew out the lamp, plunging the room into darkness. Lightning streaked across the sky. Sarah jumped. Strange shapes moved around the furniture.

She pulled the comforter up farther. Being afraid of a storm was silly. Thunder and lightning had never frightened her before. Joshua slept just down the hall. Jack resided 120 years away. She was safe.

She wished she could listen to her cassette player for a few minutes, but she feared she'd fall asleep with it on and Joshua might see it in the morning. She closed her eyes tightly to shut out the flashes of lightning. If only she could block out the booming sound that followed each flash.

She jumped as the next boom shook the windows. It seemed to be getting closer. She pulled the covers over her head. They would drown out the noise.

Stereo music swirled around her. Sarah lounged on her rose-colored couch, glad to be home. She should clean up the Chinese take-out food containers on her black marble coffee table and more importantly, she needed to get up and turn on the computer. Tomorrow she had appointments with two new clients and she hadn't finished the proposals for either one of them. Pete would be highly irritated if she blew two new accounts in one day, but she just couldn't seem to concentrate. She'd been that way for three days, ever since she'd met Jack at the local coffee shop. She'd been sitting alone eating dinner when he'd plopped down in the chair next to her and introduced himself. He told her how beautiful she looked and stated he wanted to marry her. She'd laughed, thinking he was making a joke. When she realized he was deadly serious, the hairs on the back of her neck prickled and she made a hasty departure.

Somehow he'd found her two days later at another restaurant where he had burst in on her business meeting and threatened her client, a scene that cost her the account. A shiver ran down her spine as she remembered the scene. She could still see the veins standing out on his neck as he screamed at her. She tried to stay calm and got someone to call the police. They'd escorted him out.

The police told her to get a restraining order, which she did immediately. Yesterday, when he showed up outside her office, she had called the police again. They asked him to move along. When she'd gotten home last night, she noticed his car parked outside her building. Luckily she lived in a security building that required a keycard to drive into the garage. The police told her they couldn't do anything since he'd parked on a public street and had remained a hundred yards away from her.

Tonight she hadn't seen him, but she felt him. She picked up her cell phone and called LeeAnne. A chat would settle her nerves. The answering machine clicked on and Sarah clicked off.

Sighing, she climbed off the couch and parked herself in front of the computer. Work needed doing and she'd better get to it. She watched the flickering numbers as the machine checked the hard drive and finally flashed a cursor at her. She'd just started typing when the doorbell rang.

"Damn. I don't have time for company," she muttered. Pushing on the floor with her feet, she sailed her chair across the tile floor. She spun in the chair, pushed herself to her feet, and stomped to the door. She wondered what crisis her neighbor needed to discuss tonight. Jane was lonely since her daughter had left for college. So every day at eight o'clock sharp, she showed up at Sarah's door with some crisis to talk over. Tonight, Sarah just didn't have the time or the patience.

Opening the door, she smiled. "How are you tonight, Ja . . ."

She stared up into steel-blue eyes framed by long, black hair. A shudder ran through her body. She grabbed for the door, trying to shove it closed.

Jack's hand caught the door and sent it swinging backward. "Hiding a man in here?"

"How the hell did you get in the building?" She grabbed for the door, but he leaned against it, blocking her way.

"Where is he?" Jack looked over her head.

"Jack. You're not allowed to be here. Leave." She stood as tall as she could, but she still only came to his shoulder.

He pushed her inside the room and shut the door. "You can't keep me away. You belong to me."

"Get out. I'm calling the police." She turned and walked across the living room toward where she'd left the phone on the couch cushion.

He grabbed her arm and twisted her back to face him. She tried to pull free, but his grip tightened. "Let go. Get out." She put as much force into her voice as she could, keeping it cold and calm.

He shoved her down on the couch. "You're mine. I won't have you sleeping with every man in town. Do you understand?" He leaned down with his hands on either side of her on the back of the couch.

She felt for the phone. Her fingers curled around it. She moved to slip out under his arms. He grabbed her by her sweatshirt and pulled her toward him. The phone clattered to the floor. She tried to breathe normally. If she didn't show him how afraid she was, she might gain some control.

"Jack, if you don't leave, the police are going to lock you up."

"They won't do anything. You're mine." He laughed hoarsely. "I saw you with that guy at lunch today. I know you brought him home with you. I'll kill you before I see you with another man. Now, where is he?" His grip tightened on her and she abruptly jerked backward. Jack momentarily lost his grip and she fell backward onto the couch.

"I'm not yours. I don't even know you." Her voice shook. Her heart blocked her throat so she could barely breathe. It pounded so hard she thought it would explode at any moment. She tried to claw her way off the couch but she couldn't seem to get her limbs to work. They felt so leaden and heavy, weighing her down. And before she knew it, Jack was standing over her again, glaring down at her with a cold stare.

"Who is he?"

She rolled to the right and slipped under his arm as he grabbed for her. If she could grab the phone and make it to the bedroom, she could call for help. Or the doorway. Someone had to be around. This building always had people in it.

He grabbed her by the hair and yanked her back. "Whore. You'll pay for what you did."

"No, Jack, no! Noooo. I didn't do anything," she wailed, and then she screamed as she caught the flash of a knife. She screamed again and again as cold metal pressed against the back of her neck.

Chapter 8

JOSHUA BOLTED OUT of bed and raced down the hall toward the screaming. He knocked into the table in the upstairs hallway, sending a vase smashing to the floor. A bolt of lightning illuminated the empty hallway. He threw open Sarah's bedroom door, sending it crashing into the wall. Instinctively he crouched as he approached the bed, trying to see in the dark. The lightning flashed directly into his eyes, obscuring his vision.

"Don't kill me. Please don't kill me." Sarah's screams pierced the darkness.

Joshua saw no one. He blinked rapidly, trying to peer through the dark. Clutching his knife in his right hand, he tried to figure which way to lunge. Another flash of lightning brightened the room.

She was alone.

His knife clattered to the floor as he grabbed her into his arms.

She flailed at him with her hands. "Help," she screamed.

"Cath. Wake up. It's me, Joshua. You're safe."

"No, Jack. Don't kill me. Stop. Help me! Somebody help me!"

Her screams deafened him. He shook her, then pinned her arms against her sides, holding her crushed against his chest. "Cath, it's okay. You're safe."

A breath rattled through her. She sagged against him, sobbing. "Where am I?" She tried to push herself away from him. She shook violently.

He held her tightly. "You're with me, Cath. At my ranch. You've had a bad dream."

"Oh, God." She wrapped her arms around his body and buried her face against him. "He tried to kill me. I knew he was going to."

"But he didn't."

"No." She shook her head against him. "He could have. He told me he would. He cut off my hair. Told me next time it would be my throat."

"Is that why you ran away?"

She nodded her head against him. "I knew he would. The police wouldn't do anything. Said they couldn't. They wouldn't even keep him in jail after they arrested him. Infringement of his rights since he could make bail."

"His rights? They should have hanged him. Or at the very least, horsewhipped him within an inch of his life. No woman should be treated like that." The muscles tightened at the back of his neck. If he got his hands on the son of a bitch, he'd teach him not to hurt a lady again. He'd love to have his hands around the bastard's neck right at this moment. "Don't worry, Cath," he murmured. "I won't let him hurt you."

"I know that. I'm perfectly safe here." She sighed heavily as her trembling subsided.

"I'm glad you feel that way, but what if he follows you?"

"That's highly unlikely." She relaxed into his chest.

"You'd best be careful anyway." He rubbed his hand down her back. He pulled it away suddenly, holding his hand dangling in the air, uncertain of where to put it. She didn't have any nightclothes on. Women didn't sleep without clothes. Granted she only had his shirt, but she didn't even have that on.

She snuggled closer to him. He placed his hand on her back. Her skin felt soft—as he had known it would be. Warmth flooded through him. Clad only in his drawers, he knew that if she shifted she would become aware of her physical effect on him. He wanted to nuzzle against her neck and rub his fingers across her breasts which pressed against his chest, separated only by the bedsheet. He took a long breath and let his fingers enjoy the silky feeling of her back. He never wanted a woman as much as he wanted Sarah.

He pushed her back and lifted her head to look into her eyes. They opened wide like a colt about to bolt. "Don't worry, Cath. I won't let him hurt you. I won't let anyone hurt you."

Sarah's lips looked soft and inviting, begging him to kiss them. For several seconds he continued gazing at her. Then he bent his head and captured her lips with his. Softly, at first, she responded to his kiss, then she threw her arms around his neck and returned the kiss full force. He ran his tongue across her lips until they parted and invited his entrance. His tongue did a dance with hers. He inhaled the wonderful scent of her while he tasted her. He wanted more of her. He wanted to taste every inch of her body and explore it with his hands. The heat within him grew.

He crushed her against his chest again. She was so vulnerable, so frightened. He couldn't take advantage of her. Taking in a jagged breath, he smoothed her hair down. "You're okay now."

"Better." Her breathing had become ragged.

"I'll let you get some rest. You'll be safe here. I'm just down the hall." He laid her back on the bed and covered her with the quilt.

She reached up and grabbed his arm. "Stay, please."

"I'd probably best not." He took her hand from his arm, holding it engulfed in his. "I'll light a lamp. That should make you feel better." He dropped her hand and reached for the bedside lamp.

A flash of lightning cut across the sky and thunder rattled

the windows. Sarah jumped and gasped, grasping his arm.
The sheet slipped down. Joshua dropped a lit match on the
floor. "Damn." He pulled his arm away, groping for the still
glowing match.   .

Sarah's laughter floated around him and he looked up
sheepishly. Fumbling, he finally got the lamp lit. A soft glow
pushed back the darkness of the room. Sarah lay thus with
just the sheet and quilt covering her, outlining the shape of
her body, while she shook with laughter.

"Burning down the house is not amusing."

"I know." She looked into his eyes. "I'm sorry. It's just a
nervous reaction." Her gaze moved down to his bare chest.

Quickly, Joshua sat down on the side of the bed and
pulled the bottom edge of the quilt over his lap. He tried to
look at Sarah's face, but all his mind saw was her outline beneath the sheet with her breasts pushing it up.

She reached out and touched his chest. "Thank you."

Her fingers burned their imprint into his skin. "For
what?"

"Coming to my rescue."

"Nothing to it." He shrugged his shoulders. "You weren't
in any danger." He folded her hand in his. He'd forget she
didn't belong to him if she touched him again.

"But you didn't know that."

Joshua shrugged again. "Best get some sleep." His mouth
was as dry as a desert gulch. "Are you going to be okay
now?"

"Yeah. Just leave the light on."

"Afraid of the dark?"

"Not usually." Sarah smiled at him.

Joshua smiled back. God, she was beautiful. Reluctantly,
he moved out of the bedroom and closed the door. This
should have been his wedding night. He should have been
sharing that bed with his wife. He sighed and moved back to
the other room. If only his body would get the message that
he hadn't gotten married this afternoon.

Crawling out of bed, Sarah pulled on Joshua's shirt and buttoned it, sighing. Her entire wardrobe consisted of a pair of

jeans, running shoes, a blouse, a bra, and two pairs of underwear—and all of it needed washing. She wished she'd
dragged her suitcase down the church aisle with her. At least
she'd brought an extra pair of underwear, but only because
she'd forgotten to pack it in the suitcase. Being too lazy to
open the luggage again, she'd shoved it in her backpack.

Sarah looked at herself in the mirror and tried to mat her
curls down. A little makeup would be an improvement, but
after the storm, the world felt like a sauna. She wanted another bath and clean clothes before she did her face. Shrug-
ging her shoulders, she headed downstairs to find food.
She'd slept right through breakfast. She never slept this late,
but after the nightmare and Joshua's kiss, she'd had trouble
getting back to sleep. She couldn't decide which had made
her tremble more, but while she could skip the nightmares,
she wouldn't mind a repeat of the kiss. A shiver raced
through her body and she put her fingers to her lips.

When she reached the top of the stairs, the smell of coffee greeted her. At least she could have her morning cup and
get herself jump-started—not that she had anything for
which to get started. She'd have to go back to Mrs. Westall's
today, plus face the irate buggy owner. But after that . . .
after that, she didn't know what to do. She might never be
able to get home. She couldn't make a living here and she
couldn't rely on other people's generosity forever. She'd always been self-sufficient. The fates were paying her back
for bragging about that to LeeAnne.

She walked into the kitchen and found Joshua sitting at
the table with papers spread in front of him. "Good morning.
What are you doing?" She glanced over her shoulder as she
poured herself coffee. Sitting down next to him at the table,
she glanced at the papers.

"Record-keeping. Nothing you'd be interested in. Want
some breakfast?" He turned and smiled at her.

"I'd love some."

"Steak and eggs okay? I have some bread Cookie made.
Or I can fix some flapjacks." He held the pencil poised over
the sheet on which he wrote.

She usually only ate a bagel with low-fat cream cheese

with her coffee before she sailed out of her apartment to work. She never had time to fix anything else. However, she didn't see a toaster and she knew no bagels existed, so she'd have to change her diet. "Flapjacks. By the way, who's Cookie?"

"He works for me. Feeds the men and me most of the time." He rose and went toward the stove.

"What men?"

"The ones who work for me. A cattle ranch doesn't run itself, nor is it a one-man operation." He pulled a bowl from the cupboard and poured flour in it.

Damn, he made cooking look easy. "How many men do you have here?"

"Ten plus Cookie. He does odd jobs as well as cook, though that takes a lot of his time the way the men eat. From time to time I hire drifters to help in the spring during roundup and branding." He stirred the mixture before lifting a cast-iron skillet onto the stove. "How many?"

"How many what?"

"Flapjacks."

"Depends on the size. Three or four if you don't make them gigantic." She drew the papers he had been working on in front of her. A column of numbers listed the expenses that he'd been adding up. As she flipped to the second page, she found a list of things for the house, including the bathtub and toilet. He had spent quite a lot to ensure his bride's comfort.

He set the plate in front of her and scooped up the papers. "Boring stuff." He smiled at her.

"You'd be surprised. Numbers and accounts are things I actually know something about." She couldn't remember how many accounting systems she'd set up for people on their computers and then taught them how to use.

"Most women don't have much interest in figures."

She laughed. "You are the sexist man I've ever met."

His forehead furrowed together. "The what?"

"Sexist."

He shook his head, not comprehending.

"Categorizing women as helpless except in the kitchen or

doing housework. Lots of women are interested in accounting."

"And you?"

"Something I learned in the line of business." She bit into a pancake. It tasted heavenly. And he'd made them without measuring cups or pancake mix. "If you can't read financial records, you don't know if you're being ripped off."

"Being ripped off?" He sat down next to her, coffee cup in hand.

"Robbed. You're not eating?"

"Ate hours ago."

She finished the pancakes and picked up her coffee cup. "You really are a tremendous cook. I wish I could cook like that."

"Just takes a little practice."

Sarah watched his face. He seemed to be studying her intently. "It takes more than practice. I've tried to learn. I'm just not any good at it."

"Never met a woman who couldn't cook." His statement was flat.

"Never met a man who could—at least not like you can." She smiled at him.

"I've been thinking." He stood up and went to refill his cup.

"And . . . ?"

"I'm not sure it's a good idea for you to go back to town."

"But I have to go somewhere. Do you think Mrs. Westall will let me stay with her?" Joshua's green eyes sparkled as he looked down at her. Standing above her, he seemed to stretch upward forever. It would be so easy to fall in love with him. He'd treat any woman special. But . . . this situation held no buts. She didn't like this time or this place. She'd never fit in. And when Joshua walked off into a snowdrift, she would be all alone. That would send her over the edge.

"Mrs. Westall would be more than happy to let you stay with her for a while. She's taken a liking to you. However, you can't stay there forever." He sat down in the chair across from her.

"I know I can't stay with her forever, but I don't know what else to do." Sarah sighed and took a sip of her coffee. She needed a plan. At home, she always knew what to do. She was an expert with a skill people demanded. Here, she had become excess baggage for which no one had any use. As Sarah sat contemplating her somewhat dim future, Joshua spoke again, interrupting her thoughts.

"I know you hate this place, Cath . . ."

"I don't hate this place. I just don't belong here."

"But you won't tell me where you do belong."

"I can't." She looked down at her cup. She wanted to feel his strong arms around her again. Shivering, she remembered the feeling of his hands against her bare back the night before. Heat stole through her insides at the thought of his lips against hers.

He placed his hand on her shoulder. "You cold?"

"No." She shook her head, her voice barely above a whisper. Heat permeated her skin where his hand rested. She wanted to reach up and touch his hand, but feared making the situation worse by responding to him.

"I don't think it would be wise to go back to Mrs. Westall's. It could be dangerous."

"Why? Because the town is going to hang me for being a horse thief?"

"No." Joshua laughed. "They are beginning to expect the unexpected from you. Plus my men dug the buggy out early this morning and I plan to deliver it to its owner later today. And I plan to bring whoever it is a side of beef to assure there are no hard feelings." He ran his hand through his hair. "Because of Jack."

"Jack?"

"He might have followed you. You could be in danger."

"It's highly unlikely." It went beyond highly; more like next to impossible. To do that, he'd have to figure out where she'd gone. No one would think to look for her in 1870. She barely believed it herself.

"After what he did to you, you should be careful. You'd be safer here."

"Oh, no. I can't stay here."

"Why?"

"It just wouldn't be right."

"Now you're suddenly worried about proper."

"I don't care what people say. I have done nothing to be ashamed of. I just don't . . . well, I don't want you to think because I stay here I'll marry you." The words sounded cruel. She didn't mean them to, but she wouldn't have him get his hopes up. Granted, nothing would look as bleak if she could snuggle into his arms. She wanted to touch him again. Kiss him again. But that would be dangerous. She couldn't. She wouldn't. Never would she give up her hope of going home.

Pain flashed in his eyes for a moment, then was gone. "Don't worry yourself about that. I know you have no intention of marrying me. But I won't have it on my conscience if Jack finds you and something happens to Mrs. Westall because you're staying there."

She flinched even though she knew she had deserved that one. "Believe me when I say Jack won't find me, not in a million years."

"And why should I believe that?" His eyebrows drew together as he stared at her.

"Contrary to popular belief, I have not lied to any of you."

"Just omitted a great deal of the truth." He angrily pushed his coffee cup away.

She stared back at him. He had her on that one. She shrugged her shoulders. "I'm perfectly safe from Jack anywhere in Moose Creek."

"Still, I'd feel better with you here. That way no one will get hurt."

Sarah sat quietly for a moment, staring into her cup. She had to make a decision. No matter where she went, she'd be imposing on someone. Lord, how she hated not being self-sufficient. If her great-grandparents' store was bigger, she'd beg them for a job, but it looked to have barely enough for the two of them. "I can't impose upon you."

"I've plenty of room here and I promise to leave you alone. Most of my time is spent working outside anyway."

"Then how will I be safer here than at Mrs. Westall's?"

"Because I'll make sure one of the men is about at all times to protect you." His eyes pleaded with her.

The longer she stayed here, the worse matters would be. She could get attached to this man. Then going home would be bittersweet. She intended to take her heart home with her, not his. "I don't think that would be a very good idea."

"It's better to impose on Mrs. Westall?"

"I don't want to impose on anyone. I'm used to taking care of myself. I just don't know what to do." She threw her hands up in the air. "I have to find a job. I won't be dependent on anyone. I haven't been since I turned eighteen. God, I hate this."

"What kind of a job do you plan on getting?"

"If I knew that, I wouldn't be in this predicament," she snapped at him.

"While you decide, you'll stay here." He rose to get more coffee.

"Is that an order?"

He turned and looked at her. "No. Just sensible."

"I should have some say in this matter."

"I won't have you putting Mrs. Westall in danger. Not after all the kindness she's shown you." He set the coffeepot back on the stove. "Besides, I can afford an extra mouth better than she can."

"I don't take charity from anyone."

"You're not in a position to do much else." He settled at the table once more and picked up his pencil. He studied the papers in front of him.

She stood and walked across to him. "I can sure as hell try."

He didn't look up. "You always try. You just don't seem to do a great job at succeeding."

She glared at him. "Now, I did just fine pulling my gr . . . Rachel from that building before she got shot. I'll stay, but only if you let me earn my keep."

"Doing what?" He made a notation on the paper in front of him.

"I can keep your books for you. That will give you more time to do whatever else you do."

"Women don't keep books."

"Oh, for Pete's sake, you are the most hardheaded man I've ever met. I can't do much else, but I can keep books. At least that way I won't feel like I'm sponging off you completely."

"You're what?" He looked at her.

"Taking without giving."

He stared at her.

"Is it a deal?" Sarah asked.

Joshua looked at her a while longer and finally just shook his head in resignation.

"Good. Now it's settled." She picked up the papers and walked back to the table.

"Alright, alright," Joshua muttered. "But you've got to start dressing more appropriately."

"What's wrong with the way I'm dressed?" She looked down at his shirt, which hung nearly to her knees.

"You're practically naked." He snapped his pencil in half.

"I'm completely covered. Besides, the few clothes I have all need washing."

"You have clothes in town."

"No. Catherine has clothes. Mine got left at my last stop."

"Catherine's clothes seem to fit you just fine. I'm sure Mrs. Martin won't mind if you use them under the circumstances."

"I don't like those clothes. I swelter to death in them."

"So what? I won't have you parading around in front of my men dressed like that. It'll give them ideas. Cause trouble."

Laughter erupted from her. "Sometimes you are as big a fuddy-duddy as my . . . as Henry. Living here with you is going to make everyone think we're sleeping together as it is. What does it matter what I wear?"

"It matters." He reached for his coffee cup and knocked it over. The coffee pooled across the table. "Damn." He grabbed for his papers. "The only way to stop the talk is to marry, which you have made quite clear you have no intention of doing. I can't help what people think. And after last night, no other man will have you anyway."

"Such nonsense. As a concession to you, I'll try to conform—somewhat. I won't make any promises. I won't wear a corset, however, and that is final."

"All women wear corsets. Mrs. Westall can surely fix the one you had on, but Catherine probably had a second one you can use until we find your lost bags."

"I don't own a single one. Never have. Never will. Catherine might, but I'm not putting it on. Not for you or anyone else in this world." She crossed her arms across her chest. "And you weren't listening. You aren't going to find my suitcase no matter how hard you look."

"Suitcase?" His gaze became fixed on her face.

"The thing you stuff clothes in when you're going on a trip." She stared back at him, holding his eyes with hers.

"Your trunk."

"Much smaller than a trunk. It has wheels on it and I can drag it by myself."

"Never heard of such a thing. No matter." He waved his hand in dismissal. "It wouldn't be fitting to go around without a corset on."

"What is so blasted 'fitting' about a corset? Damn thing nearly squeezed me to death."

His mouth hung open. "You are the most unconventional woman I've ever met."

She smiled at him. "I won't give in on the corset, but I'll put on more clothes if you agree to letting me do your books. I won't stay with you otherwise." She put her hands on her hips.

"You can't stay anywhere if you don't dress proper. You think the people in town are talking now." He shook his head. "We'll give it a try. Hell, I'll try anything at the moment."

"Good. It's settled."

"Then get dressed."

"In what?"

"Your jeans. You can't go into town like that." He blinked, but his eyes never left her face.

"All my clothes are dirty. You'll have to give me laundry soap so I can wash them. And I guess you'll have to get Catherine's clothes for me, or something."

"I can't leave you alone here."

"Why not?"

"What if some drifter comes by and finds you naked in my kitchen? Or someone comes to retrieve the buggy? Or my men come back?" He shook his head back and forth. "Oh, no. You're going to town with me."

"I really do want to visit the church." She nodded slowly. "Alright. I guess I could put on my jeans. They aren't that dirty. But I don't have any clean underwear."

Joshua's face matched the color of his hair. "This whole conversation isn't proper."

Sarah laughed, putting her hand on his shoulder. "I'm not as concerned about proper as I am about survival." Being that close to Joshua, she wanted to feel his lips against hers again. She brushed the hair from his forehead. Sliding her hand behind his head, she pulled him forward until she could reach his mouth with hers. His lips radiated the same warmth she remembered from the night before. It hadn't been all a dream. Leaning into him, she increased the pressure on his mouth. He grabbed her and pulled her down into his lap.

Chapter 9

SARAH HELD HER chin in her hands as she sat at the kitchen table. The papers on which Joshua wrote his accounts lay in front of her. She'd expected more paperwork on a ranch this size, but within a couple of hours she had everything added up, even without the assistance of a calculator, and until somebody bought something or payday arrived, she didn't have anything else to do.

And payday wouldn't be much, from what Joshua had said. He paid the men once a month, forty dollars each. Payroll taxes and deductions didn't exist, so all she had to do was log in the amounts next to their names and then they'd sign for the money. But Joshua had made it very clear he'd be the one handing out the money, not her.

In fact, in the two weeks since she'd agreed to stay with him, he'd made it very clear she was to stay away from the men. Not that she had any desire to make friends with them, but she wished she had somebody to talk to or something to do. She could dust, but she'd done that yesterday, and the place didn't get that dirty. Women during this time were supposed to be inundated with housework, but all she really did was sweep, dust, and do dishes. Joshua wouldn't let her do laundry, because that meant going out in the yard where everyone could see her. So instead Cookie did it, except for her personal laundry, which she did in the kitchen sink and hung in the bathroom.

She would go into town and to the church except that Joshua wouldn't let her travel on the road by herself. He feared she'd get hurt or lost. Her whole life she'd been able to go about by herself—well, at least since she'd turned ten and her father had bought her a bicycle.

Sarah sighed again. She was a prisoner—not only in 1870, but in this damned house. Perhaps if she married Joshua, he'd at least let her go out.

The only time she ever saw him was at dinner. He came in at about six and fixed her food every night. Most of the time he just sat silently eating, then went back out until dark, leaving her to do the dishes. Not that she minded washing dishes. At least it gave her something to do.

Ever since the morning she'd kissed him, he'd gone out of his way to avoid her. He rose and left the house by the time the sun came up every morning right after he fixed her coffee and biscuits for breakfast.

But she'd taken up sleeping late. She saw no reason to get up. Nothing but long, empty hours stretched in front of her. She'd stood just about enough of this. Something had to change or she'd go crazy.

She rose and trod up the stairs to her room. Dumping out the contents of her backpack, she picked up her cell phone. More than anything in the world she wanted to talk with LeeAnne. Just hearing a familiar voice would brighten her day. She clicked the phone on and listened to the familiar beep. Quickly, she punched in the number. Nothing happened. She knew nothing would. But . . . She cradled the phone against her, her head hanging. She needed to find a way home. Otherwise she'd go stark raving mad.

A pounding at the door startled her. She held the phone for a moment. Joshua wouldn't like her answering the door. He'd become such a drag. The pounding continued. She turned off the phone and shoved her belongings back into the bag.

Glancing at herself in the mirror, she groaned. Lord, she'd let herself go. She hadn't applied makeup since her arrival. Her hair stood up on end. No wonder he avoided her. As the pounding became more insistent, she patted at her hair, trying to get it to stay down. Then she shook out the yellow skirt she wore and rushed toward the stairs. She looked as good as she was going to. "I'm coming," she hollered.

As she threw open the door, Rachel and Mrs. Westall stood on the porch. She smiled broadly. Company was a welcome diversion. "Please, come in." She stepped back from the door and swung her arm in a circle of invitation.

"We came to see how you are doing," said Mrs. Westall, smiling. A basket hung from her arm.

"Much better now that you're here. Come into the living room," Sarah said.

"We aren't interrupting your chores, are we?" asked Rachel.

Sarah shook her head as the two women pushed past her.

"Why, what a wonderful room," said Rachel. "Mr. Campbell did a fine job in fixing up his house for a—"

"Now, I have to take much of the credit. The man has no sense when it comes to what makes a woman comfortable, but he spared no expense." Mrs. Westall beamed.

"Such fine furniture you have," said Rachel.

"Joshua made the tables himself," said Sarah.

"Really." Rachel removed one of her gloves and ran her fingers over the surface. "Do you think I could convince him to make me some? I've never seen finer, even in Boston."

"I'll ask him at dinner tonight." Relief flooded through Sarah. Thank goodness she'd dusted yesterday. Mortification would have set in if her great-grandmother had run her fingers along the table and come away with dust covering her fingertips.

The two women minutely inspected the room. They reminded her of military inspectors. She wondered if she'd passed the inspection.

"He made such a wonderful curio cabinet," said Mrs. Westall, running her hand over the wood. She turned to Sarah. "You'll have to find something to fill it with."

"He expected Cather . . . I'll work on that." Sarah

shrugged her shoulders. She could put her cell phone and walkman in it. That would cause quite a stir. "Won't you sit down? I'd offer you some refreshments, but all I have available is lukewarm coffee and cold biscuits."

"You haven't got to your baking for the week?" asked Mrs. Westall. "Now, Mr. Campbell doesn't expect you to cook for those hired men, does he?"

Sarah laughed. "Joshua doesn't expect me to cook for anyone. And no, I haven't gotten to the baking because I don't do baking."

Rachel and Mrs. Westall gave her a hard look. "I hear Mr. Campbell bought you a fine new stove. One any woman would be glad to have," said Rachel.

Sarah shrugged. "I never learned to cook." She smiled. "I've learned the fine art of pumping water and heating it on the stove for dishes, laundry, and a bath."

Mrs. Westall tsked under her breath. "We brought you a chocolate cake just in case you hadn't gotten to your baking. Let's go in the kitchen and I'll make us a nice pot of tea to go with it. Then we can chat."

Sarah groaned inwardly. She could just imagine what the two women wanted to chat about. But for chocolate cake she could put up with a lot. She sighed. She hadn't realized just how much she missed her one indulgence, Hershey bars with almonds. "Right this way." She turned and led the way to the kitchen.

"Isn't this glorious," said Mrs. Westall.

Rachel walked around the kitchen, running her hand over the working counter, reaching up and touching the boxes that held the flour and sugar. She stood in front of the cabinets that held the china and sighed. Finally she stopped in front of the stove. "This is truly a fine stove. Mr. Campbell must be very wealthy to be able to put so much money into making his wife so comfortable."

"I guess," said Sarah. She pulled dishes from the cupboard and got a knife and forks. She tried to refrain from drooling as she watched Mrs. Westall pull out of the basket the most delicious-looking cake she'd ever seen. She held the knife poised over the cake and debated whether or not to cut it. She really didn't want to look like a pig and Mrs. Westall had said she was going to make tea. Oh, hell, she didn't care. She wanted cake and she hated tea, so why wait?

"I'll just put the water on." Mrs. Westall pulled a teapot from the cupboard and filled it with water. She acted as though she worked in her own kitchen.

"Make yourself at home." As if the woman needed an invitation. Sarah sliced through the cake. Leaning over, she sniffed it. Nothing in the world smelled more heavenly than chocolate cake. She supposed she ought to save some for Joshua, but considering the way he'd been treating her, maybe she'd eat his piece too. Sliding three pieces onto plates, she scooted them around the table and sat. With the fork poised over the cake, she inhaled the aroma, then stuffed a large bite into her mouth. She chewed slowly, savoring the flavor. Finally swallowing, she smiled and looked at Mrs. Westall. "This is the most delicious cake I've ever had."

Rachel frowned at Sarah. "Mrs. Westall will have the tea in a moment."

Sarah shrugged. "I hate tea and I just couldn't wait. I haven't had chocolate in so long. It just makes me feel so much better." She crammed another bite into her mouth, then stood up and got cups and saucers from the cupboard.

"I could make coffee instead," Mrs. Westall suggested.

"Not on my account. I still have half a pot that Joshua left me this morning. I'll just drink some of that. I'd volunteer to make the tea for you, but you'll probably enjoy it more if I don't." Sarah sat down, intent on her cake.

Rachel glared at Sarah. "It would be better manners to wait for your guests."

Sarah looked up. "I'm sorry. You see, Joshua doesn't make any goodies. He's only made biscuits and meat for two weeks."

Mrs. Westall smiled. "I like to see people enjoy my baking. Since my Luther passed away, I haven't had anyone to bake for." She came to sit at the table while the water boiled.

Grateful that at least Mrs. Westall wasn't yelling at her, Sarah slid another piece of cake onto her plate. "I'm really being a terrible hostess. Would either of you like sugar or milk for your tea?"

"Sugar would be very nice, dear," said Mrs. Westall.

Sarah rose and searched the cupboards for a sugar bowl. She found one, filled it, and put it on the table along with some spoons. She sat back down and eyed her cake. She'd just look at and savor the sight of this piece until the water boiled. She'd be polite and eat it with the other two women.

Mrs. Westall stood, made the tea, and poured cups for Rachel and herself. She sat and stirred it after she'd put sugar into it. "This is such a lovely house. It really needs a woman to make it a home and fill it with children. You have so much room."

Oh, boy, thought Sarah. *Here it comes.*

"It truly is so roomy. Much more so than our apartment over the store," said Rachel. "Not that I'm complaining. Mr. Martin has done his very best to make me comfortable. I'm very lucky he took me."

"He's the lucky one," said Sarah. "Besides, the two of you are a perfect match and will have many long, happy years together. Not to mention raise a passel of kids, small quarters or not."

"Do you really think we'll have children?" asked Rachel.

"I'm positive," said Sarah.

"And be happy?" asked Rachel.

"Extremely," said Sarah. She picked up her fork and started on the second piece of cake. She wanted to consume it before they ruined her appetite with the conversation she knew was about to come.

"And you could be happy with a passel of children here on this wonderful ranch," said Mrs. Westall.

Sarah held a bite of cake in front of her mouth. She didn't want to be rude, but she wanted them to understand that she had no intention of marrying Joshua. She put the cake in her mouth and stood up. She went to the stove and poured herself a cup of coffee. "I don't know a delicate way of putting this. I . . . oh, hell, I hate this place."

Rachel gasped.

Mrs. Westall tsked.

Sarah returned to her seat and forked another piece of cake into her mouth.

"Now, dear," said Mrs. Westall, reaching over and patting Sarah's hand. "It can't be as bad as all that. Mr. Campbell would do anything for you. Look at this beautiful house he built for you."

"He didn't build this house for me. He built it for Catherine. I'm not Catherine." Sarah held her cup in both hands, willing them to stop shaking.

"Yes, dear, I know that. Mrs. Stedman told me the whole story," said Mrs. Westall.

"Figures," snapped Sarah. "Somebody had to 'fess up."

"But that doesn't mean he wouldn't be just as willing to take you for a wife," said Rachel. "He's a lonely man and while Catherine would have made him a fine wife, God didn't intend that."

"So I'll do as a replacement." Sarah looked from one of the women to the other. "I don't think so."

"And why not?" asked Rachel.

"Really," said Mrs. Westall. "You are a fine young woman."

"That's not what I hear," said Sarah. She pushed the cake away. It would keep until dinner. "Besides, Joshua treats me like I have the plague or something."

"And what does that mean?" asked Mrs. Westall. "I can't imagine such a fine young man doing anything unseemly."

"He doesn't do anything, except go out all day and leave me alone," said Sarah. She sighed. She really didn't want to make these women angry. She wanted to be friends with them and share things with them. She needed someone to replace LeeAnne. But they didn't have anything in common. She couldn't talk about the things they did and exchange recipes or talk about sewing. She didn't understand any of those things. Oh, how she wished her cell phone would reach across the years and she could talk to LeeAnne! Then maybe the loneliness threatening to overwhelm her would disappear the way a wave erased footprints on the sand.

"He has a ranch to run," said Mrs. Westall.

"Yeah, I know." Sarah was getting tired of this line of conversation.

Rachel took a sip of her tea, then set the cup delicately on the saucer. "Men have to make a living. That is the way of things."

"Women need to make a living, also," said Sarah with another sigh.

"The women around here take care of their men. That's their job," said Mrs. Westall.

"And when they don't have a man to take care of?" asked Sarah.

"I rent a room now and then and mend clothes for the men who don't have wives," said Mrs. Westall. "Besides, my Luther left me sufficient money to get along."

"I can't do that. I'm used to making my own money."

"What did you do?" asked Rachel, picking at her piece of cake.

"I did . . . I just did."

"Not much call for what a woman can do here in Moose Creek," said Mrs. Westall.

"So I've been told," said Sarah.

"And," said Mrs. Westall, "your present living arrangement is most unseemly." She poured herself more tea.

"Most." Rachel nodded.

"I've heard that also, but I don't have many choices. I can't stay with you, Mrs. Westall." Sarah propped her chin up with her hands.

"The itinerate minister will be back for the harvest celebration the end of next month. It would be better if you stayed with me until then," said Mrs. Westall. "I would be glad to give you cooking lessons and I surely wouldn't mind the company."

"That's not going to happen," said Sarah.

"It would be a much more proper arrangement," said Rachel. "Then after you're properly married, you can return here."

"Joshua won't let me leave," said Sarah.

"I'm sure he'd see the reason of it," said Mrs. Westall. "He is a gentleman, after all."

"And if you're to have a proper place in the community, we must do what we can to restore your reputation," said Rachel. "It wouldn't do for the kind Mr. Campbell to be saddled with a wife with a soiled reputation."

"Well, excuse me," said Sarah. "I didn't plan any of this.

Everyone is so wrapped up in proper, no one even bothers to ask me what I want."

"We're just thinking of what's best for you, Sarah," said Mrs. Westall. She took a bite of cake.

"And the only solution is to get the two of you wed," said Rachel. She ran her fingers around the edge of her cup.

"But first we have to get proper living arrangements settled," said Mrs. Westall.

Sarah took in a deep breath and stared at the women. "Number one," she stated softly, "Joshua won't let me leave here and go stay with you."

"And why not?" asked Mrs. Westall. "You'd be perfectly safe." She poured herself more tea and stirred the sugar she'd added, clinking the spoon against the side.

"He doesn't think so, and he doesn't want to put you out." Sarah sighed. "And number two, I have no intention of marrying Joshua."

Mrs. Westall shook her head, tsking under her breath. "Now, child . . ."

"I'm not a child. I'm a grown-up who makes up her own mind. And as far as marrying goes, I've made up my mind. As far as where I live, Joshua hasn't given me a lot of choices, but we have struck a bargain and I intend to live by it until I can make other sane arrangements, which doesn't seem to be likely for the moment. So as much as I want to be elsewhere, here I stay."

"What kind of a bargain?" Rachel's brows furrowed. She ran her finger down the handle of the cup and back up again as she stared at Sarah.

"I render him a certain service to pay for my keep, though it's turned out not to be much of a service," said Sarah. She picked up her coffee cup and went to the stove to refill it.

"What type of service?" asked Mrs. Westall. Her mouth clamped together in a hard line.

"Just a service," said Sarah. They really didn't need to know and spread her business all over town. "It's a business agreement."

"Well, I never," said Rachel. "I never thought Mr. Camp-

bell would be like that. Definitely we must get her away
from him, at least until the minister returns."

"And before it's too late," said Mrs. Westall.

"Too late how?" asked Sarah.

"Before . . . well, before . . . before there's a child."
Rachel's cheeks turned bright red.

"Definitely," said Mrs. Westall. "The townsfolk are already talking. That would only add fuel to the fire." She
shook her head. "Oh what a disgrace that would be."

"Let them talk." Sarah glared at them. These women had
such narrow minds. She should tell them she'd become his
bookkeeper, but their insinuations ticked her off. "No babies
are coming out of Joshua's and my agreement."

"You never can be sure," said Rachel. "Oh, Mr. Martin
would be so upset."

"Oh, hell, he's always upset," said Sarah. Her great-
grandfather was the least of her worries.

"That is part of your problem," said Mrs. Westall. "Your
language is most inappropriate, as are your actions. You cannot stay here under the present conditions."

Sarah looked from one woman to the other. In a low, terse
voice, she said, "You have it all wrong. We have a business
arrangement and nothing else."

"That's what we mean," said Rachel. Her hands lay on the
table, tightly clasped together.

"Not that kind of business arrangement. We share a roof,
that's all," said Sarah. "Everything's just as proper as can be."

"Then why is he so dead set against your leaving?" asked
Mrs. Westall.

"Because it might put you in danger," said Sarah.

"I find that hard to believe," said Rachel.

"Well, believe it. Number three is, we aren't having sex,
so you have nothing to worry about except what a lot of gos-
sips conjure up." Sarah slammed the palm of her hand
against the table, sloshing the tea from the cups.

Joshua watched as the buggy pulled up in front of his house. He
moved around the corner just out of sight and watched the two
women climb out of the buggy. Sarah would enjoy having other

women with whom to talk. She probably enjoyed having any-one to talk to her. He knew he hadn't talked to her much lately. He just wasn't sure what to say to her. And every time he looked at her, he could only remember the morning when she'd kissed him and he'd pulled her into his lap. He'd nearly lost control that morning. So he avoided her because he wouldn't force himself on her any more than he'd force her to marry him.

Of course, it would help a great deal if she didn't have such a propensity for parading around the house with nothing more on than his shirt. He'd given up eating breakfast in the house. He put on a pot of coffee and escaped to eat with the men, be-cause he knew he'd lose control if he had to sit across from Sarah at the breakfast table clad like that. It was more than a man could stand.

Even after dinner, he needed to run back out to the corral. Joshua didn't go to the bunkhouse, but just prowled around until dark. The whole situation had gotten out of hand. He wanted nothing more than to be with Sarah, but at the same time feared being with her. She had to marry him or go home. If something didn't change soon he was going to be blown apart like a dandelion in a heavy wind.

He wandered back to the corral to look at the two wild horses his men had caught the day before—caught when he should have been with them. Just like he should have ridden out with the men this morning, but he didn't like to leave Sarah unguarded at the ranch and he didn't trust any of his men to stay around and watch over her. Hell, he didn't trust himself to watch over her, which was why he was standing in the yard.

He studied the horses. The mare looked as if she'd make a good cow horse. He hadn't reached a decision about the stallion. He, like Joshua, seemed bound on self-destruction. He put his booted foot up on the fence rail and leaned against the top. All he'd ever wanted was a ranch, a wife, and children running around. He had his ranch. The rest seemed as unobtainable as a star shining in the night sky.

He'd found the woman he wanted. When he kissed her, waves of heat and desire roiled through him like a wind through the trees just before a storm. But she'd made it clear that she didn't want him and he saw no way around that.

However, he couldn't go on forever ignoring her and hiding at the corral. The men had started talking already, not only about the fact he had a woman living in his house, but the fact that as of late he hadn't been paying any attention to the business of running his ranch.

He couldn't. No matter what he did, she crept into his mind and pushed aside all other thoughts. He'd nearly cut off his foot yesterday while chopping firewood. He'd been dreaming about what was under that damn shirt rather than thinking about where the axe was going.

She was so near to him, yet so far away. She was like the calf stranded on the other side of a swollen stream and he couldn't reach her without being swept downstream and probably drowned in the attempt.

He watched the stallion try and corner the mare in the corral. "Sorry, big fella," he shouted to the horse. "She seems to want you as much as Cath wants me." Even though he had known for weeks that her name was really Sarah, this nickname had stuck with him.

He turned and looked at the house. The women were probably chattering away and indulging in whatever wonderful baked goods Mrs. Westall had brought. He'd hoped he'd have a wife who could bake half as good as her, but he'd take one who couldn't bake at all. If he joined them, maybe he could have some of the wonders in that basket before the women ate them all. At least he could enjoy that.

No, he thought, *I shouldn't interrupt them. Women need time to be with women.* He looked back at the horse. But Sarah wasn't like the rest of the women. She might say most anything. He'd better go and check before she said something to upset the two ladies. He strode up to the house and quietly entered through the back door. If they were just having a quiet women's chat, he'd sneak back out.

"We aren't having sex . . ." Sarah's voice boomed around him.

"Oh, no," groaned Joshua under his breath. "Now what has she done?"

Chapter 10

SARAH HEARD JOSHUA'S boots on the floor and turned. She smiled at him, wondering why he had come in so early. His face had turned beet red. She turned back to the two women and found their faces as red as Joshua's. *Oops, sex must be one of those improper words,* thought Sarah. *A fine mess of things I've made now.*

"Good afternoon, ladies," Joshua said, smiling and nodding to each of them. "You are so kind to pay Cath a visit. I know she's getting very lonely out here on the ranch with no other womenfolk about."

Mrs. Westall opened her mouth, but no words came out.

"Joshua, look what Mrs. Westall brought us. It is just the most wonderful chocolate cake in the world. Would you care for a piece?" Sarah stood and went to get another plate. "How about a cup of coffee to go with it?"

"That would hit the spot." He sat down at the head of the table, a smile plastered on his face. "Nice weather we're having, isn't it?"

Rachel nodded her head.

Sarah set the cake and coffee in front of Joshua and slithered back into her seat.

He took a bite of the cake and chewed while the silence
hung like an icicle from a February tree. "Oh, Mrs. Westall,
this is wonderful, as always. Thank you so much for thinking of us. I never have gotten the hang of baking a cake and
Cookie's are a great deal like chewing hay." The color in his
face didn't seem to be subsiding.

"Mrs. Westall offered to teach me how to make them if I
came to stay with her until the harvest celebration and the
minister returns," said Sarah, her hands held in her lap.

"That was very nice, but if we have chocolate cake every
day, then it won't be such a treat." Joshua continued to eat
his cake and smile at the women. "Mrs. Martin, are you getting adjusted to our little town? It is very different from
Boston, but I find it much cozier."

"Uh-huh." Rachel nodded her head. The knuckles on her
clasped hands had turned white, in sharp contrast to her
face.

"Oh," said Sarah, suddenly sitting up very straight,
"Rachel wants to know if you could make her some tables
like the ones in the living room. She said they were the
nicest she'd ever seen." The tension in the room could have
been cut just like the cake. This faux pas she wasn't going
to live down. She just couldn't keep track of all the no-nos
in this era. No one would have blinked an eye at home if
she'd said that.

"Just tell me what size and I'd be more than happy to,"
said Joshua, taking a long swig of coffee. "I think I'll reheat
the coffee. Would anyone else like some?"

"No, thank you," said Rachel.

"We're drinking tea," said Mrs. Westall.

Oh, thank goodness, they'd both found their voices again.
Joshua might just placate them yet. And she had a month before the harvest celebration for them to forget, if she didn't
commit another faux pas before then. Bribery might be
good, too. The tables might make Rachel a little more likely
to overlook Sarah's mouth.

"Cath?" asked Joshua, holding up his cup.

"I'd love some. Thank you."

"Why do you insist upon calling her Cath?" asked Rachel, looking at Joshua and acting as if Sarah no longer sat in the room. "You know her name is Sarah."

"I like Cath. It seems to fit her better than Sarah." He picked up the coffeepot and poured two cups. Setting one in front of Sarah, he sat back down.

"Ever find out what her surname is?" asked Rachel. Her voice could put frost on the steaming coffee.

"Nope. She'll tell me when and if she's ready. Doesn't matter much, anyhow," said Joshua. "What size do you want the tables? I know your living area is a mite smaller than mine. I could make them three-quarters the size."

"If you're sure it wouldn't be too much work," said Rachel, turning her face away from Sarah.

"Not at all. I haven't given you a wedding present yet and I think that tables will do nicely." He smiled at her.

"I believe you are right. Some a bit smaller than your tables would fit nicely into my parlor. I would be beholden to you for making them," said Rachel.

"Nonsense. It's the least I can do," said Joshua with a wave of his hand. "Now, Mrs. Westall, how would you like a cabinet like I have in the corner of the other room. You have all those little keepsakes about that would look lovely set in one."

"I couldn't impose upon you," said Mrs. Westall. But her face lit up.

Sarah sighed. He was quite a diplomat. And, thankfully, also a great carpenter. He'd saved her hide again. She looked at Joshua and smiled. She wished he'd kiss her again. But then, she'd be grateful if he'd start talking to her again.

"No imposition at all. After all, I never could have furnished my house properly without your help." Joshua took a sip of his coffee and his smile looked genuine. "Mrs. Martin, has Cath or Mrs. Westall shown you about? I'm really very proud of this place, but then I think Mrs. Westall is also."

"I've only seen the parlor and the kitchen. You have a wonderful stove," said Rachel, wistfully.

"I told Henry to order one for you, but he said he'd best let you pick out your own," said Joshua.

"Really?" Rachel's face brightened. "He never said a word."

"That's like Henry." Joshua push his chair back. "I'll have a talk with him the next time I'm in town." He stood. "You must see the water closet. That would be proper, wouldn't it, Mrs. Westall?"

"Oh, yes." She nodded her head. "And it is a wonder to behold."

"I told Henry he needed to put one in, but he thought I was crazy." Joshua moved across the room.

Sarah jumped up and raced for the bathroom door. She'd left her laundry hanging in there, never expecting Joshua to return before dinner. Joshua opened the door and entered first. He swung the door shut, nearly hitting Sarah in the nose. A moment later he opened the door and smiled at the ladies. "Sorry about that. Wanted to . . . adjust things so you could really get the full effect." His eyebrows drew together as he looked at Sarah.

He stepped back and let Rachel and Mrs. Westall into the bathroom. Mrs. Westall showed off the room to Rachel.

Reentering the kitchen, Rachel said, "You are such a thoughtful man. Imagine not having to go out to the necessary in the snow. You must talk to Mr. Martin about this again."

"Oh, my, look at the time," said Mrs. Westall. "We need to be getting back or Mr. Martin won't be having his supper on time."

"Thank you again for stopping by. Please feel free to visit anytime," said Joshua.

"Oh, yes," said Sarah. As if they would ever visit her again. "And thank you so much for the cake." She walked with Joshua to the door. He followed the women out into the yard and helped them into their buggy.

Sarah turned back toward the kitchen. At least it hadn't been a boring afternoon. She picked up her piece of cake and ate it with her fingers. As she licked the frosting off, she heard Joshua's steps coming down the hall.

"Thank you," she said as he entered the room.

He looked at her and remained standing in the middle of the room.

"Want some more cake?" she asked.

"Don't you ever think before you speak?" he demanded. He folded his arms across his chest.

"I didn't realize I'd give them apoplexy." She continued licking frosting from her fingers.

"Cath, you don't think. You can't say things like that in front of ladies."

"Obviously."

"Surely you don't talk that way at home?"

"Why not? Sex isn't a big secret or anything." She smiled up at him.

"Because . . . because . . . just because," he sputtered.

His face had turned red again. Sarah said, "I'm sorry. Okay. My friends wouldn't have come unhinged. I'll remember and not use the word again. Okay?" She stood and went to the sink to wash her hands.

"Nothing's okay. Nothing's been okay since you arrived on the scene." His hands fell to his sides.

She turned and glared at him. "I'd leave if I could."

"I don't want you to leave. I want you to stay. I want you to marry me." He threw his hands up in the air. "But at this rate, we'll be outcasts from the town."

"I don't know why you'd want to marry me. And I didn't mean to bring this down on you. Believe me, I'd like to fit in if I have to stay here, but obviously I don't know how to do that either." She spat her words at him. "I'll work on getting out of your way just as soon as you let me out of this prison."

"I don't mean it to be a prison. I just want you to be safe." He shrugged his shoulders. "You don't need to leave. I'll deal with the townspeople."

"So, I'll stay. For the moment. But that is all I promise. I won't—"

"I know."

"I'll try to behave."

"I have no faith in that happening." He ran his fingers through his hair.

Sarah put her hands on her hips. "You don't have to be rude about it. I don't even understand why most of the things I do wrong are wrong."

"How can you not understand?" He took a step toward her.

"You wouldn't understand that."

"I never understand anything you do." He reached into his shirt. "For example, I don't understand what these are, but I know they shouldn't have been hanging in my bathroom."

Sarah looked at him as he held up her bra and bikini panties. He looked ready to explode. His hands shook as he held the garments with just two fingers each. "Why, this," she said as she grabbed the end of her bra and yanked it from his hand, "is my bra. And those," she said, snatching the other item, "are my panties. And they were drying in the bathroom because I didn't think you'd appreciate me hanging them outside for the men to see." She started to laugh. It came from deep within her and shook her whole body.

"They're what?" He stood perfectly still, hardly breathing, his hands still in the air.

"A bra." She held it up. "It replaces a corset, sort of, and is a hell of a lot more comfortable." She held up her blue silk panties. "These replace pantaloons and they are a whole lot cooler. Any more questions, or may I put away my underwear?"

His mouth dropped open. Then he closed it again. He cleared his throat several times. Then he groaned. "Have you no sense of propriety?"

"All kinds, but everyone has underwear."

"But . . . but . . ."

"But nothing. Usually I have it put away before you come in the house to start dinner." She turned and stomped up the stairs.

Sarah flung her underwear on the bed and flopped across it. Somehow, she had managed to make everyone in her immediate world upset with her. She didn't do it on purpose.

Digging out her cell phone, she dialed LeeAnne. Cradling the dead phone against her chest, she sighed. "LeeAnne, where are you when I need you? You'd probably think this whole situation is funny. I miss talking with you. At least you could see the ridiculousness and show me the way out. Here, everyone thinks I'm crazy or a fallen woman. What am I going to do?"

Sarah stared up at the ceiling. Finally she clicked off the phone and threw it back in her backpack. A lot of good it did her, anyway. She knew what she'd do now—she'd fix herself up. It would make her feel better, anyway.

Digging through her bag, she retrieved her makeup and applied it. She threw her curling iron aside. Without electricity, she had no use for it. Dipping her brush into the washbowl, she brushed down her hair. Finally getting it in place, she sprayed it with hair spray. She looked at herself in the small mirror on the dresser. *Not so bad,* she thought. She smiled at her image.

Next she rummaged through the closet and found a white blouse and a blue skirt. She shook out the wrinkles as best as she could and changed into the outfit. Somewhere in the bottom of her bag, she had a pair of gold hoop earrings. After affixing them to her ears, she looked through Catherine's accessories and found a blue ribbon to match the skirt. She tied it around her neck, tucking it beneath her collar so she had a wide bow at her throat.

With one final glance in the mirror, she turned to go downstairs. Fixing oneself up did amazing things for one's spirits. Now she'd try fixing dinner for Joshua. A peace offering might help matters. Then maybe she could get him to talk. Things had to change before she leapt across the line to being labelled "stark-raving mad."

In the kitchen she pulled potatoes from the bin. She could do fried potatoes, steaks, and biscuits. She'd watched Joshua often enough. It really couldn't be that hard.

She grabbed his apron and tied it up under her arms so she wouldn't splash on her white blouse. Then she scrubbed and cut the potatoes. After mixing the biscuit dough just the way he did, she turned to the stove. She hardly used the one in her condo, but when she did all she had to do was turn the knob and flames appeared. But this one, she had to stuff wood into and light with a match.

Picturing the way Joshua started the stove, she followed the steps. She laid down small chips of wood and then lugged larger pieces from the box in the back room where Joshua kept his coat. She struck a match and held it to the wood chips. The match quickly burned up the matchstick to her fingers.

"Ouch," she said, throwing the match into the stove. She lit another one. The wood didn't light. The match sputtered and went out.

"All right, wood, you're going to burn. I won't be undone by a stupid bit of wood. Do you understand?" She lit another match. By the tenth try, the chips finally ignited and she smiled to herself. Brushing her hands together, she smiled gleefully. "I told you so."

She shut the door to the stove and brought down two cast-iron frying pans with a clang. Into one she scooped grease. She looked at the white blob. "Oh, my poor arteries. I can feel them blocking up with all this animal fat. A big bottle of vegetable oil would be wonderful right now." She stirred the blob as it started to melt. "If the church window won't let me go home, I wonder if it would let me send for groceries. I'd love a nice roasted, skinless chicken breast right now."

Next, she needed to find the meat. It couldn't be far away, since Joshua never left the kitchen more than a moment to get it. She went to the back door and peeked outside. No one lingered in the yard. Smoke rose from a small building just off to the right. The cookhouse? She looked around again and ran over to the building. Opening the door a crack, she peeked in. A gray-haired man with a long ponytail stood by a large wooden table, mixing something.

Taking a step in, she smiled at him. "Hi. I'm Sarah. Where can I find some steaks for dinner?"

He raised his head and looked her up and down with his deep brown eyes. "You don't belong here."

"I know. But I wanted to fix dinner for Joshua and I don't

know where he keeps the meat." She crossed over to the table.

The man glared. "Over there. Take some." He pointed, waving a large knife, to a pile of steaks.

She looked at the bloody meat and cringed. "Don't you have anything to put it on?"

"Take a plate." He pointed to a pile of tin plates across the room. The muscles in his arm rippled as he moved. "Just bring it back."

"Yes, sir. And thank you." Gingerly, she picked up two pieces of meat with two fingers and plopped them onto the plate. She held her dirtied fingers away from her and scurried back to the kitchen. After washing her hands, she found a fork and plopped the meat into the frying pan. The lard had melted. She also scraped the potatoes from the cutting board into the pan. They sat there in a lump. She stirred them, then put the biscuits into the oven.

"Nothing to it," she said out loud. "I could become a world-class cook, with time." She stirred the potatoes, checked the biscuits, and turned the meat. Standing with a fork in one hand and a towel in the other, she watched the stove.

A loud rapping sounded behind her. She turned. The front door. Someone had knocked on the front door! For two weeks there'd been no one, and now, in one day, two sets of visitors. The knocking came again, insistent.

"Oh, all right. I really don't have time for this," she shouted down the hall. She glanced back at the stove and raced for the front door. Flinging it open, she glared. "Yes?"

Two men stood on the porch. Both of them needed a bath and a shave. One had a gunbelt slung over his shoulder that held a revolver. The other sported a knife tucked into a sheath strapped to his leg.

Sarah took a step back and reached for the door handle. "Can I help you?"

"We was told there might be work here seeing as it's coming on time to move the cows to winter pasture," the man with the gun said.

"I know nothing about that." Sarah eased the door par-

tially closed. "You need to go around back and talk with
Joshua. You can't miss him. He's the one with the red hair."

"How 'bout we just come in and wait for him," the man
with the knife said, leering at her.

The hair on the back of her neck prickled. "No. Just go
around that way." She pointed to the side of the house. "Ask
any of the men you see." She shoved the door closed and
leaned against it.

A burnt smell wafted toward her. "Oh, no—my dinner!"
She raced back down the hall and into the kitchen. She
yanked open the oven with a towel. The biscuits looked fine.
She pulled them out and put them up top the way Joshua always did. After stirring the potatoes and turning the steaks,
she pulled a biscuit from the pan. The bottoms were singed.
She got a butter knife and scraped them. Then she smiled to
herself. For a first try, they weren't too bad.

She dished the steaks onto plates and lifted the pan over
to the sink. She got a bowl and started spooning the potatoes
into it. Grease came off with them. "Oh, hell, how do I drain
the grease?" she muttered. She scooped up more potatoes
from the pan.

Joshua left the barn and started for the house. He'd best be
getting started on supper. He had been getting into a bad
habit of not leaving much for Sarah to eat during the day.
Seeing her in the middle of the day made it even harder for
him to stay away from her, so he never fed her dinner. The
hour he spent with her in the evening proved pure torture as
it was. Every time he looked at her, his lips burned, remembering her kiss. And a most improper kiss it had been.

He removed his hat and fanned his face. For late September, the evenings were awfully warm.

He sped up his walking. He looked forward to supper
more than any other part of the day. He could gaze at Sarah
and wish. Then when his self-control had been stretched to
the point of snapping like a twig, he could escape outside.

He groaned. Some control had to be established in life.
He acted like a lovesick calf. Time to think about moving
the cattle to winter feed had arrived and all he could think

about was that slip of a woman in his house. And quite a woman she was. The women of the town had to be all scandalized by now over her unorthodox ways. Mrs. Westall surely would spread today's conversation all over town before nightfall. Then Sarah would have an even harder time being accepted, even if she finally consented to marry him.

Scandalous was what she was—through and through. Even down to her underwear. He rubbed his hand across his stomach, remembering the feel of that tiny piece of silk and lace she swore she wore instead of pantaloons. No proper woman would be caught dead in such a garment, let alone alive. And the thing she called a "bra" was nothing more than a scrap of fabric and lace. It couldn't possibly take the place of a corset.

Joshua stopped at the water trough and pumped water, then splashed some on his face. He also rubbed the cold water on his neck. A shiver ran through him—but not from the cold water.

Shaking the water from his face, he crossed to the back door and entered the house. He smelled food cooking. He sniffed again. He hadn't seen anyone else arrive. It couldn't be Sarah cooking.

He quietly let himself into the kitchen. Two men walked up behind Sarah. One of them toyed with the handle of his knife. Joshua reached for his pistol before remembering he'd left it in the barn. Sweat broke out on his neck and trickled down his back. "What the hell are you doing in here?" Joshua snarled.

A spoon clattered to the floor. Sarah gasped. The men stopped in their tracks.

"I . . ." Sarah said.

"We's looking for work," one of the men said as he shifted the holster slung around his neck.

"In my kitchen?" demanded Joshua. He kept his eyes on the two men. Sarah stood frozen beside him. The smell of fried potatoes greeted him.

"Your missus said we needed to talk with you, so since we could smell your supper cooking, we thought we'd wait in the kitchen. Seemed the quickest way of finding you," the man with the knife said, letting his hand fall away from the weapon.

"I told them to go around back and ask for you," inserted Sarah.

Joshua heard a bowl being set down next to the stove. "I'm not in need of any extra hands at the moment." He took a step toward the men so he was between them and Sarah. "Git."

"We didn't mean to upset you, Mr. Campbell. The people in town said you always put on extra hands this time of year. We just wanted to earn some money," the man with the gun said.

"There's another ranch about ten miles down the road. Try there." He didn't like the looks of these two. Even though he could use them, he didn't want them around his place. Not when they had the nerve to walk into his house uninvited. Unless . . . Surely Sarah had better sense than to invite them in.

"But we hear you're the best boss around and pays the best," the man with the knife said. A crooked smile crossed the man's face.

It was a smile that made Joshua feel like a snake had crawled down his back. Out of the corner of his eye, he caught a glimpse of a knife lying on the edge of the sink. He could reach it and get one of them, but probably not both. "Sarah, go out back and tell Cookie we need some of Mrs. Westall's jam to go with our biscuits."

"But . . ."

"Now, Sarah," Joshua snapped. Once she went outside, he'd only have to worry about the two men. He heard the back door shut behind him. "Now, your business is finished here. Move on along." Every muscle in his body tensed, ready to dive for the knife.

"All right, but I don't see what the fuss is all about. We didn't mean no harm. Just wanted to find you before you set down to your supper," the man with the knife said. He wiped his hands on his trousers, before his hand went back to the hilt of his knife.

"Let's go," said the man with the gun. "We'll try the ranch

down the road. No harm meant, mister." The man edged toward the hallway.

Joshua let out his breath slowly and his muscles relaxed as he heard the front door close. He looked down and realized he'd picked up the knife the second the men had disappeared down the hall. The back door slammed. Joshua jumped. Turning swiftly, he pointed the knife at Cookie, who was also armed with a butcher knife.

The old man smiled at him. "Heard you got two saddle bums in your kitchen."

"They left." Joshua let the knife drop to his side.

"The little lady kept her wits about her and quick as lightning told us the problem. The boys are out front making sure they're riding on." Cookie sniffed. "I smell burnt biscuits."

"Shush," said Joshua, smiling. "Make sure the boys keep an eye out for those two. I don't want them anywhere around. Where's the lady?"

"Right here." Sarah stepped out of the back room.

"I got men to feed." Cookie turned and stomped out.

Joshua looked at Sarah for a long moment. "Don't ever let strangers into this house."

She put her hands on her hips and frowned. "I didn't let them in. I shut the door in their faces. I can't help it if you don't have any locks."

His shoulders slumped forward. "Never needed any before, but you can bet every door in this house will be fitted with locks first thing in the morning." He smiled at her. "Seeing them coming up behind you scared ten years off my life."

A strangled laugh came from her. "Didn't do much for me when I realized you were yelling at them, not at me." She smiled. "Thank you."

He smiled and set the knife back on the sink.

"I made dinner for you. Sit down and I'll serve." She smiled at him, then frowned. "I forgot to make coffee."

"I'll start it while you serve."

Sarah set out the food and Joshua set the coffee to brew before sitting down. He picked up his fork and knife and sawed at the meat. Once he got a piece free, he popped it into his mouth. He chewed while he watched Sarah try and cut a biscuit in half to butter it. He continued chewing. He got up to pump himself a cup of water and took a swig. The meat refused to be washed down. He chewed some more while Sarah set the biscuit down on the plate, still holding the knife with butter on it. He finally swallowed and forked some potatoes into his mouth. They made a squishing sound, and grease filled his mouth.

Sarah looked at him and started laughing. She held up a biscuit. "It would make a great hockey puck."

He pointed to the steak. "Wonderful shoe leather." He burst out laughing.

Sarah stood and walked over to the cupboard, wiping at her eyes. She smiled at Joshua and held up a plate. "We have wonderful chocolate cake for dessert."

Chapter 11

JOSHUA LOOKED AT the cake. "Maybe I'd better make us some real supper first. Too much chocolate cake can't be good for us."

"Neither can all that greasy fried food," said Sarah, putting the cake in the middle of the table and pinching a small piece between her fingers. "But real food would be good."

Joshua stared at her. "Cake is real. And what's wrong with what I fix?"

"Of course cake is real, but it's not 'real' food. It's not substantial." Sarah filched another bite of cake. "And all the animal fat you consume isn't good for your arteries and you probably have the highest cholesterol level of any person I know. Animal lard is terrible for your heart."

"Are you a doctor?" Joshua began preparing dinner.

"Nope, but everybody knows these things." *Then again, maybe not.* "Cake's not so good for you, either. Too much sugar and fat." She smiled at him.

"You make no sense half the time and the other half

you're scandalous." Joshua scrubbed out a frying pan, rinsed it, and plunked it on the stove.

Sarah sighed. "I don't mean to be. It's just that sometimes my mouth engages before my mind." She got up and put the cake back in the cupboard. "Plus, I'm never quite sure what's scandalous and what isn't."

Joshua shook his head. "How can you have gotten as old as you are and never learned to cook?"

"It never interested me much. By the time I got home from work, I was too tired to cook or even think about cleaning up a kitchen. Besides, I usually brought several hours of work home with me." LeeAnne called her a workaholic. She thought LeeAnne exaggerated, but after two weeks of nothing to do—and the withdrawal seemed pretty bad—maybe she really was a workaholic.

"Someone must have fed you. Your mother?" He whipped up a batch of biscuits.

"You make that look so easy." She settled in a chair and propped her head in her hands. "I've lived alone since I went off to college. Besides, when my mother was alive, she seldom cooked. The only thing she knew how to make was Thanksgiving dinner, and then only with a lot of help from her sister. Probably why I never learned to cook either."

"So what'd you eat after all those hours of work?" He shoved the biscuits into the oven.

"Fast . . . take . . . restaurant food." *Mind over mouth,* she chided herself. He'd be shaking his head and she'd be trying to explain things that didn't exist yet. Life had gotten way too complicated.

"Isn't that expensive?" He poured potatoes on top of the grease. They sizzled loudly and grease popped up from the stove.

"I made plenty of money." She shrugged. Her nice, fat bank account waited for her if she could ever get home. Maybe the church window wouldn't mind sending some of her money through, converted to proper 1870 currency.

He turned and looked at her. "What did you do? Around here you don't seem to be very self-sufficient."

"I pro . . . owned a business." If she disappeared tomorrow, would she find references in her great-grandmother's diary about the wacko who'd shown up in the church one day? She couldn't say anything about her life that would make any sense to these people.

"What kind?" Joshua flipped the meat.

"A . . . a business."

He pulled the biscuits from the oven and set them on top of the stove. "You're not very forthright with information."

She walked to the stove and grabbed a biscuit, bouncing it back and forth between her hands to cool it. "Some things don't sound very plausible." Her voice rose at the end of the sentence.

"Try me."

"These biscuits are very good." She smiled at him.

He put his hand under her chin. "As good as you are at evading my questions?"

The warmth from his hand flowed through her. She had an overwhelming urge to reach up and kiss him. "Where's the jam Mrs. Westall made?" She fluttered her eyelashes at him.

"Oh, no, it isn't that easy." He held her chin. "Are you ashamed of what you did?"

"Of course not."

"Then why won't you tell me?"

"Because you won't understand." She stretched up and kissed him soundly on the lips. He dropped her chin as if he'd been scalded.

He stood staring at her, a dreamy look coming into his eyes. *Oh, hell,* she thought and reached up and kissed him again. She'd been right. He kissed better than any man she'd ever met. "I think the meat's burning."

"Oh," he said. "Oh!" He turned quickly to the stove.

Turning back, he looked at her. "You didn't run a . . . a saloon?"

"Heavens, no! Why would you ask that?"

"The way you dress, talk . . ."

"Though saloons probably make all kinds of money if you have the right motif and get regular return clientele— but they're just too risky. My partner and I ran an up-and-coming business without too much risk of failure. With my expert skills and his good business sense, we were looking to make a million dollars in another five years." *Ooops,* she thought. Mouth had slipped without her mind in gear. A million dollars had to be a much bigger figure now than in the future.

"How much?" Joshua choked.

"A lot." She fluttered her eyelashes at him again.

"Then what the hell are you doing here?" He banged the dinner plates on the table. No wonder she wanted to leave. He had nothing to compare with what she could provide for herself.

"I got lost, running from Jack."

"Your partner, I'm sure, wants you back."

"I'm sure Pete's beside himself wondering what happened to me."

"Then tomorrow I'll take you into town and you can send him a telegram. I'm sure he'd be willing to wire you the money to get home." Joshua pushed his plate away. His appetite had gone out the window along with his hopes.

"If it were that easy, I'd have done it the first day I was in Moose Creek." Her eyes clouded up. "I can't send him a telegram." She blinked. "Not unless they'll hold it for a while. A long while." She waved her hand in dismissal. "It doesn't matter. I'm lost. Pete will either survive or not. The business will either survive or not. I can't do a damn thing about it. I can't get unlost." She banged her hand on the table. "And I hate my life."

"Is life so bad here?" He'd promise her anything just to keep her from crying. Helplessness washed over him as her eyes filled with tears. She blinked them away furiously.

Sarah picked up her coffee cup and took a swallow. She nodded. "Yes—as a matter of fact, it is. I have nothing to do all day. You go outside and do whatever you want to while I sit. For hours I sit. I've already read the two books you own. How many times can I dust a stupid table? I hate housework. My cleaning lady came twice a week and picked up after me and made sure everything was nice. She even made sure that I had Cokes in the refrig . . . that I had what I needed. I had work to do. Work that gave me pleasure. Work that made me feel like I accomplished something." Her shoulders sagged. "Here I have nothing. I'm locked in the house all day alone. The first time I have visitors, I insult them. The next time I almost got mugged, or worse. I made a mess of dinner. I'm useless."

Joshua came around the table and sat next to her. He put his hand on her arm. "Cath, you're not useless. I just don't know what to do with you."

"I have to have something to do. I'll go nuts if I don't." Her eyes pleaded with him.

"Give me suggestions." The heat of her arm came through the cotton blouse she wore. She looked more beautiful tonight than any other time he'd seen her, except walking down the aisle of the church. Her bruises had nearly faded, so anger toward Jack didn't engulf him every time he looked at her. Joshua wanted her. He wanted to make her happy. He didn't know how.

She stared at him. "I don't know. If I did, I could tell you."

"I haven't been fair keeping you in the house all the time. Starting tomorrow, you can go out back. I'll make sure Cookie or one of the other men I trust is around to keep an eye on you. At least until we're sure those drifters have moved on." He smiled at her. "By the back door is a plot of ground. You could plant a vegetable garden or flowers or something."

"I've never tried gardening. But it's on my to-do list." A wistful smile flashed across her face. "I'd like flowers. It would be better than just sitting all day. All I'd do is get fat and depressed."

"I'll have George bring up the supplies tomorrow." He took her hand in his. "But, Cath, you have to dress proper when you're outside where the men are."

"What's proper?"

"Your jeans are fine. But you have to wash your face. They'll get the wrong idea."

"What's wrong with my face?"

"The makeup. Only saloon girls wear makeup." He liked

it, but he didn't want his men to think she was free for the taking. They wouldn't understand that she was not a whore—just different.

"Oh, for crying out loud. This ti . . . place has so many friggin' restrictions."

"You are a puzzle, Cath." A puzzle he wanted to take apart piece by piece.

"So's this life." She smiled at him and reached up her hand and laid it against his cheek. "Why'd you call me Sarah when those men were here?"

"I hoped it would make you realize just how serious the situation was." He pressed his cheek against her palm. For such a small hand, it generated an enormous amount of heat. He liked the way it branded his skin.

"I did."

"Will you tell me the rest of your name?"

"Sarah Elizabeth."

She let her hand drop into her lap.

He felt like part of him had disappeared with the removal of her hand.

"Two fine and proper names."

"For a fine and improper miss." Her eyes twinkled.

Joshua laughed. "Most improper, to the dismay of Mrs. Westall and Mrs. Martin."

She shook her head. "They'll never speak to me again."

"I hope that's not true. Womenfolk need other womenfolk to talk with. The tables and cabinet will help them forgive, if not forget. After all, they wouldn't want to upset me by snubbing you."

"You've got that much influence, huh?"

"Yep. At least in my neck of the woods."

A thoughtful smile flickered across her face. "I could make them each a present. That might help."

"What can you make?"

"I'm not a total dud. I'm really good with flowers. My one hobby. I make some very stunning dried floral arrangements. I even know how to dry flowers." Her head tilted slightly to the side in a sassy motion.

The garden may have been a bad idea. Not much would

grow in late September. He didn't want to see disappointment replace the first spark of happiness he'd seen in Sarah. "If you're planning to grow flowers in your garden to bloom now, you could be in for a big disappointment. It's awfully late in the year and only a couple of things will bloom before the snow starts."

She frowned at that.

"I tell you what. Sunday I'll take you out where you can pick wildflowers, as many as you like."

"That would be wonderful." She threw her arms around his neck and kissed him.

He let her lips brand him as hers. Then he gently sat her back in her chair and walked back to his dinner. He had no intention of branding her. Not until she agreed to marry him. And that seemed about as likely as a Wyoming winter without snow.

Sarah looked at herself in the mirror and turned from side to side. The blue dress she'd picked to wear to the harvest celebration looked really good, especially since she'd put bunches of slips under it. It swirled when she turned. Swirling on the dance floor would be neat. And it showed some cleavage. Joshua couldn't complain. Catherine had brought the dress with her, so it had to be all right.

She tucked her hair behind her ear. It needed trimming badly, but she'd never been any good at cutting it herself. The perm still held up—sort of—but she really couldn't do much with it. She wished she had one of her hair clips so she could pin it back, but those had stayed at home. In two months, it hadn't grown enough to tie back with a ribbon. It would just have to do.

She leaned forward to study her face. Without makeup she looked so blasé, but Joshua would never take her to town if she put on any. She pinched her cheeks and laughed. The last time she'd done that instead of using blush was in the seventh grade when her parents had emphatically said she was too young for makeup. Now she was too "nice" to wear it. She wrinkled her nose. She picked up her gold hoop earrings, then dropped them back on the dresser. They'd probably be unacceptable. She shrugged her shoulders and went to pick up her cape and the flower arrangements she'd made for Mrs. Westall and Rachel. Joshua hadn't allowed her to take them to town without him and he'd been busy getting the ranch ready for winter.

She practically skipped down the steps. A real social event. People would be around. She could dance and talk and hopefully not offend a single soul. She'd promised herself to be extra careful about what she said.

"You look quite beautiful, my lady." Joshua gave her an exaggerated bow.

"And you quite handsome, sir." She curtsied and laughed.

"And in a very good mood." He took her arm and escorted her to the waiting buggy.

"Why, yes, I am. I get to go to town and have some fun." And visit the church. She looked up at the sun. It shone brightly as it started its trek across the sky. She let him help her into the wagon. The back contained the furniture promised to the two women in town.

Joshua settled on the seat next to her, bouncing the wagon. He reached into his pocket, looking like a little boy who was up to some mischief. He pulled out a small box and handed it to her.

"For me?" Sarah giggled and took the box. "I just love presents." Carefully, she removed the wrapping paper from the box and smoothed it on her lap. Then she raised the lid of the box and gasped. "Oh, they're beautiful." She pulled out two pear-shaped pearl-drop earrings. She affixed them to her ears. Then she picked up a matching chain, from which hung a pear-shaped gold locket embedded with pearls. "I love them." She reached up and kissed Joshua on the cheek.

He beamed at her, his eyes sparkling. She handed him the locket and turned her back to him. "Fasten it, please." The cold chain caressed her neck, in contrast with his warm fingers. She turned back to him. "How do they look?"

"Just perfect with your gown." He adjusted the locket so it perfectly centered on her bare chest. His fingers lingered against her skin, sending a shiver through her. "I thought you might like some jewelry of your own since you seem only to have one pair of earbobs and Catherine's cameo."

"What a wonderful and perceptive man you are." As they drove along, her heart sang. This would be a glorious day.

As the buggy approached town, she saw people already bustling about, setting up tables and putting out food. The center of the street had been blocked. Joshua pulled the wagon up beside several others. "I'll tend to the horses. You can take your peace offerings to the women."

She grabbed his arm. "Maybe I should wait. They won't say anything rude if you're standing with me."

"Mrs. Westall and Mrs. Martin would never be rude—not directly anyway." He patted her hand. "Go along. If you see Henry, send him over to help me unload the furniture."

"Ugh. If I must." Holding her head high, she smiled and walked toward where the women fussed around a table. Her stomach did several flips. The few she didn't know moved aside as she walked up. "Hello, Rachel. Mrs. Westall." She nodded her head toward them. "I came to see if I could be of help."

"Extra hands are always needed," said Mrs. Westall, returning Sarah's smile.

The spring within her that was wound so tightly relaxed. "Oh wonderful. Here, I brought you a present." She handed an intricate flower arrangement of golden and leaby asters to Mrs. Westall. She handed a second one of chicory, harebell, and daisies to Rachel. "I hope you like them. I thought they might brighten your home during the winter months."

"My goodness," said Rachel. "Aren't they the most beautiful things? This will look wonderful over the sofa upstairs." The flowers were woven together with straw to make a fan shape.

"Did you make these yourself?" Mrs. Westall examined hers, carefully turning the fountain-shaped mound of flowers. "However did you do it?"

"It's one of the few talents I possess." Sarah folded her hands and let them drop in front of her.

The rest of the women crowded around Rachel and Mrs.

Westall, oohing and ahhing. "Do you think she might make me one?" one of the women asked softly.

"Ask her yourself, Trudy," said Mrs. Westall. "She doesn't bite."

The woman looked at her shyly.

"I can make more. I'm not very busy." Sarah shrugged her shoulders. Now if she managed not to offend anyone, she might have found the way into the women's hearts.

"I'll be glad to pay you a bit," said another woman, "if you'll make me one."

"That's not necessary." Sarah suddenly wanted to hide from all the attention.

Trudy reached over and gingerly touched Rachel's flowers. "You ought to have her make more and carry them in the store. I bet they'd sell real well."

"What a wonderful idea. I'll talk with my Henry about it." Rachel cradled the flowers on her arm.

"Oh, that's right—Henry. Joshua asked if he could come help unload the furniture. He has finished your tables, Rachel, and your cabinet, Mrs. Westall. Those flowers will fit perfectly in the center shelf if you want to put them there." Sarah edged down to the end of the table away from the crush of women. She'd never had a lot of female friends or spent much time in their company. LeeAnne was the only woman she really called friend. Suddenly, she had no idea of what to say or do.

Rachel came and took her arm. "Come and we'll find Henry. Then you can help me display these flowers. I'd hate to have anything happen to them."

"You two go on along," said Mrs. Westall. "We can manage just fine for a while, but don't you be gone long."

Sarah walked with her grandmother. For the first time in a long time she felt like she belonged.

"Oh, there's Henry." Rachel hollered and waved at him. Instantly he stood beside her, his eyes worshipping her. A twinge of jealousy rushed through Sarah. The look on Henry's face had more value than any other object on earth. Someday she hoped a man would look at her that way.

Rachel showed him the flowers, then dispatched him to

help Joshua. She took Sarah into the store and up the stairs. "It isn't as spacious as Joshua's house, but it's very comfortable. I have been very lucky in my choice to come west."

"Henry would give you everything you want within his power. The man is besotted." Sarah looked around the small room. Doilies covered the tables in contrast to the heavy wooden pipe rack sitting next to an overstuffed chair. For her great-grandfather, of course.

"He is a dear man." Rachel looked around the room. "Where do you think?" she asked, holding up the flowers.

Sarah turned a complete circle. A painting of a wolf standing among the trees hung on a wall next to white lace curtains. A bearskin covered the floor. A pair of tiny china angels were set up on the mantel. "You're right. Over the couch."

"We'll have the men put it up when they bring the tables. Come, sit and visit a moment." Rachel sat on the green velvet-covered couch. A lace doily covered its arm, hiding most of a worn spot. She patted the seat next to her.

Sarah sat down. The place was a hodgepodge with no overall decorating theme, but had a cozy feel that welcomed visitors. "This is very nice."

"I'm happy." She laid the flowers on the table in front of her. "Now. Have you decided?"

"Decided on what?" Sarah eyed her grandmother carefully. She wished she could read minds.

"The minister is back. We could have a wedding today." Her grandmother smiled benignly at her.

The ever-present topic. "I decided a long time ago. No wedding."

Rachel shook her head. "Too bad. Joshua would make you a fine husband."

"And I'd make a lousy wife." Sarah patted Rachel's hand. "Don't worry about me. Things will work out. How is married life treating you?"

"I'm very happy." Rachel gave her a sly look. "I guess you were right."

"About what?" Sarah tried to remember anything she'd said that she might possibly be right about.

"I'm with child." The woman glowed.

Sarah squealed and wrapped her arms around Rachel. "I'm so happy for you."

"I see all is forgiven." Joshua's voice made her jump.

"She's going to have a baby." Sarah blurted out, then slapped her hand over her mouth. So much for control. "I guess I should have let you tell." She looked at her great-grandmother with an apology. Rachel's face had turned bright red.

"Congratulations," said Joshua, patting Henry on the back.

"And what do you say to the mother-to-be? Men. They take all the credit for these things."

Joshua laughed.

Henry glared. "I see she hasn't changed in the least."

"She means well," said Rachel. "And she did bring me a beautiful present. I would greatly appreciate you men attaching it to the wall above the sofa."

"Very carefully," added Sarah.

A baby. Her great-grandmother was pregnant. The first of many. A chill ran down her spine. The first one died. Sadness overshadowed the joy. She tried to smile. Her great-grandmother's joy shouldn't be tarnished. Maybe it was something she did wrong. Sarah looked at Rachel. She didn't look pregnant. "How far along?"

Red crept into Rachel's face again. "Let me show you the bedroom." Rachel grabbed Sarah's arm and dragged her into the other room. Joshua's laughter followed them.

"It isn't seemly to talk about such things in front of men."

"Oh. Another taboo I've broken." Sarah shrugged. "Now, how far along?"

Rachel placed her hand on her stomach. "About six weeks."

"You haven't had time to put on any weight." Sarah studied her grandmother's frame.

"A little, but the corset hides it."

"You're wearing a corset? Do you realize how bad that is for the baby? You have to take it off this instant." Sarah put her hands on her hips. "This instant."

"I can't do that."

"Well, you better or you'll squish the poor little boy."

"I never heard of such a thing. Women wear corsets all the time while they are pregnant."

"And, believe me, they squish the kids." Sarah threw up her hands. "At least let me loosen it. Please."

Rachel looked at her. "It's that important to you?"

"As important as you are to Henry."

Rachel turned around. "I'll try it looser. I guess it doesn't matter if I look heavier, but the dress won't button."

"Then find another or let it out."

Sarah helped Rachel change. "Now, doesn't that feel better?"

"Actually, yes." Rachel smiled at Sarah. "You seem to know a great deal about having babies. Have you ever had one?"

"Good grief, no. I've never been married." She might say things she shouldn't, but she had no intention of being a single mother. She firmly thought babies needed two parents.

"We should go and help Edna and the others," said Rachel.

"Who?"

"Mrs. Westall."

"Oh, yes, of course. We should also check on the men. The other room seems awfully quiet." Sarah followed Rachel into the living room. Henry sat in his chair smoking a pipe. Shocked, she walked over to him and yanked it from his hand. "You can't smoke around a pregnant woman. It's not good for your wife or your baby. Go downstairs or outside with this disgusting thing." Sarah waved the pipe in the air.

Henry sat still with his mouth hanging open.

Joshua reached for the pipe. "A man has a right to smoke in his own house."

"She's right. It does make me feel sick," said Rachel.

Henry grabbed the pipe and knocked the tobacco out, extinguishing the burning bits.

Sarah linked arms with Rachel and started for the stairs. "We'll see you men downstairs. Now, Rachel, you have to remember to eat right. Lots of vegetables, fruits. We have lots of apples around the place. I'll make sure Joshua sends you bushels. And milk. You need fresh milk."

Rachel patted Sarah's arm. "You can be very sweet, when you try."

"You mean when I don't have both feet in my mouth." They walked out into the sunshine. The sun had nearly reached its midday level. "I'm going to the church for a few minutes. Will you tell Joshua for me?"

"Yes, dear. But don't be too long. You'll miss all the fun."

Forever, Sarah hoped. "I'll try not to be. But you remember: Keep that corset loose."

"I'll try." Rachel went off toward the table that had the food.

Sarah lifted the hem of her skirt and hurried toward the church. She pushed open the door, walked in, and peeped around the partition. It was empty. Good.

She turned her attention to the window. The sun shone through it. Slowly she walked down the aisle, holding up her arms. A glint flashed in her eyes. Did she imagine it, or was Jesus beckoning to her? She kept walking. "Please," she whispered. "Please. I want to go home now."

Rough hands grabbed her from behind. She tried to scream, but a bitter-tasting hand clamped over her mouth. She struggled, kicking out at the body attached to the hands that held her. The cold blade of a knife pressed against her throat. A piece of material crushed against her eyes and pulled her hair as hands knotted it in back. The person twisted her arms behind her back and tied them with rough rope which cut into her flesh.

Jack. He'd followed her somehow. Now he'd carry out his threat. Her body went rigid. She struggled for breath. He would kill her. The only way out was through the door to the street, and too many people milled about outside to carry her that way. Her only chance was escape. She pulled against her captor, freeing herself. Her skirts tangled around her feet and she lunged forward. A sharp pain shot through her head. Bright spots flashed before her blindfolded eyes. *Don't let me die,* she prayed to the window.

Chapter 12

HENRY SHOOK HIS head as he watched the two women go down the stairs. "I don't know how you put up with her. I'm sorry I ever got you into this."

"You didn't." Joshua leaned back on the sofa in Henry's living quarters. "Remember, she wasn't one of the brides we sent for."

"I know, but somehow I feel responsible." Henry cleaned his pipe and put it neatly back on the rack. "When we found her we assumed she was Catherine Hodges."

"I assumed as much as you did. I don't regret taking her home with me."

"Does she have any useful qualities?" Henry leaned back in his chair.

"She adds up numbers quicker than anyone I've ever seen and she makes great flower arrangements." Joshua stretched his legs out under the new table and crossed them at the ankles.

Henry looked up at the flowers on the wall. "It does

brighten the place. Rachel has been redecorating some, but it still looks a great deal like it did when I lived alone."

"You should have had Mrs. Westall redecorate for you like I did. Gave it a nice woman's touch rather than that lived-in look."

"She isn't leading you around on a halter, is she?" Henry looked at his friend.

Joshua laughed. "No. Most of the time she seems to be going in circles." He frowned. "She really wants to go home, but she won't tell me why she can't. I reckon it has something to do with Jack."

"Who?" Henry refilled his pipe and looked at it.

"The man who put the bruises on her."

"She probably drove him nuts with her ways." He put the pipe in his mouth. "Do you reckon the smoke really bothers my Rachel?"

"I doubt she'd have said anything if it didn't." Joshua combed his hair back with his fingers and put on his hat. "The womenfolk will be waiting. I hear the band tuning up and I figure they'll want to dance."

"Womenfolk always do." Henry picked up his matches. "Guess I'll take this along and smoke it outside so I don't smell up the parlor."

Joshua unfolded from the sofa and moved toward the door.

"I still don't know how you put up with her." Henry rose from his chair to follow.

"She keeps my life interesting. I never know what's going to come out of her mouth." *Or off her body,* he thought. At least as the weather cooled, she seemed inclined to wear a few more clothes.

"That's the truth of it."

Joshua strolled out of the shop and onto the street. "I better head over to the women and make sure Cath hasn't started a riot."

Henry chuckled and chewed on the mouthpiece of his pipe. "I'll see if Rachel is inclined to dance."

"Howdy, ladies." Joshua removed his hat and bowed to the women. "How are all of you this fine day?"

Murmurs surrounded him. He looked around for Sarah's uncovered black hair. He needed to remember to have Mrs. Westall make her some sunbonnets since she refused to wear any of the hats in Catherine's things and he didn't have one small enough to fit her head. Her face and arms had become a golden tan since he'd allowed her outside. Her garden had sprouted some winter peas, of which she was very proud. But Joshua worried about her being in the sun so much with her head uncovered. She had made a remark about running low on sunscreen, but he decided against trying to find out exactly what that might be. Sometimes he felt better if he didn't understand what she'd meant.

He couldn't see Sarah anywhere. He made his way to Rachel. "Mrs. Martin, have you seen Cath? I thought she was with you."

Rachel smiled up at him. "She went off to the church. I think she wanted to pray, or had some thinking to do."

"Thank you," he said, nodding his head to her. Of course. Sarah always wanted to visit the church. She was obsessed with it. He'd wander over and see if she might be ready to dance.

Quietly, he entered the back so as not to disturb her if she was praying. Peeking around the wall, he looked toward the altar. The room was empty. He walked down the aisle, looking at the empty seats. She couldn't have gone far. A cold chill ran up his spine. He turned and strode out of the church and back to the women. Searching the crowd of people for Sarah, his stomach clenched when he couldn't find her. Out in the middle of the street, Rachel danced with Henry. Joshua wound his way through the couples.

"Excuse me, Henry, Mrs. Martin." Joshua placed a hand on Henry's shoulder.

Henry looked up at him. "This is our first dance and I'm not going to let you cut in," he said brusquely.

"I don't want to dance. I can't find Cath. Mrs. Martin, are you sure she said she was going to the church?" He clutched his hat in his hands, curling the brim.

Rachel placed her hand over his. "Goodness, Mr. Campbell, you're going to ruin your hat. I'm sure she's fine. Probably just wandering about looking for you if she's not in the church."

"I hope you're right." He crammed his hat on his head. Stepping out of the way of the dancers, he surveyed the area. Walking around the dance area, he stopped and asked everyone if they'd seen her. The coldness spread from his back through his body. He looked back at the church. She might have been there and he didn't see her. It didn't seem likely, but . . . He headed back to the church. Swinging open the door, he strode in.

"Cath, you in here?" he called.

Silence greeted him. He walked into the center aisle, and lifted his head to stare at the church window that fascinated her so. "You have something to do with this," he said to the window. "I know you do. Once I figure it out, then everything else can be settled." Sarah was rubbing off on him and he'd started to lose his senses. Talking to the window would only add fuel to the gossip that abounded since Sarah's arrival. He kept staring at the window. He could swear the pictured Jesus frowned at him.

He rubbed his eyes with his sleeve. "You know where she's got to, don't you." Joshua sank into one of the pews. "Has she gone for good?" A black cloud descended over his mind, blocking out the joy. He propped his elbows on his knees and let his head drop into his hands. The sprightly music from outside entered the church and circled around him. He put his hands to his ears to shut it out. His dance partner had returned home. She would be happy.

He rose slowly. No one would miss him if he just returned to the ranch. They were all having fun, and his long face had no place amongst them. He stepped into the aisle. His boot crunched on something. He stopped and looked down. Her locket. He hunkered down and picked it up, clutching it. She hated this place so much she had left behind his gift to her so she wouldn't have to remember it.

The chain swung from his fingers. He started to drop the jewelry into his pocket, but then looked at it more closely. The chain was broken—as if someone had yanked it from Sarah's neck. His heart started to beat rapidly. He remembered the look on her face when she opened the box. She wouldn't break the chain and throw the locket on the floor.

He rushed out of the church and searched the dirt around the steps. Her footprints went in, along with several sets of boots. But her footprints didn't exit. Joshua walked carefully around to the side of the building. Two fresh sets of prints led into the trees behind the church. One dug deeper into the dirt, as if carrying a heavy load. Jack. He'd found her and taken her.

Joshua turned back to the merrymaking. He had to find Sarah quickly, or Jack would kill her. He made straight for Henry, nearly knocking over two other couples who danced. He muttered "sorry" under his breath and pushed his way to the middle of the moving crowd. "Henry, I need your help." Joshua stopped directly in front of him.

Henry swung Rachel around, his back turning to Joshua.

Joshua put his hand on Henry's shoulder. "Henry, listen to me."

"I'm still not sharing my wife. If you want to dance, find that woman of yours." Henry slid away from Joshua.

"Dammit, Henry. Stop and listen to me." Joshua grabbed Henry by the shoulder and forced him around.

Henry raised his hands to push Joshua away. But then he stopped once he saw the look on Joshua's face. "What's wrong?"

"She's gone. Disappeared. I need your help to find her." Joshua let his hands fall to his sides.

Henry shook his head. "Probably run off. Went back where she came from."

"No. Jack took her. And he had help. I found tracks by the church. There's two of them."

Henry looked wistfully over his shoulder at Rachel. "Probably ran off with them. If you're that concerned, take your men."

"She didn't leave of her own will. And I'd like to get her back alive. My men are fine with a bunch of cows but not one of 'em could track a buffalo after a snowfall or hit one with a shot standing five feet away. I need you. And you owe me for helping you rescue Mrs. Martin." And he didn't need to stand here arguing. Jack and Sarah had at least a half-hour head start on him. She could already be dead. He forced the thought from his mind. He had to focus on finding her and ignore the cold, hard knot that formed in his stomach.

"Who's Jack?" Henry took his wife's hand.

"The man who put the bruises on her neck. The one she ran away from and ended up here." Joshua grabbed Rachel's arm and started to hustle her out of the crowd of dancers. "All this jawing is putting them farther away from us."

Henry put his hand on Joshua's arm. "How do you know she didn't leave with him of her own accord?"

Joshua fished the locket from his pocket. "Her tracks don't leave the church. And," he held up the locket, "the chain's been torn from her neck. She wouldn't do that."

Rachel pulled her hand free from her husband. "No, she wouldn't have broken her beautiful locket. Go. She's in trouble."

Joshua started, then stopped. "I brought the buggy. I don't have my horse."

Rachel put her hand on his arm. "She will be fine. Take one of your men's horses and have him take the buggy home."

"Get an extra mount for Sarah," said Henry, heading for the stable where he kept his horse. "And get Cookie to come with us," he hollered over his shoulder.

The three men met at the edge of the church within minutes. "They headed southeast." The men rode out, looking for clues. They followed tracks in the dirt that stretched on into the distance.

They'd traveled several miles when the tracks disappeared into a creek. Joshua stopped his horse, and lifted himself in the saddle, searching up and down the stream for any sign. "Damn," he muttered. "They could follow the water for miles and we'll waste time figuring which way to go."

Cookie slid from his horse and into the water. A hunting knife bounced against his side. Joshua watched him for a moment. "Henry, head upstream and I'll go down."

"It's not a good idea to separate," said Henry. "Puts all of us in danger."

"We don't have time to search both ways. He could kill Cath by then. We have no other choice." He started moving his horse downstream.

"Hold on," Cookie barked at him. "You're going the wrong way."

Joshua wheeled his horse around. "What'd you find?"

Cookie held up a pearl-drop earring.

Joshua stopped his horse next to Cookie and took the earring. He urged his horse upstream, looking along the banks for signs of the men they tracked.

Sarah was glad to be off the horse and out of the grips of the man who smelled like last month's garbage. She struggled to sit up and lean against the tree where the two men had dumped her after removing her blindfold. She watched them. They passed a bottle back and forth, both taking long swigs from it.

A shiver ran through her when she thought how these men had put their hands on her. They were the two who had come by the ranch looking for work. Joshua had been correct in being suspicious of them. They were also the ones who had robbed the stage and killed Catherine. Listening to them now she knew that she was in deep trouble, especially if someone didn't come to rescue her soon.

"Don't know why we're keeping her around," said the man with the knife.

"'Cuz we're going have some fun first, Caleb," said the man with the gun holster slung around his neck. A raucous laugh erupted from him.

"That's what got us in trouble last time, Trent. If we'd just killed the two women and got on, no one would ever have figured us for the robbery," said Caleb.

Trent threw the empty whiskey bottle into the bushes. "That stage didn't carry anything worth stealing except the two women."

"That one weren't no fun." Caleb dug in his saddlebag for

another bottle of whiskey. "And if we hadn't run out of whiskey, we'd had the other one."

"We'll have this one. After what her mister did to Horace it's only fair we take his missus." Trent laughed loudly as he grabbed the bottle from Caleb.

Caleb cuffed him across the side of the head and grabbed the bottle back. "You had most of the last bottle. I've had to carry the woman all these miles. I'll drink 'til I'm done and you can have what's left."

"Give me a drink." Trent forced the bottle from the smaller man. "You can have the woman first." He turned to leer at Sarah. "Pretty little thing, ain't she?"

"You sure she's not sick or something? I never seen a woman with shorn hair that weren't sick." Caleb glanced over at her and stroked the hilt of his knife.

Sarah forced down the churning in her stomach, which threatened to erupt. Her body went cold at the thought of those men touching her. She took deep breaths and leaned her head against the tree. A throbbing ache ran from her temple, where she'd hit her head on the pew, down to her shoulders. Her fingers tingled from being tied behind her back for so long.

She wiggled her fingers and pain shot up her arms. Twisting as best she could, she felt the tree for a sharp spot. The bark peeled away under the pressure of her hands. Somehow she had to get her hands untied. She pulled her hands apart and tried to stretch the rope. They moved only a minuscule amount. She twisted the rope, shifting it a fraction at a time. Finally she could feel the knot in her fingers. The skin on her wrists stung and the rope had a sticky feel to it. She picked at the knot, but the ropes seemed to grow tighter.

She looked over at the men. They still swigged from the bottle.

"Somebody's gonna be missing her soon," said Caleb. "We need to get rid of her. She's slowing us down too much."

"I say we take her and leave her here for Mr. Campbell. Then we jump him," said Trent. "I want him, after him killing Horace and throwing us off his place like we wasn't good enough to herd cattle for him."

"We didn't want to herd no cattle anyhows," said Caleb. He staggered as he stood and walked toward Sarah.

"That's beside the point." Trent's speech slurred.

Caleb stood over Sarah, ogling her. He pulled his knife from its sheath and yanked her to her feet. "You tied the rope too tight. Her hands are all bloody."

"Who cares?" Trent looked at the empty bottle of whiskey and threw it down on the ground with force. The smashing of glass mixed with his laughter.

Caleb slipped the knife between Sarah's hands and sliced through the rope. He grabbed her by the arm and hauled her toward him.

Sarah's arms shrieked as the blood rushed into them. She staggered and Caleb caught her against him. The smell of whiskey made her gag. She tried not to breathe. She couldn't wait for the cavalry to come riding over the hill to save her. She had to act now, or nothing would matter. She wouldn't give in and allow them to rape her. But she didn't want to end up like Catherine either, killed while fighting them off. She had other plans for her life. She'd escaped Jack. She'd escape them, too.

Caleb ripped open the buttons down the front of her dress. Yanking it away from her shoulders, he slobbered on her neck. "She smells right purty."

"Hurry it up. We's out of whiskey again," said Trent.

"She's gonna be better than whiskey." Caleb cut off her camisole. Her dress pooled around her feet. "What the hell is that?" His grip on her shoulder lessened as he stared at her bra.

She shoved him, putting all of her weight into the movement. He staggered backward, tripping over a rock. She stepped out of the dress and ran toward where the broken whiskey bottle lay, picking up its neck.

"Grab her," yelled Caleb as he picked himself up off the ground.

Trent staggered toward Sarah. She held the jagged piece

of glass pointed toward him. "You stay away." She held the bottle piece steady, watching him carefully.

"We got a hellcat on our hands," laughed Trent.

"Just get her. Shoot her if you have to," snarled Caleb, waving his knife in the air.

Trent took a step toward Sarah. "Don't want to waste a woman with this much spirit. 'Twould be like shooting a good horse."

Sarah grabbed the top of her petticoats and slid down all but one so they formed a snowy puddle at her feet. She wasn't going to trip on all that material again. As Trent took another step, she stepped back with one foot and kicked the clothes at him with the other. They covered him like a parachute. She turned and ran for the creek. Plenty of brush grew along the banks to give her cover and as long as she followed the water, she could find her way back to Moose Creek.

Plunging into the water, her spool-heeled shoes slipped on the wet rocks. She stepped into a hole, wrenched her ankle, and fell face-first into the water. Horses' hooves sounded behind her. She scrambled up, pushing her wet bangs back from her forehead. Still gripping the piece of glass, she splashed toward the far bank. She stepped on a large rock and fell sideways into the water, then blinked away the water and started for the other bank. The whinnying of a horse came from beside her. Another horse's snorting sprayed her. She leapt toward the shore and scrambled up the rocky edge. A hand tried to grab her. She sliced at it with the broken bottle.

"Damn, hellcat," snarled Trent. His hand jerked away from her.

Sarah turned to face them. If she was going down, she was going down fighting. She balanced as best she could on the slippery soles of her shoes and brandished her weapon at them. Caleb rode toward her, his knife held easily in his hand. As he came close, she sat down suddenly, rocks cutting into her bottom. As he leaned toward her, he nearly fell from the saddle as he rode by. She jabbed up and gouged his leg with the glass, breaking off the bottle's tip.

He screamed and turned his horse to come back for her.

She ran back toward the creek. Trent turned his horse to cut off her path. Her lungs burned as she gasped for air. Grabbing the bottom of her slip, she hoisted it up around her waist and plunged headlong into the water, going down just as Trent's horse stopped in front of her. As Trent reached his hand down she raked the glass across the back of it. He kept reaching.

A shot rang out. Sarah screamed. Trent's hat spun into the water. Sarah screamed again. The horse reared. Sarah crawled backward, knees up and hands beneath her bottom, the rocks scraping her palms. Another shot rang out. She flipped to her hands and knees, crawling madly as she tried to get to the shore away from the men. She heard the sound of horses' hooves galloping away, and of more coming toward her. She'd nearly gained the bank and the bushes, where she could hide.

One horse drew up behind her and she heard a rider splash into the water. She turned, the rest of the glass clasped in her hand. "Don't touch me!" she screamed.

Chapter 13

"CATH. IT'S ME, sweetheart." Joshua bent down slowly. "You're safe."

She stared up at him, wildly waving the glass back and forth. Slowly she let it drop in the creek next to her and sagged forward, her head resting on her knees. Joshua scooped her up and cradled her against his chest. She clung to him.

Joshua hugged her tightly, wading toward the shore. He gently placed her on dry land. His shirt clung to him where she'd soaked him. "Let me look at you. Are you okay?"

She nodded her head, breathing heavily.

He pulled off his coat and wrapped it around her. "Why is it that every time I turn around I find you running around half-naked?"

Sarah looked up at him with eyes still wide with terror. Then slowly she began a low, gurgling nervous laugh that shook her body. Joshua sat next to her and pulled her into his lap, rubbing her back through his coat. She pulled up her legs and formed a small ball. "They were going to rape and kill me," she said in choked tones.

"I know, sweetheart." He laid his head against the top of her head. "They're gone now. They can't hurt you anymore."

At the sound of the hooves splashing through the water, Sarah tensed in his arms. "It's okay. It's just Henry and Cookie returning. Did you get them?"

"Naw," said Cookie. He swung down from his horse, pulling a blanket from the back of the saddle. "They disappeared like a wisp of smoke." He handed the blanket to Joshua.

Henry stood and looked down at Sarah. "You put up a mighty good fight. Something to be proud of."

Sarah peeked up at him. "Thank you," she mumbled. "I come from good stock."

He laughed.

"We need to get her back." Joshua tucked the blanket around her. "She's injured. I'll carry her in front of me on my mount."

Sarah shifted slightly in his lap. "I can ride."

"I'll carry you."

She shook her head. "Nope. If I'm going to be a Western woman, I have to learn to take these things in stride."

"Nobody takes these things in stride. Most women would have the vapors by now." Henry crouched next to Joshua.

"That's 'cause they wear their corsets too tight." Sarah leaned into Joshua.

Henry blushed. Joshua laughed. Cookie went to check the cinches on the horses.

"That's my Cath," said Joshua.

"Ain't that the truth," said Henry, rising slowly. "I've got some salve in my saddlebags for her wrists."

Sarah held out her hands while Joshua applied the salve. Then he cut off the edge of her remaining slip and wrapped each wrist.

"I'm not going to have any clothes at all if this keeps up," said Sarah.

"I thought you liked it that way," Joshua replied.

"Sometimes I have to leave the house."

Henry cleared his throat. "Who were those men?"

"The ones who robbed the stage and killed Catherine. The same ones who came to the ranch looking for work." Sarah stood up, swaying.

Joshua caught her by the shoulders. "Are you sure you can ride?"

She nodded her head.

"Why'd they grab you?" asked Cookie. He mounted his horse and sat, waiting.

"To pay Joshua back for killing their friend and not hiring them." Sarah wobbled toward her horse.

Joshua lifted her onto the saddle and tucked the blanket around her legs. "But Henry killed the man, not me."

"I guess they got confused. Thank God for that at least. If they'd taken Rachel, she might have lost the baby, or worse, been killed." A shiver ran through Sarah.

Sarah soaked in the hot water, wishing she had some bubble bath. Not one spot on her body didn't ache. The rope had rubbed her wrists raw and strained her shoulders. Hitting the pew had made a goose egg appear on her head. In the creek she had twisted her ankle, and skirting the rocks caused various scrapes all over her body. The hot bath helped to ease all the pains except for the one in her wrists.

She shifted slightly in the tub, trying to soothe her sore joints. At least one good thing had come out of her adventure. Everyone in town felt sorry for her and some of her unorthodox behavior had been pushed to the back of their memories.

A rap at the door made her jump. "Yes," she called out.

"Is the water getting cold?" Joshua's voice floated in through the door.

"A little," she called back to him.

"Want more hot water?"

"That would be nice."

The door opened and he stood holding a pot in one hand. He started to walk in, and then stepped back. "I'll just set it by the door and you can get it." He started to close the door.

"The pan's too heavy for me to lift. My arms don't want to work yet." She didn't move.

"But you're . . . you're unclothed. I can't come in." Joshua stood with the door open a crack.

Sarah laughed. "If I put a towel over me, will that help?"

"Maybe." His voice sounded hoarse.

She reached over the edge of the tub and grabbed the towel, placing it over her. "Okay, I'm ready."

Joshua slowly entered the room. He looked at his feet. Kneeling down, he pulled the plug on the tub, letting some of the water drain. The towel settled around Sarah's body, contouring her curves. He quickly replaced the plug and lifted the pan.

"Don't just dump that in." Sarah pulled up her legs. "You have to stir it with your hand to mix it with the cooler water or you're going to parboil me."

"Sorry. I wasn't thinking." Slowly he poured the water in, swishing it around. "Is that better?"

"Much." She stretched out her legs. Her foot brushed against his hand. He yanked it back.

He squatted by the edge of the tub, staring at her. She reached out and touched his arm. Water dripped down onto the floor. "Thank you for rescuing me."

He nodded. He gazed into her eyes for a long time. "I thought you'd left. Gone home. I almost didn't come."

"Thank God you did." She reached up and stroked the side of his face. "What made you change your mind?"

Joshua pulled her locket from his pocket, dangling it in the air.

She reached out and clasped it. "I didn't realize I'd lost it."

"If Cookie hadn't found one of your earrings, I would have gone in the wrong direction."

"I'm glad you gave me the jewelry before we left. It saved my life."

He took her hand in his. "Promise me you'll tell me first when you leave for good."

"I won't be able to." She stroked the side of his face. She

wanted to wipe away the haunted look from his eyes. "I won't know until I go."

"Why not?"

She shrugged. "I just won't."

"It's the window, isn't it?" His grip on her hand increased as though he were trying to hold on to her forever.

She nodded.

"Tell me, Cath."

"I can't, Joshua. I just can't."

He stood and started for the door.

"Joshua, come back, please."

"I need to know, Cath."

"I can't explain." She reached out to him. "Please. Can't we just have this moment? I can't promise any more than that."

He stood and looked at her. "Why, Cath?"

"Because. Just because."

His arms hung at his sides. "What are you hiding, Cath?"

My life. Sarah couldn't explain it to him. She didn't know how. But this man had started to matter to her. She didn't want to hurt him. She wanted him to hold her. She wanted to feel safe. She wanted the confusion to go away. She wanted her life to be sane again, but that didn't seem to be in the cards. "Nothing really important. Nothing that affects us."

"It affects us if you can't tell me why you won't marry me." His eyes implored her. "I need to know."

"Some things are best left unsaid." She stood up, holding the wet towel in front of her. "They get in the way of the present."

"I want more than the present. I want a wife."

"I know. You went to all this expense to fix up your house for a wife and then didn't get one." She waved one hand around as if to encompass the bathroom and the rest of the house. "But I'm not a substitute. I just can't fit into your world and replace Catherine. It doesn't work that way."

"You're not a substitute. I never knew Catherine. She was but a dream, a promise unfulfilled. But I liked the promise."

He ran his hand through his hair. "It's you who are the promise fulfilled. You're real, warm, caring, and—"

"And a little crazy," Sarah finished for him. She laughed softly as she stepped out of the tub, dripping water onto the floor.

"More than a little." He stared at the wet towel clinging to her body.

Flashes of desire raced through her body at his stare. She stared back into his eyes, eyes filled with lust. "I can't offer a promise fulfilled. Life's too uncertain."

"We're back to my never having a wife." He started to turn away from her.

She stepped toward him and took his arm. "I never said you weren't worthy of having a wife. You'd make a great husband and I haven't met many men I'd say that about."

"But not *your* husband." His voice came softly, achingly, to her.

"I can't promise that, Joshua. I can't promise anything." She wished she could wipe away the hurt that she knew her words caused him. He'd taken her in when he could have abandoned her in a place from which she couldn't get home—a place more foreign to her than a third-world country. But home was where she belonged and she wouldn't give up her resolve to get there. Jack might be waiting there, but at least she knew the rules of the game in her time and where she could go for help. Here she had to rely on everyone else, which she hated.

"All you'll give me is now?"

She nodded.

"No explanations?"

She shook her head.

"Why, Cath? Why?"

"Because."

" 'Because' is a lousy answer."

She smiled at him. "I know. I just can't give you a better one. Life has been off-kilter since I ended up in the church and it hasn't seemed to get any better." She shrugged her shoulders. "First I have Jack chasing me. I do a dandy job of evading him. But the world changes in ways I don't understand. Then Rachel nearly gets killed. Now, instead of one psycho chasing me and trying to cut me up, I've got two." A shiver ran through her. "I'm almost afraid to try running away from them. God knows where I'll end up next."

He put his hand on her shoulder. "Psycho?"

"Crazy people. Everywhere crazy people wait for me. It's like I have a sign tattooed on my forehead saying 'crazy men, attack here.'" She leaned her head against his shoulder and shook it.

"It isn't funny, Cath. You could have been killed." He wrapped his arms around her. His hand burned against her bare back.

"The whole situation has gone beyond funny and straight to ludicrous. I want to be home, curled up in my own bed with my own things around me. I want to be able to ph . . . talk with LeeAnne, my best friend. I want to go to work tomorrow." She sighed. "But none of that's going to happen. Maybe it never will again." She leaned away from him and looked into his eyes. "But, Joshua, I can't give up hope. I won't survive if my hope disappears. You have to understand that, even if I can't explain the situation in detail. I can't be held hostage here, alone and lost."

"You're not a hostage. You can leave anytime you want."

She sighed. "I wish. I don't want to hurt you. That has never been my intention. If I could have left as soon as I'd come, I would have. But I can't leave. I'm trapped, and I'm scared of being trapped all alone in this wilderness where I don't fit in. I can't do anything and I feel totally useless."

He hugged her tightly. "You're not alone. And I won't let anything happen to you. I'll keep the psychos away."

"For the present, Joshua. All we have is that."

He pushed her away a bit and gazed into her eyes. Determination shone from them. "After the way you handled those two ruffians, I can't believe you can't find your way home."

"Some things I can't control. Oh, hell, a lot of things are out of my control. But for now I want to be with you. Not as your wife. That wouldn't be fair. Not as a promise fulfilled, but as a memory stored against loneliness. A memory that all of this really happened."

"This is very real." She'd trapped his heart and threatened to stomp it the way the cows trampled the grass. But she'd set her mind like a bear trap and he knew that springing the trap brought pain.

"I'm not even sure of that anymore."

"I won't settle for just today. I'll never settle for that. I'll spend the rest of my days trying to convince you to marry me." He smiled at her.

"I know."

"But I'll take today, also. Memories for our old age."

She laughed. "You're dripping wet." She wiped her damp hands against his cheeks.

"And you are without clothes again."

She shrugged. "My towel's all wet, so I can't dry off and get dressed." She wrinkled her nose.

"I'd best get you another one, if you're through with your bath." He'd better get out of the bathroom until she put on clothes. His hands lingered on her bare back, balling into fists and pressing into the small of her back.

"Ooh, that feels good. Press a little higher up." She shifted, rubbing the lower half of her body against his.

"What?" He looked into her half-closed eyes.

"Press higher up on my back. I've more knots than a piece of yarn after a kitten's played with it." She turned part of the way around, exposing her back.

He gulped as he put his hands on her bare shoulders. His gaze followed the contours of her back down to the swell of her hips. Her back was amazingly white compared to her arms and neck.

She turned her head and looked back at him. "You're supposed to rub my back."

He moved his fingers gingerly against her shoulders.

"Harder. I slipped so many times in the creek, my muscles are strained."

He made a fist and pushed against her spine. She swayed away from his touch. He put his hand around her waist to steady her and worked his fist down to the small of her back. "Maybe you'd better get dressed."

"Will you rub my back some more if I get dressed?" Her voice reached up and caressed him.

"Yes." His voice became low and husky.

She turned, and standing on tiptoe, kissed him quickly on the lips. "I still need a towel."

"Yes." Joshua stared at her. The wet towel clung to her breasts. An imprint of his hand held the material to her stomach. He turned abruptly to get a towel.

He handed Sarah the towel and leaned against the doorframe. For late October, the house surely was hot. He looked over to the window and thought about opening it. But Cath was wet, including her hair, and he didn't want her to get a chill. He could go outside and chop some wood. Surely that would keep his mind off her body. He groaned. He'd probably cut his foot.

He had to do something. He could still feel the silkiness of her skin against him. He could see the outline of her shape beneath the towel. The curve of her bottom had burned itself into his mind. He would go crazy having this woman beneath his roof, so near and yet so unattainable.

Sarah walked out of the bathroom with the dry towel wrapped about her, pushing her hair out of her eyes. She stopped and looked at Joshua. The towel parted at the side, showing him bare flesh up her body with the side of her breast exposed. "I think you got me the smallest towel in the house."

He swallowed, staring at her. He swallowed again. "Not on purpose."

"I bet." She walked off, the edge of the towel bouncing up as she walked, showing the curve of her bottom. "I still expect a back rub. And my ankle, too. It stings like a son of a gun."

"Oh." The air scorched his lungs. He stepped forward and swept her up in his arms. "Then you shouldn't be walking on it." He walked into the living room and sat her down on the couch.

"My clothes are upstairs."

"I know." He knelt down beside the couch. "It's safer here."

"Are you going to get my clothes?" Her eyes twinkled at him.

"Yes." He reached over and rubbed his thumb down the side of her face. She shivered under his touch. "Are you cold?"

"Nope." She captured his hand and held it against her cheek. She turned her head and kissed his palm.

"You're beautiful."

"Thank you."

He shook his head. "Lie down and I'll rub your back."

She swung her legs onto the couch and rolled onto her stomach. He rubbed her shoulders, his gaze riveted on where the towel stopped just at the top of her legs. He put his hand on the middle of her back, the roughness of the towel abrasive against his hand.

Lifting her body slightly, Sarah tugged the towel from beneath her. "It's rubbing me."

He pulled the towel down so it draped across her bottom and the top of her legs. He rubbed up and down her back with his palms flat and his fingers splayed. Her body relaxed beneath his touch. His fingers traced down her sides and over the swell of her breasts.

She jumped. "That tickles. Rub harder."

Using the heel of his hands, he pushed against the muscles in her back, rubbing in a circular motion. "Is that better?"

"Much," she cooed.

He hesitated at the swell of her hips, then slid his fingers beneath the towel, stroking her flesh. She appeared to melt into the couch. He groaned silently. Touching her was the most exquisite torture he'd ever experienced.

"That feels wonderful," she murmured against the couch.

Every bit of his resolve shredded. "How about your ankle?" His voice came in a husky whisper.

She bent her knee and lifted one foot into the air. He took her foot into his hand and gently rubbed it, rotating it slightly. "Does that hurt?"

"Some." She lifted herself slightly to look at him, exposing most of her breast.

He put a hand in the middle of her back and softly pushed her flat against the couch. He wanted to take her breast into his hand and caress it.

He turned his attention to her ankle, rubbing it gingerly so as not to cause her any additional pain. He continued the massage up her leg to her knee and back down again. The muscles in her leg relaxed and the weight of it dropped against his hand. He lay her leg down on the sofa and rubbed the backs of both legs, moving his hands up to the bottom rim of the towel and back down. He knew he played with fire, but right now he didn't care if he got burned.

Sliding his hands under the towel, he fondled her bottom. She wiggled slightly under his ministrations. Her skin heated like a branding iron, putting her mark on his soul. The heat swirled up around him and he unbuttoned his shirt.

He smoothed her skin with his hand, absorbing the silkiness. Caressing her, he ran his hands down to the top of her legs, his thumbs teasing the insides of her legs. She shifted, moving her legs slightly apart. He increased the pressure on the inside of her legs, letting her heat envelop his hand.

He wanted her. Wanted her more than any woman he'd ever met. He wanted his brand upon her so she became his and could never leave him. She might not be wedded to him yet, but he could still make her his.

Slowly he let his hand drift up to the apex of her legs. He reined in his need and caressed her, soothed her. He wanted her to want him and need his touch as much as he needed hers.

She moaned softly as his hand caressed her. She pushed her body against his hand, demanding that he continue. He put one hand on her back and rubbed her bare skin. His hand skimmed down her side and across her breasts. His fingers pushed against her side and she lifted up slightly so his hand could take her breast. He skimmed his fingers across her nipple and it hardened to his touch. She sucked in her breath and held it.

He bent forward, turning her on her side, and took her nipple in his mouth, nipping at it and sucking. Her hand tangled in his hair, holding his mouth to her. His hand stroked between her legs, teasing her. Her body dampened his fingers and he edged a fingertip inside her and out. She groaned and tried to take his fingertip back.

He wanted to loosen his pants, but didn't dare. The ache in him threatened to wash away his resolve to ease her slowly into womanhood, the way a flash flood washed away all in its path.

Gently, he turned her and gazed at her naked body stretched out before him. He lay his cheek against her belly and watched as his hand raked through the tight black curls that guarded the entrance to her. He sought the hard nub that would bring her pleasure and began to rub it with his finger. She bent her knee and rested one leg against the back of the sofa. She moved in time to his hand, in turn taking in ragged breaths and holding her breath.

He ran his lips across the soft skin of her stomach and kissed the underside of her breasts. The swollen nipples seemed to beg him to kiss them. He took first one, then the other in his mouth as his hand stroked her underneath, building the fire within her. She stroked his neck, shoulders, and back in a frenzy. Her nails raked across his skin, stinging, searing into him. Her hand trailed around to his side and across his belly. Her fingers squeezed inside the waistband of his trousers, pinned there.

She rolled her head from side to side as he stroked and licked her. Her moisture soaked his fingers. She started to tremble. Her back arched, then she folded toward him, clawing at his shoulders. "Joshua," she gasped and her body shook. She rocked against his hand and his body. He held her tightly against him as she gasped for air. His other hand moved in a steady motion between her legs.

She clamped her legs down on his hand, trapping it. She tore at his trousers, trying to free the belt.

"Easy, sweetheart," he breathed at her.

She fell back on the sofa, still holding onto his belt. "Come to me, Joshua. Please."

He slid his hand from her and yanked his belt loose. After he kicked off his trousers, he sat beside her on the sofa. He ran his hands up and down her body. She squirmed under his touch. Sarah put her hand against his side, and her flesh burned his. She tried to pull him toward her. Her gaze begged him.

"I don't want to hurt you." Joshua pushed the coffee table out of the way and slid to sit on the floor. He reached for her and she sat up and slid into his waiting arms. He positioned her on top of him, holding her tightly so she perched above him. He begged entrance into her body, to become one with her. Slowly he lowered her, then raised her again. She tried to push against his hands and take him.

"Slow, Cath. Slow so it doesn't hurt."

She looked at him with glazed eyes. She shook her head and chewed her lip. He settled her down on top of him partway. Desire shot through his body and he forced himself to lift her away from him. He lowered her again, each time a little farther, waiting for resistance. She finally forced herself down and took him deep within her. She rocked slowly, then faster, taking him in and out of her. He matched her motion, and buried himself into her as each time she came back to him.

Her wet slick body accepted him, took him, sucked at him. The world disappeared in a mist as he watched her eyes. The trembling started deep within him and he exploded. Grabbing her, he pressed her against his chest as he buried himself in her one last time. "Oh, Lord, Cath."

She clung to him, rocking her body against his. He held her, hunting for her mouth until their lips touched. He kissed her, drawing breath from her.

As the world stopped spinning, he rolled her to his side. She snuggled her head on his shoulder and gave little tugs to the hair on his chest. She shivered against him.

"Cold?" he asked.

She shivered again. "No." Her voice came in a whisper.

He pulled the quilt from the sofa and spread it across them. "I should take you up to bed."

She wrapped her arms around him, pinning him to the floor.

He brushed her hair back from her face. "You're beautiful."

"Ummm."

He stared up at the ceiling. Her body fit with him as if the two were made for each other. She had come to him full of fire and wanting. Nothing had impeded him. As if . . . Some thought nagged at the back of his mind and he tried to retrieve it from the mist. She hadn't seemed the least bit shy about his touching her or looking at her. As if . . .

"Cath?"

"Yes?" she murmured.

"Have you been with a man before?"

"Yes." She brushed her hand across his stomach.

He took her hand in his. "Jack."

"Yuck, no."

"Then . . ."

"At college, I had a steady boyfriend for three years. We lived together for about a year and a half. Then he got a job in Chicago and I didn't want to go with him. That was the end of that." She pushed herself up on one elbow and looked into his face. With a finger, she traced a line from his forehead to his mouth. When her finger stopped, she bent over and kissed him.

He cupped her cheek in his hand and held her so he could study her face. "You lived with him. You—"

"Slept with him. Yeah, but that was several years ago and I never found anyone I wanted to start a relationship with after that."

"You act as if it were nothing." He looked into her eyes. She'd been with another man. A man who had touched her in places he didn't want any other man ever to touch. Before, now, or ever.

"I cared for him. I thought I loved him, but it sort of fizzled out in the end and we were both glad to have an excuse to end it without a scene. He walked away. I waved goodbye and we got on with our lives."

"How can you act that way?" he accused. She acted as though giving her body away was of no importance.

"Don't get me wrong. At twenty I thought he was the

most wonderful man in the world and I madly loved him. If he'd asked me then, I would have gone to the ends of the world with him." She shrugged. "But over time, things just didn't work."

"You never married him?"

"The subject never really came up."

"What?" He sat up, knocking her over.

She looked at him, blinking. "You can't tell me you've never been with a woman before."

"That's different." Men sowed their wild oats, but not with women they intended to wed. He'd never have taken Sarah now if he thought he could convince her to become his wife. He hadn't meant to take her, but touching her had lit fires he couldn't control and they had consumed him.

"Oh, give me a break. It's not like I have sex with every man I meet. One guy in college I had a meaningful relationship with for a while. We were both very young and didn't know what we really wanted. And each other wasn't it." Her eyes sparkled.

"But . . ."

"You talk too much." She pulled him back down. "Come here, shut up, and hold me, please." She snuggled against him.

Her body fit against his. He wanted to hold her forever. But . . . Her breathing had become a slow, regular motion. She was asleep. He stared at the ceiling, wondering what else she hadn't told him.

Sarah looked at the pine tree Joshua had set up in the corner of the living room. She tied another red bow and handed it to Joshua to attach to the tree. She couldn't believe Christmas had arrived so soon. The freshly cut pine tree filled the room with its scent. A fire roared in the fireplace, causing shadows to dance on the walls. She sat in Joshua's chair with the wick turned up on the lamp so she could see what she was doing.

He'd wanted to put candles on the tree, but she refused to let him. Even as a child, her mother had insisted on an artificial tree because the electric lights posed a fire hazard as the tree dried out. Real candles seemed insane to Sarah, though Joshua had just shaken his head when she'd said so, as he often did when she complained. He said understanding her defied him.

She'd never seen a more unusual tree. Instead of the shiny glass balls she put on her artificial tree in her condo, the decorations consisted of bows she'd tied and some snowflakes Rachel had crocheted and starched. On top sat an angel Edna had made for her. She'd embroidered the tiny face so that the angel smiled down. The white lace wings were trimmed with a thin gold braid.

Joshua brought a bowl of popcorn into the living room and set it on the table next to her. He handed her a needle.

She looked at him and laughed. "Know what?"

"You've never strung popcorn for a Christmas tree." He laughed—a laughter that brought joy to Sarah's heart.

"Nope." He seemed happy. He still slept in his room and she in the master bedroom, but they had been closer over the two months since the day of her kidnapping and the events of that night. A warm glow started deep inside her every time she thought of their rendezvous after he'd rescued her. But he'd seemed in no hurry to repeat it since then.

"What did you decorate your tree with?" He threaded a needle and expertly shoved it through a kernel of popcorn.

"Garlands. Ornaments. Many of them belonged to my parents."

"It seems strange not to put the candles on the tree. Henry ordered them especially for that." He continued to put one piece after another on the string.

Sarah threaded her needle and picked up a piece of popcorn. "The whole time I'd be afraid of burning down the house."

"You don't light them except when you're in the room."

She shivered. "I don't care. The tree will look beautiful without candles. The fire gives it plenty of light." The piece of popcorn she was holding cracked in half and fell into her lap. Sarah looked at it, then shrugged and popped it into her mouth. She took a second one, aiming the needle for its center. It fell into her lap instead. "Why do I always feel so clumsy when I try to do these things? You make it look so easy."

"You just have to remember the popcorn is as delicate as the flowers you work with." He grabbed a handful and threw it into his mouth.

She finally got a rhythm going. "I don't think it's fair you put packages under the tree already. Santa doesn't come until Christmas Eve." She eyed the five boxes tied up with ribbon. The last two years since her parents had died, the only presents under her tree had been from LeeAnne and Pete. She'd spent most of the day reading a book or watching movies.

"It's more fun to look at them and try and guess what's in them. Besides, I want you to appreciate all the effort put into the wrapping." He stood and stretched, letting his string of popcorn hang down. "Want a cup of hot chocolate?"

"That would be nice."

When Joshua returned from the kitchen, he sat and started on another strand of popcorn.

"What do you usually do on Christmas?" she asked.

"If it's not storming, then we all go to church in the morning. The minister always preaches in Moose Creek on Christmas Day because of the window. When we get back, Cookie fixes a big dinner. I usually order a few bottles of whiskey for the men." He picked up his cup and took a sip. "Not really a lot. But this year I have you and a Christmas tree, so I had to stick presents under it. It makes it more festive."

She smiled. Holding up her string of popcorn for his appraisal, she said, "You don't usually put up a Christmas tree?"

"Not much sense in it, me being alone."

"Don't the men have one in the bunkhouse?"

"You expect a bunch of cowpokes to decorate a Christmas tree? Heaven knows what they'd put on it. And they would probably burn down the place." He laughed. Standing, he took her popcorn string and placed it on the tree.

"Did you have one?" Joshua asked.

"Always."

"And what did you do for Christmas?" He stood near the fireplace, watching her.

"Slept late, since I didn't have to go to work. Read a book. Watch mo . . . stay in my pj's all day."

"You didn't have anyone to be with?"

"Nope. LeeAnne invited me over to her parents' home the last two years, but Christmas is really a family day. She has all these cousins and nieces and nephews. Her parents' place always has mass confusion."

"I'd think that would be more pleasant than sitting home alone. At least I had the men and could get drunk with them."

"I felt like an intruder." Her family had always been small, and so had the celebrations. Her parents hadn't stayed in touch with the rest of the Martin family. And like her, her mother had been an only child.

He knelt down in front of her. "You don't feel like an intruder here?"

"No. This place is actually starting to feel like home."

"You aren't in such a big hurry to go away?" He held her with his gaze.

"Not until after Christmas and after I see what's in those boxes."

"Greedy wench, aren't you?" He leaned forward and kissed her.

She draped her arms around his neck. When he released her, her eyes twinkled. "You betcha. I just love presents. I always wanted a tree with so many presents around it you couldn't see the base anymore."

"All for you." She'd seemed less miserable as time went on. She smiled more, and she tried to adhere to society's conventions. But she still wouldn't commit herself to him. Even after he'd bedded her. Unfortunately, no child had come of the union. Then she would have had no choice. But then, he didn't want her to marry him just because she carried his child.

"No. I'm willing to share." She leaned her forehead against his. His breath caressed her face.

"Obviously your parents didn't spoil you."

"They didn't believe in that. Besides, my father was a bit of a Scrooge."

"A what?"

"Scrooge. From *A Christmas Carol* by Charles Dickens."

"Umm. He didn't want to spend the money."

"Not on silly things. If I needed something, he bought it for me immediately. I never lacked for anything."

"Didn't that bother your mother?" He stood and scooped her into his arms. Sitting back down, he held her in his lap. She fit so well. Even with the billowing red skirt which buried his legs, she seemed made just to sit in his lap.

"My mother had other concerns. She wasn't much of a holiday person. She only did Christmas because as a little girl I expected Santa. After I was sixteen, I mostly got checks to go buy what I wanted." She leaned her head against his shoulder.

He stroked her hair. Finally it had grown down to her shoulders, but in uneven lengths that always seemed to be in her face. He liked the soft feel of it against his skin. "Didn't you go to church on Christmas?"

"My parents weren't very religious. In fact, I don't ever remember them being in church. They were married by a judge." She traced circles on the back of his hand. "We're not getting the tree decorated."

He looked around her. "We're close to done. It only needs a few more strands of popcorn."

"So who's going to string the rest of the popcorn? The elves?" She pulled her legs up so they rested over the arm of the chair.

"I guess so." He nuzzled her neck. "You seem mighty comfortable, so I guess you aren't going to be inclined to get up and do it."

"If you keep that up, the Christmas tree will be the farthest thing from my mind." She trembled against him and leaned her head back.

He nibbled down her neck. Her hand came up and stroked his cheek. He pushed against it with his face, soaking in the taste and warmth of her body. After only a few months, she had become as important to him as the rising of the sun. She couldn't leave him. If she went home, his reason for living would go with her. "Cath," he said softly, "marry me on Christmas Day."

Chapter 14

SARAH PUT HER finger against his lips. She snuggled her head against his shoulder and kissed his neck. The question could hang in the air, but she would not acknowledge it. She wouldn't let it tarnish Christmas.

His hand stroked her arm and stoked the fire in her. Weeks had passed with nothing between them except a kiss. With her hand, she turned his face to her and captured his lips. She played her tongue along his lips until he opened them. Putting both arms around his neck, she pulled him backward so he leaned over her. "Why don't you carry me up to my bedroom?"

"Sarah Elizabeth." His tone held shock. His eyes, desire.

She traced his ear with her fingertip. "So you really *do* know my name." She pressed her lips against his, holding his head with her hands.

"I have no intentions of sharing that bed with anyone but my wife." He looked at her for a moment, then bent and captured her lips again. She slid from his lap onto the floor,

breaking the contact between them. He reached out and
stroked the side of her face.

She grabbed him by the hands and pulled. He sat, unwill-
ing to move, just watching her.

"Come on now, you have to help some. You weigh too
much for me to move you without your cooperation."

A mischievous grin flitted across his face. "And if I have
no intention of cooperating?"

She knelt in front of him and began to unbutton his shirt.

"Cath, what are you doing?"

"What do you think? You won't come to my bed, we'll
use the floor again. At least we have a fire going this time."

"You're . . . you're . . ." His broad smile made his eyes
crinkle.

"Scandalous. And you love it." She ran her hands over his
bare chest, tweaking his nipples. His muscles beneath her
hands tensed. She unbuttoned the front, pulling the shirt off
his shoulders, but was unable to get any further as Joshua
firmly clamped his arms down on either side and refused to
help her. "Well, hell, this isn't working." She gave up and
leaned her head against his chest.

Joshua's arms went up immediately and encircled her.
She wrapped her arms around his waist. "Not on the floor,"
he whispered.

"Then come and lay next to me and snuggle." She looked
up into his face. Taking his hands, she pulled him to the
floor and laid her head against him.

His arm went around her. He started to open his mouth
and she placed her finger against it. "Just hold me."

For a long time, they lay before the fire entwined in each
other's arms. Her hand rested against the side of his neck.
The hair on his chest tickled her cheek. She sighed.

"What are you thinking about, sweetheart?" Joshua
asked, hugging her.

"Wondering what's in those boxes around the bottom of
the tree." She giggled.

"I'll see if I can give you something else to think about."
He rolled her off his chest and leaned over her. Kissing her

soundly, his hand cupped her breast and teased her nipple through the material. "Now what are you thinking about?"

"Not those presents." She moaned softly.

His mouth traced a pattern around the top of her dress. Her breathing became more rapid. He rolled her to her side. "Let me get those buttons."

"Don't rip them all off. I'm running out of clothes."

He nibbled at the back of her neck and she squirmed beneath him. "I'll sew them all back on for you." His kisses followed his hand that was undoing the buttons. The dress fell forward and his hand slipped inside, gently squeezing her nipple. She shuddered.

He rolled her back to him and looked into her eyes. He wanted to take her. He wanted to sink himself into her once again and feel her heat and moisture engulf him. But he'd promised himself he wouldn't. Not until she married him. He would have her for his wife. But he couldn't stop touching her and feeling her body ask for more. He stripped her dress down to her waist. He studied her bra. "I know how to undo a corset, but this is beyond me."

She laughed. "Just a little hook right there." She placed a finger between her breasts.

He looked at it and tried to slide it open. The damn thing defied him. He reached up and pulled the straps down around her arms so the material didn't hug her so tightly. He captured one breast in his mouth and sucked gently. She moved beneath him and reached for his shoulders.

He lifted her slightly and pulled her dress and slips down around her legs. He traced a path down her stomach with his mouth. She arched against his kisses, pulling at his hair. Gently he pulled the bit of silk material down from her bottom and stared at her. She was glorious. He couldn't imagine a more beautiful woman.

She pulled one leg out of the mound of clothing. Slowly he slipped her panties down one leg, letting his fingertips caress her skin as he went. She quivered and rolled toward him. Removing the material over her foot, he let it drop against the other leg. He rubbed her leg, starting at the ankle and working his way up. He stretched out and cradled her against him as he cupped her bottom in his hand. He captured her lips with his and moved his hand around until it rested between her legs. She twisted and raised one knee. He stroked her gently with his finger as her body tensed against his. She moved in rhythm with his finger.

She pulled her mouth away from his. She gasped for air. She buried her head against his shoulder, clasping at his back. He continued to rub faster and faster. She threw her head back. Her body arched against his and she cried into his shoulder. He continued stroking her while her body arched again, letting her hair caress him. Violently, she threw a leg over him and clung to him.

"Come to me," she whispered.

He crushed her to his chest, letting her body move against his. Grabbing her by the back of the head, he kissed her long and hard, bruising her swollen lips. Her hand moved down his chest and pulled at his belt. He wrapped his fingers around her hand and held it still. She pushed her body into him. "Shhh," he said, stroking her back slowly. Her back radiated more heat than the fire. He kissed her cheek.

"Come to me."

"Not tonight, Cath. Not tonight." He'd brand her with his heat, but not with his seed. When she agreed to marry him, it would be because she wanted him.

He shifted and grabbed the quilt from off the couch. Throwing it over her, he cradled her against him. He was of a mind to fill the tub with cold water from the tap and drown himself in it. That would be the only way the heat that she created in him would escape.

Her breathing became more regular. "Cath, I should take you up to bed."

"Hmmm." She snuggled closer to him.

"Are you awake?"

She nodded her head against his chest.

"Cath."

"I'm trying to sleep here."

"Then I will take you up to bed."

"Only if you're going to stay and hold me," she mumbled.

"No." Holding her naked body against him on the floor pushed the ends of his resolve. He wouldn't share her bed.

"Then I'm sleeping right here."

"We'll both have aches in the morning." And his were not going to be caused by the hard floor.

She drew her arm across his chest. "It's worth it."

"Cath, I have to be up at first light tomorrow."

"It'll come in the windows."

"I'm riding out with the boys."

"That's nice. Be quiet so I can go to sleep." She moved her leg which rested on top of him.

"We'll be gone three days."

"As long as you're here for Christmas or I'm opening the presents without you."

"I wouldn't miss it." Her breath caressed his chest. He needed to move from beneath her. Sweat started to bead on his forehead. "But I don't want you here at the ranch alone. Tom's going to take you into town and then join up with us."

"I'm not going to town," she purred against him.

"Yes you are. It will be safer if you stay with Mrs. Westall."

"I want to stay home. I'll finish the tree while you're gone."

"You can't."

"Of course I can finish the tree. I got the hang of stringing popcorn."

"Cath, you aren't making any sense."

"That's your fault."

He sighed. "You're going to Mrs. Westall's."

She reached up and put her fingers against his mouth. "Nope. I'm staying home."

He kissed them. She'd called his place home. A warm glow added to the heat she stoked in him. "Cath, those two men might still be about."

"Moose Creek doesn't keep enough whiskey for them."

"Cath, you're going."

She didn't answer him. Her fingers lay limply across his face and poked him in the nose. He should move her upstairs.

He could hold her until morning.

• • •

Sarah woke and wondered why the bed was so hard. She pulled the quilt up around her shoulders and reached for the pillow. Her fingers rubbed across the rug. Rolling on her back, she looked up at the Christmas tree. Tucking the quilt behind her, she leaned on one elbow and eyed the packages. Pretty ribbons tied up each box. She could probably use the ribbons in her hair or as chokers after she opened the packages.

What could he have bought her? She felt about five years old, which was probably the last time she'd been excited about Christmas. LeeAnne always bought her jewelry. Pete always gave her a new briefcase. The fact she still used the first one he'd given her and that she had six more stuffed in the closet didn't seem to faze the man.

But Joshua . . . in this little bit of a place, what could he possibly have bought? She wanted to lift the packages and shake them. He'd frown if he caught her. She looked around. She smelled coffee, but didn't hear any noises from the kitchen.

She stood and pulled the quilt around her. The coffee smelled wonderful. With the quilt dragging behind her, she wandered into the kitchen. A plate of biscuits sat on the stove, along with the coffeepot. But the kitchen was empty.

Joshua had said something about riding out with the men. Or had she dreamed that? Probably not. He'd said they needed to get the cattle down to winter pasture before the snow started in the foothills. That must be where he was.

She poured herself a cup of coffee and sat at the table. Three days. Three long days, especially since she had to eat her own cooking. But then it would be Christmas. She still needed to wrap the gloves she'd bought with the money she'd made from selling her floral arrangements. Henry had ordered them, assuring her Joshua would like them. And she did have to finish the tree. She'd find something to do. Like look at her presents.

She picked up her coffee cup and trailed the quilt back to the living room. Setting the cup on the table, she reached for one of the packages. A knock sounded at the back door. She squealed, dropping the quilt and clutching her hand against her pounding heart. "That'll teach me to peek."

The rapping came louder. No one should be about. And she didn't have any clothes on. She'd never get her dress buttoned in time to answer the door. It usually took her half an hour and a lot of cussing over the buttonhook that lay on her bed upstairs.

The back door creaked open. "Miss Sarah, it's me, Tom. I came to take you to town."

"Great," she muttered. "I'm not going," she called to him.

"Mr. Campbell said I wasn't to take no for an answer." She heard footsteps coming across the kitchen.

"Don't come in here." She grabbed the quilt and wrapped it around her. She kicked her clothes behind the chair.

"We need to leave now. I've got the buggy out front. I'll carry out your bag for you." The footsteps came closer.

"I'm not ready." Sarah looked around the room. Her panties lay under the Christmas tree. She quickly picked them up, threw them onto the seat of the chair, and plopped on top of them. Tucking the quilt around her, she pasted a smile on her face.

The skinny young man with brown hair stopped at the edge of the living room. He held his hat in front of him. "How long are you going to be?" He stared at her.

Sarah glanced down. The quilt covered her, but her hair probably stood on end. "I can't possibly be ready before noon, if then."

"Mr. Campbell said you're to go first thing this morning." Tom weaved back and forth from foot to foot.

"He didn't wake me up and I'm not ready. I can't go at the moment." She needed a bath before she got dressed. Plus she had to finish the tree and wrap Joshua's present. There wouldn't be time when he got back.

Besides, at Mrs. Westall's she'd have to use the outhouse and go without a bath. She didn't want to go there. The likelihood of those two men returning was nil. And if she kept Joshua's rifle with her and the doors locked, she'd be just fine until he got back.

"He said I'm to take you no matter what you say."

She looked him straight in the eye. He couldn't be but eighteen and looked as nervous as a rat in the sights of a cat. "Oh, well. He didn't consult me. I'm not going, so go along and do whatever you have to do."

"I have to stay right here until you're ready to go. Mr. Campbell made that very clear."

"He did, did he? Well for your information. I was about to take a bath and believe me, I'm not dressed to go to town. So you're going to be waiting quite a while."

"I don't think Mr. Campbell would like it if I waited while you bathed, ma'am." The boy looked down at his toes. "That wouldn't be proper. So we'd best go now."

"Dressed in a quilt? Give me a break."

The boy's face turned as red as her hidden dress. "Yes, ma'am." He continued to stare at the tips of his boots. His hat brim curled in his fingers.

"I'm not going. Period. I have things to do. If you're determined to stand guard, fine, but you have to do it outside." She shoved her panties down the chair cushion, stood, and moved toward Tom.

He backed up several steps. "Mr. Campbell's gonna be real angry."

She pushed past him and headed down the hall. "It won't be the first time, and he'll get over it."

She heard Tom's boots click against the floor as he followed her. She reached one hand out from under the quilt and grabbed a pot, then went to the sink and pumped water into it. Carefully lifting it, she carried it to the stove to heat. "Would you like a cup of coffee?"

"No, Miss Sarah. I really think we should be going. Mr. Campbell will be expectin' me to catch up with them 'for noon."

"Oh, well." She poured herself another cup of coffee and sat at the table to drink it. After she soaked out the kinks from sleeping on the floor with a nice bath, maybe she'd be in the mood to consider whether she'd give in and go to town. But not before a bath.

She lay her head on the table next to the cup and shut her eyes. A nap seemed like an even better idea. Using Joshua's body for a pillow had been wonderful, but she still felt bone weary.

She pushed the coffee aside, stood up, and removed the water from the stove. "I'm going to take a nap. Make yourself at home—as long as it's downstairs." She walked over to where Joshua kept his rifle, hoisted it up, turned, and walked out of the kitchen.

Sarah stretched her legs and arms. She looked at the string of popcorn lying across her lap and wondered how many hours she'd been sitting stringing the stuff. Shaking it out, she got up and placed it on the tree. She stood back and surveyed her work. It looked good.

She smiled to herself. She'd tucked her present to Joshua behind the ones he'd put out for her. The tree was finished and she was ready for Christmas. Darkness had crept up on her and her stomach grumbled. The time to fix dinner had come. She wondered what had become of Tom. The last she knew, he still stood on sentry duty outside the back door. She could at least try and feed the young man without poisoning him.

The back door slammed open. She grabbed for the rifle and cocked it. She stood frozen, listening, pointing the rifle toward the hallway.

"Cath." Joshua's voice boomed down the hallway and flooded the living room. "Cath, where the hell are you?"

She let the rifle point dip toward the floor. "In here," she called back.

He stomped into the room. Stopping at the door, he glared at her. "Why didn't you go to town?"

"And hello to you too." She stared back at him.

"Answer the question." He crossed his arms and tapped his foot.

"Don't take that tone with me, buster." She flounced past him, snatching his hat from his head. "And remove your hat in the house." She flipped it down the hallway toward the kitchen.

He made a grab for her and she twisted away. "Cath," he yelled after her.

Tilting her head upward, she walked into the kitchen and banged a frying pan onto the top of the stove.

His footsteps echoed in the hallway behind her. "Cath."

She turned and glared at him. "What?"

"You're supposed to be at Mrs. Westall's. Why didn't you go?" His voice came in angry tones.

She turned back to the stove.

He took her by the shoulders and turned her to face him. She pushed away his hands. "Do not touch me," she spat at him.

"You didn't have any objection last night," he snapped.

She moved away from him, still clutching the rifle in her hand. "Don't ever touch me in anger." She raised the tip of the rifle.

"Why don't you ever do what you're told?" His hands balled into fists at his side.

"Because you're not my boss and I'll do as I please. If that doesn't suit you, then I'll leave. But if I leave, I won't be coming back."

His eyes flashed. "You're not going anywhere."

"I thought I was supposed to be gone."

He walked over and wrenched the rifle away from her. Leaning it against the side of the cupboard, he looked back at her. "I didn't want you to be alone."

"I had things to do and I don't want to go to Mrs. Westall's."

"You're the most pigheaded woman I've ever met." He picked up the frying pan and slammed it back down on the stove. The clanging noise bounced off walls all around the room, carrying the force of his anger.

Sarah squared her shoulders and straightened her back. "You ain't seen pigheaded yet." She turned and stomped toward the hallway.

"Cath . . ."

"What!" she hollered over her shoulder.

"Cath, come back."

"Go to hell."

She stomped up the stairs and slammed her bedroom door. He could be so irritating.

A loud rapping came at the door.

"Go away."

"No."

"Then go to hell."

"Cath, open the door."

"Or what? You'll break it down?" She sat down in front of her dresser, her arms crossed on the surface.

"No."

She listened to the silence. She didn't hear his footsteps leaving.

The rapping came again. "Cath, I want to talk with you."

"No."

"Cath . . ."

"Go away." She glared into the mirror.

"No."

She stomped over to the door and flung it open. It crashed against the wall. "What?"

"You scared the wits out of me." He looked down at her. His eyes threatened to swallow her.

She put her hand against his chest, puzzled. "What do you mean?"

"When Tom didn't show up, I thought something had happened to you!"

"I told you I was staying here."

"I didn't believe you."

"A fine time to start thinking I wouldn't do what I said." She shook her head. "When have I ever not done exactly what I said I would do?"

"Never." He smiled at her.

"So why would you think this time would be different?" She patted his chest.

He captured her hand and kissed the palm. "Because."

"That's a lousy answer."

"Isn't it, though?" He looked at her for a long moment. "It isn't safe here alone."

"I kept the doors locked and the rifle with me. I'd have shot any strangers coming in." She tilted her head and smiled at him.

"You can't stay here by yourself."

"I had Tom."

"I need him." He kissed her hand again.

"Then you should have taken him with you. And you should have locked the back door when you left. He walked in on me before I had time to get dressed."

Joshua's eyebrows rose.

"I had a quilt." She started to laugh. "It was a good thing, too. He'd have died of mortification if I hadn't."

"Will you please go to Mrs. Westall's tomorrow, for me? So I can get my work done without worrying myself half to death. Cookie says I'm worthless as it is." His eyes pleaded with her.

"I'll think about it." She slipped her arm into his. "Will you fix me dinner?"

"I'll think about it."

She slapped him on the arm. "You'd better feed Tom, too."

Christmas Eve had arrived and Sarah had a date with LeeAnne to go shopping. LeeAnne loved fighting the crowds for last-minute bargains. Sarah had no plans to buy anything, but LeeAnne wanted a new ski suit for her jaunt to the mountains with Paul, the new man in her life.

Sarah sipped coffee at the outdoor cafe, waiting for LeeAnne. She spotted her coming through the crowd. Her blond hair bounced and a smile lit up her face. She put her hands on her hips, coming to a stop in front of Sarah's table. "Let's go. I've got two presents to buy, plus what I need for my trip. Time's a-wasting."

Sarah smiled up at her. "You're always in such a hurry. Let me finish my coffee."

LeeAnne cocked her head to one side and grimaced. She reached for the cup. "You drink too much of that stuff." Turning, she tossed the cup into a trash can.

"Thanks a lot." Sarah grabbed her bag and fell into step beside LeeAnne. "Where to?"

"Robinson/May." LeeAnne practically skipped down the mall. "Do you have any shopping to do?"

"No. The stores don't get rich off me at Christmas." Sarah

looked at the Christmas tree in the center of the mall. It stood at least fifteen feet high and the lights flashed. Large gold balls with red bows stood out against the white flocking. "That's a fire hazard," she remarked.

When she got no answer, she turned. LeeAnne had vanished. Turning slowly in a circle, Sarah looked at the storefronts trying to figure out which one LeeAnne had rushed into. Something on sale must have caught her eye.

Completing the circle, she stared where the tree had been. A dark hallway now extended in front of her. LeeAnne wouldn't have gone that way. Sarah looked back over her shoulder. The darkness surrounded her. Footsteps sounded behind her. Footsteps made by cowboy boots. Clutching her purse to her, she hurried ahead. The boots followed her. She started to run. Her breath came in ragged gulps and her heart pounded in her ears.

At the end of the dark tunnel, a dim light shone. Sarah kicked off her heels and ran for it, her stockinged feet soundless against the floor. The light didn't come any closer. Her side ached. She paused and leaned against the cold, damp wall and tried to pull breath into her lungs. She could hear the footsteps coming closer.

Sarah started to run again. She dropped her handbag, but didn't stop to pick it up. The footsteps would catch her if she stopped again. The hair on the back of her neck prickled.

A crash sounded far away.

Sarah sat straight up in bed, her hand over her mouth. She gasped for breath. Clutching the quilt to her, she peered into the semidarkness. She let out a sigh. Another bad dream. Still, they didn't come as often as they had before and at least Jack hadn't been in this one. She listened. The fire still crackled in the fireplace. An owl hooted outside. She jumped at the sound.

Such silliness. She fell back on the bed and pulled the covers up. The darkness pressed down on her. She scooted to the edge of the bed and patted the table with her hand, searching for the matches to light the lamp. When she found them, she started to strike one—then paused.

The floor downstairs creaked. The hallway only made

that noise when someone walked across it. Someone was prowling around down there.

Joshua. He'd gone down to the bathroom. She listened. The noise sounded like boot steps. Joshua wouldn't wear his boots to the bathroom.

Chapter 15

SARAH LEAPT FROM the bed and raced to the door. Slowly, she opened it a crack and stared into the hallway. She listened, hearing the kitchen door bump into the hallway wall. She flew down the hallway, quietly opened the door to Joshua's bedroom, and slid into the room. She leaned against the closed door, her hands behind her still clutching the knob. Outside a large tree blocked the window, allowing precious little moonlight into the darkness of his bedroom. A tiny glow came from the fireplace but did little to illuminate as well.

She blinked, trying to make out any shape. Making out the shape of the bed, she jumped on it and threw her arms around Joshua's neck.

"What?" His voice boomed around her. He sat straight up, carrying her with him.

She clamped her hand over his mouth. "Be quiet. Someone's in the house. Downstairs." She clung to him.

"Huh?" His arm went around her and he pulled her down on the bed as he fell backward.

She shook him. "Wake up."

"I'm awake," he mumbled.

The table in the hallway crashed. Joshua shoved her aside and she rolled off the bed with a thud. "Stay down," he hissed at her.

Sarah flattened herself on the floor and crawled under the bed. Scooting to the edge, she raised the skirt that hung to the floor and peered out. They were upstairs now. A silhouette crept toward the door clutching a knife. She heard her bedroom door bang against the wall. She curled the material of the bedskirt in her hand. Joshua silently opened his bedroom door and crept into the hall.

Edging out from under the bed, Sarah crawled after him. At the doorway she stopped, peeking around its edge. Three silhouettes graced the hallway, one crouched, the other two erect.

"The woman's gone." She recognized Caleb's voice.

"Can't be far," Trent answered him.

Joshua hugged the wall, moving stealthily toward the other two shapes. Sarah held her breath. Trent would have a gun. Joshua carried only his knife. His rifle still leaned against the cupboard in the kitchen. The house didn't have a back stairs so she could creep down and retrieve it.

The two men continued down the upstairs hall and opened the next door to an empty room. Joshua moved toward them.

"Damn," muttered Caleb. "We're going to have to get a lantern. She must have heard us and hid."

"Try the rest of the rooms first," said Trent.

"I'm tired of wandering around in the dark. I've banged up both of my shins. Go back and get the lantern out of the bedroom. She obviously slept in there until I fell over the damn table. She didn't go downstairs 'cuz we would have collided, so she's got to be hiding in one of these rooms," Caleb said.

Trent disappeared into Sarah's room. She stood and held onto the doorframe as she looked out. The air rushed from her lungs as Joshua lunged for Caleb. Both men thudded into the wall and fell to the floor. As they tumbled over each other, Sarah couldn't distinguish one man from the other.

She stepped back into Joshua's room. She could hide under the bed, but that would be the first place someone would look. Or the closet. Except it was a wooden wardrobe and barely large enough to conceal her. She could try crawling out the window and getting Tom to help. But she'd probably break her leg jumping from the second story—and Joshua could be dead by then.

"What the hell . . ." She heard Trent's voice.

Her hand rested on the dresser next to the door. She picked up the washbowl and looked into the hallway. The two shadows still rolled on the floor. The third silhouette came out of her bedroom. With the tiny bit of light coming from her room, she could see Trent's pistol in his hand. He pointed it toward the rolling bodies. A hand came up from the fracas, holding a knife, and stabbed back down. A groan came from the jumble of men.

"No!" she screamed. She flung the washbowl as hard as she could toward the standing man. It splintered against the wall.

"Damn," yelled Trent. The report of his pistol reverberated down the hall and the flash blinded Sarah. As she stepped back into Joshua's room her fingers wrapped around the handle of the water pitcher that had been resting on the dresser next to the washbowl. Raising it above her head, she started into the hall.

The two figures on the floor had separated. One lay still. The other knelt on one knee, his head hanging, his hand searching for something.

Joshua couldn't be dead. She wouldn't be responsible for his death. She should have gone to Mrs. Westall's—then this wouldn't be happening.

Trent started to move toward the kneeling figure, his gun raised. "Caleb, that you?"

Sarah let out the scream that had been building since she'd first heard the footsteps. It swirled out and around and down the hall, increasing in volume. Holding her nightgown in one hand and the raised pitcher in the other, she raced straight for Trent. He stopped dead in his tracks. As the pitcher crashed into his head, splinters of porcelain flew about them. He crumpled to the ground and passed out.

She swiveled and pointed the broken handle at the figure on the floor. "Don't you move," she hissed.

The bent figure stopped the search of the floor with his hand. "Cath, it's okay." Joshua's voice reached out and caressed her.

Sarah dropped the broken china to the floor and hurled herself at him. They fell backward in a heap. Joshua's arms went around her, hugging her to his body.

"Are you okay?" she asked, kissing his face.

"Fine."

"I thought that you were dead and I was next." She hiccupped.

Joshua laughed softly. "Hell, if you hadn't clobbered the man, you would have scared him to death with that scream." He pushed them up to a sitting position.

"He was going to shoot you." She nestled against his shoulder.

"Poor man didn't stand a chance." He kissed her.

She smacked him against his chest. "Poor man, indeed."

"I'd better get a lantern and see to these two." He picked her up and started toward his bedroom.

A violent pounding started at the back door.

"I'll let Tom in," Sarah said as he set her down inside his room.

"You'd better put on my boots first or you'll cut the bottom of your feet on the broken porcelain." He ruffled her hair. "Thank you."

"For what?" She wrapped her arms around his chest and hugged him.

"For caring." He held her tightly for a moment. The pounding continued. "Best answer the door before he breaks it down. And tell him to bring me plenty of rope."

"What are you going to do with them?" Sarah asked.

"The one you called Trent we'll take to town and send for the circuit judge. The other one's dead." Joshua's voice was cold.

A shiver ran through Sarah. The pounding continued. "I'm coming," she shouted. "I'm coming."

Sarah snuggled deeper under the blankets. Time seemed to have settled into a slow, steady rhythm since both Christmas and the two stage robbers had made their appearance. Trent had been locked in Henry's basement until after the new year when the judge could come to town. Both she and Rachel had been called to testify. The trial had been swift, with a guilty verdict handed down on all three counts: murder, stage robbery, and kidnapping. The finer points had been swept away along with yesterday's dust.

The hanging had taken place the next day. Even though a storm had just passed through and the temperature was bitter cold, everyone who could showed up. Everyone except Sarah, that is. She had no desire to watch someone hang. It all seemed rather macabre to her, especially the party afterward. She'd stayed at the ranch. Joshua, being one of the town council, had gone as a witness.

Since then, nothing much had happened except lots of winter storms. For what seemed like the first time in months, the sun peeked through the window hitting Sarah's face as she lay in bed. She was more than content just to lie there and let the sun's faint warmth run all over her. In the past weeks, the snow had blown into enormous piles surrounding the house and the temperature had dropped to the point where she never wanted to get out of bed. More than ever, Sarah longed to be back in her own world with her sweats, fuzzy slippers, and central heating.

She peeked over the top of the blanket at the fireplace across the room. Sometime in the middle of the night the fire had burned out, leaving the room freezing. Even with her long nightgown, she couldn't bear leaving the warmth of the bed long enough to get dressed.

The smell of coffee brewing crept around the edges of the door. She knew Joshua was already in the kitchen, fixing breakfast. He expected her downstairs.

"Cath, it's ready," he called from the bottom of the stairs. She groaned. Keeping the blankets around her, she rolled

over to see if she could reach her jeans without getting out
of bed. She pulled them on under her nightgown. Taking a
deep breath, she threw back the covers and jumped out of
the bed. Shivering, she pulled on a pair of Joshua's socks,
three slips, and a skirt. She pulled a blanket around her while
she got up the courage to pull off her nightgown and put on
a shirt. She could light the fire, but by the time the room
warmed up, breakfast would be cold.

Quickly she threw the nightgown toward the bed, ignoring it as it slithered to the floor. She yanked on a camisole,
a blouse, and one of Joshua's heavy shirts. She reminded
herself of a bag lady who wore everything she owned. Her
teeth chattering and her arms hugged about herself, she hurried downstairs to the kitchen.

She went and stood next to the stove and held her hands
out over it.

"It's not that cold," said Joshua.

She turned to look at him. "Maybe not to you."

He laughed. "At least it keeps you clothed."

She stuck her tongue out at him. She poured herself a cup
of coffee and sat down at the table. Joshua placed a plate of
flapjacks in front of her. She lowered her head so the steam
embraced her face.

"What are your plans for today?" Joshua took a sip of his
coffee.

She shrugged and picked up her fork. "I don't know. I've
read all the books this town has. I've run out of dried flowers. Your accounts are caught up."

"The storm's over for the moment, though another seems
to be gathering on the horizon. We could go for a ride."

She groaned. "No more snow. I can't take another storm."

"It'll be over soon and spring will be here." He rocked his
chair back.

"One of these days you're going to fall over and crack
your skull." She chewed on her pancakes. Pointing her fork
at him, she asked, "How soon is spring?"

"We've just come into March. A few more weeks. Unless
we get a really late snowstorm."

She stopped chewing and stared at him. "March. Already?"

"Yes, Cath. You've been here nearly six months. It's time you made some decisions about what you're going to do. You don't seem set on hurrying back to where you came from and things can't go on the way they are." He let the chair settle back on its four legs and propped his elbows on the table.

She waved her hand at him. "What day in March?"

"The fifth. That got a special meaning?"

Her mind flashed back to her grandmother's diary. Rachel's first baby had been stillborn on the fourth of March, born way too early. No one had come to notify them. But the wind had only let up some time during the night. "Can we get into town?"

"Not by buggy." He watched her.

"By horse?" She let her fork drop onto her plate with a clang.

"If we want, but I don't know what's in town. Rachel already has more flower arrangements than she'll ever sell. Unless you want to visit the church again."

"No." Sarah rose from the table. "I don't think the church window likes me." She walked around to him and pulled on his arm. "Come on. I have to see Rachel."

"Why?" He took her hand and held it.

"I can't explain. I just have to see Rachel."

"Cath, you can never explain." He frowned at her. "I thought we could spend the day together. I could show you how glorious the countryside is when it's blanketed by snow."

"Yuck. I hate snow. That's why I lived in Southern California." She wrinkled her nose. She had to convince him to take her to town. She knew Rachel would be all right, but she'd need a shoulder to cry on. She'd need other women around her.

Sarah needed to see Rachel.

"More snow's coming. I don't think it's a good idea to head for town. We could get caught in the storm before we get back."

"Please take me to town to see Rachel." She looked down into his green eyes and suddenly realized just how much she missed the green trees and grass. When he walked away into a blizzard next winter, she would be alone in this horrid, cold place with no one. The thought bore down on her like the snow weighed down the trees. "Please."

He looked at her for a long moment. "It's that important?"

She nodded her head. "Yes."

"Alright. A short visit only. We have to be home before the next storm hits."

"Okay. Let's get going."

"Then you best get dressed to go."

"All I need is boots." She smiled at him and tugged at his arm. "Get up and get the horses."

"Don't you think you should put on pants rather than a dress?"

She lifted her skirt. "They're under here." She headed for the back door. She pulled on one of his jackets, shoved her feet into the boots he'd given her for Christmas, then wrapped her cape around her.

"You are the most unusual woman. In the summer, you can't keep on clothes. In the winter, you wear more clothes than any person I've ever met."

"It's cold out there."

Joshua watched Sarah swing her leg over the horse's rump and slide to the ground in front of the Martins' store. Something had put a burr in her saddle. She couldn't even wait for him to help her dismount. All the way to town she'd given him one-word answers and chewed her bottom lip. Something worried her, he knew, but she wasn't going to be forthcoming about it. She was inside the store before he could dismount.

Joshua tied the horses to the hitching post and followed her into the store. He removed his hat and looked for her. She stood in the back hugging Rachel. Then she stepped back and looked Rachel up and down.

"You're fine?" Sarah asked.

"Just as fine as can be." Rachel disentangled herself from

Sarah. "I don't know what you were worried about. The babe isn't due until nearly summer."

"I know. I was just worried." Sarah turned around and looked at Joshua. She smiled. "Rachel's just fine."

"I can see that. I rode all the way through the snow with a storm forming in the mountains just so you could tell me that." He walked up to the two women. "The least you can do is buy me a piece of licorice for my troubles."

Sarah looped her arm through his. "The baby's just fine. He's kicking and everything."

"Babies do that," Joshua replied, reaching for the candy jar.

"I'm surprised to see you," said Henry as he came from the back room. "We haven't had any business since the storm started. We're just tidying up the place. About to close up for the day. Why don't you come upstairs for a cup of coffee?"

"I'd love that," said Joshua.

"Or we could go out in the back room and smoke a pipe." Henry looked at Joshua.

"I'll join you if the women want to go upstairs and chat." Joshua hugged Sarah.

"I'm sure they will," said Henry. "What are you doing in town in this weather?"

"Cath was worried about Rachel and nothing would do but to bring her to town to check on your missus. We're not staying long, though. We have to head back to the ranch before the snow starts again."

Sarah took her arm away from Joshua and moved over to Rachel. "You're sure you're feeling fine?"

"Absolutely." Rachel smiled at her. "Let's go upstairs and I'll fix you a cup of coffee while the men jaw."

"You're not drinking a lot of coffee, are you?" Sarah asked as she pursed her lips together.

"No. I've been drinking milk and only one cup of coffee in the morning and a cup of tea at night." Rachel took Sarah by the arm.

"That woman of yours sure does fuss a lot over having a

baby," said Henry. He pulled his tobacco from beneath the counter and tapped it into the bowl of his pipe.

"She's not mine." Joshua looked at Sarah. With all her clothing, she took up twice as much space as usual. Her eyebrows pulled together and her mouth turned down as she questioned Rachel. With the answers, a smile lit up her face. Maybe someday he'd understand her but he didn't count on it.

Sarah turned to Joshua. Her eyes sparkled. "I want to go to the church."

"You said the church didn't like you." Joshua shook his head. Women weren't made for understanding. That was the fact of it. Even at age one hundred he'd never figure out what action to expect next.

"How can a church not like you?" asked Rachel. A puzzled look crossed her face.

"Best not ask that one," said Joshua. "Sometimes it's just better to let things lie with Cath."

Sarah glared at him. "I'm going to the church."

"Not alone. Last time you went alone, those two men ran off with you." He held out his arm to her. "I'll go with you."

"I want to be alone." She looked up at him, not taking his arm.

"Fine. I'll stand guard outside the door." Joshua nodded his head to Rachel and Henry. "Start the coffee. We won't be long, I don't think."

"Not long," Sarah said over her shoulder, waving her hand at them.

"That is the prayingest woman I've ever seen the likes of, considering she won't properly marry Joshua," muttered Henry.

"Figuring her out is half the fun," Joshua replied.

Sarah pinched his arm.

Sarah walked into the church and stared up at the window. Slowly she walked down the aisle. The sun had disappeared and the window had a dull, muted look. "Not a day to go home, is it?" she said softly.

She sank into a pew. "He stole my heart and it's your fault

because you wouldn't let me go home." She rested her chin on her hands against the back of the pew in front of her. "I don't know what to do. I've changed things. My coming here has made everyone's life different than before. First my great-grandmother got kidnapped in the stagecoach holdup. Now the baby seems fine. I know she should have miscarried yesterday." Sarah sighed and studied the window.

"You aren't going to give me any answers, are you?" She leaned back and stretched out her legs. "It isn't so terrible here, except I don't have much to do. I don't want to be a housewife. But I want to be Joshua's wife. Tell me. Have I changed that part of history, too?"

She studied the window. Practically no light came through it and Jesus had become little more than a shadow. "You're not going to reveal any secrets. Not today. Not any day." She closed her eyes and remembered home. Of everything and everybody she'd left behind, she missed LeeAnne the most. LeeAnne always knew how to cheer her up and make her laugh. She kept her from being just a computer geek and got her out and about to enjoy life.

She did miss her job and Pete. Pete would find someone to help him once they'd figured out she wouldn't return. They'd probably blame Jack, but without a body, it would be hard to prove murder. She'd just hope they didn't mourn her too long. If only she could get a message to them.

Things here were the same, yet different. Her grandparents were still happy, which was a good thing. The child she descended from wouldn't be born until a year from June. That baby had to come. And she saw no reason why it wouldn't.

She looked up at the window again. The darkness grew. "I guess you're not going to let me leave. You brought me here to stay, didn't you?" She stared, looking for any sign. Receiving none, she said, "I guess I'd better make some decisions and figure out how I'm going to get on with life."

Sarah sighed and stood. Taking one last look at the window, she left the church. Joshua was waiting outside. She looped her arm around his and together they walked down the steps. Snowflakes drifted down and sprinkled them with white.

"If we leave this instant, we might make it home." Joshua looked up at the sky. "But probably we'd get stuck somewhere along the road. I hope Mrs. Westall will put us up."

Sarah patted his arm. "You're not upset, are you?"

"Naw. A night in town won't hurt, but the sleeping arrangements might be a bit difficult. Mrs. Westall only has one spare room and she isn't going to let both of us occupy it."

"Henry and Rachel will put up one of us."

Joshua pulled her to a stop and turned her to face him. Lifting her chin, he looked into her eyes. "Did you find what you were looking for in the church? You seem lost in thought."

"I guess I am. Being in the church gave me a lot to think about." She smiled at him. "Come on. I'm freezing to death." She stared up at him for a moment. "Do you think I'll ever get used to the cold?"

"I don't know, but I promise I'll buy you extra clothes if you don't." He took her hand and led her to the store.

Henry had left the door unlocked and they let themselves in. Joshua secured the door behind them and followed Sarah upstairs. A roaring fire greeted them. Sarah draped her cape and his coat over a table and went to stand in front of the fire. She held her hands out to warm them.

"I have coffee for you," said Rachel.

Sarah turned and took the cup. "Thank you. I'm just so cold all the time. Sometimes I don't think I'll ever defrost." She let the steam rise into her face to warm it. Rachel sat on the couch and picked up her knitting needles. Henry sat in his chair, watching his wife. He fiddled with his pipe. Joshua sat down on the other end of the couch and balanced his hand on his knee.

"We're going to have to impose on someone's hospitality for the night." Joshua picked up his cup of coffee. "The storm's moving in fast and I don't want to get caught in it."

"We'd love to have you stay for supper." Rachel looked up from her knitting, but her fingers never slowed. "I planned on fixing fried chicken."

"That would be a nice change from beef." Sarah watched

them. Everyone seemed so relaxed, as if drop-in company happened everyday.

"We'll put Sarah up and you can go to Edna's after supper if the snow's not coming down so hard you can't see," said Henry. "If that happens, I guess you can bunk on the sofa."

Rachel held up the tiny sweater she knitted and examined it. "Guess it's about time to put on supper. Come along, Sarah, and you can help me."

"I'm not much use in the kitchen except to peel vegetables." Sarah unbuttoned Joshua's shirt and removed it. Finally the heat from the fire had warmed her to the bone.

"That's the truth." Joshua laughed.

Sarah wrinkled her nose at him. "I try."

"And you're getting better. The last piece of meat she fixed me I could cut." Joshua stretched out his legs. "But I'd be glad to help."

Rachel set her knitting aside. "Men just get underfoot."

"Not always," said Sarah. "It's a good thing, too, or we'd starve."

Everyone laughed.

Sarah shrugged her shoulders. "I can't help it. My mother couldn't cook, so she didn't teach me."

"A curious family you come from," said Henry. He rolled a match between two fingers.

Sarah laughed. "More curious than you realize." She took a deep breath. "Has anyone ever thought about starting a school in this town?"

"Not a lot of young'uns about." Henry laid his pipe down.

"I've seen ten or twelve who appear to be school age." Sarah looked from one man to the other.

"The town doesn't have money to pay a teacher or to get supplies," said Joshua. "We thought about it a while back but, quite honestly, we couldn't find anyone who wanted to come here and teach. I guess we don't have a lot to offer."

"How do the children learn?" Sarah gripped her hands behind her back.

"Their mothers teach them." Rachel rose from the couch.

"If their mothers can't read and cipher, then they don't learn either."

"That's a shame," said Sarah.

"As the town grows, there'll be more of a call for a school," said Henry.

"But wouldn't you like to have an established school for your children?" asked Sarah.

"We've got plenty of time." Henry reached for his pipe and started to rise. "Joshua, let's go downstairs so I can have a smoke while the women fix supper."

"I'd like to start a school," said Sarah. She held her breath.

Henry dropped back into his chair. "That wouldn't be seemly."

"And why not?" Sarah looked him straight in the eyes.

The color rose in his face. "Most folks accept you because of Joshua. But they wouldn't accept a woman like you teaching their children."

"And what kind of woman am I?" Sarah demanded.

"Now, Sarah," said Rachel. "My Henry doesn't mean anything. But with you living under the same roof as Joshua and not being wed and all, it doesn't look proper. Makes people nervous."

"Is that the only reason?" asked Sarah. She looked at Joshua, who just smiled.

"You haven't any experience that we know of," said Henry. "We'd want a good teacher."

"Cath went to college," Joshua stated.

Rachel looked at her. "I didn't realize that, dear. Which college did you attend?"

Oooops. Now I've stepped in it. She tried to think of a college on the West Coast that had been around for a long time, but she hadn't the faintest idea when any of the colleges had been founded. "One in Los Angeles. I haven't taught, but I'm sure I could."

"Why would you want to?" asked Henry.

"Because I'm bored. I need something to do and I'm a bust at cooking and cleaning." She crossed her arms in front of her and held her body rigid. If she was stuck in this place, she had to find something to do besides sit around all day.

Joshua stared at Sarah. His mouth drew into a thin line.

"The town can't afford to pay," said Henry.

"Each child could pay what they could afford. I'm sure we could find some books or buy a few. Maybe we could have a fund-raiser." She picked at the sleeve of her dress. Joshua just kept staring at her, not saying a word.

"A what?" asked Rachel.

"Have a party and everybody pays something to come. Or sell cakes and pies or knit goods or something to raise money for starting the school." Sarah looked at Joshua. His expression didn't change.

"Might work," said Henry. "It's something to think about, anyway." He rose from his chair.

"Does this mean you're planning on staying?" Joshua's voice froze as it left his mouth.

"If I'm to become the teacher, I'd have to stay." She smiled at him.

"And move into town and support yourself." Anger shone in his eyes.

She looked at him for a long moment. "Actually, I thought I'd make an honest woman of myself and marry you."

Chapter 16

Rachel rushed across the room and threw her arms around Sarah. "That's wonderful."

"It's about time," grumbled Henry.

Joshua stared at Sarah. She watched him. His eyes grew dark. Suddenly he stood, crammed his hat on his head, and stormed out of the room, slamming the door behind him.

Rachel turned to look in the direction of the door. "What's the matter with him?"

Sarah shrugged. She'd thought he'd be happy she'd finally decided to marry him. She couldn't count the number of times he'd asked her. He repeatedly said he wanted her to be his wife. She'd held out because she wanted to go home, but the hope of that faded with each day. And now that Rachel hadn't lost her first child, a new hope sprang up. Joshua might not be lost in the snowstorm next winter. She held to the hope they'd have a long life together.

She'd made up her mind. With Joshua, she could survive in this time and place.

Henry started for the door. "I'll see what's chewing at

him." He put his pipe in his mouth and held a box of matches in his other hand.

"Wait," said Sarah, softly. "I'd better go after him and straighten this out. I'm the one who messed things up again."

"As you wish—but I'm going down and have a smoke." He stomped out the door.

"Now whatever is the matter with him?" asked Rachel.

"With men, who knows?" Sarah reached for her coat and cape. "He probably doesn't think I should marry Joshua."

"Henry can be a bit rigid at times, but he'll come around. If Joshua is happy, that's all that matters to him." Rachel patted Sarah's arm. "Now you go and straighten things out with Joshua while I start supper." She smiled and hugged Sarah.

Sarah walked down the stairs, trailing her hand along the railing. She guessed she'd best approach this situation head-on. Joshua stood on the porch in front of the store, looking out into the storm. As she opened the door, a blast of cold air cut into her. She wrapped her arms around herself and walked over and stood next to Joshua. "You want to tell me what's the matter with you?"

He turned and looked down at her. Then he turned away, stepped off the porch, and started across the street.

"Joshua Campbell, you come back here. Don't you dare walk away from me." Snow flurries whipped around her.

He stopped. "Go back inside, Cath, before you freeze to death."

She stepped into the street and grabbed him by the arm. Roughly, he pulled his arm free. "I'm not going in until you talk to me."

"Leave me be, Cath." He crossed his arms across his chest.

"I thought it would make you happy if I decided to marry you." She shivered in the cold and wiped snow from her eyes.

He turned to face her. His eyes were as cold as the weather. "You might have consulted with me before you blurted it to the world."

"I didn't blurt it to the world. Just Rachel and Henry. And they're friends." She glared back at him.

He stood for a long time staring at her. The snow covered the brim of his hat. "Why?"

"Why what?"

"Why now? You've been adamant about not being my wife. You've made that very clear. Now suddenly you make this grand announcement."

"I changed my mind. Can't I change my mind?"

"Not without one hell of a good reason."

She waved her hands in the air. "I *have* one hell of a good reason."

"So you can be a schoolteacher. You can marry me, then be respectful enough to get a job."

"One has nothing to do with the other."

"I don't see that. You can't teach school and live with me the way you do now. People wouldn't let you." The muscle along his jaw twitched.

"I know that. But the school was just an idea, because I need something to keep busy." She tapped her foot. "You have the ranch. I have nothing."

"Being my wife should be enough."

"It isn't. Being a wife doesn't take all day. You're gone most of the time. I get lonely."

"You could learn to do what other wives do."

"Yeah, right. We both know how good I am at that."

"And how do you know you'll be any good at teaching?"

"I don't." She crossed her hands and pulled them to herself, trying to keep out the cold. "But at least I've had more practice at that than cooking. I used to tutor for extra money in college."

"Fine. Be a teacher. Mrs. Westall will keep you so you'll be close to town." He turned away again.

"Joshua." He kept walking.

Sarah ran after him. "Stop. Please stop."

He stopped abruptly and she bounced off his back, falling down in the snow. She picked herself up and dusted off her skirts. "Being a teacher isn't the prime motivating factor here."

He looked at her blankly.

"We were talking about getting married. If you're that dead set against my being a teacher, well . . ." She shrugged her shoulders. "I'll find something else to do. I haven't gone completely stir-crazy yet."

"You're talking about getting married. I had no say in the matter."

"Is that what you're so angry about?" She studied his face. His jaws were clenched so tight that the veins bulged in his neck and it looked to Sarah like his head might split in two.

"I never agreed to marry you."

"No, you didn't, but you asked."

"Not for months."

"I'm sorry. I shouldn't have assumed. It's just . . ." She let her hands fall to her sides. "If you don't want to get married, then so be it."

"I didn't say I didn't want to get married." He took his hat from his head and knocked the snow off of it.

"Then what is the problem?" Sarah felt that their disagreement ran in circles, neither of them coming to the same point at the same time.

"A man likes to ask." He ran his fingers through his hair and placed his hat back on his head.

"So ask."

"You haven't told me why you had a sudden change of heart."

"I'm staying."

"Just like that."

"I guess I was staying since I arrived. It just took me a while to figure it out."

"So, now you figure that since you're trapped here with no way to go home, you'll give in and consent to marry me."

"I didn't mean it to sound that way." Sarah tucked her hands under her armpits for warmth.

"You'll do so because you have no choice."

"I never said that."

"Sounded that way to me."

"If I remember right, after Catherine died, you told me I'd do fine as a substitute."

"That was different."

"In a pig's eye. You wanted a wife and I happened to be handy, so I'd do. I didn't want to be just a substitute." She stomped her feet, trying to get the blood flowing. "I waited to see if I thought we'd make it as a couple."

"And?"

"Yes. I think we'd be good together."

He looked into her eyes. "Maybe I don't want a wife, now."

"What?"

"Why should I marry what I can have without?" Joshua smirked at her.

Sarah looked at him. Her mouth fell open. She sputtered.

"I have you now if I want you. Then when I'm tired of you and find a woman who makes a proper wife, I can be rid of you."

"Why, you pig!" Sarah slapped him across the face with all of her strength. She turned and stomped across the street, into the store, and up the stairs. After she threw herself down on the couch, she crossed her arms and huddled in its corner.

Rachel came out of the kitchen. "What's the matter?"

"Men. I hate them."

Rachel sat down next to Sarah and took her hand. "You don't mean that."

"I most certainly do. He . . . he . . . he called me a . . . I'm never speaking to him again." For the first time in her life she was truly alone. When her parents had been killed, LeeAnne had been there. Her work had kept her busy. Now she was stranded in a time and place where she had nothing. And now, no one. She'd have to move in with Mrs. Westall until she could figure out where she'd go. And how would she make a living to support herself? Hopefully Mrs. Westall would take credit.

Her world had abruptly become as dark and cold as the one outside.

"Now, Sarah, you don't mean that." Rachel's voice held

the familiar tone she used when trying to smooth things
over.

"Oh, yes, I do. I'll move in with Mrs. Westall as soon as
the storm lets up. Then I guess I'll take the next stage to
somewhere."

"Sarah, I know Joshua wants you for his wife. He's said
so often enough." Rachel wiped her hands on her apron. "A
good meal and you'll feel better."

"What he said and what he meant don't quite come together. He wants a proper wife and I don't fit the bill." She
remembered why she'd shied away from men. They were a
lot more trouble than they were worth.

"I'll have Henry talk to him. He'll be fine."

"The man's a pig. I have no intention of going back to
him." Sarah looked at Rachel. "Don't let it upset you. That's
not good for the baby. I'll survive. Not long ago I told my
best friend I could survive anywhere. I guess now I'm about
to find out if it's true. When's the next stage due?"

"Not until spring," said Rachel.

"Swell."

Joshua mounted his horse and headed toward the ranch. He
had no desire to be in anyone's company. He'd finally gotten his wish. Sarah had agreed to marry him. And what had
he done? Made a jackass out of himself. He certainly wasn't
going to stay around and listen to Henry tell him so or see
the look of confusion and hurt in Sarah's eyes.

He wanted her for his wife. So why had he blown up like that
and said those things? Deep inside he still didn't believe
that after all these months she had finally decided to marry him.
She'd been so set on going home. Something had made her
change her mind and until he knew what, he wouldn't believe
she really meant she wanted to stay.

The horse slowed to a walk, picking his way through the
snow. He probably should have gone to Mrs. Westall's, but
by now, even with the storm, the whole town would have
heard about his fight with Sarah. Hell, arguing in the middle
of the street as they did, they'd probably given the town gos-
sips enough to keep them busy for weeks. He rubbed his

face. It still stung where she'd slapped him. A well-deserved slap, he had to admit.

The ride home would give him time to cool off and to think. He pulled the collar of his coat up around his ears and yanked down on his hat. The snow pelted him unmercifully. He kept his head bent.

Tomorrow, when the snow stopped, he'd have to make the trip back into town and apologize for the remarks he'd made. He'd tell Sarah he'd accept her announcement. He needed something to give her to make up for his stupidity. Flowers were out of the question. Hopefully, Henry had something in the store he could buy. A dress length of fabric would not bring a smile to Sarah's eyes either.

The snow grew worse. The wind whipped against him. He hadn't thought the storm would turn into a blizzard. His stupidity had grown to stampede proportions. Not only had he insulted the woman he wanted for his wife, but he'd ridden off in the middle of a blizzard.

But the question of why she'd changed her mind still worried him like a burr under a saddle. It just didn't feel right. And before he agreed to take her as his wife, he'd have to know the answer.

Sarah awoke with a start. The darkness of the room confused her. She couldn't remember where she was. Brushing her hair out of her face, she looked about. This wasn't home. Not hers. Not Joshua's.

It all flooded back. Her announcement. Joshua's anger. The fight. His rude remarks. Her slapping him.

The aloneness crashed in on her. Rachel said she could stay a few days until Joshua came to his senses, but Sarah didn't know if she wanted that. She'd been bounced around enough. She thought he cared for her, that she'd become more than a substitute for the dead Catherine. But his attitude and remarks belied her belief. And she didn't care if she was stranded in 1870. She wouldn't take that attitude from any man.

She crept out of bed and pulled the quilt with her. Her great-grandparents' house was colder than Joshua's, if that could be possible. But what she missed most was the bathroom. Chamber pots were the most disgusting things anyone had ever invented, though they ranked somewhat better than trying to go to the outhouse in this storm.

She wanted to go home. Not to Joshua's, but to her condo. Even though she still had a psycho after her back in her own time, she'd have heat and a flush toilet. And she'd gotten pretty good at handling psychos. Anything had to be better than being on her own in 1870 Moose Creek, Wyoming.

She pulled on her dress and wandered out. She could smell coffee and bacon frying. Joshua never made bacon. He never fixed anything but beef. But then, he had a constant supply.

In the kitchen she poured herself a cup of coffee and sat at the table. "Good morning." She tried to smile, but it took more energy than she could muster.

"Morning," Henry answered.

"Are you feeling better this morning?" Rachel stood at the stove cooking. She made it look so easy.

"No." Sarah took a sip from her cup.

"I still don't know what all the fuss is about." Henry reached for a slice of toast.

"The man is a . . . You wouldn't understand." Sarah looked at her grandfather. "Hell, I don't even understand what happened. All I know is Joshua walked off and made it very clear he didn't want me for his wife and I'm not staying around here to be kicked in the teeth."

Henry shook his head. "If you'd be more ladylike, he wouldn't have any objections."

"Oh, give me a break. The man had no objections at all until I said I'd marry him." She stood up and stomped toward the living room.

"Sarah, dear, come back and eat your breakfast," Rachel called after her.

"I lost my appetite." Sarah plunked down on the couch and sipped her coffee.

"Now see what you did. You upset her." Sarah could hear Rachel scolding Henry.

"Me. What'd I do?" Henry asked.

Just like a man. They never knew what they did. Sarah never could understand them.

She heaved a sigh. She had to make plans. If she went somewhere else, she could start over with an untarnished reputation. She'd have to leave the church and the window behind, but she didn't think the window would agree to transport her home, anyway.

She could try Los Angeles. There must be something she could do to survive. Getting there would be the problem. She didn't have enough money for a stage ticket. She'd made five dollars from her flower arrangements, but had spent three on Christmas presents for Joshua. Two dollars wouldn't take her very far, even in 1870.

She listened to the wind whistle around the building. The storm seemed determined to last forever. Maybe she should just walk out into it and get lost. No one would miss her.

"I'm going over to Mrs. Westall's and fetch Joshua." Henry stomped by her. "We need to get this straightened out if I'm ever to have some peace and quiet again." He shook his head as he walked. He clutched his pipe in his hand.

"You can't go out in this storm." Sarah watched as he pulled on his coat.

"It's better than sitting here listening to two women go on." He slammed the door as he left.

Sarah walked back into the kitchen. "I didn't mean to cause a fight between you two."

Rachel turned and smiled at Sarah. "You didn't, dear. My Henry never fights with me. He always sees the reason of doing what I want."

Sarah laughed. Never in her wildest dreams had she imagined her great-grandfather as henpecked. But then, she'd never imagined many things about her great-grandparents. They were a matched pair, to be certain.

"Sit and eat. You can't make any decisions on an empty stomach." Rachel set a plate in front of her.

Sarah picked at her eggs and bacon. She really wanted a bagel and cream cheese. She wanted her cell phone to work so she could dial LeeAnne. She wanted this damn snow to stop and the weather to get warm.

Rachel sat at the table with her. "I think your plan for the school is a fine one. Every town should have a school."

"I don't think I'll be around long enough to see it to fruition."

Rachel patted her hand. "Sometimes men can be difficult, but with a little time, they can be managed."

"You know, you're nothing like I expected you to be." Sarah pushed her plate away.

Rachel gave her a quizzical look. "What do you mean by that, dear?"

Henry stomped back in. "He's not at Edna's. Never showed up last night."

"What do you mean he's not there?" A knot gripped Sarah's stomach. He didn't get lost in a blizzard this winter. Her arrival couldn't have moved the event up a year. That wouldn't be fair.

"He didn't go there. Probably rode back to the ranch." Henry turned and walked out of the room. "I'm going for a smoke."

"He wouldn't be that stupid, would he?" Sarah looked at Rachel.

"Don't worry. Joshua knows where he's going and can take care of himself." Rachel stood and picked up the plates from the table.

"I'll do the dishes."

"Nonsense. Sit and enjoy your coffee." Rachel started to pump the water.

"It's the least I can do to pay for your hospitality. You should sit and rest some, anyway." Sarah took Rachel by the shoulders and turned her around. "You go knit."

"Nonsense. I'm not sick. I don't need to rest."

"You'd better enjoy it while you can. Soon you'll be chasing a passel of children and won't have any time to rest." Everything had turned into such a muddle. Rachel's baby had survived, so far, but Joshua had ridden off into a blizzard. Things weren't supposed to happen this way.

She wished she'd never left Los Angeles.

• • • •

It had been a week, and the snow had finally melted enough that Sarah figured she could ride out to the ranch. She needed to get her clothes. After a week in the same ones, she could hardly stand it.

But mostly, she had to make sure Joshua was okay. No one had heard from him since the night he'd ridden off into the storm.

Henry had gone down to the store to open it up while Rachel cleaned up the breakfast dishes. Sarah had told Rachel where she was headed. She went down the steps and slipped out while Henry waited on an early-morning customer. Hopefully someone would be at the stable to saddle her horse for her, because that she couldn't do by herself.

She stepped off the porch and collided with Joshua. She wanted to throw her arms around his neck and kiss him. Never in her life had she been so glad to see anyone. She stepped back and looked up at him. "Why did you pull such a stupid stunt?"

"And hello to you too." He gave her an exaggerated bow. "I was just coming to find you."

"Do you realize you scared me half to death? I thought you'd been lost in the blizzard and were dead." She crossed her arms and tapped her foot.

"Now why would you think that?"

"Because you disappeared in the worst storm of the winter."

"I'm glad to know you care." He smiled at her. "I've come to take you home."

"Just like that."

"Yes." He reached for her arm.

"I don't think so." She stepped away from him.

"I'm sorry, Cath. I shouldn't have said what I did." He took off his hat and held it in his hand. "You just caught me by surprise."

"You're damn right you shouldn't have said what you did." She turned her back to him.

He circled around her. "Cath, please forgive me. Come home and we'll talk."

"I'm not going home with you. I'll send for my clothes.

"I'm moving in with Mrs. Westall until the stage comes in the spring. Then I'm leaving."

"You can't leave." He grabbed her by the shoulders.

She shook him off. "I can do anything I want. And I can tell you, buster, I'm not staying where I'm not wanted."

"I won't let you go to Mrs. Westall's."

"You have no say." She swiped at her eyes. Never would he see her cry.

"Cath, be reasonable."

"I am being reasonable."

"I thought you were going to marry me."

"You made it very clear you didn't want me."

People had started to gather around the front of the store.

"You're creating a scene." Sarah turned to walk away.

"I'm going to follow you wherever you go. To the ends of the earth if I have to." Joshua's voice rose in volume.

"Will you be quiet?" she hissed at him. "People are watching."

"Let them. I made a jackass out of myself the other night. If I could, I'd take back everything I said." He held his hand out to her. "I want you to come home with me."

She batted away his hand. "No."

He bent down on one knee. "Sarah Elizabeth, will you do me the honor of becoming my wife?"

She stared at him. "Get up."

"Not until you say yes."

"No. Now get up out of the dirt." She turned and walked toward Mrs. Westall's house.

"Cath, please," Joshua called after her.

"Go away, Joshua Campbell." She covered her ears. "I can't hear you."

"Marry me, Cath."

"No." She turned and looked. He followed her on his knees.

She hung her head and shook it. The crowd by the store had grown. For the life of her she couldn't figure out where all these people had come from. In fact until now, she had never known that so many people actually lived in Moose Creek. Heat flushed her face. "If I say yes, will you get up?"

He nodded as he crept closer to her.

"Yes," she whispered.

"What?"

"Yes."

"Yes, what?"

"Yes, I'll marry you."

He placed his hand behind his ear and cocked his head. "I can't hear you."

"Yes, Joshua Campbell, I'll marry you," she yelled at him. "Can you hear me now?"

He smiled, stood, and took her into his arms, kissing her. The crowd cheered.

"Now will you sneak me out of town?" she whispered in his ear.

He laughed, then picked her up and swung her around in a circle. Calling to the people on the store steps, he asked, "When is the minister due?"

"In about two months," replied Henry. "He left just before the storm."

Sarah looked around the kitchen. This had become her home. Here she is, here she would stay for the rest of her life. She poured a cup of coffee and sat down at the table. Life had fallen into a quiet routine. The weather had finally started to warm with the coming of April.

Mrs. Westall and Rachel had consented to make her a wedding dress. Not the white satin of which she had always dreamed, but a pale-green dress trimmed with lace and roses. The two women had chosen the material and told her she could use it for festive occasions after the wedding—as if anything in Moose Creek required getting dressed to the nines! But the dress would be beautiful when they finished, and they were delighted.

Rachel had tried to teach Sarah to knit and, after a fashion, she was getting the knack of it. Sarah had made a baby blanket for Rachel. The design had been rectangular, but the blanket defied all of her attempts at making it so. Mrs. Westall said Rachel would love it anyway.

For the first time in her life, Sarah had more than one

woman friend. She rather enjoyed the exchanges, even though they took place at irregular intervals because Joshua still wouldn't allow her to ride into town by herself.

Sarah stretched, feeling lazy. She guessed she'd better enjoy it. The idea of a school had been met with great enthusiasm by the townspeople. They decided they would like it started by September. Getting things ready would keep Sarah busy.

But first, she would get married. The minister would be back in a month. She didn't have much to do in the meantime. Mrs. Westall and Rachel did all of the planning. And Sarah decided she *would* master the fine art of making biscuits before she got married. It just didn't seem fair that something everyone else made look so simple proved to be so complicated for her. She could set up a networking system with computers without blinking an eye, and yet she couldn't produce an edible biscuit.

She stood up. Now was as good a time as any. Joshua had ridden out two days ago with his men except for Tom, who had stayed behind to keep a watch on her and the ranch. However, he kept to himself so she didn't have to worry about anyone observing her pitiful attempts at cooking.

Sarah pulled the bowl from the cupboard and set it on the table. She was alone. And homesick. She loved Joshua, but she still missed her old life, especially LeeAnne. She'd always imagined LeeAnne as her maid of honor at her wedding. She sat back down and pushed the bowl aside. At least when Joshua was around, she didn't get as lonely. She could ride into town, but Joshua would have a fit when he found out, and he would find out.

She wanted to go home to her old life. She wanted to stay and marry Joshua. She laid her head on her arms on the table. "This is ridiculous," she chided herself. Self-pity would get her nowhere.

But . . .

Upstairs in her backpack lay her Walkman. She could listen to it and no one would bother her. Joshua wasn't due back for two more days. She could bring her Walkman downstairs and listen to her music while she cooked. She'd only used it once or twice, and for very short periods of time. The batteries should still work.

She jumped up and scurried upstairs. She put on the headphones and turned the machine on. Music floated out. "Yes!" She clipped the small CD player to the waistband of her jeans and danced her way back to the kitchen.

This was much better. She lit the stove, then picked up the bowl from the table. Sliding across the room in her socks, she pursed her lips while she measured in the ingredients. She stirred the mixture with a spoon and wondered if she'd gotten the amounts correct. It would help her a great deal if people would use measuring cups instead of a blob of this and a pinch of that. What a way to cook.

It didn't matter. No one would be subjected to the results except her. She picked up a pitcher of water and placed both it and the bowl on the table. Slowly she started pouring in the water, stirring in time to the music.

Joshua opened the gate to the corral and released his horse into it. He'd find Tom to take care of the animal, then surprise Sarah. His crew needed more supplies, since Cookie had dumped a bag of flour off the wagon into a stream. Joshua could have sent one of the men, but it gave him an excuse to go back to the ranch house and see Sarah for a few minutes. He couldn't stay long. His men would be wanting their supper.

He opened the back door and could hear Sarah singing loudly. Placing his hat and coat on the pegs, he opened the kitchen door. She stood at the table, mixing something. He smiled. Hopefully, she wouldn't poison herself while he worked on the range.

He stopped and watched her. She bounced from side to side, then shook her bottom. Holding the spoon above her head, she waved it, singing a song he'd never heard before. She shook her whole body, bouncing from foot to foot. It appeared she was dancing. At least he guessed it must be a dance of some sort.

She did a spin, clutching the bowl to her chest. She stopped dead, her mouth hanging open, her eyes wide, star-

ing at him. Quickly she set the bowl on the table. She
yanked at her shirt, untucking it. It bunched at one side of
her waist. She swept her hand through her hair. Music blared
across the room. She fumbled at her waist and the music
stopped.

"Hi." She smiled at him, not moving.

"What are you doing?" He walked toward her.

"Practicing my biscuit-making." She moved to the stove.
"Want some coffee?" She poured two cups and slid into the
chair at the end of the table.

He stood beside her and rubbed his finger from the bridge
of her nose downward. "I can tell you've been in the flour.
You're wearing it."

"Really." She made no move to wipe her face.

"What did I hear?"

"I don't know. What did you hear?" She blinked up at
him.

"Strange music."

"Really?"

"Cath, I want a straight answer." He bent over and lowered his face to hers.

"If you heard music, then you heard music." She tried to
scoot the chair back, but Joshua grabbed the back, pinning
her between his arms.

"What is that thing?" He nodded his head toward her
waist.

She clamped her elbows to her waist and looked around
the room. "What particular thing are you talking about?"

He pulled her out of the chair. He realized he'd walked in
on something he wasn't supposed to see. More than biscuit-
making had been going on in his kitchen. And it had something to do with all those months of unanswered questions.

He reached for her waist and pulled off the strange,
slightly oval box. A cord wound up and around her neck.
She stood perfectly still while he gently took the cord and
the tiniest little earmuffs he'd ever seen from her neck.
"This. What is this?"

Sarah looked at him, expressionless. But her eyes flashed

as if she were trying to figure out what to say. Instead, she just stood there.

He pushed one of the buttons on the box. Music roared from the earmuffs. His fingers slipped from the box and he held it suspended by its cord. Sarah jumped for it.

"Please be careful. It'll break if you drop it." She looked at the box wistfully.

He handed it back to her. "It means a lot to you, doesn't it?"

She nodded.

"Then tell me what it is."

She looked up into his face. "It's a CD player."

He stared at her. She cradled the player against her chest. He didn't understand. He wasn't sure he wanted to. That strange box could mean the end of everything as he knew it. A shiver ran up his spine. That box could bring disaster. "What's it for?"

"To play music." Her tone sounded as though she talked about how much flour they should buy at the store.

"I figured that much out on my own."

Silence settled between them like fog on an autumn morning. He knew the right questions to ask hid in his head somewhere. He just couldn't find them.

"Where'd you get it?"

"I brought it with me." She clipped the box back to her jeans and hung the wire about her neck. She fiddled with something on the box, and the music came out again, softer.

"Music doesn't come out of boxes, Cath. It's like a whole band is inside that little thing." Joshua's head started to throb. He ran his fingers through his hair. Often he hadn't understood Sarah, but what he saw now was impossible.

She nodded her head. "Where I come from it does."

"And where do you come from?" He held his breath. Something about the look on her face told him he shouldn't have asked that question. He didn't want to know.

"From the future."

Chapter 17

JOSHUA SAT DOWN abruptly and stared at Sarah. He shook his head. No doubt existed in his mind. She'd escaped from an asylum, which explained many things.

Sarah wiped her hands on her pant legs, then crossed her arms. She watched him carefully, suddenly sitting down at the table and picking up her coffee cup.

Their silence covered them like a shroud, echoed by the mournful music from her box as background.

She sipped her coffee. Banging the cup on the table, spilling her coffee, she said, "I can't stand it. Say something."

"What, Cath? What is there to say?"

"I don't know. Laugh. Yell. Have some reaction. Don't just sit there and stare at me."

"Is this why you wouldn't tell us who you were and where you came from?" He reached out and took her hand, patting it. She was delusional, crazy.

"I came from Los Angeles just like I said. I'm Sarah Elizabeth." She held his gaze, never wavering.

"And Jack?"

"Jack's a psycho killer who was stalking me. It's all his fault. If he hadn't been obsessed with me for no reason, I never would have come to Moose Creek and . . . and . . . oh, hell, I don't know and what." The wailing music leaked sadness into the room.

Joshua shook his head. He had to get help for her. "Can I contact someone in Los Angeles? They must be worried about you."

She laughed, a hysterical edge tingeing the sound. "I'm sure LeeAnne and Pete are worried sick. They probably figure Jack caught up with me and hid my body somewhere after he cut me up." She shivered. "But no one I know in Los Angeles is even born yet."

"It'll be all right, Cath." He continued patting her hand. She had been bruised when she arrived. Had whoever been her caretakers hurt her? He'd heard asylums were dark, dreadful places and horrible things occurred in them. Was that why she'd run away? Jack could have been just a delusion or possibly another inmate. "I'm sure whoever you ran away from was just trying to help you. I'm sure they didn't mean to hurt you."

"Excuse me!" She jerked her hand away. "Jack was trying to kill me. That kind of help I don't need."

"What's your surname, Cath?" He reached for her hand, but she pulled it out of his reach.

"Cath?"

"What?" She clasped her hands together in her lap, the knuckles turning white.

"Are you going to answer me?"

"No."

"I'm going to send Tom out to the camp with the supplies." He stood and walked toward the back door. "Then we'll discuss this some more." He could never tell the Martins the truth of the situation, or Mrs. Westall, unless he wanted the whole town to know Sarah's mind was unbalanced.

But he had to tell them something about the upcoming marriage. Under the circumstances, he couldn't marry Sarah until he found out who she really was, whether she was dangerous, or whether she just lived in a fantasy world she'd created.

Joshua could send a telegram, but then he'd have to take Henry into his confidence. Henry disliked Sarah enough already. He'd have her locked away. Joshua wouldn't let them put Sarah in Henry's basement while he sorted through this. If she had escaped from an asylum, he'd return her himself. Or find a way to care for her. He'd have to write to Los Angeles, to the sheriff. The sheriff would know who to contact to find out if someone missed Sarah.

But while he waited for the truth, he had to make sure she never had an opportunity to hurt anyone. Just in case. He'd stay with her when she went to visit Rachel. He couldn't take the chance that Rachel or the baby would come to harm.

Not until he was sure about Sarah.

He looked at her sitting at the table drinking coffee. She appeared perfectly normal. As normal as she ever did in her jeans and his shirt, covered with flour.

But thinking she came from the future belied the picture.

Sarah rose to refill her cup while Joshua went to find Tom. She had to think of some way to convince him she wasn't a candidate for a rubber room. Hell, if Joshua had said to her he'd traveled through time, she'd have been pretty skeptical herself, up until she'd met the church window. Now, she could just about believe anything.

Joshua sat back down at the table and reached for her hand. She liked the rough feel of his skin against hers. She'd become rather accustomed to his little touches when they shared a meal or just sat and talked.

But the look in his eyes foretold doom. He didn't believe her. She wondered if he would make plans to lock her away. If the roles were reversed, she'd have already called 911 to get the "men with the white coats." She giggled, making a strangled, hiccupping sound.

"Cath, I don't see anything funny."

"You're not looking at it from my perspective." She

grinned at him. "I realize you think I'm loony, but I can prove I'm from the future."

Joshua just shook his head.

She could tell him things that would really make him shake his head—like walking on the moon. Recounting her history wouldn't be very convincing, though. He'd have no way to confirm it. "What do you want to know?"

"Where you really come from."

"The Los Angeles area a little more than a hundred and twenty years from now."

"Cath, that isn't possible."

"Believe me, I'd have said the same thing before I found myself in the church with Mrs. Westall clucking over me. Talk about a head rush." She looked into his eyes—eyes filled with questions. Questions to which he feared the answers. "At first I just thought I'd gotten caught in a bad dream because of all the stress I'd been under thanks to Jack."

"Why would you come to Moose Creek, of all the places you could choose from?"

His expression didn't change. She pulled her hand from his, a creepy feeling running up her spine. Rubbing her hands against her jeans, she tried to figure out the best way to explain everything without getting herself into more trouble. "I had family from Moose Creek. I wanted to trace my roots."

"Anyone I know?"

"Yeah." She stood and put more wood into the stove, then flipped back the top of the coffeepot and peered into it. "Want more coffee?" She walked over to the sink and pumped water. The time had come to tell him who she was, but she didn't know if she was ready.

"Who?"

Sarah set the coffeepot on the stove and turned to look at him. She crossed her arms, hugging herself, hoping this world wouldn't crumble. She had nothing else. "Maybe it would be best if we went upstairs. I have things in my bag to prove who I am." She walked out of the room.

Joshua stood to follow her. When they got to her room,

he sat down next to her on her bed. He'd planned on sharing this room with his wife. Maybe Sarah had been right. He never would get married. First Catherine had been killed, now this.

She took her brown leather backpack and dumped it upside down on the bed, its contents spilling out. Turning off the CD player, she laid it with the rest of her belongings. She smiled at him. "Not much to show for who I am but it's all I've got." She picked up a small black object and hugged it to her. Then she flipped open the front and pushed a button. A beep sounded. "This is a cell phone. It doesn't work, though." She sighed and handed it to him.

"A cell phone?"

"A telephone. To call people, only portable."

He handed it back to her and shrugged.

"No phones yet, huh? Okay." She pursed her lips together, grasping for an explanation. "Like a telegraph line, but instead of just transmitting clicks, you can actually hear the other person's voice. I can talk to people all over the world with a phone. Cell phones, though, are more limited because they don't transmit along lines in the same way, but through cells."

He gave her a blank stare. "Voices can't be transmitted. Especially not through the air."

"Not now maybe, but they can in the future. The first phone will be invented by Alexander Graham Bell within the next twenty years."

This wasn't working. She sighed again and picked up a tan leather wallet. "Let's try this. You asked what my surname was. Well, it's Martin, Sarah Elizabeth Martin." She pulled a card from the wallet and handed it to Joshua.

He stared at the hard, shiny card. A colored picture of Sarah was embossed on one corner. Printed at the top in large letters was California and DMV. Next it stated "driver license" with a number printed below that. SARAH ELIZABETH MARTIN was printed in small black letters. A faint picture showed behind the printing and when he turned the card in the light he could see the picture repeated, or the letters DMV. "Expires 11–03–99" appeared above the picture. He ran his fingers over it. It was shiny and hard, unlike anything he'd ever seen before. "What's it for?"

"It's a driver's license. So I can drive a car." She clutched the wallet.

"A what?"

"A car. A horseless carriage."

"Really, Cath. You can't expect me to believe that." He stared at the colored picture of her and the black ink.

"Why not? Steamboats run on engines. Ford just made a smaller version, an internal combustion engine, so you don't have to stoke it with coal—which would be extremely awkward when you're driving." She was rambling to keep the silence at bay, trying to get something, anything, to register on his face except blankness.

"I can prove it." She pulled two heavy pieces of paper from her wallet. "Here. Pictures of LeeAnne alone and LeeAnne with me and Pete in front of my car when I bought it."

He took the photographs and looked at them. LeeAnne wore short pants and a pink camisole. Pete leaned against a large, blue object. He'd seen photographs before, but never colored ones. "How did you get the color in these?"

"Most photos are in color in my time. But see my car?" She placed her finger on the Camaro. "It's a sports model that's supposed to go like one hundred and fifty miles per hour, but I'd never go that fast because I'd crash and die if I didn't scare myself to death first. I'm a really cautious driver because insurance is so expensive and you really don't care." She looked into his eyes. "You don't believe me, do you?"

"I'd like to." He really wanted to believe what she said, but how could he. It pushed his imagination beyond the possibilities he knew. Telegrams with voices and buggies without horses that went 150 miles per hour. Trains couldn't even go that fast. He turned the photographs over. "January 6, 1997" was printed on the back. He turned it back and stared at the two women in the picture. One was definitely Sarah, only with long hair. "I see you're not the only woman who likes to go about undressed."

Sarah leaned forward and looked at the picture. "We're dressed just fine. Shorts and tank tops are acceptable clothing in the nineteen-nineties."

Joshua was lost in thought. Women parading around half-dressed. Objects that played music. Strange things this future of hers held. But . . . could she have made this up? He looked at her. "Why'd you pick the name Martin?" He held up the driver's license.

"My dad was a Martin and since I've never been married, I still go by the name." She pulled her credit cards out of her wallet and handed them to him. "See? Martin on every one of them. That's who I am. Sarah Elizabeth Martin, grandchild, several generations removed, to Rachel and Henry."

"Cath . . ."

"I know it's hard to believe. But I found Rachel's diary in my grandmother's attic when she died. It fascinated me. So when Jack wouldn't leave me alone, I decided to take a vacation and see if Moose Creek still existed and if the church window remained. Rachel wrote about how magnificent it appeared. It seemed like a really good idea at the time. I figured Jack would never think to look in Moose Creek. No one had ever heard of the place. I could hide out for a few days, play tourist, and then when Jack fixated on someone else, I could go home." She raised her hands and let them drop into her lap. "It's just that the window won't let me go home. And . . ." She smiled at him. "I don't want to go home anymore. I want to stay here with you."

He reached over and patted her hand. "I know, Cath, but—"

"But, what? Don't you want to get married?" She glared at him.

"I have to think." He handed her back her things and stood up. "I have to sort things out. Maybe we should wait a bit longer before we get married." Tomorrow he'd send letters to Los Angeles. Maybe something would come back to explain all of this. He knew she said her name was Martin, but he didn't believe it. He didn't believe any of it. He couldn't explain the cards, the photographs, or the music, but he couldn't accept her story either. After pondering on it a while, maybe it would make sense.

"And what are you going to tell Rachel and Mrs. Westall? As we speak, they're preparing the finest wedding this town has ever seen." She clasped her pictures to her heart.

"I'll think of something." He turned and walked toward the door. "I have some work to do in my study, then I'll fix supper."

She watched him walk away. Holding up the picture of LeeAnne, she grimaced. "You know, I wouldn't believe me either, LeeAnne. Where are you when I need you?"

Sarah rolled over and laid her head on her arm. Life kept taking the most bizarre turns. Just once, she wished it would stop destroying her world the way the paper shredder in her office tore documents to bits.

Joshua walked Sarah into the Martins' store. Rachel waddled over to her and gave her a big hug. "Have you managed to change that man's mind about the wedding yet?"

"No." Sarah shook her head. "How are you feeling?"

"Tired. Awkward. Ready for this little one to be on his own." Rachel rested her hand on her belly.

"Come with me to Mrs. Westall's," said Sarah, pulling gently on Rachel's hand. "I need to visit with her for a minute and I'm sure Henry can survive without you."

Rachel looked at Henry, who nodded his head. "Joshua coming with us? He hasn't let you out of his sight for six weeks."

"No. He's staying here and visiting with Henry so we women can have a chance to talk without him sticking his nose in." Sarah took Rachel's arm and moved her toward the door.

Joshua followed them as far as the door and watched them walk across the street. Once they'd disappeared into Mrs. Westall's house he knew Rachel would be safe. Sarah and Mrs. Westall were giving Rachel a surprise baby shower and plenty of women would be in attendance. He turned back to Henry.

"Got some letters here for you." Henry held the envelopes out.

" 'Bout time." Joshua had never figured on it taking six weeks to hear back from the sheriff in Los Angeles about Sarah. He'd been hard put to come up with an excuse not to marry Sarah when the minister had shown up last week. Rachel and Mrs. Westall were still miffed about it. They hadn't believed him when he'd said some business in Los Angeles had to be straightened out for Sarah before the wedding could take place. He thought he'd be hog-tied and carried into the church protesting. Never for a minute did he doubt the two women thought of doing just that. And he wouldn't have blamed them. Sometimes he believed it was his mind that had become unseated instead of Sarah's. He'd watched her constantly and she seemed just as she always had, except she was miffed at him, too, and seemed to bang pans often when she did dishes. Maybe she did come from the future.

But how could she?

The letter had to hold the answer. Then maybe his thoughts would stop flipping like flapjacks on a grill. The minister would be back July 4 and Joshua had to figure out what to do before then.

"I don't know why you don't just marry the woman," Henry said.

Joshua looked up at him. "I have my reasons."

Henry lit his pipe. "Can't see what a little business has to do with anything. Either you're going to marry her or you aren't. And the way you look at her, you might just as well marry her and be done with it already."

Joshua laughed darkly. "I wish it were that easy, old friend."

"What more is there?" Henry took a long drag on his pipe. "You suppose the women will be gone a while so as the smoke will be gone before they get back?"

"Knowing them, they'll be gone for hours. Give a woman an excuse to be with other women and they don't hurry." Joshua stared at the letters. Now that they had arrived, he didn't want to face what they might tell him.

"Good." Henry took another draw on his pipe. "Means business will be slow and I can enjoy my pipe." He leaned against the counter. "You going to open those letters or try to read them through the envelopes?"

Joshua ripped open the one from the sheriff. The man's scrawl was hard to decipher. But the man hadn't heard of Sarah under her name and no one fitting her description had been reported missing.

Joshua looked at the other letter. It came from the asylum. He ripped it open. The neat and precise handwriting stated no patients had escaped their institution and no one had ever heard of Sarah. The letter did state, however, many folks kept troubled family members locked up at home, and the hospital had no way of knowing about those people.

Joshua crumpled the letters in his hand. They offered no help to his dilemma. He didn't know where else to inquire. She said she came from Los Angeles, but she could just as well have come from Texas or New York. He'd never be able to write every sheriff in the country. He'd never find the answer. His decision would have to come from within. His heart said to take her at her word and marry her. His head screamed that she was a raving lunatic.

He placed the paper in Henry's flour scale and struck a match.

"What are you doing? I measure food in that." Henry reached out to stop Joshua.

"It'll wash." Joshua held Henry's hand away and laid the match on the letters. "I never received these, all right?"

Henry stared at Joshua. "Being around that woman is affecting your mind."

"Could be." She didn't seem dangerous. She'd never tried to hurt anyone except in self-defense. He watched the paper curl on the edges and turn to ash. The fire took not only the paper, but his hopes of ever finding out exactly who Sarah was.

He wanted her for his wife. Since the first time he'd seen her, he'd wanted her. But he didn't know if he trusted her. She told such strange stories and he'd been regaled with many in the last six weeks as she kept trying to convince him she came from a distant time.

Harmless and delusional would be no problem. But what if the delusions grew worse and she harmed any children they bore together? A decision had to be made, and locking her away from the world tore at his heart.

But what if she wasn't delusional?

"Well," said Henry, "are you going to marry the woman or not?"

"I've got until the Fourth of July to decide. I'll let you know."

"You still don't believe me, do you?" Sarah sat next to Joshua in the buggy on the way back to the ranch.

"No."

"I don't know what else to say. I've shown you physical evidence. I've told you about my life, my job, my friends, computers, cars, planes, telephones. What can I say that will make you believe me?" She looked at him. He stared straight ahead at the horses' backs.

"I don't know, Cath. I want to believe you, but it's all so . . . so impossible."

"You think I don't know that? We've been arguing for weeks about this. We should have been married by now. All the women are talking. Rachel took me aside at the party and told me everyone thinks you won't marry me because of my tarnished reputation, which, she stated, didn't hardly seem fair since you had tarnished it." She clasped her hands in her lap. Something had to change. She'd had enough of being treated like a criminal and having her every movement watched.

He held the reins loosely. "You know that's not the reason."

"I know, but what am I to say? 'Oh, it's not my reputation. It's the fact I'm from the future and he thinks I'm insane and can't make up his mind whether to commit me or marry me.' That would go over really well." She picked at the end of one of the fingers of her gloves. "I've had enough. It's time you got off the fence and made up your mind. Either we're getting married or I'm on the next stagecoach to wherever. I'm not sitting around for the rest of my life wondering when you're going to lock me away."

"I don't want to do that, Cath." His voice was low.

"Then what do you want?"

He pulled the buggy to a stop and turned and looked at her.

"I don't know."

"Do you think I'm crazy?"

He nodded his head, then he shook it.

"Great." She let her head drop so her chin rested against her chest. "What am I to do?"

"I don't know."

"Do you think I'm dangerous or something?"

He took her chin in his hand and lifted her face to look at him. "I can't answer that."

She pulled away from him. "Oh, give me a break. I've given you no reason to believe I would hurt myself or anyone else."

"But anyone who thinks she's from the future . . . Cath, what am I to think?" He reached out and took her hand.

"That I'm telling the truth." She gave him a wry smile. "Or, if you can't handle that one, that I've got one hell of an imagination and what I left behind was so terrible I couldn't bear to tell anyone the truth. Either would work for me." Just having him not always look as if he expected her to start howling at the moon would be an improvement.

"Is that the truth?"

"Which?"

"The second."

Sarah looked him straight in the eye. The time had come to set things in motion. She'd grown tired of limbo. "I know the truth. What you care to believe is up to you and I can't change that. I'm not dangerous and you know it, no matter what you try to convince yourself of. I'm the same person you found in the church last September. In most ways, anyway. However, over time I've become rather fond of this place and the people in it. One in particular."

"Cath, why did you suddenly change your mind about

marrying me? You were adamantly set against it, saying you wanted to go home. Then, suddenly, you want to stay."

"I honestly don't think I can go home, and while I still don't feel like I fit in here one hundred percent, I've found someone to treasure—you. And I have hopes of a long life with you. I couldn't stay here without you."

"In the beginning, I promised you as long a life as anyone could."

Sarah thought of Rachel's diary. "Yeah, but I knew it wouldn't be as long a life as you thought. I don't mean to sound cold, but I was terrified of being stranded here as a widow."

"That's a strange assumption for you to make." He laid his hand on her leg.

"Not really." She covered his hand with hers. "Remember I told you I found Rachel's diary."

"Yes." He nodded his head thoughtfully.

"One entry states you disappear in a snowstorm at the end of March eighteen seventy-two, never to be seen again. I wanted out of here before I got too attached to you and you died and left me on my own. Taking care of myself in this time scares me to death and I hate that." She entwined her fingers in his and squeezed them.

He stiffened. "Why the sudden change of heart if I'm due to die in less than a year?"

"Because many things aren't occurring exactly like in the diary. Originally, Rachel never got kidnapped in the stage holdup, nor did she carry the baby to term. The baby was supposed to come prematurely in March but didn't, which gives me reason to hope we have a future together."

His face had that expression it wore too often lately. "Cath, that makes no sense."

"Nothing makes sense. Are we going to get married or not? I need to make some plans."

"I'm trying to sort this out, Cath. I really am. I don't know the answer to that question." His eyes were steeped in sadness.

Sarah heaved a big sigh. "I can't go on this way. I won't. So, you either decide we're getting married on July fourth when the minister shows up, or I'm out of here. Rachel will loan me the money to take the stage wherever I wish."

He squeezed her hand. "You can't leave, Cath. I won't let you."

She yanked her hand away, straightening her back. "Watch me, buster."

Sarah stood holding Little Henry cradled in her arms and watched while they loaded her trunk onto the stagecoach.

"You don't have to leave." Rachel laid her hand on Sarah's arm. "Just because Joshua won't marry you doesn't mean you have to leave Moose Creek. We'll miss you so much."

"And I'll miss you, but I have to go." Sarah had given Joshua two weeks after their conversation in the buggy to make up his mind. He still wavered, unable to say whether he would commit to marrying her or not. She still saw the uncertainty and disbelief in his eyes and she'd rather be somewhere else, even all alone, than see that look anymore.

"Now, you know, the town council voted last week to start a school in the fall with you as the teacher." Henry frowned and crossed his arms. "Even though Joshua tried to convince us we were making a mistake, the rest of the town voted him down."

"That's the right of it." Mrs. Westall brushed at her skirt. "We women voted for you. We all know it isn't your doing that the two of you aren't married."

"The women? I didn't know women could vote," said Sarah.

"As of two years ago," said Rachel.

"And Rachel and I take being on the council and voting very seriously," said Mrs. Westall. "I just can't understand Joshua. He takes advantage of your situation and ruins your reputation, then refuses to stand by you. And you left with no place to turn." She tsked under her breath. "I've never seen the likes of it. I, for one, think we should get Henry's rifle and march Joshua down the aisle. He just doesn't know what's good for him."

Sarah had to laugh. These two women would do it, too.

Bouncing the baby gently, she shook her head. "It wouldn't do any good. Besides, I won't be married to a man because he's been forced into it. I've more pride than that. And I don't need Joshua Campbell." At least she *hoped* she didn't need him. Once she was on the stage, she would be on her own, alone in a foreign place and not knowing where she would end up. But anything was better than the present situation.

"You'll write and let us know how you're doing." Rachel took the baby from Sarah.

Sarah leaned over and kissed Little Henry on the head. "You be good for your mama, little one." She hugged Rachel and climbed aboard the stage. "I'll send you the money you loaned me just as soon as I can."

"Don't you worry none about that." Henry flashed her the first genuine smile she'd seen directed toward her. "I'll just add it to Joshua's bill."

"You can't do that." Sarah leaned out the window of the stagecoach. "It would be illegal to pad his bill without his knowing."

"Oh, he'll know, all right." Henry took his wife's arm. "I'll tell him right after I tell him what a fool he's been forcing you to run off this way. He won't stand by you, then he can pay for you to start over. It'll give him something to think about."

The stagecoach driver yelled to the team, and the coach started down the road. Sarah bounced in the window as she leaned out and waved good-bye. "I'll write. I'll never forget you."

She sank back into the seat. The coach hit a pothole and nearly threw her to the floor. Holding onto the upholstery as best she could, she braced her feet against the opposite seat. Wherever she ended up, it would be a long and bruising ride.

And when she finally got off the stage, she had no idea what she would do. A woman alone in 1870 was suspect and damn near helpless. Maybe she could find a school along the way in need of a teacher. Surely Henry would wire her a recommendation, under the circumstances.

Sarah leaned her head back and let it bounce against the

seat. She forced pictures of her future from her mind. To-morrow held whatever it held, and worrying wouldn't change that fact. If only the church window had let her go home this morning, she wouldn't have needed to set off by herself.

But she'd been alone before and survived. She'd do it again. Fishing in her bag, she pulled out her cell phone and turned it on. It didn't beep. The batteries had died and with them, her hope. She cradled the phone against her chest and softly started to cry.

"I need your advice, LeeAnne. Please, tell me what to do. Please."

Joshua jumped from his horse in front of the Martins' store and slammed the door open on his way in. "Where is she?"

Henry looked up from behind the counter, then lowered his head and continued tallying his customer's bill.

Joshua stomped across the store and placed his hand on top of the paper. "Where is she, Henry?"

"I'll be with you in a moment." Henry shoved his hand aside.

"*Now,* Henry! Where is Cath? Upstairs with Rachel?" Joshua turned and stomped toward the stairs.

"Joshua Campbell, you get back here. If you wake the baby, Rachel will have both of our heads. You're not to be going upstairs and hollering and carrying on like a bull in heat." Henry slammed his pencil down on the counter, then turned red in the face. "I'm sorry, Mrs. Hamilton. I didn't mean to say that in front of a lady."

Mrs. Hamilton nodded, but her gaze was riveted on Joshua. "No matter, Mr. Martin. I couldn't have said it better myself."

"Remove your hat in my store," snapped Henry.

Joshua swept his hat from his head. "Cookie said Tom drove her to town and she took her trunk. I want to know where she is."

"Why?" Henry crossed his arms and stared at Joshua. "So you can bully her some more?"

"I never bullied her." Joshua ran his fingers through his

hair. "I just came to take her home. It's where she belongs. Where she's safe."

"I don't think she figured it that way, nor do a lot of other people. You can't keep her locked up forever on your ranch. People are talking, and not about her."

Mrs. Hamilton nodded her head. "That's the truth of it."

Joshua stared at the woman for a moment. "Cath's not a prisoner. But the ranch is where she belongs for everyone's sake. Now if she's upstairs with Rachel, I'll go up quietly and fetch her."

"She's not," said Henry.

"Mrs. Westall, of course." Joshua turned and headed for the door.

"She's not there either," Henry hollered after him.

Joshua turned at the door and looked at Henry.

"Then where is she?" His hand rested on the doorknob.

"Gone."

"Gone where? No one else has room to put her up." He started opening the door. She had to be hiding at either Mrs. Westall's or the Martins'. "You can't hide her from me."

"Took the stage about half an hour ago."

"She *what*?" Joshua gripped the door tightly. Sarah'd said she would leave if he didn't agree to marry her, but where could she go? She couldn't take care of herself. "Where to?"

"Don't rightly know. She bought a ticket, but couldn't decide how far she wanted to travel. She'll probably light somewhere between here and Los Angeles."

"She can't be gone." She had to stay here where he could protect her. She belonged here with him. He had to find her. He had to bring her back.

"Well, my hardheaded friend, she's gone and she's not coming back." Henry leaned against the counter. "Not to the likes of you."

An emptiness swept over Joshua. His Sarah had left him. Left him to the loneliness of a life vacant of hope. He might as well walk off into a snowstorm.

Chapter 18

As THE STAGECOACH hit another rut in the road and Sarah went airborne, she came to the conclusion that she had to get off at the first town, or every bone in her body would be shattered. Unfortunately, the next town wasn't any bigger than Moose Creek, and she knew she'd never find work. Plus, it was still too close to Joshua.

Her legs ached from bracing herself on the seat. She lay down and tried to hold herself down by sheer willpower. That worked as well as anything else did. The coach bounced and she landed with a thump on the floor. She folded her legs. The coach wanted her on the floor, so she might as well stay there. She tried to smooth down her skirt. It would have been so much more practical to travel in her jeans, but that would have raised eyebrows everywhere she went. She really wanted to look the part of a demure lady desperately in need of a teaching job.

It would beat the hell out of trying to work in a saloon. She'd never been a waitress and, from what she remembered from the movies, saloon girls did more than wait on customers, and she wasn't having any part of that. Of course, she might be able to convince some saloonkeeper or even a storekeeper that she could make his life easier by hiring her to do his bookkeeping. It was a possibility, no matter how remote, and she had to keep her options open.

She picked at the button on her glove. She had no idea where she was going or what she was going to do. Life stretched before her, dark and foreboding. She couldn't even cling to the hope of going home anymore. She'd left the church window behind.

And she wouldn't return to it.

She sighed, then groaned as her head banged against the seat. Stagecoaches looked much bigger and more comfortable in the movies than they were in real life. She couldn't believe anyone survived traveling in this fashion.

But then her great-grandmother had come from Boston, not knowing what she'd find in Wyoming. Sarah straightened herself as best she could, wedged between the seats on the floor. She came from stubborn stock who survived. She wouldn't let her grandparents down. She'd make them proud of her.

Some wonderful adventure awaited her out there. She'd focus on that thought and nothing else.

The sound of fast approaching horses filtered through the groaning of the stage. Somebody chased them. Bandits. Rachel had nearly gotten killed as the result of a stage holdup. Just because those bandits had been caught didn't mean others didn't lurk around some bend.

Or Indians. Had Indians ever attacked the stages in Wyoming? The Battle of Little Big Horn was sometime in the 1870s, she remembered. But that had been Colorado and they hadn't gone far enough to leave Wyoming yet. Right now she wished she'd paid a little more attention in history class so she'd know what she was in for.

She scrunched down against the seat. She wouldn't go without a fight, no matter who opened the stage door. The driver didn't seem to be hurrying the horses any, so maybe a lone rider just happened to be on the same trail.

She wanted to go home. Home, where everything made sense.

The stage started to slow down and Sarah lifted herself to the seat. She had no place to hide, so she might as well face the unknown.

The stage came to a stop and Joshua yanked open the door. "Get out," he ordered.

She glared at him. "Go to hell."

"Cath, that is no way for a lady to talk." His large frame filled the doorway.

"I don't care. I'm not going with you." She turned her head away from him.

"The lady doesn't have to go with you, mister. You're holding up the coach, so get along," the driver called down from his seat.

"In a minute." Joshua reached in for her.

Sarah moved to the farthest corner of the coach. She slapped at his hand. "Don't touch me."

"Cath, you can't leave."

"Why? Because I'm crazy and you want to lock me away? Or do you just want to keep me as your mistress forever?"

"Now, Cath . . ."

She swung her head back and glared at him. "Don't you 'Now, Cath' me. I've had enough of this. I won't be treated as some sort of freak, and if you can't accept me for who I am, believe it or not, then I have no use for you, Joshua Campbell." She pulled herself up as tall as she could and crossed her arms across her chest.

"You need me," said Joshua.

"No. I don't."

"You can't do anything to take care of yourself." He started to climb into the coach.

"I'll manage." She lifted her chin and turned her head away from him. "Get out. You don't have a ticket."

"Not until you agree to come home with me."

"I got to go, mister. Either pay for a ticket or get off," yelled the driver.

"We're both getting off," Joshua called back to him.

"No. I'm staying. You're getting off."

"What do I have to do to convince you I want you to come back with me?"

Sarah turned and, holding her head tilted upward, looked down her nose at him. She said sarcastically, "I don't know, Joshua. I can't make up my mind."

"I guess I deserve that." He held out his hand. "Please, Cath, come back with me and we'll sort this out."

"It's been sorted to death. I'm finished with it. I've made my decision. I won't stay where I'm not wanted."

"I want you, Cath. Really I do."

She looked at him. For the first time in weeks he didn't look at her as if she resembled some strange creature. He might have changed his mind, but she'd hoped that too many times already. She couldn't go back. She'd never have the strength to leave again. "I don't believe you, Joshua."

He knelt between the seats. "If you come back with me, I'll spend the rest of my life trying to make up for how I've treated you. I don't know if I believe you. I don't know that I disbelieve you. I can't make sense out of it." He reached over and took her hand. "But I do know I need you in my life."

"I need more than to be just 'in your life'." She let his hand lay on top of hers.

"Will you marry me, Cath?"

"What's to stop you from changing your mind again?"

"I give you my word."

Sarah studied his face. He'd always done what he'd said he would. But all she had left was trust and she surely didn't want to ride off into the unknown. Surviving life in the 1870s was tough enough. "Okay."

"Okay, what?" A smile started to creep across his face.

She smacked his arm. "I think I'll stay where I am."

"Cath, please."

"Yes, Joshua, I'll marry you. But if you aren't in that church ready to say 'I do' when the minister next arrives, I'll let Henry shoot you."

• • •

Sarah stood in Mrs. Westall's bedroom while Mrs. Westall and Rachel finished dressing her. She couldn't believe the Fourth of July had arrived so quickly. She realized Joshua still didn't believe she came from the future, but since he'd retrieved her from the stage, he'd stopped treating her like she had three heads and seemed genuinely happy about the wedding that would take place in an hour.

"Turn around so we can check your skirts." Mrs. Westall pursed her lips and held her hands at her waist. "Rachel, I haven't seen a more beautiful bride since you wed Henry."

"We did a right fine job on that dress." Rachel smiled as she held her month-old son.

"Let me look at Little Henry again." Sarah walked over and peeked under the blanket covering the baby's face. She reached for him. His sweet little face gave Sarah renewed hope of a long and happy life with Joshua. She'd changed things for the better for her grandparents. After all, Baby Henry's birth foretold of good things to follow, like Joshua hopefully not disappearing in the middle of a snowstorm next year. She was due for something to go right. The fates couldn't always be against her.

"Now, you don't think we're going to let you hold the baby before the wedding, do you?" Mrs. Westall took Sarah's arm and moved her in front of the mirror. "He'll make a mess on your dress as sure as the snow will come next winter."

Sarah smiled at herself in the mirror. She was about to become Mrs. Joshua Campbell, to be tied to him for always. Which was the way it should be because she couldn't imagine life without Joshua in it.

She turned back to the two women. "I'd like to go to the church for a few minutes by myself before the wedding."

"That should be just fine." Rachel shifted the baby from one shoulder to the other. "Joshua is with my Henry and knowing Henry, they're in the back of the store where he can smoke his pipe in peace. I won't let him light it in the house around the baby."

"Good for you." Sarah turned and took one last look at herself in the mirror. Sometimes she still had trouble getting used to the reflection she saw, makeup missing and all. No longer the modern woman, she had become a nineteenth-century woman. For today she had even consented to letting the women tie her up in a corset, though not as tight as last time.

She left the bedroom and walked across the street to the church. Slipping inside, she checked to make sure she was alone. The women in the town had decorated the pews with wildflowers. Pink, yellow, and white blossoms filled the small church with a wondrous smell.

Slowly she walked up the aisle toward the window and studied it. The sun shone through as it had on the day she'd arrived. She stopped halfway to the altar and stood gazing up at the window. "I don't want to go home anymore. Not without Joshua. He's my life and since I can't have him in my own time, I'll stay here. I hope that's okay. Of course, you've never been in much of a hurry to send me home anyway. By now, I'm sure everyone's assumed I'm dead and buried in the desert somewhere. Don't get me wrong. I miss them terribly and my old life, but I'd miss Joshua more." She stared at the figure of Christ. "So, if it doesn't make any difference to you, I'll just be staying here."

She reached out and caressed one of the flowers tied to the pews. The room looked so different from the first time she'd seen it. The pews were still somewhat rough and un-polished, unlike what they would become in the future. No carpet graced the floor to soften footsteps. But she liked it better this way. This was the church of her great-grand-mother—the church she'd imagined when she'd read Rachel's diary.

She sighed. She wished she'd thrown the diary in her backpack instead of leaving it on the front seat of her Camaro. Then she could check and see what Rachel had to say about Joshua and the coming winter. But she would just have to trust—trust that everything would be all right.

She looked up at the window again. Jesus seemed to smile at her, but his arms didn't beckon. "I've made my decision and I'm happy with it. I'll become Mrs. Joshua Campbell and learn to be somewhat of a decent wilderness bride. A cookbook would be nice if you could send me one." She started to laugh. Maybe Joshua was right. She might be just a little off center, but then after what had happened, who could blame her?

"Sarah." She heard Rachel call her.

Sarah turned from the window as her great-grandmother came around the partition carrying her great-uncle. She smiled.

"Oh, good, you're still here." Little Henry started to whimper and Rachel patted his back. "I'm afraid I have some bad news for you."

Sarah groaned. "What? Joshua changed his mind and rode off into the sunset?"

"Hardly. It's barely noon. Sometimes you still say the strangest things." Rachel bounced the baby as his cries became more insistent. "I do believe he's hungry. It seems to be a constant condition with him, just like his father."

"And the bad news?" Sarah walked toward Rachel and lifted the baby from her arms. She patted him on the back and he quieted.

"He certainly does like you." Rachel straightened her jacket. "The minister's not coming."

"Oh, good grief. And why not?" Sarah stared at Rachel. This couldn't be happening. Not again. Her wedding had to hold some record for the most postponements. Too bad Guinness hadn't started his book of world records yet.

"He was thrown from his buggy and broke his leg. Henry just got a wire saying he couldn't travel, not for at least six to eight weeks. Doctor's orders." Rachel took Sarah's arm and led her toward the door. "He's lucky the accident happened where they have a doctor."

"Can't someone else marry us?" Sarah saw Joshua coming toward them as they exited the church.

"The judge can't be here for a month. Besides, it's best to wait for the minister. Much more proper." Rachel took Little Henry from Sarah. "I'll go and feed him, then join you at the celebration." Rachel walked away.

"Some celebration," muttered Sarah.

Joshua stopped in front of Sarah. He shrugged his shoulders. "I don't know what to say."

She leaned her head against his chest. "I guess there isn't much anyone can say."

"You always said I'd never marry." He lifted her face and kissed her.

Putting her arms around him, she leaned into him. Breaking the kiss, she said, "I don't always have to be right."

Joshua looked up at the sun as he rode across a gully. The afternoon was nearly spent and he should be heading back to camp. Most of the strays had been found and driven back to the main herd.

He took off his hat and wiped the sweat from his brow. The September sun bore down on him. It had been nearly a year since Rachel and Catherine had been due to come in on the stage. A strange year, full of unexpected surprises, not all of them pleasant. He hoped the next year would be better. In three days' time, he and Sarah would try to get married again. The minister had telegraphed, confirming he'd be here the day after tomorrow.

By then the roundup would be complete and he would leave Cookie in charge while he took Sarah to San Francisco. Away from everyone, they could start their new life. He still didn't know if she came from the future or not, but somehow it didn't matter anymore. He knew she was as sane as he was. That was all that mattered. That and the fact he could share a bedroom with his wife.

His wife. He'd finally have a wife. Something he'd dreamed of for more than two years. A dream started by Henry's plan to send for mail-order brides. He hadn't gotten what he'd expected, but he'd gotten a fine woman, if an unorthodox one.

He looked up at the sun again. His cowboys would be breaking camp and herding the cows to pastures closer to the ranch. Tomorrow the branding of the calves would start. He didn't expect them to be finished by the time he left for San Francisco, but it didn't matter. The boys knew what to do.

And he'd made a good deal with the army, who would be picking up their beef the day before the wedding. All in all, things seemed to be going along just fine.

He turned his horse to head back home. A sharp rattle sounded in front of them. He grabbed for his rifle. The horse reared. He pulled on the reins, trying to calm the horse. The animal reared again and bucked. Joshua flew into the air and landed with a thud against a rock. A sharp pain shot up his leg. The horse bolted. The snake made for cover. Joshua aimed his rifle and shot.

Then he collapsed backward on the ground. He tried to move his leg. The pain brought blackness.

Sarah paced back and forth across the kitchen, her arms clutched across her chest trying to smother the pain in her heart. She turned as the door opened, hoping Joshua would walk through it. Instead Tom stood in the doorway, crumpling his hat. "I'm sorry, Miss Sarah. No one's been able to find Mr. Campbell."

Cookie came busting in the back door. "Now don't you be worrying her. Joshua can take care of himself. He's just fine. It's a long walk home. He'll be here soon."

Sarah looked at the two men. Cookie's expression belied his words. Three days ago Joshua's horse had come racing in without him. The men had been combing the hills ever since, but so far, no Joshua. A pain shot through her heart. Today they were to be married. Mrs. Westall had her dress all laid out for her. Rachel would be pacing with the baby wondering why they hadn't arrived.

Sarah wiped at her eyes. No wedding would take place today or any other day. Joshua had never married, but had died a bachelor. Now, instead of walking off into a blizzard, he'd been killed in September during a roundup. She realized she'd changed things, but this was not how she wanted to change them. She wanted to marry Joshua and live out her life with him.

Nothing had gone right since the day Jack had accosted her at that restaurant.

"Tom, saddle my horse. I need to go into town." She turned to go upstairs.

"Miss Sarah, I think you should wait right here for Joshua," said Cookie. "He'll be expecting you here when he returns."

"And the minister expects to marry us in a couple of hours. I can't just leave him hanging." She stopped in the doorway and looked at the two men. She didn't want to take away their hope of finding their boss. But she knew in her heart that when they found him, he would be dead.

"I'll send Tom to tell them." Cookie wiped his hands on his pants. "If you're not afraid to be here alone, I'll join the rest of the men in the search."

"I need to go to town. If you should find Joshua, you can send Tom. He doesn't need to ride with me."

"Joshua would have my hide if I let you go into town by yourself." Cookie put his hat back on his head. "I'll have Tom get the horses ready if you insist on going. When we find Joshua, we'll send a message to the store, then clean him up and bring him along."

"Thank you, Cookie." Sarah gave him a wan smile before turning and going upstairs. She changed into her jeans and one of Joshua's shirts. She packed her backpack with everything she'd brought as well as the presents he'd given her. She took the fragile china angel he'd given her for Christmas and wrapped it in her tank top. Packing it carefully away so it would not break, she went downstairs and left the house.

Once Sarah reached town, she slid from her horse and walked slowly into the store. She hated having to tell the Martins what had happened. Just before she shut the door, she glanced down the street one last time, hoping to see a rider coming fast to let her know they'd found Joshua and he was fine. She sighed and let the door bang behind her.

"Why, here you are," exclaimed Rachel, coming toward her with Little Henry in her arms. Rachel stopped halfway across the store. "My goodness, you're as pale as a sheet. Whatever is the matter?"

Sarah opened her mouth, but the words refused to come. She blinked rapidly and swallowed twice.

Henry came from the back room. "I thought you'd given up wearing pants."

"Hush, Henry, something's the matter." Rachel walked over and put her hand on Sarah's arm. "Now tell us what it is."

The bell above the store door jangled. "What are you doing over here, Sarah?" asked Mrs. Westall.

"Trying to spit something out," said Henry. He reached over and took his son.

Sarah looked at all of them. Tears welled in her eyes and she brushed them away. Her heart burned as though someone had stuck a knife in it and twisted. "He's gone," she blurted out.

"Who's gone where?" asked Mrs. Westall.

Sarah shook her head and shrugged.

"You don't mean Joshua's run off," said Henry.

"Henry, Joshua wouldn't run off and leave Sarah waiting at the altar." Rachel glared at him.

"I know that." Henry patted the baby on the back. "Now, Sarah, what are you blithering about?"

"His horse came back three days ago without him." Sarah hiccupped. She waved her hands in front of her.

Rachel took her hands and held them tightly. "Now that doesn't mean anything except he's on foot somewhere. Joshua knows how to take care of himself."

"That's what Cookie said." Sarah held onto Rachel's hand like a lifesaver thrown to a drowning person.

"We should be out searching," said Henry, his voice gruff.

"The men have been since his horse came back. They can't find him." Sarah suddenly sat on the floor.

Rachel sat next to her and hugged her tightly, rocking her as she did the baby. "It'll be all right. They'll find him and then you two will be married. We'll just make sure the minister stays around a few days if need be. Mrs. Westall can ply him with chocolate cake."

"Let's get her upstairs," said Henry. "Then I'm going to ride out to the ranch and see if I can help."

Mrs. Westall took the baby. "You go on ahead, Henry. We'll tend to Sarah." She nuzzled her cheek against the baby's head. "You send the fastest rider in as soon as you find Joshua."

Sarah sat upright and looked at Henry. "Thank you. Take Tom with you. I know he hates being saddled with me when he could be out looking."

"Don't you fret now, dear," said Mrs. Westall. "We'll go have a nice cup of tea while the men do the looking. That Cookie is the best tracker in these parts."

"I don't understand," said Sarah. "I thought he was just the cook."

"He's the only man out at the ranch besides Joshua who *can* cook. He's getting too old to ride herd on those stupid beasts—but when someone's lost, Cookie is the first person we all turn to." Mrs. Westall started for the stairs. "Now come along."

Sarah stood up. "You go ahead. I want to go to the church for a minute, first."

"I'll fix you a nice cup of coffee," said Rachel. "And I have some apple pie left from last night's supper. Why don't you come upstairs with us now? Being alone and brooding is hard on the soul."

Sarah walked over to Mrs. Westall and kissed Little Henry on the head. "You're such a sweet thing. You grow up big and strong now, you hear?"

"Such a thing to tell a babe." Mrs. Westall tsked at Sarah.

Sarah hugged her. "Thank you for being such a good friend." Then she walked to Rachel. She hugged her and whispered, "I love you."

Picking up her backpack, she left the store and walked toward the church. One year ago today, she'd arrived in the Moose Creek of 1870. Now she had no reason to stay. Joshua was dead. Rachel and Henry were happy and on their way to having a huge family. Maybe she'd changed events enough so that Mrs. Westall would survive the next winter and not die from the flu. She hadn't been able to save Joshua, but perhaps Mrs. Westall would live. But she didn't care to stay and find out.

She entered the door of the church and dragged her booted feet across the floor. Slinging her bag over her shoulder, she moved slowly down the aisle, her gaze fastened on the glimmering stained-glass window. Jesus extended his arms toward heaven.

"I want to go home now," she said softly. "I know I've said that before and you've ignored me. And I know I told you I wanted to stay. But I've changed my mind and this time I mean it when I say take me home. I can't survive here now that Joshua's gone."

The sun glinted through the window. She stared at it, but nothing changed.

"Please," she begged, "you have to take me back to where I belong. My heart is torn in two." She fell to her knees and rocked back and forth. "I can't stay here. Not without the man I love. Don't you understand that?"

She stared up at the window and raised her hands to it. The sun glinted off the halo above Christ's head. But He ignored her.

Her hands clenched into fists and she shook them at the window. "This is all your fault. You brought me here. I hate this place. Take me home. Please, take me home."

The sun continued to shine benignly at her. "Dammit!" she screamed. "Why don't you listen? Take me home! Take me home now!"

The world began to swirl around her as the sun flashed in her eyes and blinded her. She thought she saw Jesus stretch out his arms to her.

Chapter 19

JOSHUA AWOKE WITH a start. His leg throbbed and he wished he had some of those tablets Sarah had given him for pain when he'd been injured before. The cold of the early morning seeped into his bones and made the throbbing worse. The fire had burned out sometime while he'd slept, if that was what he'd really done. He seemed to drift between here and someplace far away. He preferred the place far away where Sarah beckoned to him from that strange machine she called her car and the pain no longer plagued him.

He shivered convulsively. Using his rifle for leverage, he pushed himself into a sitting position against a large rock. He'd start the fire again, but he'd used all the brush within his reach and he had no more matches. At first he'd tried to keep track of how long he'd lain in the gully, but after a while the hours ran into days and it became a fog. He was sure he'd been here at least three days. If so, Sarah would be waiting for him at the church. It would be the day they were finally to be married. He would realize the dream he'd held for two years—he would have a wife. But he thought he'd been here longer than three days. Four. Maybe five.

The men who worked for him should be looking for him. He'd expected them to come before the first night fell. He'd managed to cook the rattlesnake that he'd shot and eat part of it. He'd saved some just in case they didn't find him until the next morning.

He'd eaten the rest of the rattlesnake the day before yesterday or possibly the day before that. Hunger had gnawed at his belly, but even it had given up in despair. His throat felt as dry as the dust in which he lay. A small trickle of water still ran through the gully, but to get to it meant dragging his leg across the rock-strewn ground.

He leaned back against the rock. The strength to move had departed with the hope his crew would find him. Too many days had passed. No one knew exactly where he had ridden to and the ranch covered too large an area for the men to search everywhere in time. Eventually, they'd find him.

But by then he would be dead.

He hoped they would find him soon—if not for his sake, for Sarah's. It frightened him to think of her being alone.

As he lay there he wondered what she was doing at that moment, and if she missed him yet. He pictured her in his mind. The soft, dark hair falling to her shoulders. The warmth of her skin against his. He'd been a fool. He should have married her earlier. Then at least he would have died a happy man.

He hoped she could get home. She would be miserable alone on the ranch. She needed to return to where she'd come from. Her life would be in the future. His future held nothing.

She would miss him. He knew that for a fact. She said she wanted to be Mrs. Campbell.

Never had she said she loved him.

Did she?

He'd never considered love. He'd wanted a wife and she had crept her way into his heart and his life. He couldn't imagine not having her about his house or in his life, turning things topsy-turvy all the time. But he'd never told her he loved her.

But he did. Fervently. Passionately.

And his one regret was he hadn't told her.

But his last thoughts would be of her.

He leaned his head back against the rock and closed his eyes. He let himself float away from the pain and the cold. He pictured Sarah gliding toward him in her wedding gown. She looked like an angel. She reached out her hand to him. He tried to take it, but he couldn't reach her. He tried to move toward her, but the distance between them increased. The sounds of horses neighing came from the side, but he couldn't take his eyes off of Sarah. If he looked away, she would vanish and he'd never be able to touch her again. He stretched out his hand.

"There he be." Cookie's gruff voice swirled through Joshua's dream.

Sarah smiled and put her hands to her lips. She blew him a kiss and turned away from him. "Come back," he hollered. Looking over her shoulder with a wistful smile on her face, she vanished into thin air. "Come back. Please. Don't leave me."

"We're right here, boss," Tom said.

Something cold pressed against Joshua's lips. He didn't want the cold to return. He wanted Sarah to stay.

"Drink." Henry's gruff voice cut through the dream.

Joshua opened his eyes partway. Henry hunkered down beside him, a canteen in his hand. Cookie stood over him. He closed his eyes again and sipped at the water.

"Get a blanket," Cookie shouted.

The heavy material enveloped him, warming him. He blinked his eyes. "What day is it?"

"The day after you were to be married." Henry moved to Joshua's leg, and ripped at the material. He carefully ran his hands up Joshua's leg.

Joshua bit his lip and choked down the pain.

"Yep, it's broken. Tom, cut some straight branches for a splint. Then start working on a travois so we can get him back to the ranch." Henry looked up at Cookie. "You want to hold him while I straighten it?"

Cookie grabbed Joshua's arms and pinned them to his sides. "All right."

Henry's hands pulled at Joshua's ankle. Blackness swirled around him and the pain faded in the dark.

The bouncing woke Joshua. He looked up into the blue sky and watched the white clouds float overhead. The travois banged across rocks, and he grimaced, biting down on his lip.

"I see you're back with us." Henry rode beside him.

"Sarah?" asked Joshua.

"Worried sick. She's with the missus and Edna. I promised we'd send a rider as soon as we found you. Tom's headed for town. He'll have her back at the ranch before we have you there."

Joshua closed his eyes. He would have a chance to tell her he loved her after all. "What about the minister? Is he gone again?"

"Naw," said Henry. "The womenfolk are holding him hostage until we can get you to the church. But we may have to bring everyone to the ranch. You're going to be laid up for a few weeks."

"Fine." Tiredness flooded through Joshua and he let himself slip back to the dreaming place of no pain.

As hands picked him up, he opened his eyes. "Cookie's going to make you some food while the boys and I get you upstairs," said Henry.

"Where's Cath?" Joshua placed his arms around Henry's and Sam's necks as they lifted him. He looked around and saw Tom standing to the side, curling the brim of his hat in his hand.

"Don't know," Henry answered as he and Sam carried Joshua into the house.

"Tom," yelled Joshua, "where's Cath?"

Tom hung his head and dragged his boots in the dirt as he trailed behind the other men. "Don't know, Mr. Campbell."

Joshua grabbed the doorframe leading into the kitchen,

nearly unseating himself from the men's hands. "What do you mean you don't know? Damn it, Henry, turn around."

Tom faced Joshua. He chewed on his bottom lip and shrugged his shoulders. "Mrs. Martin and Mrs. Westall said Miss Sarah went off to the church right after Mr. Martin left to search for you. No one's seen her since." He twisted the brim of his hat. "They've looked everywhere. No one saw her come out."

"The church." Joshua made a low, strangled sound.

"Get him upstairs. Tom, take the buggy and get Mrs. Westall." Henry balanced Joshua's head against his shoulder. "Have Cookie ride into town and see if he can find out anything."

The curtains whisked back and the morning light flooded the bedroom. Joshua looked up out of half-open eyes to see Mrs. Westall standing over him, her hands on her hips.

"Joshua Campbell, you bestir yourself right now. You've been lying in this bed for two weeks and it's time to be up and about."

Joshua turned his head away. He saw no reason to get up. His desire to continue living had gone with Sarah. "Leave me be."

"I most certainly will not." Mrs. Westall yanked the covers back. "I'm tired of toting food up these stairs for a man disinterested in eating. I'm also tired of your foolishness."

Joshua reached for the covers. "I'm no good to anyone with my leg stove up the way it is. Leave me be."

"All right, boys. Let's get him downstairs. I've made up a bed for you in your study. That way you don't have to manage the stairs and I don't have to empty any more chamber pots." She turned and stomped from the room. "His breakfast is ready, so hurry it up."

Joshua glared at the two men standing next to the bed. "Go back to work."

"Oh, no. You're going downstairs," Sam said.

"You work for me and you'll do as I say." He turned his back on the men.

George pulled back the covers and lifted Joshua to a sit-

ting position. "We may work for you, but I, for one, ain't
gonna cross that woman. Now, we can help you put on your
pants, or you can go to breakfast in your nightshirt."

Joshua stared at them. "I could fire you."

"Yes, sir, you could. But you'd still be going downstairs,"
said Sam. "When that woman speaks, everyone jumps. The
only reason you don't is 'cause you can't." He held Joshua's
pants out to him. One of the legs had been slashed open.

Joshua sighed. It made no difference to him. "Help me on
with my pants."

"Smart move," said Sam.

The two men lifted him and carried him to the bottom of
the stairs. They set him in a wicker wheelchair and wheeled
him into the kitchen.

"Now that's much better." Mrs. Westall smiled at him as
she set a plate in front of him. "Henry had the idea of getting you a chair. And a wonderful idea it was. Now you can
move about the house." She turned back to the stove and
poured herself a cup of tea. Sitting next to him, she reached
over and patted his hand. "I know you miss her, Joshua. But
that's no reason to give up living. She wouldn't want you
to."

He looked at Mrs. Westall, then pushed his plate away.
"I'm not very hungry."

She pushed it back. "You need your strength to get well."

"Where'd she go?" In his heart, he knew. She'd gone to a
place where he couldn't follow. Did she think he had died
out on the range? Now he wished he had.

"I don't know. Cookie found no untoward tracks about
the place." She sipped her tea. "It's as though she vanished
into thin air just the way she seemed to come out of it a year
ago."

"I want to go into town." Joshua picked up his cup of coffee. He had to know for himself.

"Not with your leg the way it is." Mrs. Westall went to the
sink and started to wash the dishes.

"Have Tom bring the buggy around. I'm going now."
Joshua pushed his chair away from the table. "And have two
of the men come along."

Mrs. Westall turned to look at him. When she saw the determination on his face, she went to the back door.

Joshua sent the men away and wheeled himself down the aisle of the church. He stared at the window. He remembered finding Sarah collapsed on the floor before Rachel and Henry's marriage. She'd said she wanted to go home and couldn't and she kept looking at the church window. Much later, she'd told him it had brought her here from the future.

Now it had taken her back. He finally fully believed her story.

"It's your fault," he railed at the window. "You brought her to me and then you took her away. Why?" He shook his fist. "Bring Cath back to me. I need her. She's to be my wife." His head sank to his chest. "Please, bring Cath back to me."

Joshua sat at his desk and finished his books. He hadn't been able to work at the kitchen table since Sarah had vanished. He looked out the window. The snow had mostly melted. March had come around, and still he missed Sarah. The house stood so empty without her to fill it. He seldom came in it anymore except to do his books. He took his meals with the men and had even started to sleep in the bunkhouse.

Rachel, Henry, and Mrs. Westall tried to convince him to find another mail-order bride or to marry the Conklin girl on the farm west of town. But she wasn't Sarah. And only Sarah would fill the void and make the sun shine bright again.

He'd gone to the church many times and asked the window to bring her back, but it hadn't. It simply wouldn't.

Joshua chewed on the end of his pencil. Maybe he'd been asking the wrong question. If he wanted Sarah in his life, he would have to go to her. He'd find her somehow.

But what if she'd found someone else?

He opened the desk drawer and pulled out a sheet of paper. He'd never know if he didn't try. The ranch held nothing for him without her. His heart had traveled to the future with Sarah. This time and place offered him nothing but loneliness.

And he'd do his damnedest to follow his heart.

Taking up his pen, he dipped it in the ink. Across the top of the paper he wrote, "The Last Will and Testament of Joshua Campbell." He'd leave the ranch to Henry and Rachel. With another child on the way, they needed more room. And Sarah said they would have six offspring.

When he finished he walked into the kitchen and left the paper on the table. If this didn't work, he could put his will away when he returned. If it did, then someone would find it.

He saddled his horse and rode into town. The wind started to whip around him. He looked off to the horizon. A late storm brewed and he needed to beat it to town. He kicked his horse into a gallop.

Once at the church, he slid from his saddle and threw the reins over the hitching post. Walking into the church, he removed his hat and stared up at the window. The snow had already started to fall, but a small ray of sun shone through the window just above Jesus's head.

He walked slowly up the aisle, crushing his hat in his hands. He stared at the window and breathed deeply. What awaited him? Sarah? He'd never know if he didn't take the chance.

He bent down on his knees and looked up at the window. "I know you won't bring her back to me. I've tried that." He ran his fingers through his hair. "I love her. She's part of me. Please take me to her."

The light flashed into his eyes and he could see the Christ figure beckoning to him. The world swirled around him. "Thank you," he murmured.

Finally, thought Joshua, trying to make his way to the bar by pushing his way through the crowd watching the dancers. It had taken him months, but he'd finally found Sarah. She didn't know him, but he would woo her again, and do it right this time. There wouldn't be any of the mishaps from before. He'd make her fall in love with him again.

The window had a warped sense of humor and had sent him forward—just not far enough forward. He could hardly believe it had been nearly a year since he'd fallen from his horse and Sarah had returned to her own time. He now knew why she'd acted so strangely when she'd first arrived in Moose Creek. Even after listening to all her stories, he'd been out of step with his surroundings and could understand her frustrations when she'd been in his time. He'd faced plenty in her time. And she hadn't begun to tell him the difficulties of not being "legal" in this century. Thank God for Pedro, who'd helped him.

One of Henry's great-grandsons still owned the Crazy C Ranch and while cattle work had changed somewhat, he'd still been able to do it well enough to get a job. He'd spent his first two months working on the ranch, trying to figure out what to do and how to act in this strange future.

Finally with Pedro's help, he'd come to Los Angeles to look for Sarah. Los Angeles had turned out to be bigger than he ever could have dreamed. It held things for which even his time in Wyoming hadn't prepared him.

Then he remembered Sarah telling him of the place LeeAnne had taken her dancing. He'd been hanging out in the place for a week, wondering if she'd ever show.

And tonight she had.

His heart nearly stopped beating when he saw her sitting on the bar stool. His first instinct had been to rush over to her and sweep her into his arms. His second instinct had prevailed. He'd asked her to dance and called her Cath.

Now he was sure he'd arrived before she'd ever visited Moose Creek—and if he had his way, she never would.

He picked up the drinks for the two women and started back to the table. His heart stopped. A man dragged Sarah across the floor. Jack. The man who had tried to kill her. He blocked the man's way. "Let her go. She doesn't want to leave with you." He kept his voice even. He had to get her away from the man.

"Get the hell out of my way." Jack shoved Josh and he lost his grip on the drinks, sending them flying into the onlookers.

He balanced on the balls of his feet, ready to spring. "Let the lady go."

Jack brandished a knife at him.

Joshua held his hands in front of him. "Calm down."

Jack pushed Sarah in front of him and propelled her toward the door, still waving the knife. Her eyes met Joshua's, pleading for help.

The crowd swirled around them and Joshua lost sight of the two figures. He jostled his way to the door. He had to reach her. He bolted out and witnessed Jack slamming Sarah against his truck, then pounding his knife on the roof. Onlookers blocked Joshua's way. He tried to force his way past them. His heart raced. He screamed for people to move. Sarah kicked and clawed at her assailant. She started to sag. Joshua threw a bystander to the side and charged Jack. They toppled to the ground. "Run, Sarah," Joshua commanded.

Sirens filled the night air. He held Jack pinned to the ground and watched Sarah drive away into the night.

"Damn," he muttered.

Joshua pulled Pedro's green pickup truck into the parking lot of the Moose Creek church and stopped it next to Sarah's blue Camaro. For three days he'd been two steps behind her. He had to catch her before she walked down that aisle. He jumped from the truck and ran up the stairs, his keys jangling in his hands. Throwing open the door, he grabbed the partition to propel himself into the main room of the church.

"Sarah," he yelled.

The sun glinted down the main aisle of the church and swirled in a pattern. Sarah, caught in the swirling light, faded before his eyes.

Chapter 20

JOSHUA SANK DOWN into a pew and laid his forehead against the cool wood. She'd left him again. "I love you, Cath," he called after her.

The swirling lights faded. He leaned back and looked up at the window. "I'm really beginning not to like this church much, or you either. Can't you get the timing right?" he said out loud.

A year. Sarah had spent a year in the Moose Creek of 1870 and 1871. And he'd be spending the next year in modern Moose Creek waiting for her.

Another year. Already he'd been alone for a year. How many more would he have to wait before he finally could have Sarah for his wife?

He could go back to the ranch, but they didn't expect him for another two days. He really didn't have anywhere else to go. This Moose Creek didn't have the Martins' store to stand around in or Henry to jaw with while they stood and smoked. Mrs. Westall's house had disappeared with the years. The church and the window were still the center of the town.

If people only knew the truth about the window, they'd probably pull down the place.

He could follow her, but he had no way of knowing what time he'd travel to. He could be chasing her through that window forever. It was best to sit tight and wait for her. At least when she did return he wouldn't have to woo her—do one hell of a lot of explaining, yes, but surely she'd still be willing to marry him, even in this century. She'd said she didn't have a beau in her present time.

He took one last look at the window. "I really hate you." He shook his fist in the air. Slowly he rose and walked toward the back of the church. "Might as well go back to work. At least I know when to expect her back." And one year from today, he'd be waiting in the church for her arrival.

He stood at the partition and ran his hand down the wood. So many times he'd come to this church. The first time he'd seen Sarah, he'd been standing behind the partition and Mrs. Westall had been trying to hide Sarah from his view.

That had been two years ago. Two years filled with love, hope, misery. And ahead of him stretched another long year of loneliness. "It's all your fault, Henry Martin. You and your mail-order brides and your crazy relatives. Rachel was right. Sarah surely does look a great deal like you. If I had realized that earlier, and that she spoke the truth, then maybe some of this craziness could have been stopped." He sighed and took one last look at the window.

The light swirled in the aisle and nearly blinded him. He gasped. Sarah knelt in the middle of the swirling light. Slowly she stood and walked out of the light, dressed in her blue jeans, and carrying her leather backpack. Her head hung and she dragged the bag behind her. Her shoulders drooped.

He blinked his eyes. She'd just left him. But this was not the Sarah who had left. Her black, shoulder-length hair fell forward, obscuring most of her face. She wore one of his shirts from the 1870s.

He stepped away from the partition. "Cath?" he said softly.

She stopped and looked at him. She stared, not moving. He took a step toward her. She dropped her bag and launched herself into his arms. Her tears dampened his shirt and she clung to him.

"Thank God," she gasped. "I thought you were dead."

"Not quite." He laughed and swung her around. "I came after you. I couldn't live without you." He set her down on the floor.

She leaned away from him, reaching up to touch his face. "When you didn't show up earlier today for the wedding, I thought you were dead." She reached up and kissed him. "I'm so glad they finally found you. Where have you been? I was so worried. Rachel and Mrs. Westall kept telling me it would be okay. I need to go and tell them we need to get ready for the wedding before the minister rides off again."

"We can't do that, Cath."

"Joshua Campbell, you haven't changed your mind again, because if you have, you're going to wish you were dead." She tried to pull away from him.

"No, Cath, I still want to marry you more than anything else in the world."

"Then what's your reason now? I know the minister hasn't left." She pulled against his hold.

"He left a long time ago." He laughed, and she frowned at him. "I never made it to the church for the wedding. I fell off my horse and broke my leg. It took them days to find me and by then you were gone." He caressed her hair, then hugged her to him again. "I was beginning to believe I'd never catch up with you."

"I don't understand."

"When I didn't show up, you left. You went home." He ran his finger down the side of her face.

"I tried to a few minutes ago." She blinked at him. "You finally believe me, don't you?"

"Oh, yeah."

She shook her head. "I asked the window to take me

home because you were dead." She smiled at him. "I'm glad it didn't listen to me. I turned around and there you were."

"It did what you asked, Cath. You're home."

She looked around the church. The fine linens covered the altar. The brass cross sat atop them. She looked at her feet and saw the rust carpet beneath them. "I'm truly home again." Her voice came as a breathy whisper.

Joshua nodded.

"I don't understand. How can you be here?"

He laughed. "I used the same travel agent you did." He inclined his head toward the window and briefly told her his story.

She hugged him again. "I don't care what century we're in. I'm just glad we're together." She'd been afraid she'd never see him again. Maybe the fates had never intended for him to marry in his time—but in her time, things might be different.

"I'm just glad I didn't have to wait another year."

She looked up at him. "What are you talking about?"

"You've only been gone a few minutes. I watched you leave."

"That's not possible."

"In this place, anything's possible." He looked up at the window and grinned.

She followed his gaze and stared at the window. "I have to say, this is one adventure I don't think I'll ever tell anyone about. Not even LeeAnne."

A door slammed behind them and both of them jumped at the sudden noise. Sarah turned to see who their unexpected visitor was, only to see Jack charging up the aisle toward her, a maniacal gleam in his eyes.

He pulled a knife from his boot and brandished it in the air.

"How'd you find me?" she gasped.

"Your girlfriend told me all about this nice little town. It didn't take much persuasion." Jack laughed hollowly, creeping even closer to Sarah and Joshua.

Sarah stepped back against Joshua, trying to put as much distance between her and Jack as possible. "How did she know? I never said a thing to her." She had survived so much to return to this. After everything else, she refused to let Jack defeat her.

"I told her," whispered Joshua. "I never dreamed it would put her or you in danger."

Sarah glanced up at him, then back at Jack who continued to advance toward her. "I'll call the police again. I have a re-straining order against you."

"So? You can't keep me away, Sarah. You belong to me." A wicked smile played across his face. "And as soon as I take care of this bastard, we'll be together forever. Just you and me."

"No." She shook her head. Could she get the window to take her and Joshua to safety? Life in a different time far outweighed death in the present. She glanced up at the window, but the sun had dimmed. "No!" she screamed. "I won't ever go with you."

Joshua pushed her behind him. "Look for a chance to run and get to your car."

"I won't leave you," she hissed.

"I told you no other man could have you. You're mine and I'm not letting you get away again." Jack snarled as he moved toward them. He looked at Joshua and narrowed his eyes. "You're the same jerk who tried to move in on my ter-ritory the other night. This is the last time. I told you to stay away from her and now you will—permanently."

Joshua shoved Sarah into one of the pews and stood blocking her from Jack. He wished he had a weapon, any-thing. Jack lurched at him and he tried to back up, but the end of the pew blocked his way. The knife slashed along the back of his wrist. A burning sensation shot up his arm. With his other hand he slugged Jack in the jaw and the man stag-gered backward.

Joshua yanked Sarah from between the pews and pushed her toward the back door. "Run. Get out of here. Get help."

Jack came at him again, the knife slashing the air. Joshua moved in a circle, trying to draw Jack to the front of the church and away from Sarah. He kept his gaze on the knife.

The sun glinted off of it. Jack rushed him and Joshua stepped slightly to the side. The knife raked down his arm.

He yelled in pain but refused to give up. There was no way he would leave Sarah now that he had finally joined her again. Joshua grabbed Jack's arm and pounded it against the top edge of one of the pews. The knife clattered against a pew as it fell to the floor. He swung at Jack and sent him reeling toward the altar.

A streak of light came through the window.

"I wish Jack were gone," Sarah screamed. "Far away from here. Back in a time where he can't hurt anyone."

The light swirled in the aisle and Jack's falling body faded from sight. Sarah threw her arms around Joshua's neck, nearly knocking him over.

"I told you to get out of here." Joshua hugged her to him.

"So, when did I ever listen?" She kissed his face. Stepping back, she looked at him. "You could have been killed."

"So could you."

"I wasn't deserting you this time. We're a team." She smiled up at him. Looking down at his arm, she frowned. "You're bleeding."

"It's nothing. Let's get out of here." He took her arm. "Where do you suppose the window sent him?"

"Back to the beginning of time, I hope, with no way back."

Joshua laughed. "It'll take him a while to figure out what's happened to him."

"I'm taking you to a doctor, then I'm calling LeeAnne. She has to be worried sick."

Joshua kissed the top of Sarah's head. "I'm sure she is."

Sarah sat next to Joshua on the examining table in the doctor's office waiting for the doctor to arrive and stitch up his wounds. "It won't hurt much. They'll give you a local to deaden the skin."

"I've been stitched up before." Joshua shrugged his shoulders. "Without benefit of this local you talk about."

She shivered. "Yuck."

"Glad to be home?" He reached over and brushed her hair back from her face.

She kissed the inside of his arm. "More than you'll ever realize."

"I don't think so."

"Do you want to go home?" She looked into his soft green eyes.

"Not without you, and you're happier here." He leaned over and kissed her.

"But your friends, your ranch, your life. All of those are back in 1870. I know what it's like to give up everything."

"You told me I had no future after March of eighteen seventy-two. Remember?" He smiled. "Besides, I gladly gave up everything to have you."

She reached into her bag and pulled out a worn, brown book. She held it up. "Rachel's diary."

"Does it still foretell doom?" He reached over and touched it.

"You know, this is all we have left of them now." Sarah's heart twinged. "I miss them, too." She opened the diary. "Let's see what I changed."

She started to read out loud.

September 22, 1870

It has been a glorious day. After everything that happened, I am finally married . . . Henry insisted since the minister will not return to Moose Creek for two months and I have nowhere to live except with him.

My sorrow extends to Joshua Campbell. He seems such a nice man and would gladly have wed the strange woman who appeared in town out of nowhere. However, she refused his hand and he is most distraught, as is Henry. . . .

"Strange woman, indeed. What a way for her to talk about me." Sarah looked up at Joshua.

He laughed. "Remember, she'd just met you. Everyone thought you were a little strange."

Sarah smacked him on the knee before turning back to the diary. "Let's see what else she's added."

June 4, 1871

> I bore our first son today. I am truly glad the ordeal is over, but feel very blessed to hold my strong, healthy baby. He looks so like his father. We shall name him Henry Joshua Martin. Being named for two such strong and honest gentlemen will give him a fine start in this harsh land where he must grow to manhood.
>
> I am very tired and should be abed, but I had to record this momentous occasion. Henry and Mrs. Westall would scold me if they caught me sitting at my desk, but I feel it worth the risk.
>
> Happy birthday, my son.

"Now that's one change I enjoy reading." Sarah flipped the pages. "Oh, here's another one about me."

June 10, 1871

> Sarah nearly left us today. I would have sorely missed her. Although she is still a bit unusual, she is a fine friend and in this place, those are hard to find.
>
> Joshua finally came to his senses and has agreed to marry her at our July Fourth celebration. Everyone is delighted.

"Came to my senses." Joshua snorted and looked indignant.

"And it was about time, too." Sarah giggled. "You know, Henry was set on a shotgun wedding."

"The man didn't even like you."

"He loved me. After all, he was my great-grandfather and he thought you acted very badly."

"Me? I wasn't the one going around saying I was from the future."

"But I didn't lie, did I?"

His eyes twinkled. "No, my darling. You definitely didn't lie. Find the entry about me and the snowstorm."

"Okay. Okay. Be patient." Sarah flipped a few pages into the diary. "Oh, listen to this one."

September 22, 1871

Thank God they have finally found Joshua. His leg is broken in several places, but he will be fine. Mrs. Westall has gone to take care of him.

The joy is tinged with great sadness. Sarah has disappeared. No sign exists that someone has taken her. I shall sorely miss her, for she has brightened many hours for me.

"I miss Rachel, too." Sarah snuffled and wiped her eyes with the edge of her sleeve. "I'm glad someone appreciated me."

"Everyone did after you'd been there a while." Joshua moved his arm gingerly.

"Do you want me to see what's keeping the doctor?" She laid her hand on his leg.

"No. He'll be here when he gets here. Keep reading. I want to hear something nice about myself."

"Joshua, you're terrible."

He leaned over and kissed her nose. "I've taken lessons from you."

"Excuse me? I'm the sweetest person around." She blinked her eyes at him. For the first time in a very long time, she was truly happy. "Okay. Let's see. Here's an interesting one."

"About me?"

"No. Mrs. Westall. And one that makes me glad."

November 19. 1871

Mrs. Westall has finally returned from Joshua's ranch.
She says he is gloomy as a winter's night and we must
find him a wife before he withers away.

Selfish as it sounds, I am glad to have her back in
town. With the store and Little Henry to care for, plus
another babe on the way, I find it too difficult to ride to
the ranch to visit her. I have been exceedingly lonely
with Sarah gone and her caring for Joshua.

I still think of Sarah often and wonder what became
of her. I hope wherever she is, she is happy. We all
loved her dearly.

I think Mrs. Westall is right. We must find a wife for
Joshua. He is not a man meant to be alone.

"Oh and did they ever try to find me a wife." Joshua
grinned at her. "I had my pick of several."

"And I see whom you chose." Sarah shifted on the table.
"I'm really glad to read that entry. Originally Mrs. Westall
died from the flu in November eighteen seventy-one."

"She didn't have time to get sick. She was too busy running my ranch and my life."

Sarah laughed. "Here you are at last."

March 30, 1872

Henry found Joshua's horse wandering loose in town
today after the terrible snowstorm. It is strange the animal would be alone. With no sign of Joshua, we are
very worried. Henry, Cookie, and several other men
will go looking for him tomorrow.

April 3, 1872

It has been four days and we still cannot find Joshua.
We fear the worst. Our friend may be lost in the snow.
We may never know.

But, we are certain he will not return to us. He left his will on his kitchen table, leaving his ranch to Henry and me. It is a strange occurrence and we would rather have him than the ranch.

The only explanation is his heart never recovered from losing Sarah and he has chosen to leave life. I hope God will forgive him and finally grant him peace.

"I didn't realize you left your ranch to my great-grand-parents. That was sweet."

"I couldn't just abandon the place, and with all the children you said they would have, they needed the space." He gave her a boyish grin.

She leaned over and hugged him. "That was nice." Straightening up, she looked into his eyes. "Other than the last two paragraphs, the rest about you is the same."

"No wonder you feared marrying me."

"Committing to a man you know's going to die is a little difficult. Especially one you don't know all that well."

He caressed her cheek and she leaned into him. "Read some more while we wait."

Sarah was more than happy to oblige, content in the fact that Joshua was back and that they were, after everything, still together.

Sarah sat at her desk in her office across from a very stern-looking lawyer. Joshua stood behind her and she clutched his hand, which lay on her shoulder. When she'd called LeeAnne, she'd been told the lawyer had been calling her since the day she'd left Los Angeles. He had made it very clear that the matter was of the utmost urgency and he had to complete his business as quickly as possible.

It amazed her how much more self-assured she felt wearing a business suit, nylons, and high heels. She'd had her hair and her nails done and sat ready to face any adversary. She wondered what he could want. If one of her customers was unhappy and had filed a lawsuit, her attorney would handle it. She probably should have called him instead of dealing with this man herself. If she mucked things up, Pete would not be happy with her.

"Now, Miss Martin, this is a private matter," the gray-haired man said. "I don't feel it is proper for this person to be present." He waved his hand toward Joshua.

She straightened her shoulders and put her hands on her desk. The polished wood gave her confidence. "This man is my fiancé and whatever you have to say, you will say in front of him or you'll leave." The word "proper" grated against her nerves. She'd been told often enough in the past year how improper she was and she wasn't going to take it anymore, especially now that she was back in her own time.

"Very well." He humphed. "It's a matter of reading a will, and you are the sole beneficiary. I've already wasted four days waiting for you and I don't intend to waste any more of my time in Los Angeles on this matter."

Sarah leaned back in her chair and looked up at Joshua. She didn't know anyone who would leave her money.

"I don't know if you realize it or not, but Charles Martin died just over a week ago."

"Who?" asked Sarah. "I've never heard of the man."

Joshua suddenly sat up. "He's the one who owns the Crazy C Ranch."

"One of Henry's descendants?" asked Sarah.

"Yeah. One of his grandsons. I knew the man was getting along in years, but when I left the Crazy C, he looked fine to me. That was only two weeks ago." Joshua stared at the attorney. "Are you sure he's dead?"

"Of course, I'm sure. He had a massive heart attack." The man snapped his fingers. "Gone. Just like that." Obviously unhappy at being interrupted, he frowned at the two of them. "He had no children and was estranged from most of his family. He left the Crazy C ranch to you, Miss Martin, and all of his other holdings."

Sarah looked at Joshua and started to laugh. "Isn't that just the strangest twist of fate."

Joshua bent forward and whispered in her ear, "We're right back where we started."

"Excuse me. I'm not finished," said the attorney.

"Only without Rachel, Henry, and Mrs. Westall." She placed her hand on top of Joshua's. "It won't be the same without Cookie or Tom."

"You should see the house. They have a real modern bathroom, electric lights, and a gas stove. Someone even put in heating and air-conditioning." Joshua laughed. "The structure itself is pretty much the same. Even the cabinet I made is still in the corner of the living room."

"I can put the angel back in her spot."

"Listen to me." The lawyer's voice came louder, annoying, like the buzz of a mosquito.

Sarah waved her hand at him in dismissal.

Joshua swung Sarah's chair around and pulled her to him. He looked into her eyes. "This isn't the strangest thing that's happened."

"Listen, now," the lawyer screeched. Turning red in the face, he lowered his voice. "If you would please come back to the matter at hand instead of rambling on about nonsense, I have some papers for you to sign. And I have a buyer lined up for the ranch. He's willing to open escrow immediately."

Sarah turned her head and looked at the lawyer. "I have no intentions of selling."

"What would a city girl like you want with a ranch?" The man looked at her over the top of his glasses.

"You'd be surprised." She looked at Joshua. "We can go home."

He nodded his head. Holding her hand, he bent down on one knee. "Sarah Elizabeth Martin, I love you. Will you marry me?"

She pulled him to his feet. "Of course I will, Joshua Campbell." Wrapping her arms around his neck, she whispered, "I love you, too."

If you liked *Yesteryear's Love,*
you won't want to miss

IREBIRD

The stunning new novel from Janice Graham

Coming in August from Berkley Books

One

So far as we know, no modern poet has written of the Flint Hills, which is surprising since they are perfectly attuned to his lyre. In their physical characteristics they reflect want and despair. A line of low-flung hills stretching from the Osage Nation on the south to the Kaw River on the north, they present a pinched and frowning face to those who gaze on them. Their verbiage is scant. Jagged rocks rise everywhere to their surface. The Flint Hills never laugh. In the early spring, when the sparse grass first turns to green upon them, they smile saltily and sardonically. But as spring turns to summer, they grow sullen again and hopeless. Death is no stranger to them.

—JAY E. HOUSE
PHILADELPHIA PUBLIC LEDGER (1931)

Ethan Brown was in love with the Flint Hills. His father
had been a railroad man, not a rancher, but you would have
thought he had been born into a dynasty of men connected
to this land, the way he loved it. He loved it the way certain
peoples love their homeland, with a spiritual dimension, like
the Jews love Jerusalem and the Irish their Emerald Isle. He
had never loved a woman quite like this, but that was about
to change.

   He was, at this very moment, ruminating on the idea of
marriage as he sat in the passenger seat of the sheriff's car,
staring gloomily at the bloodied, mangled carcass of a calf
lying in the headlights in the middle of the road. Ethan's
long, muscular legs were thrust under the dashboard and his
hat brushed the roof every time he turned his head, but
Clay's car was a lot warmer than Ethan's truck, which took
forever to heat up. Ethan poured a cup of coffee from a
scratched metal thermos his father had carried on the Santa
Fe line on cold October nights like this, and passed it to the
sheriff.

   "Thanks."

   "You bet."

   They looked over the dashboard at the calf; there was
nowhere else to look.

   "I had to shoot her. She was still breathin'," said Clay
apologetically.

   "You did the right thing."

   "I don't like to put down other men's animals, but she was
sufferin'."

   Ethan tried to shake his head, but his hat caught. "Nobody's gonna blame you. Tom'll be grateful to you."

   "I sure appreciate your comin' out here in the middle of
the night. I can't leave this mess out here. Just beggin' for
another accident."

   "The guy wasn't hurt?"

   "Naw. He was a little shook up, but he had a big four-
wheeler, comin' back from a huntin' trip. Just a little fender
damage."

   She was a small calf, but it took the two men some mighty

effort to heave her stiff carcass into the back of Ethan's truck. Then Clay picked up his markers and flares, and the two men headed home along the country road that wound through the prairie.

As Ethan drove along, his eyes fell on the bright pink hair clip on the dashboard. He had taken it out of Katie Anne's hair the night before, when she had climbed on top of him. He remembered the way her hair had looked when it fell around her face, the way it smelled, the way it curled softly over her naked shoulders. He began thinking about her again and forgot about the dead animal in the bed of the truck behind him.

As he turned off on the road toward the Mackey ranch, Ethan noticed the sky was beginning to lighten. He had hoped he would be able to go back to bed, to draw his long, tired body up next to Katie Anne's, but there wouldn't be time now. He might as well stir up some eggs and make another pot of coffee because as soon as day broke he would have to be out on the range, looking for the downed fence. There was no way of telling where the calf had gotten loose; there were thousands of miles of fence. Thousands of miles.

Ethan Brown had met Katherine Anne Mackey when his father was dying of cancer, which was also the year he turned forty. Katie Anne was twenty-seven—old enough to keep him interested and young enough to keep him entertained. She was the kind of girl Ethan had always avoided when he was younger; she was certainly nothing like Paula, his first wife. Katie Anne got rowdy, told dirty jokes, and wore sexy underwear. She lived in the guest house on her father's ranch, a beautiful limestone structure with wood-burning fireplaces built against the south slope of one of the highest hills in western Chase County. Tom Mackey, her father, was a fifth-generation rancher whose ancestors had been among the first to raise cattle in the Flint Hills. Tom owned about half the Flint Hills, give or take a few hundred thousand acres, and, rumor had it, about half the state of Oklahoma, and he knew everything there was to know about cattle ranching.

Ethan had found himself drawn to Katie Anne's place; it was like a smaller version of the home he had always dreamed of building in the hills, and he would tear over there in his truck from his law office, his heart full and aching, and then Katie Anne would entertain him with her quick wit and her stock of cold beer and her soft, sexy body, and he would leave in the morning thinking how marvelous she was, with his heart still full and aching.

All that year Ethan had felt a terrible cloud over his head, a psychic weight that at times seemed tangible; he even quit wearing the cross and Saint Christopher's medal his mother had given him when he went away to college his freshman year, as though shedding the gold around his neck might lessen his spiritual burden. If Ethan had dared to examine his conscience honestly he might have eventually come to understand the nature of his malaise, but Katie Anne had come along, and the relief she brought enabled him to skim over the top of those painful months.

Once every two weeks he would visit his father in Abilene; always, on the drive back home, he felt that troubling sensation grow like the cancer that was consuming his father. On several occasions he tried to speak about it to Katie Anne; he ventured very tentatively into these intimate waters with her, for she seemed to dislike all talk about things sad and depressing. He yearned to confess his despair, to understand it and define it, and maybe ease a little the terrible anguish in his heart. But when he would broach the subject, when he would finally begin to say the things that meant something to him, Katie Anne would grow terribly distracted. In the middle of his sentence she would stand up and ask him if he wanted another beer. "I'm still listening," she would toss at him sweetly. Or she would decide to clear the table at that moment. Or set the alarm clock. Mostly, it was her eyes. Ethan was very good at reading eyes. He often wished he weren't. He noticed an immediate change in her eyes, the way they glazed over, pulled her just out of range of hearing as soon as he brought up the subject of his father.

Occasionally, when Ethan would come over straight from a visit to Abilene, she would politely ask about the old man, and Ethan would respond with a terse comment such as, "Well, he's pretty grumpy," or "He's feeling a little better." But she didn't want to hear any more than that, so after a while he quit trying to talk about it. Ethan didn't like Katie Anne very much when her eyes began to dance away from him, when she fidgeted and thought about other things and pretended to be listening, although her eyes didn't pretend very well. And Ethan wanted very much to like Katie Anne. There was so much about her he did like.

Katie Anne, like her father, was devoted to the animals and the prairie lands that sustained them. Her knowledge of ranching almost equaled his. The Mackeys were an intelligent, educated family, and occasionally, on a quiet evening in her parents' company when the talk turned to more controversial issues such as public access to the Flint Hills or environmentalism, she would surprise Ethan with her perspicacity. These occasional glimpses of a critical edge to her mind, albeit all too infrequent, led him to believe there was another side to her nature that could, with time and the right influence, be brought out and nurtured. Right away Ethan recognized her remarkable gift for remaining touchingly feminine and yet very much at ease around the crude, coarse men who populated her world. She was the first ranch hand he had ever watched castrate a young bull wearing pale pink nail polish.

So that summer, while his father lay dying, Ethan and Katie Anne talked about ranching, about the cattle, about the land; they talked about country music, about the new truck Ethan was going to buy. They drank a lot of beer and barbecued a lot of steaks with their friends, and Ethan even got used to watching her dance with other guys at the South Forty, where they spent a lot of time on weekends. Ethan hated to dance, but Katie Anne danced with a sexual energy he had never seen in a woman. She loved to be watched. And she was good. There wasn't a step she didn't know or a partner she couldn't keep up with. So Ethan would sit and drink with his buddies while Katie Anne danced, and the guys would talk about what a goddamn lucky son of a bitch he was.

Then his father died, and although Ethan was with him in those final hours, even though he'd held the old man's hand and cradled his mother's head against his strong chest while she grieved, there nevertheless lingered in Ethan's mind a sense of things unresolved, and Katie Anne, guilty by association, somehow figured into it all.

Three years had passed since then, and everyone just assumed they would be married. Several times Katie Anne had casually proposed dates to him, none of which Ethan had taken seriously. As of yet there was no formal engagement, but Ethan was making his plans. Assiduously, carefully, very cautiously, the way he proceeded in law, he was building the life he had always dreamed of. He had never moved from the rather inconvenient third-floor attic office in the old Salmon P. Chase House that he had leased upon his arrival in Cottonwood Falls, fresh on the heels of his divorce, but this was no indication of his success. His had grown to a shamefully lucrative practice. Chase Countians loved Ethan Brown, not only for his impressive academic credentials and his faultless knowledge of the law, but because he was a man of conscience. He was also a man's man, a strong man with callused hands and strong legs that gripped the flanks of a horse with authority.

Now, at last, his dreams were coming true. From the earnings of his law practice he had purchased his land and was building his house. In a few years he would be able to buy a small herd. It was time to get married.

Two

Ethan pulled the string of barbed wire tight and looped it around the stake he had just pounded back into the ground. It was a windy day and the loose end of wire whipped wildly in his hand. It smacked him across the cheek near his eye and he flinched. He caught the loose end with a gloved hand and finished nailing it down, then he removed his glove and wiped away the warm blood that trickled down his face.

As he untied his horse and swung up into the saddle he thought he caught a whiff of fire. He lifted his head into the wind and sniffed the air, his nostrils twitching like sensitive radar seeking out an intruder. But he couldn't find the smell again. It was gone as quickly as it had come. Perhaps he had only imagined it.

He dug his heels into the horse's ribs and took off at a trot, following the fence as it curved over the hills. This was not the burning season, and yet the hills seemed to be aflame in their burnished October garb. The copper-colored grasses, short after a long summer's grazing, stood out sharply against the fiercely blue sky. They reminded Ethan of the

short-cropped head of a red-haired boy on his first day back
at school, all trim and clean and embarrassed.

From the other side of the fence, down the hill toward the
highway, came a bleating sound. *Not another one,* he
thought. It was past two in the afternoon, and he had a desk
piled with work waiting for him in town, but he turned his
horse around and rode her up to the top of the hill, where he
could see down into the valley below.

He had forgotten all about Emma Fergusen's funeral until
that moment when he looked down on the Old Cemetery, an
outcropping of modest tombstones circumscribed by a rusty
chain-link fence. It stood out in the middle of nowhere; the
only access was a narrow blacktop county road. But this afternoon the side of the road was lined with trucks and cars,
and the old graves were obscured by mourners of the newly
dead. The service was over. As he watched, the cemetery
emptied, and within a few minutes there were only the black
limousine from the mortuary and a little girl holding the
hand of a woman in black who stood looking down into the
open grave. Ethan had meant to attend the funeral. He was
handling Emma Fergusen's estate and her will was sitting on
top of a pile of folders in his office. But the dead calf had
seized his attention. The loss, about $500, was Tom
Mackey's, but it was all the same to Ethan. Tom Mackey
was like a father to him.

Ethan shifted his gaze from the mourners and scanned the
narrow stretch of bottomland. He saw the heifer standing in
a little tree-shaded gully just below the cemetery. To reach
her he would have to jump the fence or ride two miles to the
next gate. He guided the mare back down the hill and
stopped to study the ground to determine the best place to
jump. The fence wasn't high, but the ground was treacherous. Hidden underneath the smooth russet-colored bed of
grass lay rock outcroppings and potholes: burrows, dens,
things that could splinter a horse's leg like a matchstick, all
of them obscured by the deceptive harmony of waving
grasses. Ethan found a spot that looked safe but he got down
off his horse and walked the approach, just to make sure. He
spread apart the barbed wire and slipped through to check

out the other side. When he got back up on his horse he glanced down at the cemetery again. He had hoped the woman and child would be gone, but they were still standing by the grave. *That would be Emma's daughter,* he thought in passing. *And her granddaughter.* Ethan's heartbeat quickened but he didn't give himself time to fret. He settled his mind and whispered to his horse, then he kicked her flanks hard, and within a few seconds he felt her pull her forelegs underneath and with a mighty surge of strength from her powerful hind legs sail into the air.

The woman looked up just as the horse appeared in the sky and she gasped. It seemed frozen there in space for the longest time, a black, deep-chested horse outlined against the blue sky, and then hooves hit the ground with a thud, and the horse and rider thundered down the slope of the hill.

"*Maman!*" cried the child in awe. "*Tu as vu ça?*"

The woman was still staring, speechless, when she heard her father call from the limousine.

"Annette!"

She turned around.

"You can come back another time," her father called in a pinched voice.

Annette took one last look at her mother's grave and knew she would never come back. She held out her hand to her daughter and they walked together to the limousine.

TIME PASSAGES

__CRYSTAL MEMORIES *Ginny Aiken*   0-515-12159-2

__A DANCE THROUGH TIME *Lynn Kurland*
                                          0-515-11927-X

__ECHOES OF TOMORROW *Jenny Lykins*   0-515-12079-0

__LOST YESTERDAY *Jenny Lykins*   0-515-12013-8

__MY LADY IN TIME *Angie Ray*   0-515-12227-0

__NICK OF TIME *Casey Claybourne*   0-515-12189-4

__REMEMBER LOVE *Susan Plunkett*   0-515-11980-6

__SILVER TOMORROWS *Susan Plunkett*   0-515-12047-2

__THIS TIME TOGETHER *Susan Leslie Liepitz*
                                          0-515-11981-4

__WAITING FOR YESTERDAY *Jenny Lykins*
                                          0-515-12129-0

__HEAVEN'S TIME *Susan Plunkett*   0-515-12287-4

__THE LAST HIGHLANDER *Claire Cross*   0-515-12337-4

__A TIME FOR US *Christine Holden*   0-515-12375-7

Prices slightly higher in Canada   All books $5.99

Payable in U.S. funds only. No cash/COD accepted. Postage & handling: U.S./CAN. $2.75 for one book, $1.00 for each additional, not to exceed $6.75; Int'l $5.00 for one book, $1.00 each additional. We accept Visa, Amex, MC ($10.00 min.), checks ($15.00 fee for returned checks) and money orders. Call 800-788-6262 or 201-933-9292, fax 201-896-8569; refer to ad # 680 (2/99)

Penguin Putnam Inc.	**Bill my:** ☐Visa ☐MasterCard ☐Amex _____ (expires)
P.O. Box 12289, Dept. B	Card#_____
Newark, NJ 07101-5289	
Please allow 4-6 weeks for delivery.	Signature_____

Foreign and Canadian delivery 6-8 weeks.

Bill to:

Name_____

Address_____City_____

State/ZIP_____

Daytime Phone #_____

Ship to:

Name_____	Book Total	$_____
Address_____	Applicable Sales Tax	$_____
City_____	Postage & Handling	$_____
State/ZIP_____	Total Amount Due	$_____

This offer subject to change without notice.